TH
UNCANNY
RAVEN
WINSTON

Book Two

Of

The Cassie Black Trilogy

TAMMIE PAINTER

The Uncanny Raven Winston
Book Two of The Cassie Black Trilogy

You may contact the author by email at
Tammie@tammiepainter.com
Mailing Address:
Daisy Dog Media
P.O. Box 165
Netarts, Oregon 97143, USA

First Edition, April 2021
also available as an ebook

ALSO BY TAMMIE PAINTER

What Readers Are saying About the Trilogy...

The Undead Mr. Tenpenny is a clever, hilarious romp through a new magical universe that can be accessed through the closet of a hole-in-the-wall apartment in Portland, Oregon.

—**Sarah Angleton, author of *Gentleman of Misfortune***

Man oh man, did I love this book! ...The plot was great, and got even better as things progressed.... I think the biggest pro of this book is the characters.

—**Jonathon Pongratz, author of *Reaper: Aftermath***

...suffused with dark humor and witty dialogue, of the sort that Painter excels at...a fun read for anyone who enjoys fast-paced, somewhat snarky, somewhat twisted, fantasy adventures.

—**Berthold Gambrel, author of *Vespasian Moon's Fabulous Autumn Carnival***

I was unable to put this down when I started reading it. The author combines humour with a fast paced murder mystery all packed into a funeral home.

—**Amazon Reviewer**

It's a bit "Pushing Daisies" meets Hogwarts, which makes the novel a fun and entertaining read. Great wit too.

—**Carrie Rubin, author of** *The Bone Curse*

When I saw the book title...my first thought was, "another zombie apocalypse". A wonderful surprise greeted me with an entertaining story that was written with humor, a great story line and new twist on the undead.

—**J. Tate,** *Eugene Reviewer*

Wow and wow again! I absolutely loved this book! You get such a feel for the characters and the story is so fast paced you don't want to put it down.

—**Goodreads Reviewer**

The whole story was a bit of wild ride, but it was a ride I wanted to stay on all the way through! There is mystery that actually kept me guessing, there's humor, magic, and a unique storyline.

—**Goodreads Reviewer**

This book is dedicated to David (aka "Mr. Husband"), to whom I owe a debt of gratitude (and maybe a vacation) for putting up with my 24-7 work schedule while creating this trilogy.

It is also dedicated to my grandmother, Bertha, who would have approved of my use of the word "floozy" in this book.

THE
UNCANNY
RAVEN
WINSTON

AUTHOR'S NOTE:
TOWER TERMINOLOGY

The majority of this book takes place in the Tower of London. The Tower of London has many towers...which is a little confusing, so let me explain how I use the term "Tower" in this story.

The Tower of London is a large complex that includes walls, living quarters for the Yeoman Warders, and structures like Wakefield Tower, Salt Tower, and the White Tower (the castle that started it all).

In this book and in *The Untangled Cassie Black* (Book Three), I use the word "Tower" by itself only when referring to The Tower of London as a whole. Other towers within the Tower are referred to by name.

I don't know if this will help dispel any confusion, or add to it, but there it is.

To get an understanding of the layout of The Tower of London, take a gander at the excellent map provided by the Historic Royal Palaces website at: *www.hrp.org.uk/media/1587/tower-map-2018.pdf*

Oh, and if you aren't familiar with the "Shoop Shoop Song" mentioned in the story, you can see Betty Everett's rendition on YouTube at: *https://www.youtube.com/watch?v=4L7WTpxcPfQ*

PROLOGUE
THE REPORT

"Report in from the Yanks, sir."

The grey-haired woman glanced up at the stout, somewhat hairy man who'd just stepped into her office.

No, she thought upon noticing his hands had only four digits. Not a man. A troll. Judging by his lack of a bulbous nose, and with ears that didn't stick straight out from the sides of his head, he was only half troll, but he still possessed that frustrating troll trait of being difficult to train out of a habit. Once a troll got an idea stuck in his or her head, it was near impossible to get it back out.

It's what made them excellent guards. You simply made them promise to keep whoever they were meant to guard alive, and that became their primary focus, even if some of them went about it in unconventional ways. However, this sticky-idea quirk was also why you always had to be careful when working with them.

"I've told you before, I'm not a sir. *Ma'am, mum,* even just *Olivia* would be fine."

"Yes sir, mum," he said, mumbling the two titles together.

Olivia Waylon rolled her eyes and, even though she made a great effort to hold it in, let out an exasperated sigh. It was too early in the day for this, and someone — probably one of the pixies they hired as cleaners — had hidden the cords for all the electric kettles. Which meant Olivia was not only having to deal with a pile of troubling information that had surfaced about the Starlings, but also with a dim-brained half-troll without the benefit of caffeine from the tea department of Fortnum & Mason.

No witch should have to endure so much before ten a.m.

Olivia pushed back from her desk. The chair's wheels stuttered over the stone slab floor.

"What is it?"

Before the troll could begin, a man entered her office. He appeared to be in his mid-thirties and was slim with cheek bones so sharp they could slice cold butter.

"Ah, you've heard the report, then?" Rafi said, taking a seat in one of the chairs before Olivia's desk.

"Not yet."

"Chester, why haven't you told her?" he asked, speaking in a tone of mock reproach as he twisted his lithe frame around to grin at the troll. "Never mind. Tell her now."

"The Mauvais is back," Chester said as flatly as if delivering a weather report.

"Damn, Chester, you could've eased into it," Rafi chided. Olivia caught a hint of Rafi's sandalwood scent as he turned back to face her.

"Sorry," said Chester. "That was the report, though."

Olivia's dark cheeks had paled to an odd shade reminiscent of a paper sack left in the sun too long. Did this have anything to do with the information she'd just received on the Starlings? The single sentence from Chester — and the lack of any tea — left her head pounding. She rolled forward, put her elbows on the desk and began rubbing her temples.

"Never mind, then," Rafi told Chester. "Go to the next person on your list and relay the news."

14

"Yes sir. Goodbye, sirs." Chester gave a little bow and touched his three fingers to his forehead in a salute.

"You do know we're only supposed to use them as guards," Olivia criticized as soon as Chester's heavy footsteps could be heard thumping down the hall.

"I know, but I keep thinking there's more to them. I mean, with their level of dedication to a job, it just seems with the right training..." Rafi's words trailed off under Olivia's it's-not-going-to-happen stare.

"So, what's this about?" Olivia asked. She couldn't shake the idea that whatever Rafi had to say had something to do with the file humming under her fingers. Her throat went dry, and she swallowed hard to relieve it.

"Turns out some American girl—" Olivia scolded Rafi with her eyes. "Sorry, a young American *woman* woke up the watch, brought some dead people back to life, and this alerted the Mauvais's senses as to the watch's location. He'd already been on the hunt for the watch, but we assumed he lost the trail when Corrine Corrigan shut down her messenger portal."

"That was an inconvenient fiasco." Olivia watched Rafi's face. He met her scrutiny with a patient, level gaze. "There's more, isn't there?"

"The Mauvais got the watch." The words rushed from his lips in a tumble of syllables as if, like ripping off a bandage, he could make delivering the news less painful if he did it as quickly as possible.

Olivia burst up from her desk. "What the hell, Rafi?"

In rapid, angry strides, she paced the office from one tapestry-lined wall to another. With each step she mentally listed everything that needed to be put into place immediately. When she realized her head was going in circles with tasks, she stopped at the desk, hovering over Rafi like a hawk over its prey.

15

"The Mauvais has the watch? Don't you think that's what you should have led with? The wizard who wants to rule us Magics and enslave the Norms has regained the incredibly powerful, the insanely dangerous object that could allow him to do that very thing. And you send me bloody half-troll Chester with the news? Why are we not on full alert?"

"First off, if I can't call her *girl*, you can't go around pointing out Chester's impure bloodlines in such a disparaging tone."

Olivia no longer wanted tea. Who cared if it was only ten a.m., she needed scotch.

"Sod the bloody semantics, Rafi. We need to activate all the defensive tactics we have ready."

"No, we don't." Rafi leaned back and put his feet up on the edge of Olivia's desk. He wore a grin that made Olivia want to scream. The only thing holding her back was that she hated revealing the tiny drop of banshee blood she carried in her veins. Well, and the fact that she could kill Rafi with her scream.

Not that she wasn't tempted. Her fingers twitched with the urge to wrap around his long neck. But since being a frustrating twat first thing in the morning wasn't a punishable offense, she restrained herself. Instead, she shoved his feet off her desk.

"Need I remind you I have the authority to set your hair on fire?" Olivia said through tight lips. "Which I will do if you don't explain things more clearly right this very second."

"The Mauvais had disguised himself. He got his hands on the watch, but the watch is useless because the girl absorbed all the power out of it. Supposedly she's got a knack for magic, even though she only started training a few weeks ago."

The lurch within Olivia's stomach had nothing to do with hunger. Too many issues, problems, and rumors were snapping together to create a tower of concern.

16

"Where did this take place?" she asked, although she was willing to bet she already knew.

"Portland community. Busby Tenpenny, he was one of the people she brought back."

"Busby's dead?"

"Not anymore."

"This girl—"

"Young woman," Rafi corrected.

"Whatever. She doesn't happen to be named Starling, does she?"

"No, Black. Cassie Black." With a heavy exhale of relief, Olivia dropped into the chair opposite Rafi. He then added, "But she is the daughter of a couple Starlings. Name got changed somewhere along the way, I guess."

Once again, Olivia pressed her fingers to her temples and worked them in small circles.

"What's her name matter?" Rafi asked, his voice suddenly full of confused worry. Olivia was one of those people who were never shaken. She was a steadfast rock who radiated confidence and authority without being overbearing. For her to show this much distress made him wish he'd left Chester to deliver the information.

"Because I just received a stack of reports from various sources indicating Simon and Chloe Starling may still be alive."

"She's their kid?" Rafi asked, awe replacing his concern for his boss. "The people who got the watch from the Mauvais in the first place?"

Olivia nodded.

"And based on the information I've just received," she said, tapping the folder in front of her, "they could indeed be alive. If they are, they would be in extreme danger. Until you and Chester came in, I'd been thinking we might put a team together to sift through the files, sort out their exact location, and extract them." Rafi's mahogany skin went a shade more in the direction of pine. Olivia raised a hand as if wiping a slate clean. "Sorry, not extract as in *extraction*. Although, that may have already happened. I mean, *extract* as in get them out. Rescue them. If we can. They deserve our care after what they did for the community at large."

"How can they not be dead after all this time? It's been what? More than twenty years, yes?"

"Twenty-four. If they are alive, it won't have been a thriving existence. They're nothing more than pawns to whoever has them. Likely kept just enough alive. Again, assuming these reports aren't false leads, if the Starlings aren't dead, it's quite likely they wish they were."

"You're thinking the Mauvais has them." Chills went up Rafi's arms.

"I haven't had time to sort out what I'm thinking, but from what you've just said, if this daughter of theirs has tricked the Mauvais and it turns out they're being held by him, he's going to use them to get to her. He'll dangle them in front of her then throw them away once he has what he wants. What I don't understand is why wouldn't he just go after her directly? What good do the parents do him?"

"He tried." Rafi's voice carried a hint of amused pride. "He was trying to get the watch, but she beat him."

"Her years of training have really paid off. Remind me to commend the Portland community." Rafi, an enigmatic grin lighting up his face, shook his head emphatically. "What?"

"I just told you. She wasn't trained. I mean, she was, but only for a couple weeks. Before that, she had no idea she was one of us. Think about it," Rafi said, clearly impressed, "barely trained and she beat him. Of course, she had been hopped up on donuts, but it's still impressive."

Olivia's stomach growled at the mention of food. She stood up, flipped open the report cover, and looked at the photo of a lanky, dark-haired white woman. Barely trained and she had survived going toe to toe with the Mauvais.

"But you said the Mauvais had the watch. That doesn't sound like she won."

Rafi's face beamed like a pre-teen gushing over the latest boy band. "She pulled all the power from the watch into herself. The Mauvais got the watch, but it's nothing more than a decorative trinket now. He'll be fuming once he finds out."

Barely trained, and she now held the watch's power within her. "We need to call her in," Olivia said with grim decisiveness.

"Are we locking her down or inviting her to work with us?"

Olivia closed the folder.

"We'll see."

CHAPTER ONE

HOME DESIGN

I hate it when Fiona looks at me like that. I mean, I expect it from Dr. Dunwiddle, but when Fiona gives you that I'm-so-frustrated-I-could-smack-you glare, you know you've screwed up.

Okay, I admit the book I was supposed to be shelving — hands free, mind you — might have traveled a bit farther than I intended. And, well, there might now be a book-sized hole in Fiona's wall.

In my defense, I had offered to put it away using good old Norm muscle power. She's the one who insisted I use my magic to place the book back on the shelf.

You know when you reach into the fridge and lift up an opaque jug thinking it's full to the brim with orange juice, cashew milk, wine, or whatever liquid suits your fancy? Your muscles prepare themselves to heft a certain amount of weight. So when you lift the jug that your roommate/spouse/child/self put back nearly empty, you end up overdoing it and banging the damn jug right into the top of the fridge while your muscles are shouting, "Hells yes! We are so strong!"

That's pretty much what I've been doing with my magic these past couple weeks.

Again, in my defense, the book was really thick and looked like it should have weighed at least six pounds. When I gave it a magical little lift and push...*Bam!* It went straight through the drywall, through the insulation, then through the siding of Fiona's schoolroom that makes up most of the ground floor of her house.

I couldn't figure out why she was so agitated. I mean, Fiona now had a perfect peekaboo view of Spellbound Patisserie, along with the tantalizing smell of baked goods wafting through her home.

I also couldn't figure out why it mattered so much to me that I'd annoyed her. After all, a month ago I wouldn't have given a flying rat's fart about upsetting any human on Planet Earth, except for Mr. Wood — my boss at the funeral home where I illegally put makeup on dead people for their final show.

In fact, I took personal pride in being able to put up someone's hackles against me in less than eight minutes. I was like the rodeo queen of keeping people at a distance. Now, here I stood worried, bothered even, that I'd upset Fiona, one of the few Magics who had shown an enormous amount of patience and understanding with me.

So far.

Oh, by the way, while there are supposedly flying cats in MagicLand, there are no flying rats. Although they can be very aerodynamic if you ask them to tuck up their paws while you magically zip them around through the air.

Probably best if you keep that one from PETA.

"Really, I think it's an improvement," I said, looking appreciatively at the damage.

"Cassie, you put a hole in my wall," Fiona said with controlled matter-of-factness.

"But now you have the tasty scent of cake filling your home."

"Since I should really lose a few pounds and ought to stay away from Spellbound's product line, I don't see how that's a benefit." She almost, *almost* tapped her toes with impatience, but then seemed to think better of it. Even so, Fiona standing with her hands on her round hips and arms akimbo was a clear sign of her frustration level.

"Still, when you do get the urge to go, now you can check to see if there's a line before you head out." As I looked through the hole to demonstrate this excellent new amenity, my heart jumped. Before I could control my mouth, I said, "Look, there's Alastair."

I blurted this too brightly, trying in some weird way to use good cheer to cover up my confusion over this man. He was one of my instructors. He had known my parents. But he had also known the person who may have killed my parents. And while he had seemed to want to help me in my fight against the Mauvais, something about his involvement that day and his actions in the two weeks leading up to it, left my suspicion systems on high alert.

Unfortunately, while Team Brain was trying to be analytical about all this, Team Heart stubbornly refused to listen. Even though Alastair couldn't match a pair of socks to save his life, he was devilishly good looking, he had a shy charm, he had great taste in sweet treats, and my attraction toward him was bulking up like a boneheaded jock who's chugged too many protein shakes.

And our class time together wasn't helping one bit with this confusion. See, the Mauvais — that's this evil wizard who wants to go all Voldemort on the world — would love to capture me to tap into my magic for his own nefarious purposes. A comforting thought if ever there was one. As such, it was imperative to get me trained in how to protect myself. But I also needed intensive and immediate instruction on how to control my magic since my powers were currently overflowing like a leaky diaper.

As part of this more rigid, more in-depth training, my lessons with Alastair these past couple of weeks were no longer the back-and-forth banter sessions over cake they had been before my showdown with the Mauvais. They were now physical and focused primarily on defense.

As with any defense-oriented class, there were plenty of awkward moments of close contact. This close contact also led to a few near kisses, from which Alastair would — after a couple tension-filled seconds — catch himself, fumble his way backward, and launch into some tidbit of magical history no matter how out of context it was for the lesson at hand. All the while, his embarrassment would bring the most adorable sparkle to his eyes...

Ugh. See how ridiculously enamored I've become. Pathetic, right?

However, in my most recent sessions with Alastair, it seemed he wasn't jumping back quite so quickly. Which would be fine if I was your run-of-the-mill Magic, but I'm an absorber. That means I can suck away someone else's magic without even trying. As an absorber, you're supposed to be taught from a very young age how to tame your abilities so you don't end up draining your entire neighborhood.

Thanks to missing out on my magical formative years and thanks to my recent overdose of magic, my absorbing side was running as wild as a lion who's just escaped from the zoo. Just as it would be dangerous to hang out with that rogue lion, it was risky for any Magic to be near me too long.

Which meant Alastair's willingness to spend time with me, and spend that time in close proximity to me, was creating a battle royale between Team Heart's ever-intensifying crush and Team Brain's incessant questions regarding his true motives.

Of course, when I was around Alastair, Team Heart usually

won out and all these doubts fell right out of my head. Especially when he would lean in close to adjust my hands into a spell's proper sequence and his breath on my neck would send goosebumps all down my arm...

Sorry, where was I? Oh right, I was telling you a story about a hole in a wall.

"Yes, I'm aware Alastair is there," Fiona said, distracting me from drooling as Alastair shifted a square box under his arm. He checked both ways, then darted across the street and headed straight for my remodeling job. Realizing I was staring, I turned away. Fiona had a knowing look on her face. "Look, Cassie, a few people, including Alastair, are coming by. We need to talk."

"Somehow I don't think the topic is about getting a team together for the Starlight Parade this year," I said, referring to a silly bit of annual fun in the non-magical Portland world.

"No," she said so crisply you could have topped the word with cheese and served it as a savory snack.

"Is this about my parents?"

I can't tell you how much I wanted her to say yes. Every part of me wanted to find them, wanted news about them, wanted to be reunited with them.

My parents, who I'd thought abandoned me to a childhood trapped in wickedly nasty foster homes, turned out to be heroes in the magic world. Everyone believed they had died in action, but the Mauvais hinted they might be alive. As had Dr. Runa Dunwiddle, who is not the kind of person to tell you lies just to boost your mood.

"No, it's not, and I know you think we're not taking the rumors seriously, but it is being looked into. So, please let the matter of your parents be handled by proper investigators. You poking around and playing detective is exactly how the Mauvais will get his hands on you."

"Then what—?"

"Hello!" Alastair called through the hole in the wall. At the sight of him, Team Brain responded by tensing my shoulders, while Team Heart did a couple cartwheels in my chest. Welcome to the Infatuation Roller Coaster, everyone. "I like what you've done with the place, Fiona."

I smiled and raised my eyebrows at Fiona as if to say: See, everyone's going to love this new, innovative feature in home design.

In a curt tone, Fiona told him to go around to the front door then focused her stern, green eyes back on me. My smile dropped.

"That," she pointed to the hole, "is what's going to be discussed."

CHAPTER TWO

TOO MUCH MAGIC

Once inside the house, Alastair lifted a lemon cake decorated with summer strawberries from the box. Fiona directed him to take it upstairs to her sitting room, telling him we'd join him shortly. With Fiona following, I went into her kitchen to make coffee under her careful scrutiny.

Thankfully, she was too busy welcoming the no-longer-dead Busby Tenpenny to notice when my Boiling Charm went too far and instantly turned an entire kettle of water into steam. I quickly refilled the appliance and opted to use the on/off switch just like normal people do to heat water for the French press. I then pulled down a tray and arranged five sets of cups and saucers on it, as well as cake plates and forks.

Without breaking a single thing.

And let me tell you, that really was a feat to be proud of. See, even though the bones of one of my hands had recently been crushed into a billion pieces, that hand refused to give up its delusions of being functional.

As such, it kept reaching for things, only to bash into them and send shocks of pain up my arm. It was annoying and embarrassing, but since Dr. Dunwiddle insisted there was no such thing as Skelegro, I was stuck waiting for the hand to heal the old-fashioned way.

Fiona, apparently not wanting her dishes to go flying through any walls, carried the tray upstairs, where Mr. Tenpenny doled out the treats. Cake and caffeine sorted, I took a seat in an agonizingly stiff, wooden chair, while Fiona, Dr. Dunwiddle, Alastair, and Busby sat in plush chairs passing judgmental stares over me. Okay, Alastair's stare was more mischievous than judgey, but the others? Very judgey indeed.

"I'll get right to it, Cassie," said Fiona just as I'd taken a bite of the cake and was preparing to swoon in strawberry bliss. "You're too powerful and you aren't learning to control it."

"I am," I said, gulping down my forkful of cake. "I can change a feather into a rock just as quickly as the advanced students."

"But there's an inconsistency," Fiona insisted. "When you trained with Lola you were able to show excellent control." She was referring to my lessons with Lola LeMieux during which Lola had turned me into her personal Magic Maid service. But I had to agree that even after I'd spent two weeks dusting, vacuuming, and rearranging furniture, Lola's walls had remained free of any unexpected new openings. "Now, you're demonstrating no finesse."

"Look," Dr. Dunwiddle said, cutting me off from muttering my excuses. She used to hate me, but ever since I proved myself against the Mauvais, she had switched gears to only mildly disliking me. "We're not blaming you."

"It certainly feels like you're blaming me," I said, my defensive instincts throwing up a barrier so extensive and sturdy it would have put the Great Wall of China to shame.

"This isn't an accusation or implication," said Mr. T, "but you pulled in a great deal of power from the watch when you fought the Mauvais. Your magic levels are off the chart. Since you're barely trained as it is, the extra strength makes it harder to manage."

"So, how do I get my magic levels under control? Could you just prescribe me some magic statins," I quipped, and I thought it was a pretty clever quip, but there was Dr. D giving me the stink eye.

"I feel it's my fault," Alastair said. "After giving her the donuts, I should have stuck by her side when she went to Vivian's."

Yes, about that—

I darted my gaze between my other three interrogators, hoping one of them would ask what I'd been finding myself unable to. Really, why had they not addressed this before?

Alastair had fed me a heap of donuts on the day he believed I would be coming face to face with the Evil One. In addition to being an absorber, I'm an even rarer Magic who's also a giver, meaning I can donate magic. Or have it taken from me against my will. Alastair had to have known those sugar bombs would boost both the absorbing and the giving side of my magic.

So the question remained: Had he given me them to strengthen me for the fight ahead? Or had he hoped the Mauvais would capture me and use my sugar-charged magic to strengthen himself?

My eyes locked on Mr. Tenpenny's. I raised my eyebrows in a prodding way. He gave a slight nod.

"After enhancing Cassie's magic with sugar, you let her walk into danger. Is that what you intended?" Mr. T said, voicing my own thoughts in his rich, posher-than-the-Queen accent.

"I did not," replied Alastair, clearly offended. "I wanted her to have an advantage if something happened. I'd planned to be there, but Cassie and the Mauvais found each other first. Fiona, if you recall that day, you're the one who stopped me to tell me how Cassie's draining went. Remember how impatient I was?"

"You could have just said something," Fiona said.

"I wasn't certain what you'd think. I mean, I didn't know

Cassie would steal the watch, but I did know she was up to something. I had hoped to keep it between me and her because I didn't want to stir up trouble for her."

He stopped and took a sip of tea, watching me over the rim of the cup. The deep blue eyes were now serious, all hint of the earlier mischief gone. "Maybe it was foolish of me, but I thought with a little help from the donuts, she and I could work together to face the problem, but by the time I did get there. Well..."

He let the sentence trail off, holding back from telling them I was the one who didn't let him in. I was the one who refused his help, unsure if he'd come to fight with me or against me. "Anyway, she was doing well. When I did get in, I was merely helping finish up what she had started."

I don't know, it may be my inability to trust, but this sounded a little weak to me. Still, when Alastair next met my eyes there was sincere apology and maybe a hint of guilt in his look.

"This is beside the point," said Dr. Dunwiddle. "The sugar in the donuts not only kept her from being able to be fully drained, but it also amplified the power she absorbed from the watch, which would have been a huge dose for even the most capable Magic."

"So, maybe I just cut back on sugar for a bit," I offered, hating the idea the moment I said it.

My ability to absorb may have allowed me to pull the trick with the watch, but Dr. D was right, the watch's power had thrown my magical strength into overdrive. If I'd wanted to, I could have probably sucked up all the magic in the room, swirled it into a tornado, and funneled it into Alastair's cake box.

But I had been making a sincere effort in my training over the past couple weeks. Part of this effort stemmed from not wanting the Mauvais to turn me into a rechargeable magic battery, but also because if it turns out Alastair's not on the side of evil and I do allow myself to succumb to this force between us, it would be nice not to completely de-magic him.

Which I did nearly do during our last class. See, the timer failed to go off. I'd just nailed a Shield Spell for the first time when Alastair started swaying woozily. I thought it was me. Well, it was me, but only the uncontrolled magic part of me, not the sweeping-men-off-their-feet part — if I even had one. We'd only gone thirty minutes over our time; it took Alastair the rest of the day to recover.

But look at him now, he looks fine.

Really fine.

"You can try adjusting your diet," Dr. D said, jerking me away from gawking at Alastair, "but I want you to bear in mind that you now have more power than any Magic should. And a fair deal of that is the watch's power."

"And it's a worrisome power at that," Mr. Tenpenny added, "because if the Mauvais does capture you, he will use you against us. Against everyone."

I slumped in my uncomfortable chair and shoved a hunk of cake into my mouth. So much for the diet.

"We can help," Runa offered. "We can intensify your training and we can hope to drain some of the magic from you, but that could be dangerous."

"Dangerous how?" I asked.

"We should have asked Gwendolyn to explain this," Fiona said. "Basically, magic can stay separate in an object, but once magic goes into a person, it combines. The instant you took in the watch's magic — most of which is the Mauvais's magic — you intertwined your power with his. Much like butter and eggs being mixed into sugar for a batch of cookies, it's near impossible to separate the components once they've blended. We don't know what exactly to do with you. We've been hoping these past couple weeks might have given us some answers, but we're at a loss. The more we try to tame your magic, the wilder it gets."

"You make me sound like a freak." Which I was used to, but it still hurt, especially since during my time in MagicLand — my not-so-clever name for Rosaria, the secret underworld of the magic community of Portland, Oregon — I hadn't felt quite as freaky as I used to.

"No, not a freak," Mr. Tenpenny said, "but like a very talented pupil who's been assigned teachers who only know how to instruct mediocre students."

"Not exactly how I'd put it," Dr. Dunwiddle grumbled.

"So, what? You're kicking me out of Hogwarts?"

Mr. T bristled. He hated Harry Potter. *Hate* can't even describe it. It's more of a personal assault on him every time there's a Harry Potter reference. I've tried to control the habit in his presence, but one slips through now and then. Still, he can't complain too much. After all, I did bring him back from the dead. Twice.

"No, we're not kicking you out," said Fiona. "Right now, you're kind of like a clumsy kid with an elephant gun, but I'm certain with enough time and patience, we can turn you into something more akin to a marksman with a fine-tipped arrow. But if there are any further incidents, something will have to be done."

"I understand." I didn't. I couldn't help but have this magic and I'd been working really hard, so what more could I do?

"Good. I hope you do. Because if you don't show more control, I honestly don't know what we'll do with you."

And with that, with the feeling I was an unwanted knickknack only being kept around until they could find time to list me on eBay, I finished my cake in silence, my magic buzzing with every bite.

CHAPTER THREE

NUMBER THREE

After my you're-a-freak intervention session, the other three Magics volunteered to help Fiona tidy up. With one hand broken and with my new habit of destroying things by over-magicking them, no one tried to cajole me into kitchen duties. I bided my time browsing Fiona's bookshelves while Runa, Busby, and Alastair followed Fiona downstairs with the dirty dishes.

I felt like a halfwit. I felt like I would never fit in anywhere or make the right decision about anything. I thought I'd been helping with the watch trick. Instead, I'd only turned myself into a bigger misfit.

So, once their voices were bouncing off the walls and high ceilings of Fiona's vast country kitchen, I slipped down the stairs and out the door, dashed over to the next building, and hurried through my portal.

Or rather, tried to hurry.

I had recently succeeded in straightening up my coat closet, which is where my portal to MagicLand had been installed. However, to keep the main living area of my apartment somewhat clean, I have a habit of simply tossing things into whatever cupboard or drawer is handy. So, it had only taken a few short days for my briefly tidy closet to revert to its usual tangle of coats, bags, and shoes.

Once I'd waded through the disarray and into my apartment, I dropped into my secondhand (or was it third?) wingback chair and sulked. But even that self-indulgent moping wasn't to be. Pablo, my formerly deceased feline who I'd gotten from a formerly deceased Hispanic lady, barely had time to rub across my legs and beg for a treat before my phone pinged to let me know messages were waiting.

For some reason, although I can make calls out of MagicLand, incoming messages seem unable to make it past the barrier. Luckily, I'm not very popular, so the task of sifting through the notifications rarely takes more than twenty seconds.

This time, however, there were four voicemails from Mr. Wood, all sent within the space of two minutes. I didn't bother to listen to them. That many messages in a row could not be good. My boss had repeatedly expressed his utter boredom in his convalescence, but it's not like he was going to call every thirty seconds just to chat. Something was wrong. And with the way things had been going at the funeral home lately, it was likely my fault. I handed over some cat crack to Pablo, then hustled down the stairs to the door of my apartment building.

Where I was promptly met by my landlord.

You remember Morelli, right? Hairy shoulders, dirty tank tops, missing pinky on each hand, and a fan of television reruns. Other than keeping the garden gnome out front looking spiffy, Morelli didn't do much in regards to building maintenance, but he did get a kick out of informing me, his only tenant, when my rent was due down to the exact minute. He could also, without a lick of effort, block a doorway with the prowess of an all-star hockey goalie. That's not to say he was fat. He had a paunch, but thanks to his favorite tank top revealing more than I cared to see, he appeared to have rock-solid muscle underneath those hairy shoulders.

"We need to talk about your lease, Black."

"Not now," I said, shifting to the left then the right, trying to find a gap I could squeeze through.

"Yes, now. You canceled your lease, but yet you're still here. I could call you in as a squatter. Plus, I know you got a cat in there."

"Hey, I never signed anything. I only verbally canceled." Mind you, that cancellation had been made while I was having a bit of a temper tantrum. "And I think you need some fresh air to clear that thick skull of yours, because if you remember correctly, my lease allows me to have a pet."

He narrowed his eyes, and I wondered if he did strength training to develop the muscles in his face. The squint was menacing and intimidating, but I didn't back down because I knew I was right. Although Morelli had recently threatened to raise my rent by a ridiculous amount, he now possessed a legal document that guaranteed I could stay in my apartment for the next five years without a single rate increase. That same document also stated I was allowed to keep a cat, free of charge.

And no, I wasn't in the habit of memorizing rental agreements. All this information was fresh in my mind because a few days ago, while Morelli was out bench pressing cars, eating an entire cow, or whatever it was he did to pack so much bulk onto his bones, I "adjusted" my lease by moving around a few ink molecules on the document. Which does prove I can control my magic. Although I don't think Fiona or the others would exactly approve of that particular use.

"I've still got a matter to settle with you, Black."

"And I've got an emergency." I made a step-aside motion with my hands. If he only knew that move — with the right intention behind it — could fling him through the wall, maybe he'd drop the scowl and show a bit of respect.

34

Something in the set of my jaw must have told him I wasn't fooling around because his eyes relaxed, he reeled in the finger he'd been pointing at me, then crossed his arms over his chest.

"We're talking about this later," he grunted as he stepped aside.

"Looking forward to it," I said cheerily and hurried past him.

* * *

After race walking the five blocks to Wood's Funeral Home, a stab of guilt hit me when I saw the sign posted in the window announcing we were only open limited hours due to illness.

Actually, that illness was the only reason we were open. Although I'd initially started my magic training in an effort to save his business, I'd ended up delivering danger right to Mr. Wood's doorstep. Danger that resulted in an unconscious, nearly dead Mr. Wood being taken away in an ambulance after the Mauvais, or one of his minions, had shattered various bones of my boss's body.

Despite receiving injuries that should have warranted surgery and at least a three-week stay in the intensive care unit, Mr. Wood's hospital trip lasted only a single night, and I suspected one of the Magics had repaired some of his extensive damage. Thanks to this head start down the road to recovery, Mr. Wood was showing daily improvements. Still, he was nowhere near to being fully recuperated.

Although my boss was now physically out of the worst trouble, he was chin-deep in financial woes due to the insane cost of health care. Mr. Wood had no intention of driving up any sort of credit card debt or of starting a Go Fund Me campaign (my suggestion), which meant he had to take on clients just to make the minimum payment on his hospital invoice. Luckily, local families had been using Wood's Funeral Home for generations of cadaverous care, and that loyalty had been keeping the business afloat.

So far.

As ever, Mr. Wood's role in the funeral home was to meet and greet, to arrange events, and to consult with family members about their final wishes for their loved ones. Other than fatiguing by midday, his injuries didn't greatly interfere with that work.

As for me, well...

While I could still apply makeup with only one good hand, shifting my clients onto my work table or moving them from table to coffin couldn't be done single-handedly. I was tempted to magic them around, but with my recent power boost there was a high risk I might send a body hurtling through the door and into the nearby park if I used any form of Lifting Charm on them.

As such, I had to have a babysitter. Oh sorry, a *mentor*.

Mr. Tenpenny had volunteered for the job. As part of this mentorship and training in magic control, I was allowed to use a Lifting Charm on the dead, but only when Mr. T enlisted his own spell to increase the gravity near the walls of my workroom. If any bodies did go flying, they'd immediately find themselves grounded before ever clearing the runway.

We'd managed to bring in five clients in the past couple weeks. It wasn't a pace that would keep Mr. Wood rolling in dough, but it was enough to keep him from drowning in a flood of medical expenses.

We probably could have taken on more clients, but in addition to Mr. Wood's broken limbs, we were also having a nasty case of the undead. But that's not exactly something you announce on a sign in the window of a funeral home, is it?

As Dr. Dunwiddle and the others had pointed out, unlike

before when I only had a little bit of the watch's essence in me, during my tussle with the Mauvais I had pulled in the watch's power. All of it. I was now basically the watch.

And that watch had some special features: It enhanced magical strength, it could control time, it could give the possessor the power to steal magic from others. Oh, and in the wrong hands (meaning my clumsy mitts) it could make the dead come back to life. And I had a feeling that's what all of Mr. Wood's messages and calls were about.

The moment I approached the building, I knew that feeling had been right.

Since Mr. Wood couldn't do much for himself in his condition, he needed a live-in nurse. And to ease a little worry from his shoulders, I'd taken on the responsibility of hiring them.

Did you notice I said "them" up there? It's so hard to find good help these days, or at least help that doesn't panic when faced with the Zombie Apocalypse.

See, with my new watch-fueled strength, our clients who were supposed to be resting in peace kept waking up. And even with strict instructions of where the nurses shouldn't go, and even with my workroom door being firmly locked, there had been a few incidents.

Apparently there'd been another, because as I came around from the side of the building, Nurse Number Three stood outside the funeral home's front door. Her arms were crossed over her sturdy bosom and her face was doing its best to look tough-as-nails. But the sweating brow, the greenish tinge to her pale skin, and the frantically wide eyes revealed the telltale signs of zombie-induced terror.

The second she saw me, she bustled across the parking lot toward me.

"I am going to the authorities with this. You have—" She gasped, then jutted a trembling finger at the funeral home. "You have a dead person in there."

"We are a funeral home," I said slowly as if she wasn't the brightest bulb in the marquee. "That big sign you're parked next to might have been your first clue."

"You know very well what I mean. I've heard about this place. I was told there were strange things going on, but I ignored it because you were paying double the usual rate."

"Who told you what exactly?" I thought I'd made it clear that lips needed to be kept sealed when Nurses One and Two departed.

Mr. Wood's business was already on probation after the Mortuary Board recently got wind of odd sightings and of a possible missing body. Responding to this, one of their investigators had doggedly tried to shut us down. He eventually came to his senses and declared that nothing was amiss, but we still had to keep our noses clean to avoid any further inquiries.

And with this recent spate of waking dead, I didn't think we could pass such scrutiny if an inspector was called in a second time. I mean, twice in less than a month? They'd have to be suspicious, right? That suspicion, and any subsequent investigation, would lead to the funeral home being shut down permanently.

"None of your business," Nurse Three snapped. "I'm quitting. Pay me now so I can go to the police."

"You can go to the police for free. Why do I need to pay you?"

"You know what I mean. Never mind. Withhold my pay. I can visit the Bureau of Labor and Industries after I finish with the cops."

"And I'll report you to the Nursing Board."

"For what?" she asked, fixing me with a defiant stare.

After pulling out my phone from my pocket, I swiped through to the correct screen as I said, "You've been knowingly practicing nursing without a license."

As if I'm one to talk. Mr. Wood had saved me from homelessness by hiring me to doll up the dead despite my own lack of a mortuary license. It's part of why I felt I owed him so much.

"Your nursing license expired six months ago," I said, watching her challenging expression slacken into self-doubt. My finger hovered over my phone's PayPal app, ready to send Nurse Three's paycheck through from Mr. Wood's account.

"My paperwork is in good order," she said with just enough uncertainty in her voice for me to know I'd won.

"Look," I said, putting on a sympathetic yet business-like tone, "I let it slide when you applied. I assumed you'd get things in order at some point. Now, if I can keep quiet about that, you can keep quiet about any delusions you had while here. Plus, if you start rambling on about what you think you saw, you'll never get that license reinstated. So, what were you saying about the cops?"

"I— Nothing," she said, sounding slightly overwhelmed by what was happening. I tapped the phone. Hers pinged, signaling the payment had gone through just as a crash sounded from inside the funeral home. Nurse Number Three jumped six inches backward. "There's something not right in there. I'm glad to be done with it."

She fumbled her keys from her bag, scurried away from me, and threw herself into her Hyundai hatchback.

Did Number Three really have an expired license? She did for now. As with certain clauses of my rental agreement, I'd used a little magic to alter our nurses' license expiration dates to *convince*, shall we say, them not to blabber about our little zombie situation. I suppose it really was a terrible trick, but it did guarantee their silence. And I always changed the license back to being valid. I'm clever, not evil.

As the Hyundai squealed out of the parking lot, the clanging crash of several pieces of metal hitting tile came from inside the funeral home. I sighed heavily. Magic would be so much more convenient if it would just stop waking up the dead.

CHAPTER FOUR

BACON BOUQUET

As soon as Number Three's hatchback bullied its way into traffic, I hurried around to the rear door and let myself in to find my latest client missing. Mr. Green was supposed to be spread out on my work table, waiting for an application of Dewy Beige foundation and Sunshine Rose blush.

Instead, he'd not only figured out which door he needed (this wasn't often the case, my first dead-alive person ended up in the storage closet), but he'd also navigated his way around the lock on my workroom door. From the workroom, he'd headed straight to the kitchen. Where he had pulled out drawer after drawer and upended the contents onto the linoleum. When I burst in, Mr. Green had his hand on the pull for the drawer that held the kitchen's knife collection.

"Cassie?" Mr. Wood called from his office where he was currently camped out. His living quarters were above the funeral home, but stairs tend to be tricky when your lower limbs are in more pieces than they should be.

"Be right there, Mr. Wood."

I approached Mr. Green. I couldn't screw this up. If anything went wrong with him — for example, if he wandered away and got hit by a bus — Mr. Wood's business would end up deader than our most recent clients. Although that was already a

41

distinct possibility. After Mr. Green's funeral, we had no other work scheduled. It was not good times for Wood's Funeral Home. And yes, I was consuming extra portions of guilt pie over all of Mr. Wood's current problems being entirely my fault.

But enough wallowing. There's a zombie to catch.

Mr. Green stopped in mid-pull, but not soon enough to keep the knife drawer from slipping out of its cubby. A Kershaw chef's knife went tip first through the center of Mr. Green's bare foot. I grit my teeth as an electric spark of phantom pain plunged deep into my own toes. I made a note to myself to get safety stops installed on the drawers.

"Mr. Green, I'm pretty sure being stabbed in the tarsal bones wasn't your last desire."

When the dead return to life — my dead anyway, I can't vouch for other zombies — they come back to satisfy one last bit of business they left unfinished when they died. Oddly enough, for each of the five clients we'd had over the past couple weeks, this last desire turned out to be a food craving.

Or maybe it wasn't so odd. Think about it, you deny yourself for years in an effort to stay healthy, but yet you still end up dead. You can't blame a corpse for reanimating with a major case of the munchies.

Even though the additional grocery shopping had added an extra chore to my work schedule, I wasn't complaining. Feeding hungry zombies was far easier than my previous waking dead who wanted to settle affairs with their significant others, or as in Mr. Tenpenny's case, to find their murderer.

Still, back then, in the good old days, my power hadn't been supercharged by the watch and only those people with truly compelling desires woke from their final sleep. This new, stronger power had the nasty side effect of waking up every dead person who came through our doors. But thankfully, none of them had a score to settle other than to give the middle finger to their calorie trackers.

I pointed to a magnetic chalkboard I'd stuck on the fridge and to the piece of chalk hanging from a string. I then realized I should have stopped to pull out the knife first.

As Mr. Green stepped away from his impalement, there was a cringe-inducing tearing noise. While the knife remained sticking up like a sundial in the linoleum, Mr. Green's foot ripped in half from mid-foot to middle toe. It was going to be a challenge to get that into a shoe for the funeral.

Mr. Green, oblivious to his future footwear issues, picked up the chalk and jotted down, "Bacon."

"I thought you were Jewish," I said. He shrugged in that way that said, "Yeah, but it's bacon." Luckily, with Mr. Wood being a junkie for BLTs, there was a bag full of cooked bacon in the fridge. "Is having it cold okay?" I asked, holding out a handful of bacon strips for Mr. Green.

Mr. Green nodded eagerly and snatched at the bacon bouquet. I let him have two pieces at a time, forcing him to delay his gratification while using the other pieces as a lure to get him back into the workroom. By the eighth slice, a look of bliss had filled his face. By the tenth, he had willingly laid himself out on the slab once more. After the final slice, he died happy. Hopefully, for the last time.

"May you have eternal dreams of porky goodness, Mr. Green," I said as I covered him with a sheet. I then left the workroom, hopped through the obstacle course of cutlery in the kitchen, and hurried to Mr. Wood's office.

Mr. Wood isn't one of those guys who gets angry. With his rotund figure and perpetually jovial demeanor, he would've made an excellent Santa Claus. So, to enter his makeshift living room and see him scowling at me, wasn't just a slap in the face, but a full-throttle walloping.

"Cassie, this can't go on. You…" He shook his head. "I'm going to have to fire you if this keeps up. Alice is scared out of her wits and I don't even know if she's remembered my BLT. Did you see her in there?"

"Alice has tendered her resignation," I said carefully, hoping to bedazzle him with big words so he'd ignore what I was saying. It didn't work. The scowl only got deeper.

"Not another one. I'm sorry, Cassie, but this is the last straw. Is Mr. Green…?"

"Satisfied. Dead."

"And who do we have scheduled after his funeral tomorrow?"

I swallowed hard. Mr. Wood organized the calendar. He knew exactly who we had after Mr. Green. "No one," I said, staring at my boots. I wiggled my toes to shake off the lingering, ghostly tingle from Mr. Green's little mishap.

"Exactly. I'm mobile enough to get my meals. I still can't get up and down the stairs, but if you can bring down a few of my things, I should be fine taking care of myself for a couple days. But as soon as I find another nurse, if nothing changes with your, well, with this situation, you're going to have to go."

"I don't know if the agency will send another." My ruse with the licenses had worked so far, but there's only so many times you can get away with the same trick before someone starts asking questions.

Mr. Wood let out an exasperated puff of air then turned his wheelchair around to stare at the blank screen of his television rather than look at me, at the person who was destroying a business that had been in his family for three generations.

I didn't want to leave Mr. Wood alone. Even if he was healing, I'd still worry. The Mauvais, or someone working for him, had attacked once. What if he came back? The Mauvais had done this to Mr. Wood because he thought the watch might be somewhere in the funeral home, and even though the Mauvais now had the watch, what if he used Mr. Wood to get to me, to take revenge for me tricking him?

"What if there was another way?" I asked.

"You've figured out how to stop this—" Mr. Wood waved his hand vaguely toward the kitchen. "This problem? Wasn't that what you were supposed to be doing the past few weeks?"

I walked around behind the TV so I could speak to him face to face. "No, but I might have an alternative to hiring another live-in nurse."

"I am not going to a care facility."

"No, of course not. I was thinking of live-in care, just in someone else's home instead of here."

"Whose?"

"You remember Mr. Tenpenny?"

"The dead guy?" he asked as if we had a stream of Mr. Tenpennys coming to the funeral home. Busby Tenpenny was my third experience with the dead refusing to stay dead and had quite literally introduced me to a whole new world.

"At least he's not going to be scared of dead people," I said with a grin, hoping to rally Mr. Wood's normal good cheer.

"That's not funny," he said gravely, but the corners of his eyes lifted ever so slightly. I watched as he seemed to rummage through his mind for arguments against the proposal until he finally said, "Fine. I'll give it a try."

"Just give me a bit to clean up the kitchen. Mr. Green did…" I hesitated, my feet shifting as if they could dance me into the right word. "Well, he did a bit of rearranging." I shouldn't have said that. Mr. Wood groaned and dropped his head into his hands in disappointed disbelief. "I'll be going now."

"Just remember to bring me my BLT when you come back."

CHAPTER FIVE

NEW ROOMMATES

Once I'd gotten the kitchen back in order, I pieced together a couple BLTs that were lighter on the bacon than Mr. Wood normally preferred. But I think he'd agree it was worth sacrificing some bacon to keep the place from being ransacked by a corpse.

I gathered up a few of Mr. Wood's belongings, placed the bag in his lap, then double checked that Mr. Green was still dead. With one sandwich in hand and another in his belly, Mr. Wood remained silent as I wheeled him out the front door.

I could have magicked Mr. Wood from his chair into his Prius, but the funeral home parking lot was clearly visible from the street and the neighboring houses. Using magic in front of Norms was a no-no except in emergency situations.

But the real problem was that, as with my clients, my unsupervised use of a Lifting Charm risked flinging my boss clear across the Willamette River. Which would not win me any points with him or with the fine folks of MagicLand. No, the best course would be to wheel Mr. Wood the five blocks back to my place. Seriously, you had to do a lot of thinking when you were hopped up on magic.

Once to my building, I entered the code on the security keypad, then performed some gymnast-type moves to get Mr.

Wood's wheelchair through the doorway while also trying to keep the door from closing and locking again. Mr. Wood barely had time to comment on the gnome out front when I looked up to find Morelli leaning his bulk up against the stair railing.

"I know for a fact that your lease says no roommates."

Not yet, I thought, and bit back a smile.

"He's not a roommate. He's just staying until a friend picks him up."

"And how are you planning to get him up the stairs?"

Inwardly, I groaned. It's annoying when you start relying on magic, then you can't use that stupid magic without risk to life and property.

"You lift at the front and I wheel him up backwards?" I asked encouragingly, like we helped each other do things like that all the time.

"No," Mr. Wood insisted and shifted his hands against the arms of the chair as if he might try to stand despite his left leg still being fully encased in a cast.

"Sit," I commanded. "We'll figure this out." I had been planning to take Mr. Wood through my portal. From there, I could wheel him the few MagicLand blocks that separated my place from Busby's, as opposed to the few miles that separated our homes on the non-magic side of Portland. I guess I missed the part of the equation where I got him to my portal in the first place.

"How about he stay at my place?" Morelli suggested in a very creepy, very if-this-were-a-horror-movie-it-would-be-time-to-run kind of way. But Mr. Wood couldn't run. The tips of my fingers vibrated, the magic surging to them in preparation for a fight.

"His friend won't be looking for him there," I said cautiously.

Morelli leaned in. I expected to be hit with the stench of sweat or stale cigars, but instead I smelled a certain something.

Spicy, but not peppery. Ginger?

He whispered, "I know you changed your lease. And I know how."

"You're—?"

"Not exactly," he said with a snide grin. "But I know what you are."

And like my own brain giving me a slap in the face, I recalled the way he and Fiona had exchanged glances when they first met. Or when I'd thought they'd first met. If I had a bit higher social IQ, I might have realized it had been a look of recognition that had bounced between them.

A sudden chill ran through me. Morelli despised me. Could he be an ally of the Mauvais? I told myself it wasn't likely. First, I'd like to think Fiona would have known and warned me. Second — and far more convincing — was Morelli had had plenty of chances to do me harm, but he'd never done anything more than verbally threaten me with eviction. Well, and offend my eyes on a daily basis, but that was the least of my worries lately.

Before I could stammer out any of the gazillion questions popcorning around in my head, Morelli said, "You left your magic stink all over your lease papers. Not that I wouldn't have figured it out, anyway. You messed with the wrong guy, Black."

"What does that mean?" I asked, my certainty that he wasn't plotting to kill me crumbling to dust.

"My specialty is detecting forgeries in the community."

"Is that why you're such a jerk to me?"

"Nah, that's because you're such a pain in the ass. Plus, me treating you like dirt kept your *talent* on the back burner."

He filled the word *talent* with utter derision, and I had no idea what he meant about back burners, but that was a question for later. Right now, Mr. Wood had already had a busy day of recuperating and dealing with freaked-out nurses and self-mutilating corpses. I wanted to get him settled.

"Do you happen to have a door? And do not point to the one right behind you. You know what I mean. I need to get to Busby's."

"Is that where you're taking him?"

"He needs a caretaker for a little while."

"Why? You scare away all the nurses?"

Mr. Wood laughed. "Something like that."

"You want to stay with me?" Morelli asked Mr. Wood.

"I hardly know you."

"I like to crochet and I make the meanest BLAT in Southeast Portland."

"BLAT?" Mr. Wood asked eagerly. "What's the A stand for?"

"Avocado."

Mr. Wood perked up. With eyes wide and eager, he sat a little straighter in his chair.

"Well, if you don't think I'll be in the way."

"He needs care," I insisted, "not just sandwiches. He also needs protection."

"You ever see anyone near my door? Even a salesman?" I shook my head. "I got protections. And as for care, I served in the Medi Unit of the Magical Armed Guard Elite during the worst of the Mauvais period. I know care."

Before I could even fathom, comprehend, or file away the extra two thousand questions I had regarding the Magical Armed Thingamajig, Mr. Wood was agreeing to stay if it wasn't too much trouble. Morelli said it was no trouble at all and wheeled Mr. Wood into his apartment. He stopped and turned to me once he'd gotten the wheelchair over the threshold.

"When you're ready to come by and discuss that lease, my portal's on the side of the pink house at the end of Lola's street."

CHAPTER SIX
PIPPI PROBLEMS

I told Mr. Wood I'd come by in the morning and collect him for Mr. Green's funeral, then grumbled out a thanks to Morelli who replied with a snorting chuckle. Before Morelli had even closed the door, the two men, who had forged an instant friendship based on pig products, were already discussing the perfect crispiness of bacon for a BLT, or a BLAT. I trudged upstairs. I was just pouring Pablo a few treats from the bag when my phone's alarm squawked.

I rolled my eyes. I mean I'd just intimidated a hard-working nurse, filled a corpse full of bacon, faced the possibility of soon being jobless, and learned my landlord had connections with MagicLand. You'd think I deserved at least fifteen minutes for a donut break. But nope, it was time for another class. I let out a long, weary sigh, scratched Pablo behind the ears, clambered back through my portal, and high-tailed it to the kitchen classroom within Spellbound Patisserie.

After facing down the Mauvais, I had asked to be properly trained. Since prior to this I'd been doing my damnedest to get rid of my magic, the request shocked a few Magics, but my actual lessons came as a shock to me. I foolishly thought I'd just continue on with the private tutelage I'd been receiving when my only goal had been to rein in enough of my magic so I could be drained — that being the process in which a Magic gives up his or her power, whether that giving up is forced or done willingly.

Although I was still attending some of my one-on-one lessons, it turns out when you say you'll start training, you literally start training like any other Magic. This was terrible for what little pride I possessed, because most Magics begin their training at a young age. All that is to say, there I was, a self-sufficient, twenty-eight-year-old woman having to attend classes full of thirteen-year-olds.

By the time I reached Spellbound's classroom, all the kiddies were sitting in pairs at their workbenches, their faces bright and eager as Gwendolyn stood at the front of the room explaining what they'd be doing that day.

Gwendolyn, baker of delicious desserts, was even taller than me, with short, brown hair that grew in untamed corkscrew curls. She didn't have the eastern seaboard accent, but she still reminded me of Julia Child, the famous chef.

Like Ms. Child, Gwendolyn had a talent for baking, but somehow I don't think Julia Child ever dreamed of her culinary talents spilling over into becoming the best potions instructor MagicLand ever had. Well, the best until I came along and blew apart, not only Gwendolyn's kitchen, but also her confidence in her teaching skills.

I had improved, though. With the past couple weeks of slow and careful instruction, I could now turn any mouse a perfect shade of pink with my concoctions. Something I couldn't muster at all when I first started brewing magic juice.

Still, I'd never been one for cooking, so Potions Making would never be my favorite class. Plus, I swear all these kids had been raised beside a cauldron and could tell by smell alone exactly how much eye of newt or scale of cobra was in a sample they were expected to re-create. As if *that* had any application in the real world. To be honest, I would have rather had Gwendolyn teach me how to bake up the perfect eclair than the perfect elixir, but I wasn't given a say in my curriculum.

As Gwendolyn called roll, I tried to sneak in. I know, what was I thinking? I'm tall. I'm clumsy. I don't sneak. I ended up tripping over the threshold from the main kitchen into the classroom. Gwendolyn's words cut off and fifteen giggling heads whipped in my direction. I don't know why they were so amused, I did this nearly every time I passed from the kitchen into the classroom whose wooden floor sat just one inch higher than the main kitchen's tiles. I mean seriously, these people were magic, you'd think they could get the floor from one part of the patisserie to sit evenly with another part.

"Oh good, Ms. Black has arrived. We were one short." Gwendolyn pointed to a bench table to the left of the room. The girl seated there looked away, clearly mortified that she was getting stuck with me for a partner. Can't blame her for that, really.

I wove my way through the tables to sit beside the girl. From her hair to her freckles it was like her parents had given birth to Pippi Longstocking. And judging by her smock dress and mismatched undershirt, they were doing their best to enhance that look. They hadn't inserted wire to curl up her coppery braids, but I'd bet they'd considered it.

"Today we'll be working on a recipe that will make a vampire's teeth soft so they can't bite you."

I didn't earn any points when I asked Gwendolyn — who I was now supposed to call "Ms. Morgan" — why if a vampire had bad teeth, wouldn't he just carry a pocketknife to make a couple tiny slits in your neck and turn you into a blood-filled juice box.

This comment extracted a gasp from Pippi, much nervous shuffling from the rest of the class, and a stern glare from Gwen— Ms. Morgan.

Apparently vampires were very scary business in MagicLand because the cheeks of every kid, from the darkest skin tones to the lightest, went as white as Gwendolyn's ivory complexion.

"Please everyone," Gwendolyn said reassuringly, "Ms. Black just has an odd sense of humor. Vampires do not carry knives, and Ms. Black would know that if she had kept up with her studies of magic culture. Because as we all know, vampires have not been allowed to carry sharp objects of any kind since, when?"

Pippi shot up her hand.

"Yes, Inga?"

Okay, so not Pippi.

"1964 in the Vampire Tolerance Act," not-Pippi recited.

I rolled my eyes. Would knowing that help me defeat the Mauvais? Maybe if I wanted to bore him to death.

"Very good, now if everyone could begin to slowly add the corn syrup to the marshmallow-acid blend, we will practice the incantation that will turn dentin into rubber.

I can't be blamed for what happened next. I still feel bad, but I refuse to take full responsibility for it.

I was perfectly willing to let Eager Little Inga do the whole spell, but Gwendolyn, in an attempt to make sure everyone (namely me) was taking part, declared that the shorter person at the bench would do the pouring and the taller person would do the incantation.

Inga measured and poured and mixed and followed Gwendolyn's instructions to add a couple flavorings until the mixture smelled like root beer. Then it was my turn.

Over my time in MagicLand I've learned I'm a hands-on kind

of witch. Give me a Shoving Charm any day, but do not ask me to do an incantation. I feel silly muttering words hoping they'll do something. I far prefer the more practical stuff where I can picture the physics of the magic doing its work. Potions was more like chemistry, and I'd never done well at chemistry. I tried to imagine the molecules of the ingredients blending together, but since potions only work after they've been administered to their intended victim, it's not the same as the immediate effect of shifting a book from here to, just for example, the other side of a wall.

But I knew I needed to try. I needed to get a handle on my magic if only to keep Mr. Wood's clients from roaming around. So, feeling like an utter fool, I spoke the words and concentrated my magic onto the mixing bowl in front of me.

Yes, a mixing bowl, not a cauldron, which still disappoints me.

When the brew started bubbling, I glanced around. Okay, good. There was bubbling going on in other mixing bowls as well. I kept on with the incantation and closed my eyes to fully picture the magic and the end goal. I had in mind Edward Cullen coming in for a glittery bite of Bella's neck and then finding himself in need of Vampire Viagra.

And then Inga was screaming. Everyone was screaming. And Gwendolyn was shoving me aside, shouting at me to get Dr. Dunwiddle immediately. When I finally got a glimpse past Gwendolyn's frantically fussing frame, my mixing bowl had bubbled up and over and the contents had somehow gone off like a geyser all over Pippi/Inga.

Okay, the tiny and short-lived spark of pride I experienced was probably inappropriate, but you have to give me credit for making the potion work. Problem was, it worked a bit too well because Inga now lay on the floor in a pool of red braids and gingham fabric. Most of her bones had turned to rubber and her unsupported muscles were wobbling in a way that reminded me of something from a Jell-O ad.

Unfortunately, as a land-dwelling vertebrate, a rigid skeleton really is handy to hold all the squishy bits of the body in place. Inga's eyes rolled out of their sockets and the twin sacks of her lungs fluttered under her dress with her panicked breath.

"Go get Runa," Gwendolyn ordered. When my legs refused to move, she shouted, "Now, Cassie!"

Like some sort of verbal Shoving Charm, her words jerked me out of my shock and sent me running.

CHAPTER SEVEN

FACING THE FIRING SQUAD

Ignoring the disgruntled looks being hurled at me from passersby, I sprinted to Dr. Dunwiddle's clinic. I didn't explain. I just said (okay, screamed) that there was a pool of Pippi on Gwendolyn's floor. Dr. D gave a disdainful shake of her head that not only left her hovering glasses scrambling to keep up, but also told me she'd been expecting this and was not happy about it.

"Stay right there," she barked. "Don't move from that spot and do not touch anything in this clinic." She then grabbed her bag and dashed down the street.

I waited. And to prove I was a trustworthy individual despite my earlier thievery, I obeyed her order not to touch anything. Not even the packets of sugar cookies that were beckoning my name as dinnertime came and went. I toyed with the idea of hurrying home for a quick bite to eat and to get some comforting cheek rubs from Pablo, but I knew if Runa came back and I was gone, I'd be in even more trouble.

The light outside changed from daytime bright to that rosy, Pacific-Northwest-summer evening glow, turning the robin's egg blue walls of the clinic a curious shade of lavender. From behind me came the tinkling chime of the bell that dangled above the entryway. I turned, doing my best to stay in the exact spot where

I'd been when Dr. D took off. At the sight of who had stepped in, a tiny fruit bat thrummed its wings inside my stomach.

"Why are you standing there?" Alastair asked, his face a mix of sympathy, amusement, and curiosity.

"Runa told me not to move."

"I'm sure she wasn't being literal."

"It's me we're talking about. She's probably got the place booby trapped against me."

Alastair pointed to the chairs in the waiting area of the clinic. My feet were throbbing and my legs ached from standing. The offer was too good to refuse. The moment I sat down, my toes cheered with relief.

"Any news?" I asked, rubbing my knees to stir them back to life.

"I only know that Runa's working on it," said Alastair as he sat in the chair next to me. He didn't ease back, but remained perched on the edge of the seat. I knew he'd get up soon and move away to protect himself from my magic ShopVac, but I appreciated the gesture. And since my worry over Inga/Pippi was pushing aside any suspicious thoughts, having him there was comforting.

The comfort disappeared as quickly as a slice of cake in front of a spell-weakened Magic when Dr. Dunwiddle returned. As soon as she stepped through the door, I jumped up from my seat. Runa narrowed her eyes when she saw me. The mint-and-honey scent of her magic filled the room as her glasses flew over and quickly scanned the shelves before they zipped back into her breast pocket. Mr. Tenpenny and Fiona followed in the wake of her annoyance.

"Well?" I asked, the word barely coming through my dry throat.

"Inga's going to be okay," Runa said, setting her bag on the counter near the register. "But she's going to be in Intensive Care for several days at the very least. It's just a good thing Gwendolyn followed protocol and told me what lessons she was doing this week, otherwise I wouldn't have had the proper equipment on hand to save the girl."

"What happened? It was just a simple potion."

I don't know why I asked. I knew what had happened: Cassie Black had happened. There were no simple spells, no simple potions, no simple incantations with me.

"You nearly dissolved all her bones. Luckily, those long legs of yours got you here in time for me to stop it. There were enough bone cells left to rebuild, but if it had gone on just a few minutes longer, she'd have died."

I dropped back into the wooden chair. Elbows on knees, I leaned forward and pressed my palms over my face. This was way worse than blowing up a kitchen or accusing an Untrained of using the Exploding Heart Charm on his grandfather. I looked up at the three of them through my fingers.

"You're going to kick me out, aren't you?"

"We wouldn't kick you out," said Fiona. It made me feel a little better and put a tiny amount of air in my balloon of belonging. "You're far too dangerous to be set loose." And the balloon deflated again. "Alastair, you might want to change seats."

Alastair got up, gave my shoulder a squeeze, then went over to lean against Dr. Dunwiddle's main counter. Not that he could ever look awful, but even in the warm pink of the evening light, his skin looked paler, duller, a little worse for wear from sitting beside me.

"So what happens now?" I asked. "Magical Prison? Forced Draining?"

A little noise came from Mr. Tenpenny's throat. It reminded

me of his efforts to speak when he first decided being dead really wasn't for him. I didn't know what he might have to say, but I couldn't meet his eye.

When he had first told me I was a witch, I'd wanted nothing to do with it. I wanted drained and I wanted to go back to a simple, solitary life. I didn't see the point of magic since it certainly hadn't done me a lick of good for well over twenty years of my life. I also most definitely did not want to be part of this community, of any community for that matter.

But after meeting these people and recognizing the kindness of their efforts to teach and help me, for the first time since meeting Mr. Wood, I'd felt a sense of belonging. And although my natural instinct was to keep other humans at a distance, I kind of wanted to make an effort to be a part of this group, which was a very icky and very unfamiliar feeling for me.

Now, with the people I'd grown closest to staring at me with that what-should-we-do-with-her look on their faces, I realized that belonging and fitting in wasn't in the cards for me. Whether it was intentional, accidental, or my typical rash behavior, my every action did nothing but chisel away at my chances of being accepted here. Again, I don't know why I was surprised. It wouldn't be the first bridge I'd burnt in my life.

Well, maybe I'd dissolved this particular bridge.

"Look, I can't be trusted. I'm a magic menace. I can understand if you're thinking of extracting me."

Extracting, in case you've forgotten, is like draining but to the most extreme degree possible. It removes all of a Magic's power and tends to have nasty side effects that make a botched lobotomy look like a fun day out at the zoo.

"We're not going to drain you or extract you," said Mr. T.

"Not yet," Dr. D muttered. She may have just put in a grueling few hours encouraging a handful of bone cells to get their act together, but she wasn't too tired not to despise me all over again. And we'd been getting along so well.

"So what are you going to do? You can't put me back in class with those kids. I won't go," I said, feeling stubbornly heroic. "And you yourselves said I can't go around without being trained."

"An opportunity has come up," said Fiona in a way that made *opportunity* sound like a euphemism for "lucky break for us."

"Opportunity?"

"Headquarters has sent a letter," Mr. T said. "They've heard about you and the watch, and they think it's best if you go there where you can be properly trained." He spoke tentatively, as if he was selecting just the right words. Or as if he wasn't certain how much he was allowed to say. That bat that had been fluttering in my belly? It now seemed to be climbing up my spine with its tiny, clawed feet.

"Properly corralled is more like it," Dr. Dunwiddle said under her breath. Mr. Tenpenny gave her a scolding look, but she merely shrugged it off.

"Anyway," said Fiona, "it would require you studying with another community. One that has more stringent training methods."

My hackles went up faster than an overexcited kitten who's just rounded a corner to find a German Shepherd staring him down. I'd barely gotten comfortable with being in the Portland community. I did not want to go to headquarters where I'd be thrown in amongst a bunch of new Magics, where I'd be Freak Number One all over again, and where I'd likely be subjected to at least a dozen embarrassing types of scrutiny.

"And if I refuse?"

"We think it's best you go," Mr. T said, but there was the tiniest bit of hesitancy in his voice.

I was feeling vulnerable. I was feeling stupid. I was feeling afraid of another upheaval to my routine. As such, that tiny bit of hesitancy sparked a wildfire of stubborn self-defeat within me. What comes next is not my proudest moment in MagicLand.

"Look, just drain me," I whined. "That's what all this is going to amount to, right? Despite what some of you claim, I am not a natural at this. I'm too old to be properly trained, and it's too late for me to learn how to control this much magic. Drain me, then put whatever comes out in a piece of magic Tupperware so someone in need can have the leftovers and I can go back to my life."

"Is that really what you want?" Fiona asked in that tone you use when you're pretty sure someone is just lashing out. Which, in all fairness, I was.

I darted a glance at Alastair. His color had returned, but there was anxious concern in his eyes. I looked away. Alastair was a messy variable that I couldn't bring into this equation.

I thought of what Vivian had offered when she lured me to her boutique to hand over the watch, and what she'd said before our little showdown. She had hinted my parents might be alive and Runa had later confirmed the possibility. They were supposed to have been killed by the Mauvais, but they may not have been and that spark of hope was part of what left me eager to make an effort with my magic and with the MagicLand community.

Now with this, with all of them looking at me and talking about me and contemplating fobbing me off to be someone else's problem, any sense of wanting to stay was getting shoved far to the back of my mind. On top of being upset over melting Inga/Pippi, I felt like I was being ganged up on. So, I did what comes naturally to me: I stayed stubborn and even raised the stubbornness ante.

"Yes, drain me. Go on, do it." I held out my arm as if ready to give blood.

"You know it doesn't work like that," Dr. Dunwiddle said, rolling her eyes. "It would take at least an hour to get everything set up and I'm too tired to do it today. Come back tomorrow."

"Ohhh-kay." I stretched out the word, a little thrown that my offer had been accepted. I mean, I expected them to refuse, to argue against the very idea, to cajole me back into feeling like I was one of them. Merlin's beard, I had really screwed up, hadn't I? "So, should I go home now?"

"That's probably for the best," Runa said wearily. "You can meet us back here tomorrow morning."

Putting on my I-don't-need-you face, I stomped over and yanked open the door, self-consciously cringing at the noise of the entry bell.

Of course, my resolve to hate everyone faltered the moment the bell ting-a-linged my departure. I tucked down my head to hide the prickling tears of confused disgrace I was desperately trying to hold back. With head tucked and shoulders hunched, I zigzagged my way out of Runa's neighborhood, moving as quickly as possible toward the side street where my portal was located.

A little tip: Although walking with your head down fully emphasizes your I'm-so-morose air, it's terrible for your back and shoulders. It also makes it really hard to see other sidewalk users. Which is why, in my hunch-y haste, I collided into Tobey Tenpenny.

Apparently the gods of magic had decided my day hadn't already been horrible enough.

CHAPTER EIGHT
LETTER FROM HQ

Tobey had been walking hand in hand with Daisy, who was impossibly gorgeous. Come to think of it, it was completely possible since she was a witch who could charm her skin into its super smooth, gleaming perfection as well as add a magic bounce and sheen to her long, blonde, shampoo-ad hair. It also helped her appearance that, unlike me, her eyes weren't brimming with tears and her nose wasn't burning red with a surge of emotion-induced snot that threatened to burst through at any moment.

"Cassie, I heard they want to train you at headquarters," Tobey said excitedly. "That's great news."

Have I mentioned MagicLand isn't big on privacy?

"Yeah, well, I'm not going."

"Are you a moron?" All his excitement changed to the offended irritation I was used to from the early days of our frenemy-ship. "Do you realize the opportunity you're being given?"

Tobey is an Untrained, that's a person who should be a Magic but, for whatever weird quirk of genetics, isn't. Having grown up with a grandfather who was, before his death, a talented wizard who ranked rather high up in the magic world, Tobey knows what he's missed out on. And he seemed to take it as a personal insult when other people, namely me, didn't see the magic in being a Magic.

"I melted a girl today, okay? I've changed my mind. I can't handle this magic crap anymore, so why don't you run along with Malibu Barbie and stop judging what I do with my life."

This earned me a deservedly nasty look from Daisy. I was lucky she didn't zap me with a Wart Charm, but maybe that was only because she didn't have any toad skin in her purse. See, I do pay attention in potions class. I'm just not good with putting what I've learned in that class into practice.

"You're a real piece of work, Cassie." Tobey tugged Daisy by the hand to pull her along as he huffed away from me.

To her credit, Daisy yanked her hand out of his and threatened to magic all his hair out if he ever dared to drag her like a dog again. If I didn't hate everyone at that moment, I might have wanted to make friends with her.

Once I got to my portal, I rushed inside and tripped my way through the mess of coats and shoes until I tumbled out of my closet door. I was never more glad to be back in my rat-trap apartment. Pablo purred at the sight of me, a bag of kettle corn was calling my name, and I had a freshly filled growler in the fridge. I poured a glass, filled up a bowl, and plunked down on my battered couch with Pablo and a novel that had nothing to do with magic.

Just as I was getting into the story, a knock sounded from inside my closet. I got up and tiptoed over to the flimsy door. I half-expected it to be Dr. Dunwiddle ready to drag me away to my draining. Or perhaps it was Inga's parents come to hurl insults and pain-inducing magic spells at me (even though this was entirely illegal according to the guidelines set by the Council on Magic Morality).

Unsure whose angry face might be lurking behind the door, I leaned closer to it and took a sniff. I chided myself over how quickly this had become a habit, and an image of me as a droopy-faced bloodhound sprang to mind. And just so you know, this isn't some weird fetish or compulsive behavior I've developed. See, all Magics carry on them a defining and unique scent that varies depending on who's doing the smelling.

Through the door, I detected chocolate and an underlying hint of raspberries. After all our time together, I should have become fully acclimated to that scent. But as with everything else, the watch had boosted my magical sniffer.

Despite wanting to stew in my bad mood, despite wanting nothing to do with magic or the magic community, and despite a lingering know-it-all voice in the back of my head telling me I shouldn't be alone with him, I smiled as the fruit bat in my belly fluttered his wings again.

"I thought you were supposed to stay away from me," I said when I opened the door, pushed aside my jackets, and invited Alastair in.

"I need to keep my distance, but this should help," he said, lifting up a white box decorated with blue and silver flourishes. I raised my eyebrows, asking a silent question. "Chocolate cupcakes with raspberry filling and hazelnut whipped cream frosting," he answered. So, maybe it wasn't him I had scented. Maybe I'd caught a whiff of those baked beauties.

"You do have a way with words," I said as Pablo strolled over to rub a couple thousand hairs all over the lower portion of Alastair's dark blue slacks.

As Alastair started one of his timers — a mechanical penguin this time — I poured him a glass of beer. I also refilled my own mug because nothing goes better with decadently sweet chocolate than a wickedly bitter IPA. When I brought the drinks, Pablo was eyeing the timer as it waddled back and forth across my shabby coffee table.

With me on the couch, Alastair in the wingback chair, and Pablo inching closer to the penguin, we made small talk, finished off two cupcakes, and consumed half the growler before Alastair got around to the real reason he'd stopped by. "I think you should do the training at HQ."

I rolled my eyes. Of course this couldn't just be a friendly little chitchat over cupcakes.

"Just because I'm practically drunk on sugar, which I'm not supposed to be having, by the way, doesn't mean I've lost my senses. I need to be drained. It's the only way for me to move on with my life and for all the little Wyrd children to stay safe."

Wyrd being the official name for Magics in the Portland community. Or maybe all communities. I suppose I should fact-check that.

Pablo leapt onto the table and took a swipe at the timer. I was about to scold him, when the penguin waddled just out of the cat's reach.

"Maybe you want to read the letter first," Alastair said, then slid a precisely folded sheet of paper across the coffee table. I took it, and something about the feel of the smooth paper under my fingers woke up a spark of hope I thought had gone dormant. Or maybe it was the buzz from so much IPA.

"Are you supposed to have this?" I asked. More importantly, was I supposed to have it?

"No, so don't mention it to any of the others."

I unfolded the letter and recognized Alastair's sharp handwriting. I looked up at him questioningly.

"After reading the original, I copied it out as soon as I could. It might not be word for word, but it's close."

Secret messages? Subterfuge? My curiosity level ratcheted up several notches. While Pablo kept up his attempts at penguin hunting, I read the letter.

Dear Mr. Tenpenny and Friends:

It has come to our attention that a Ms. Cassie Black has joined your community and that she has faced the Mauvais. We also understand she allowed the Mauvais to take the watch, but was quick thinking and skilled enough to pull the magic from the watch before it ended up in his hands.

While we are impressed with this show of talent, you must realize how dangerous she may be. She is now the watch, and if the Mauvais catches her, he will use her for any purpose he sees necessary to regain his power, which we believe to have been greatly diminished when the Starlings acquired the timepiece from him.

As such, we would ask her to come to Headquarters to evaluate and train her. Here we can better protect her, and in turn, protect Magics and non-magics alike. We understand this is an unusual offer, but this is an unusual circumstance.

This didn't seem all that eye-opening. I already knew I was a powder keg of magic and that my training was now focused on reining some of it in. I lowered the letter and reached for another cupcake. Alastair playfully smacked my hand and pulled the box away.

"Not until you finish that," he said, glancing meaningfully at the sheet in my hand.

"You could have just copied out the good bits." I drained the remaining swig of beer from my mug then went back to the letter.

Another matter has also come to our attention about your Ms. Black. If she is indeed the daughter of the Starlings, you may wish to inform her that some sources have reported the Starlings may not have died.

This may only be rumor and we are not making it public knowledge until we gather more concrete information. If they are alive, we cannot guarantee what condition they are in; they may have been extracted. We are looking further into this and have been consulting with Dr. Runa Dunwiddle on the matter as she has done the most studies regarding draining and extractions.

We cannot insist strongly enough that Ms. Black comes to HQ. She is both a danger and in danger. She should have been sent here sooner, and we will intervene if she doesn't come willingly. We welcome you to join her. You knew the Starlings well, and it's been too long since your last visit. Although we hear you are a little changed since last we saw you.

Sincerely,

Olivia

I didn't like all the "insisting" and "we will intervene" language, but I couldn't dwell on that portion of the letter. I scanned the second to last paragraph once more, then stared at Alastair. My mouth may have been gaping in stupefied surprise.

"So my parents might really be alive? Vivian wasn't just making it up?"

Like a child unwilling to give up her belief in the Easter bunny, I desperately wanted to believe these two people I'd never met were still among the living. But the cynic in me had kicked and punched at this tiny bit of optimism so often and so brutally that it had remained cowering in a far corner of my mind.

However, if they were alive, if the rumors were circulating not just between a few people in the Portland community but at HQ as well, if there really was evidence of their not being dead, my inner cynic might just let that little spark of optimism get up and wander around a while.

"Why didn't the others mention this earlier?"

"I asked them about it after you left. That's why I didn't leave when you did. I told them this was a sure way to get you to go, but they said since finding your parents alive is such a slim possibility, they didn't want you going for that reason alone. They want you to go out of a desire to become a better Magic.

"I don't agree. I think anything that can convince you to go and get a handle on the insane amount of power you've taken in would be good for you. You need to be able to protect yourself. And," he added, "it would be nice for other reasons." His cheeks warmed and his gaze dropped to the frosting on his cupcake, a charmingly shy grin on his lips.

"Could they be alive? I mean, even if their brains have been magically scrambled?" An extraction, especially one done by an evil wizard, does not leave the brain in Mensa-level condition.

"I can't say with any certainty. But if there are reports or even rumors, I think it's worth you finding out what's behind them and who's making the claims. I probably shouldn't tell you this, but you'll find out anyway. HQ isn't far from where your parents were last seen." He pointed at the growler and I gestured for him to go ahead. With Pablo now more fascinated with my guest than the timer, Alastair poured us both half a glass. After he took a sip, he cautiously said, "Busby will go with you. And I was thinking of going as well."

"You would go with me? Even though—"

"Of course I would," Alastair said, and then it was my turn to fiddle with my cupcake to hide the heat in my cheeks. With a cheeky smirk in his voice, he added, "You know, for moral support."

"Is that what the kids are calling it these days?" I asked as I picked up my mug.

"Look, at some point you would have found out about this." He tapped the paragraph about my parents with his long forefinger. "And I know you'll want to pursue it."

"The thought may have crossed my mind."

"Exactly. And from what we saw during your little stunt with Vivian, I have a feeling you'd rush in without fully considering the consequences." I pursed my lips, ready to go on the defense. "Don't pull that face. What you did was incredible, but also incredibly stupid. I would go as one of your instructors, but I also want to go to help you find your parents."

"Why you? Busby is the one who worked with them." I hated how harshly the question came out of my mouth. Why when we were having such a lovely evening full of grins and cupcakes and beer did I have to puzzle over whether Alastair had ulterior motives? Did he already know where my parents were? Would he somehow use them to deliver me to the Mauvais?

The warm, open look on Alastair's face clouded over. "They were my friends. I want to help find them, but we do it my way."

"Which is?"

"Methodically, not with your smash-and-grab style. Also, I happen to know where the best cake shops are near HQ." He paused, letting this tempting offer settle over me. "So will you go?"

What can I say? I was curious. Not just about the cake shops, but about my parents as well. The very idea of finding them, of seeing them, seemed crazier than the existence of magic. And yes, I was also curious about Alastair. I just hoped that old saying about the murderous qualities of curiosity wouldn't prove to be true.

Speaking of curiosity, Pablo was casting sly glances at the timer, his muscles twitching with patience and preparation.

"Fine, I'll go. But if I hate it, if we find out these tales about my parents really are nothing more than rumors, we're coming home."

"Agreed," he said and clinked his glass to mine.

Just then the timer went off. Pablo launched and batted the penguin across the table. Witnessed by humans for the first time, a penguin flew. But only a couple feet before it crash landed on the floor. Pablo pounced, knocked the timer around a few times, then as he was prone to do, flicked his toy under the couch.

"Bad cat," I scolded. "Sorry, I'll get it."

"It's alright. I've got a dozen of them. The penguin ones aren't the most accurate, anyway. Always going off early." He checked another timer on his phone, then turned the screen to me. "See, six more minutes."

I swirled some frosting onto my finger. I was just about to lick it off when a question stopped me.

"Where is HQ, anyway? No, let me guess, it's in the basement of the Portland Art Museum and I've been unaware of it all this time."

"Not quite," he said, arching an eyebrow with wry amusement. "HQ is in London."

CHAPTER NINE

THE FINAL SHOW

"London?" I said once I'd picked my jaw up off the floor. Only then did I recall Busby mentioning London in connection to my parents' last mission.

"Sure. Sorry, I thought you knew."

"Why would I know that? I didn't even know MagicLand existed until a few weeks ago."

"True. I sometimes forget you're new to all this. Anyway, I'll tell the others you've agreed. It'll take a day to make arrangements, and well…" He rubbed the back of his neck and gave me a sheepish look. "You're kind of suspended from classes for now, so you'll have the day free to get ready." Which was good since I still needed to squeeze Mr. Green's flayed foot into a shoe and get everything in place for his afternoon funeral. "You should probably pack what you'll need for a couple weeks."

"But what about Pablo?"

Pablo, who had been staring under the couch with his tail swishing back and forth, perked up and started purring at the sound of his name.

"He could stay with Lola. She'll love having him around."

And no doubt she'd figure out some way to get him to push a vacuum around by the end of his stay.

When Alastair left, we did that awkward pausing thing you do when you don't quite know whether or not to finally sneak in that first kiss. Or, in my case, to take the risk and ask if the person who was turning your heart into an Olympic gymnast on crack, if he was working for your mortal enemy.

Just as my lips began to tingle — whether in preparation to smooch or to blurt out an accusation, I still wasn't sure — Pablo broke the tension by scratching in his litter box a single time then launching from it as if the litter had just become electrified. In a small apartment it didn't take long to realize what he was fleeing from. Alastair and I both groaned, slapped our hands over our mouths and noses, then cursed the cat. Nothing like the stench of poo to kill the mood, am I right?

To save him from any toxic fumes, I pushed Alastair out of my apartment and through the portal. After cleaning the box, I flung the windows wide open and lit a dozen candles. I then settled down and tried to get back to my book, but not a single sentence made its way from my eyes to my brain.

I suppose I should have been filling my head with packing lists, what sights I'd get to see in London, and where we'd be staying, but unlike the Great Stink of Pablo, the reality of the trip refused to take hold.

Knowing I needed some sort of distraction as well as practice, I worked on a Light Capture Charm, a spell that allowed you to draw in photons even in the dark. It was a strange bit of quantum physics that relied on entangled light particles whose partners might be bouncing around on the other side of town, or even the other side of the universe.

Fiona, while she'd been adding extra protections around my apartment to keep my magic from being detected, had told me the spell worked best if you didn't concentrate too much on it, otherwise you risked blinding yourself with a sudden surge of brightness. Which meant my thoughts were free to circle a country dance around the topic of Alastair.

How could I like him in *that* way and suspect him at the same time? Was I on skeptical overload out of my own fear of emotional involvement? After all, from every experience I'd had, liking someone, caring for them even just a little bit, ended up with one of you getting painfully hurt. Or was my resistance some sort of magical instinct kicking in, warning me away from a wizard who might be plotting to deliver me on a platter to the Mauvais?

I know, it's complicated. What relationship isn't? But when you toss in a side of magic fries with that shake, it makes a tangled mess of everything.

I hated myself for these thoughts. But like the photons streaming in to form a shining cloud that hovered over me as I stretched out on the couch, the questions wouldn't stop flowing.

Betty Everett's "Shoop Shoop Song" — the one from the 1960s that declared if a guy really loves you it'll be revealed in his kiss — kept running through my head. The eyes deceive, the face charms, but the kiss will let you know. With Betty's back-up singers shoop-shooping and images of me and Alastair smooch-smooching, I eventually released the photons. Not long after they dispersed back into the ether, I drifted off to sleep.

* * *

As much as I hated the idea of going anywhere near Morelli's apartment, I had to collect Mr. Wood the next morning to prepare for Mr. Green's funeral. It took me several stunned moments to get over the shock that Morelli's apartment was clean, didn't smell like the wrong end of a donkey, and was filled with modern furniture softened with color-coordinated, hand-crocheted accents.

I then waited while Mr. Wood finished his breakfast of two eggs sunny-side up, three strips of bacon (no surprise there), and two pieces of what looked like homemade bread. With a bright glow to his cheeks and the familiar sparkle back in his eyes, Mr. Wood was looking more lively and acting more chipper than he had since his attack.

"Cassie, you would not believe how wonderful BLATs are," Mr. Wood said, then nipped off a piece of bacon. "The avocado, it just..." He stopped talking, a look of pure culinary bliss on his face. He swallowed the bacon and mopped up some egg with his bread. "And look, I've been trying my hand at crochet. I think I'm a natural."

With the yolk-coated bread he pointed toward some mounded clumps of knotted yarn on the table. I had no idea what they were meant to be. Yarn rocks? Bird nests? Mangled heads? But he seemed too proud of them for me to burst his creative bubble.

"They're lovely. Now, hurry up, we've got a show to put on in a few hours."

Which was the wrong thing to say. Mr. Wood dejectedly pushed his remaining slice of bacon around on his plate.

"And after that? Has anything been scheduled?"

As I've mentioned, Mr. Wood took the calls, he made the appointments, he consulted the families. He had to know no work had come in since yesterday. Or did he think I'd been out hustling funereal services last night to surprise him?

"No. Not yet. But I need to take off for a little while, so it's good timing."

"You're leaving?" Morelli asked.

"Don't get too excited. I'm coming back." Well, I hoped I was coming back. "You'll be okay staying here while I'm away?" I asked Mr. Wood.

"Where are you going? What if we have a client?"

"I have to go to London for some special training."

"HQ?" Morelli asked, his voice lowering with concern. I nodded. "You be careful there, Black. They don't go easy on trainees. And you aren't exactly known for winning people over," he added snidely.

"London? HQ? What's this about, Cassie?"

"It will help with our little problem."

"I've heard that one before," Mr. Wood said, sounding strangely like Morelli with the comment. I could not let these two hang out any longer than necessary.

"This really will work. After I get done, you'll be feeling better and we can take on more work. In the meantime, I'm sure Morelli would be glad to help you with any clients. Won't you?" I asked my landlord, placing a hint of threat behind my words.

"I don't know mascara from eyeliner." I gave him a warning look as Mr. Wood sopped up the last of his egg. "But I suppose I could figure something out."

After he finished his breakfast, I wheeled Mr. Wood to the funeral home. An hour later, he was rolling alongside the florist, chatting non-stop as they worked together to get a dozen floral arrangements in place. Meanwhile, I dealt with Mr. Green's Kershaw-inflicted injury.

Turns out, duct tape can hold a split foot together well enough for you to get said foot into a highly shined loafer. You know, just in case that's something that ever comes up as one of your life's challenges. The funeral went off without a hitch, meaning Mr. Green stayed in his coffin despite the smell of bacon lingering on Mr. Wood's shirt.

After the funeral, I tidied up while Mr. Wood finished some paperwork. Without anyone waiting for their final show and without any prospect of new clients coming in, the funeral home felt quieter, emptier than usual. I was sinking this mortuary ship, and I knew, despite his stern words the day before, that Mr. Wood wouldn't have the heart to fire me to save it. For him, if for no one else, I had to get my magic under control. And if I couldn't, I had to quit my job.

During the walk home, we both remained silent. The only sound was the rumble traffic and the hum of Mr. Wood's wheels rolling over the sidewalk pavement.

CHAPTER TEN

PACKING UP PABLO

That evening, as the scent of bacon and the sound of male laughter wafted up from Morelli's apartment, I crammed toiletries and clothes and a few books into a bag. A message from Mr. T came through on my phone, and I wondered if he was texting from home or if he had some sort of magical cellular plan that allowed him to truly talk and text anywhere, even in Rosaria.

> *After you drop your cat off at Lola's, meet us at Runa's at 9 a.m. Reply to let me know you received this.*

I replied with a smiley-face cat emoji and a thumbs up. I wasn't in the mood for words.

The next morning, knowing he wasn't going to like what was soon going to happen to him, I buttered up Pablo with a can of his favorite wet food, which looked and smelled as disgusting as every other type of cat food.

While he ate, I went down to say goodbye to Mr. Wood. Despite Morelli's hulking frame, when he answered the door, I could see just past him. Mr. Wood was standing on his cast-bound leg, not steadily, but standing nonetheless.

"What is he doing?" I demanded as I barreled past my landlord.

"Standing," Mr. Wood said with pride as he plopped back into his chair.

"Well, you shouldn't be. Your leg. Your back."

"Feel wonderful. Strong."

I whipped around to Morelli.

"What did you do?"

"Told you I worked for the Medi Unit."

"You can't magic a Norm back together," I said under my breath as Mr. Wood picked up his crochet hook. "It's illegal, isn't it?"

"So is changing rental agreements." He raised his thick eyebrows to drive home his point.

I didn't push the matter. If Morelli got fined by the Magical Morality folks, it was no skin off my nose. I made my goodbyes to Mr. Wood and told him to stay in touch, then went back upstairs full of trepidation of when I might see him again.

The cat dish was empty when I got back, which meant it was time to get Pablo ready for a little vacation with Auntie Lola. I took a deep breath, preparing for the fight ahead.

I picked up the lanky cat, cooing at him and stroking him behind the ears. Trying to be gentle, trying to do all this with one hand in a cast, I pointed him head first into the carrier he'd come with. He hadn't had the best experience his last time in that carrier and his body instantly tensed. He scrambled backward, splaying his legs like a cartoon character that refuses to be shoved through a door, and howling like a demon all the while.

"Please, Pablo," I begged him as he dug his claws into my forearms. I probably could have magicked him into the carrier somehow, but the sound of his yowling pushed aside all my magical instincts. Instead, I just kept hold and kept pushing.

Stubborn brawn won out over feline fury and the moment he was in, I slammed the metal cage door and latched it tight.

And he wailed even louder.

"Black," Morelli shouted, pounding on my door, "what is going on in there?"

I jerked open the door. Morelli stepped back half a pace at the sight of me.

"Morning exercises," I said through clenched teeth as I smoothed down my hair. Pablo shrieked and clawed at his cage. Morelli looked over my shoulder. He then snapped his fingers and Pablo keeled over. "What the hell! Did you just kill him?"

"Of course not, you dolt. He's just asleep until you get him settled. Unless you're enjoying that sound?" I shook my head no. "Have a good trip, then. And remember what I told you about keeping your toe in line. Also, wash your arms so they don't get infected."

I glanced at the six thousand or so scratches on my forearms and mumbled a thanks. As I washed up, I reminded myself to be a very quiet tenant from then on.

With my bag slung over my shoulder and the carrier for my zombie cat in my good hand, I entered MagicLand. My first stop was Chez Lola. I'd spent the majority of my previous lessons with her, serving time as her personal maid. Now that I couldn't lift a broom without sending it through the window, she was having to do her own tidying. The place wasn't a mess, but let's just say that Lola clearly preferred to have someone come in and do the dusting and vacuuming for her. A woman right up my alley.

The moment she opened the door, Lola's cumin scent filled my nostrils and I was surrounded by the aura of warmth and comfort that radiated from her. Not for the first time I wondered what my life would have been like if I'd been raised by this woman, as I might have been if I hadn't been stolen from MagicLand as a child.

I was constantly filled with questions about how she could have managed to lose me and who had taken me right from under her nose. But whenever I got near her, her very presence enveloped me in cozy feelings and I promptly forgot my quandaries.

Pablo woke the moment Lola took him from the carrier. He too must have sensed her power, and immediately began purring. As she cuddled him to her ample bosom, she promised him they were going to have a great time together. To which he purred even more loudly.

I was a little miffed at this behavior. I mean, who kept him brushed? Who fed him treats and scooped his stinky box? Who brought the ungrateful wretch back to life? Me, that's who.

After my traitorous cat made himself perfectly at home on an overstuffed armchair, I handed over his bed and his favorite toy, Fuzzy Mouse. Unable to avoid it, I allowed myself to be pulled into one of Lola's nostalgia-inducing hugs before heading off to Dr. Dunwiddle's, and to whatever awaited me at HQ. My stomach twisted so tightly with nerves, I didn't even consider tearing into the packet of coconut-almond cookies Lola had slipped into my pocket.

Cassie Black without an appetite? That says all you need to know about how much I was looking forward to my first trip to London.

CHAPTER ELEVEN

PASSENGER LIST

The bell above the door chimed its cheery greeting when I entered Runa's clinic. Dr. Dunwiddle, who'd been arranging boxes on her shelves, turned at the sound. Her hovering glasses — always a little slow to keep up — followed along with the movement of her head as best they could. I was surprised to see her look of consternation when she caught sight of my travel bag.

"Sorry," I said, "you'll have to magically lobotomize me some other time."

"I have never wanted to lobotomize you."

"That's not really true, is it?"

She actually produced a little chuckle at that. "Maybe just the once. Or twice."

"So why the grim face? I thought you'd be glad to be rid of me."

"Just promise me that once you get to HQ, you will be very serious about your studies."

Runa said this, not with her usual disdain, but with true concern. First Morelli, now her. My least favorite people were worried for me. That could not be a good sign.

"Yeah, sure."

"There'll be no 'yeah, sure'," she snapped. "You will study and you will—" She cut herself off, signaled for her glasses to go to the counter, then said in her no-nonsense way, "The others are in my office. They have something to discuss with you."

That didn't sound promising and her tone seemed even more ominous when I entered the office to see only Fiona and Mr. Tenpenny waiting. Alastair hadn't shown up to this little gathering, which bothered me more than I cared to admit. I wondered if maybe they objected to him joining in on this trip to HQ. But I didn't think he would volunteer to go if it was going to be an issue.

Maybe they'd wised up, realized they didn't want me out and about in the magic world, and had changed their minds about the trip altogether. I mean, even I'd be the first to say I wasn't exactly the best representative of the Portland community. Uncertain what insults were going to come out of their mouths, I once again stepped into what felt like an interrogation room. A feeling that was enhanced by the disconcerting way they watched me as I took a seat.

"So what's up?" I asked tentatively.

Fiona and Busby exchanged a glance, as if deciding who should speak.

"A couple days ago you seemed unwilling to go to HQ," Fiona said. Before I could respond, she added, "So why have you decided to go?"

"Because you me told me I should," I said, my voice rising into a question.

Dr. D snorted. "Since when have you done what we wanted you to do? Out with it, we need to know why you really want to go."

"Maybe we ought to start with our concerns," said Mr. Tenpenny in a more reasonable tone.

"Look," I said. "I promise not to intentionally do anything to embarrass you. I'll even wear a t-shirt that says, 'Don't judge Rosaria by my behavior'."

"No, we think you'll do well. We hope you will." I didn't have time to dwell on the vague way Fiona said this because she quickly added, "And Busby's going so you'll have an ally there."

"Alastair's going too, right?"

"He is," Fiona said tersely.

"I'm still not seeing the concern, then."

"The Mauvais has always had a close tie to London," Runa explained. "His lair, for lack of a better word, was very near HQ. And prior to the Mauvais turning up again here in Rosaria, his last strike was in London."

"By last strike, you mean my parents," I said pointedly to see their reactions. Fiona shifted uncomfortably. Why wouldn't they just tell me about the contents of HQ's letter? Why not give me some hope? I guess Magics could be just as big of jerks as normal people. "Mr. T has already told me about the Mauvais-London connection."

"Then you'll also have considered that you might be placing yourself near to the Mauvais when you should be doing everything possible to stay away from him," Fiona said.

"But the Mauvais doesn't seem all that strong. I mean, I know it would be bad if he got his hands on me, but I beat him once."

"Once," Busby said emphatically. I was still impressed that his speaking abilities had come so far in so little time. When he first came back to life, he could barely put two grunting syllables together. "And that was after he'd spent months fooling us with a Morphing Charm — a spell that takes a fair amount of strength. He should not have had that much strength." I furrowed my brow in confusion. I thought the Mauvais was supposed to be this all-powerful wizard who struck fear into the hearts of Magics. Mr. T continued, "When your parents took the watch from the Mauvais, they weakened him."

"How?" I asked, remembering the letter from HQ mentioning the same thing.

"Because he had placed the majority of his magic into it."

"Why would he do that? Seems a bit risky if you know people are after it."

"The watch contains, or used to contain, a great deal of power. And as you've seen," Busby flourished his hands to indicate himself, "it has some rather unique qualities. But the watch's key feature is to amplify any magical strength put into it. By storing his magic in the timepiece and taking out only what he needed as he needed it, he was continually strengthening, enhancing his power."

"Okay, but he didn't have the watch when he made himself into Vivian. If he didn't have much magic in him, how did he do the Morphing Charm?"

Mr. T shrugged his shoulders. "He had to be getting power from another Magic. Not a great deal. Just enough to maintain the spell. It was always suspected he might be working with someone, possibly someone in HQ. That someone could have transfused him with power. But another person's power isn't as, I don't know, *sticky* for lack of a better word. It's like wearing someone else's shoes. They just don't fit right. He wants, he needs his own magic to return to full strength. Magic that is now in you. Magic that, because you have some giving qualities, could be taken from you and passed to him without your even knowing it."

"Then why did you tell me about HQ's request in the first place? Do you suddenly think their message is fake?"

Worry gripped my mind. Alastair. How had he memorized

such a long letter so quickly? Why did he really want me to go to London?

"No, the letter they sent is official," Fiona said. The hand of worry eased its hold slightly. "We've verified it hasn't been tampered with and it came on proper HQ stationery. But it is a danger to you, to everyone, to have you closer to the Mauvais than necessary."

"That's assuming he's there. The last time I saw him, he was limping down the streets of Portland on broken stilettos."

"He could have gone back to where he feels a connection to his past," said Fiona.

"A couple days ago you were all keen for me to go. When I didn't want to, you weren't happy. Now that I do want to go, you're acting like you don't want me to. You guys send some serious mixed signals."

"We do want you to go," Dr. Dunwiddle said. "And not because we're trying to get rid of you, so lock that snappy retort inside your lips. But there are risks you should be aware of." She gave a meaningfully hard stare at Busby. He glanced away. Runa shook her head disapprovingly, then continued, "Which is why we want you to go for the right reasons: to corral your magic, to contain your power."

"And what are the wrong reasons?" I asked.

"To go looking for your parents," Busby said.

"Who are meant to be dead, according to you." I tried to meet Runa's eyes, hoping she would back me up on this, but she was busy cleaning her glasses.

"You've already told us Vivian used the possibility of your parents being alive to lure you to her boutique," said Mr. T. "And, as you say, you know of the Mauvais's connection to London. It wouldn't be much of a leap for that sharp mind of yours to guess that if your parents are alive, they might just be in or near the last place they were known to have been."

For someone who had recently been dead, Mr. T's logic centers were pretty keen.

"Why shouldn't I try to find them? If there's information on them, if they could be alive, then shouldn't I try?"

"No, you shouldn't," Busby said.

"Why?" I asked irritably.

"Because you could kill us all if you did," he barked, then caught himself in a moment of bad manners. He adjusted his shoulders and smoothed down his jacket before giving an apologetic nod.

I glanced around, goading one of them to explain.

"You're already a strong Magic," Runa finally said. "You then took in the watch's, and therefore the Mauvais's, magic. All of that power is swirling around inside your barely-trained cells and is possibly getting stronger by the second."

"Of course," Fiona added, "we don't believe you can do everything the watch is capable of. The watch itself is merely a catalyst for the dark magic it allows the possessor to perform. Much like having a car, but with an empty gas tank. In this case, you would be the fuel. The Mauvais has the watch, but without you he can't rev its engine. However, if he does get a hold of you, he could use you to boost his own power for years to come."

"Or," said Mr. T darkly, "he could simply take what he needs from you, reactivate the watch, then discard you."

"And by discard, you mean kill."

Mr. Tenpenny gave one nod of his steely grey-haired head.

In theory, I knew all of this, but it was hard to accept the reality of it. After all, I'd fought the Mauvais and had come out alive. Maybe at one time the Mauvais was something to fear, but now? Not so much.

Don't get me wrong. I wasn't underestimating the Mauvais. I

knew what he needed me for, I knew he was a ruthless wizard, and I knew I might not survive if he caught me. I wasn't about to go after him on purpose. I'm not suicidal, after all.

But I did have a primal urge to find my parents. There was no logical reason this desire should be so strong. I'd never known these people, I had no memories of them, and I hadn't grown up with a picture of them in my back pocket that I'd mope over during fits of nostalgia. Nevertheless, something deep in my double helix of nucleotides was driving me to find them. If they were alive, I wanted to rescue them.

And if the Mauvais happened to get in my way—

"I have no intention of seeking out the Mauvais," I said, speaking with the confidence of someone telling the truth, if only the truth by omission. "I need to control my power and make myself less of a danger to my fellow Magics. And their walls," I said to Fiona, but the expected grin didn't appear. "And I plan to take my studies seriously." This did earn a smile, but it was Runa smiling with relief, while Fiona twisted her hands in her lap.

"Yes, you will," Runa said when Fiona remained silent, "which is another reason why Busby is going with you."

"So he's my babysitter?"

"Him and Tobey."

I may have groaned at this point. And rolled my eyes. And slumped dejectedly in my seat.

Was it too late to change my mind? I didn't mind Busby going with me; he had definitely been my port in the storm through all this — even if he is the one who dragged me out to sea in the first place. But Tobey? I couldn't begin to explain our relationship. One minute he despised me, the next minute I was insulting him, the following day we're sort of friends, and now it seemed like we'd gone back to verbal jabs like a couple of feuding siblings.

"Why would Tobey even want to go?" I asked.

"He volunteered," Busby said. He then added with pure British pride, "It's a rare person, Magic or Norm, who passes up a trip to London."

I wasn't thrilled, but from foster parents to teachers, I'd dodged the watchful eye of many a guardian in my day. How hard could it be to slip away from a zombie and an Untrained?

"So," I said brightly, "when do we leave?"

CHAPTER TWELVE

NO PASSPORT REQUIRED

Tobey stood waiting in the pharmacy/shop portion of Runa's clinic. When he saw me, he gave a forced smile that didn't touch his eyes. So, it was one of those days.

And yes, my ridiculously confused heart leapt when Alastair walked into the clinic soon after I gave Tobey my own stiff greeting.

"Have you got the tickets booked?" Busby asked his grandson who responded by holding up four sheets of paper with flight information and bar codes printed on them. "And Cassie, I hope Alastair reminded you to bring your passport."

What the hell was this about? Tickets? Passports? I'd assumed we'd be traveling through a portal. I mean, what's the point of being Magic if you have to fly coach for ten hours to get to Heathrow?

"I don't have a passport."

"What do you mean you don't have a passport?" Tobey asked.

"It's not like I've had a lot of extra room in my budget for travel."

"But everyone has a passport," he said.

"Clearly not," I growled at his snide disbelief. I looked around at the others. "Does someone have one I can borrow? I can just," I waggled my fingers, "over it and change the info."

"Won't work," Mr. T said. He looked very smart in a crisp suit that was too well-fitted not to be tailor made. He'd also draped an expensive trench coat over his arm, and his shoes were shined to the point they might blind you if the sun reflected off them at the right angle. People just didn't dress like that to travel these days.

"Why not? I'm quite good at it."

"Yes," Dr. Dunwiddle said, "why am I not surprised that one of your specialities is somewhat criminal in nature."

"I can throw things really well, too."

"You must be so proud," said Tobey. I gave him my watch-it-or-I'll-twist-you-into-a-human-balloon-animal look, and then wondered if there was a spell for that. If magic was primarily about rearranging molecules, it might just be possible.

"Immigration control agents are Magics who've been specially trained in forgery detection," Fiona said, interrupting my daydreams of spell crafting. "They'd smell the fake before you even got to the desk."

I leaned against the cashier counter and crossed my arms over my chest. "So, is that it? No magic door. No—"

"Don't say it," Mr. Tenpenny warned. Tense muscles trembled across his jawline. "If you dare say flue powder—"

"The thought never crossed my mind." It so had. "But unless you want to wait a couple months for my passport to appear in the mail, you're going to need to come up with another option."

"Corrine," Alastair said. "She could get permission to use her international portal if HQ knows what it's for."

Corrine Corrigan was my former boss during my brief stint as a bike messenger. Had she managed to keep her business doors open one more hour, had I been able to leave with her the last package I'd been unable to deliver, I would have never known a thing about Magics. I'm still undecided if that might not have been for the best.

"I saw her at Spellbound on my way here," said Fiona.

"Good." Mr. Tenpenny picked up his small, leather suitcase. "Runa, please contact Olivia and let her know there's been a change in plans and to temporarily reactivate Corrine's London portal."

Runa, the stolid, no-nonsense woman who seemed to take everything in unwavering stride, hesitated. Her cheeks blushed and her tongue seemed to trip over itself when she said, "Olivia. Yes, of course."

I recognized that reaction. I'd experienced it myself more than once around Alastair. Did our little Runa have a crush on this Olivia? Then again, she might just be balking over the expense of an international phone call.

"Shall we, then?" Mr. Tenpenny said. As the bell jingled us out of Runa's clinic, I glanced over my shoulder to see Runa mouthing words as if practicing for her call. I hoped I'd be back to tease her about it.

We wended our way toward Main Street, but before we stepped out from Runa's side street, Mr. T and Fiona lingered back. I waited with them, uncertain what we were doing. Did we need to give Runa time to ring HQ? Had they forgotten the way to Spellbound Patisserie?

"If you don't mind," Mr. Tenpenny said and waved his hand for me to move along. I glanced to Fiona, then to her hand. Which Mr. T was holding. Ah, so that's how it was.

I picked up the pace to join Alastair and Tobey. We didn't say a word to each other as we strained to eavesdrop. From behind us I caught Mr. Tenpenny telling Fiona he'd miss her, that he'd call her as soon as he was settled, and that he'd be back as quick as he could.

I couldn't help but smirk when Mr. T rejoined us.

"There will be no comments from you, young lady."

It was too much. I burst out laughing, as did Tobey and Alastair as we followed the tantalizing scent of baked goods to Gwendolyn's bakery.

Corrine's bright red hair could be seen from down the block. She'd taken up residence at one of the outdoor bistro tables where she was picking at the last crumbs of something I'm sure had been delicious. We stopped at her table, hovering over it like begging pigeons. I passed a suggestive look between my travel companions, but no one seemed to take my hint that we should grab a snack before diving into any further vacation planning.

Mr. Tenpenny explained the situation and told Corrine that Runa was making arrangements for access to her international portal. With a wistful sigh, Corrine complained that she had been looking forward to a batch of huckleberry muffins that would be coming out of the oven in a few minutes. Alastair, who was well-versed in Spellbound's product line, assured her that if we hurried, she could probably get back before the warmth of the oven completely left the muffins' fluffy interiors.

On the non-magical side of Portland, Corrigan's Courier had been a run-down hole in the wall of a place. Her shop in MagicLand, located on the Old West-themed street, had a rustic wooden façade, wood plank flooring, and a tidy interior with square cubbies from floor to ceiling.

I didn't have time to take much in. However, it was hard to miss that packages and letters — without any of them being touched by human hand — were popping into existence in a few of the empty cubbies several rows above head height. Then, once a row of cubbies was filled, that row moved downward to be at eye level with the clerks who took the items, slipped them into red canvas satchels, and either dashed out the door or zipped over to another part of the office to put the item into a different cubby from which it would soon vanish.

This all struck me as amazingly efficient, but as with any post office, the customers lined up waiting to ship packages were called up one by one to be assisted by a clerk who seemed annoyed that anyone would dare to make use of the courier service during his shift.

"Cassie, come along," Mr. T said and I hurried after the group to a back area.

"Now, the thing to keep in mind," Corrine was saying, "is that this isn't intended for people. Just packages. But the portal panel is wide enough for you to squeeze through. Assuming they've unlocked this thing." She pointed to a metal door about half the size of a card table and with a handle at the top. Corrine grabbed the handle and gave a tug. With a creak of metal hinges, the door opened. "Ah good, Runa must have got through to HQ. Alright, luggage first."

After pulling the portal door fully open, Corrine had us drop two bags in at a time. She banged the door shut, waited a moment, then we repeated the process with two more bags. Only after seeing mine disappear did I wonder where the portal put out at. I mean, was my bag sitting in the middle of a Tube station? Had it popped out in some royal bedroom? Was Prince Charles rifling through my socks and toiletries at this very moment?

"Alastair will go through first," said Mr. T. Alastair stepped onto a stool in front of the oversized mail slot. Before he could climb in, Busby asked, "Alastair, what are you thinking?"

This seemed like a rude thing to ask, but he wasn't probing Alastair's deeper thoughts. It was a lesson. Everything was these days.

"For me it works best if I imagine myself in an airplane seat, since that's usually a reliable way to get to the U.K.," he added sarcastically. "Other people like to visualize a long slide, but that can add to the disorientation. I've also heard just picturing yourself as a package does the trick. Anything to give your mind the idea that you will be traveling. Long-distance portals aren't like stepping through local ones. If you go in without mentally preparing, it can be uncomfortable."

He gave me an encouraging smile, then tucked his long legs into the mail bin. When he said he was ready, Corrine closed the door. As you do, she quickly re-opened it to make sure her package had gone through. I had inched my way closer by this point, but when I peeked over her shoulder, the only thing I could see was that Alastair had indeed disappeared. I was hoping I might catch a glimpse of Big Ben or Buckingham Palace, but the inside of the portal was completely black.

"Cassie, are you ready?" Mr. T asked.

My gut gave a lurch. "Can't you go? I think I could use another demonstration."

"No," Tobey blurted so abruptly I flinched.

"You'll do fine," Mr. T assured me.

I wasn't sure how my tall frame was going to fold itself into the slot, but with a little guidance from Corrine (and snorts of laughter from Tobey), I managed to situate myself, protecting my wounded hand by holding it tight to my body.

I'd never been on a plane before, but I had been on the half-hearted little roller coaster at Oaks Amusement Park in the Sellwood neighborhood of Portland. I figured that was close enough to a slide, so that's what I pictured in my head when Corrine asked if I was ready. In response to her question, I nodded, my throat too dry to speak.

The moment the slot clanged behind me, I promptly forgot what it had been like to be on that roller coaster. Come to think of it, I never did make it out of the gate. The ride had broken down soon after the conductor had buckled me in.

Instead of chugging up an incline and whizzing down a descent, I ended up being jerked around, tossed aside, chucked into what felt like midair with gut-dropping speed, tumbled, shoved, squeezed. And all of this in bitterly cold darkness.

I realized I was a package. I was being treated like an uninsured box of Christmas cookies sent by the cheapest ground shipping available. A taped up, re-used box of treats that would be three months stale and broken to bits by the time Grandma got them.

Besides the pain, Alastair was right, traveling this way was disorienting and my stomach was doing more flips than a playing piece in a Tiddlywinks tournament. Then, with a sudden burst of warmth, I tumbled out onto a concrete floor. Eye level with Alastair's mismatched argyle socks, I had enough sense to turn away from his tasseled, leather loafers just before what felt like an entire week's worth of food rushed back out of my mouth in a great big *plop*.

"So, you didn't fly first class?" he asked, squatting down beside me and magicking away the mess I'd just made.

"I think I came by Pony Express. Drunken Pony Express."

"It'll be easier next time."

Alastair helped me to my feet and handed me a packet of cookies from Runa's shop. The sugar mostly stopped my head spinning. And I'm so glad it did because I wouldn't have wanted to miss what came next for anything.

CHAPTER THIRTEEN
ARRIVALS HALL

Tobey, as I may have mentioned, has no magic. I had seen him use portals in MagicLand, but my keen observation skills had noticed that, while he could return to Real World Portland on his own, he always needed a Magic with him to get into MagicLand. But I hadn't given this much thought when we'd all been lining up to be mailed to London.

Clearly, it takes a fair amount of magic to cross an entire continent and an ocean in less than five minutes without the aid of virtual reality or psychedelic drugs. Without any of his own power, Tobey needed help. And if my journey had been any indication, the ride could be bumpy if you weren't careful. Which meant holding his grandpa's hand, as he did when using Portland portals, wasn't going to work.

Instead, Tobey and Mr. T had been taped together with Tobey in front and Mr. T behind him as if they were getting ready for a bargain-basement, tandem parachute jump.

Despite my still-woozy head, I couldn't stop laughing at the sight. I tried to help undo the half roll of packaging tape Corrine had used, but the fits of laughter were eating up too much of my motor control to do much good.

"I'm glad you enjoyed that," Tobey said in a disgruntled grumble that only sent me into another giggling fit.

"Believe me," I said, wiping tears from my eyes, "no matter what happens, that sight is going to make this trip completely worthwhile."

A few giggles kept bubbling up, and while I tried to get control of myself, I took in my surroundings. We were in a basement of some sort, and from somewhere nearby there came the clattering, whooshing noise of a conveyor belt.

"Are we in the post office?" I asked.

"No," Mr. T said, almost reverentially. "This is the British Library."

I raised an unimpressed eyebrow. This place looked industrial, not somewhere that should inspire awe, stimulate minds, and draw tourists with its papery treasures.

Busby caught my judgmental look. "It's only the underground levels where items are sorted. Must you always be so cynical?"

The British Library has a collection storage facility that extends deep underground. Not "the Underground" run by Transport for London, but just underground, with a lowercase U. And not only are there miles of shelves down there, but also a system of equipment to sort, store, retrieve, and deliver books to eager readers on the upper levels.

It also, as I later learned, happens to contain the courier portals to most other magic communities around the world as well as one of the few portals into London's Magic HQ. And with all the conveyor belts looping around, the best way to get to that portal, according to Mr. T, is to climb aboard one of the belts.

We trundled past dozens of mail slots. A few of which were popping out small packages or letters, and in one case, a golden cage draped in purple silk with a yellow bow on top. The silk was slightly parted in front, providing a peek inside the cage where I caught a glimpse of a raven, gleaming black except for a small white patch above one eye that gave him a quizzical expression. As the cage rolled past, its occupant tapped its beak on the bars as if in greeting.

I tugged Alastair's sleeve and asked, "Did you see that bird?"

"What bird?" he responded distractedly as he watched our progress. I glanced back at Mr. T with my own quizzical expression. He looked in the direction I indicated, but by now the cage had gone past and only the covered back of it could be seen.

"Some communities like to send gifts to HQ, especially when they're nearing evaluation."

"Eval—" I started to ask, then cut the question off. Even in MagicLand, it seemed you couldn't escape bribes and bureaucracy. "Never mind, I'm sure I get the idea."

I half-expected to ride straight through another mail slot to get into HQ, but just like a baggage claim belt at the airport, this conveyor system only ran in an elongated oval. I wasn't sure exactly where we were headed, but when Alastair said, "Hop off," we all did.

Trouble was, when I jumped, I forgot to grab my bag and had to chase the belt a few lengths to snatch it. Unfortunately, I used my bad hand for this and cursed at the pain as I darted forward and barely managed to grasp the bag's handle before the belt disappeared into an opening in the wall.

When I rejoined my travel buddies, Tobey was doing a very bad job at holding back his laughter.

"Oh yes, Cassie's in pain, how amusing."

"Serves you right for laughing at me earlier."

My hand throbbed too much to argue, so I ignored him as we crossed the room. Alastair and Mr. T had stopped in front of a huge door that looked like it should be attached to a castle. It had that rounded top thing going on, wood slats that looked like they'd been made from entire oak trunks, and big iron bolts and hinges holding it all together. If it had been set inside a thick, stone wall, it would have seemed perfectly in order. But this door was set in what appeared to be your basic office building drywall that had been painted an industrial shade of taupe.

"Do we knock?" I asked.

"No, we wait," replied Mr. Tenpenny.

"For…?"

Heavy footsteps sounded from behind the door. Metal thunked heavily against metal and the door creaked open. I wondered if the creaking noise was just a bit of magical theatrics since it would seem that if you could transport humans over five thousand miles in only a few minutes, you could cast a spell that would quiet noisy hinges. But that's just me. I'm cynical, remember.

"Him," Mr. T said brightly. "Chester, so good to see you."

Chester was— Well, I wasn't sure exactly what Chester was. Big. Rather ugly with a squashy, bulbous nose that didn't sit quite straight on his face, a tiny fringe of red hair hanging over a heavy brow, ears that wanted to stick straight out from the sides of his head but were just managing not to, and, gripping the door's edge, a hand with only three fingers and a thumb. Except for the red hair and the tie and jacket instead of a dingy tank top, he reminded me of Morelli.

"What's that?" I asked Alastair in a whisper as Chester greeted Busby with a crushing hug like they were long-lost pals. I did wonder if Mr. T's suit was going to need to be pressed again after the encounter.

"Troll. Well, probably half troll from the look of him," Alastair said quietly. "Best gate keepers you can find. They also work well at guarding bridges."

"Chester the Troll?"

"They're named for the town they come from. Works well

since they get lost fairly often."

"Right." I drew out the word as Chester's arms swallowed up Tobey in an enthusiastic greeting. "And why does he remind me of my landlord?"

"Morelli is part troll."

That would explain so many things.

"Where's the town of Morelli," I asked.

"That's just a surname he chose. His first name is Eugene."

I grinned and couldn't wait to call him that the next time he blocked my stairway.

Once Chester had finished his boisterous welcomes — which ended up leaving a trail of troll snot on Tobey's shoulder — he took my bag for me then ushered us into London HQ.

The moment I stepped through the doorway, I hesitated. The industrial basement was gone, and I was now staring down a dark passage with dank, stone walls. As we trailed after Chester, a sensation of humming buzzed through my bones. But just as I wondered if this sensation was caused by magic in the air, something very furry and far too big for my comfort scuttled past my foot. This was immediately followed by a heavy stomp, a squishy splat, and the sound of crunching bones.

"Got him," Chester said proudly.

"Got him?" I whispered to Alastair.

"Rat. Trolls have a sort of pest-control instinct. Even half trolls can't resist the pull."

Which I suppose might explain why my apartment, no matter how terrible I was at keeping on top of the cleaning, had no mouse or cockroach problems.

"Is this a dungeon?" I asked Alastair. I may be wrong, but he seemed stronger already and had even dared to take my hand to guide me through the darkness.

"Well, yes, actually. We're in the Tower of London."

"*The* Tower. As in where many queens' heads have rolled?"

"It was only two queens," Mr. T said defensively.

"Three if you count Lady Jane Grey," added Chester.

"We do not count Lady Jane Grey," Busby said emphatically.

I'd always wanted to go to London. I've watched dozens of documentaries about the city, and have done a fair amount of armchair traveling thanks to my library card. We had just gone from the British Library to the Tower of London, a distance of about three miles, in only a few steps. If tourists only knew how easy it was to get from one side of London to the other, Transport for London's visitor pass scheme would crumble.

With Chester stomping a few more unlucky vermin and me cringing with every crushed bone, we continued along the gloomy underpass/dungeon thing until we came to a spiraling set of stone stairs that were worn almost to a U in the center. I don't know how far down we were, but my head was spinning and my thighs were burning by the time we emerged onto a courtyard bathed in deliciously warm sunlight.

"I thought it rained all the time here."

"Cassie," Mr. Tenpenny said critically, "when this is done, you really must see more of the world."

"I'll add it to my to-do list, right after working forty hours a week and barely scraping by."

"Things can be arranged," he said in an annoyingly vague way.

Just as I was about to ask him to elaborate, we slipped through a cluster of tourists and I caught sight of something I never expected to see on the grounds of any historic site.

"Garden gnomes? Isn't that kind of tacky?"

"Don't be so rude, Cassie," admonished Mr. T. He seemed about to say more, but Chester was directing us through another doorway and into a tall, glimmering stone structure. The White

Tower, I recalled from a Rick Steves's video. Once inside, and after a jaunt down a poorly lit hallway at the end of which was a small, thickly paned window, we reached a vast room with high ceilings and walls decorated with gorgeous tapestries depicting scenes from British legends.

At a sleek, modern desk on which perched an enviably recent model of the MacBook Pro, sat a woman with silvery-grey hair in rows of braids whose ends were decorated with beads. I later discovered (because I'm rude and prone to staring) these weren't beads; they were very tiny snow globes, but instead of snow, they rained down infinitesimally tiny silver flecks every time she moved.

"Olivia," said Mr. T with a warm familiarity that spoke of a long friendship.

Olivia slid out from behind the desk in a move as graceful and slinky as a cat. She wrapped her long arms around Mr. T for a brief hug, then held him at arm's length as if examining him.

"Busby, I'm so glad you're well," she said in a voice that held a hint of a Scottish brogue underneath an accent just as posh as Mr. T's.

"I'm dead."

"So I heard, but looking remarkably fit for all that. And Tobey." She reached out for Tobey and shook his hand in that two-handed grasp that always seems affected, but which Olivia had the poise to pull off. "Alastair," she said, stepping over to him. He hesitated just a moment before letting her kiss him on the cheek. She whispered something that made Alastair blush and laugh at once, and I felt a stab of intimidation, jealousy, and irritation with this languidly elegant woman.

She then turned to me and I caught a whiff of her magic which carried the woodsy, tangy scent of spruce. "And you must be Cassie Black," she said, a neutral smile on her face.

"I must be. Nice to meet you," I said, and curtly gave a little wave as I backed up half a step to show I wasn't into the European style of personal-space-invading greetings.

"Shall we," she said, then snapped her fingers. Where there had only been two chairs before her desk, there were now four. In the shuffle, I ended up sitting between Tobey and Alastair. Chester left my bag near the door, said his goodbyes, and headed back to, I assume, his rodent hunting.

"Now," Olivia began, "because of the special circumstances, starting tomorrow Cassie will take formal training with private tutors." I just love being talked about as if I'm not sitting right there. "She will be tested after her second week so we can assess her. Once that is sorted, and once we ensure she's not going to hurt anyone, she can be brought up to speed with the current cohort of students. No matter how well she does in her assessment, we will want to see vast improvement within a month."

On the final words, Olivia's gaze darted to Busby, and from the corner of my eye I could see him give the tiniest shake of his head. Olivia's lips twitched and something like disapproval crossed her face, but she was too professional to reveal anything further and continued with her instructions.

"Busby, there are papers we need to go through together. Alastair, you will continue the defensive work you've started with Ms. Black, and you will also be glad to know we have some newly uncovered archives for you to study to bring your current knowledge of historical magic innovation up to date. You might also be able to add something to them."

"I would be honored to look them over," Alastair said in that formal manner Americans adopt when talking to Brits. Especially posh Brits like Olivia.

"And Cassie." What, who me? Oh, that's right, the person you've been talking about for the past five minutes. "One of our people will work with you throughout your studies and she will be the one evaluating you."

"Is that—?" Alastair began, sitting forward in his seat as if ready to challenge her, but Olivia cut him off with a sharp *tsk*. Alastair scooted back, but I could feel the tension radiating from his shoulders.

"You'll meet her tomorrow after you've settled in."

"Settled in where?" I asked. It was a fair question. The Tower of London was a castle, but it was also a prison. Plus, it was a huge tourist attraction. How in the world was I meant to sleep, eat, and partake in magic classes right under the selfie sticks of half the world?

"You'll find the White Tower is much larger than it appears. Now, if the gentlemen wouldn't mind leaving, I'd like to speak with Ms. Black privately."

CHAPTER FOURTEEN

A CHAT WITH OLIVIA

The "gentlemen" made sounds of assent, and Alastair gave me a reassuring smile as they filed out. I noticed Alastair took my bag with him and wondered if we'd be sharing a room. I didn't think I was quite ready for that level of, well, whatever was going on between us, but since I didn't know how far away our rooms might be, I wasn't going to argue about free porter services.

"Now, Ms. Black, I'm aware you've been having difficulties with your magic, as is to be expected with taking on so much power so quickly. The Portland community should have been aware of the *strain*, shall we say, it would put you under, but," and here she spoke with utter sincerity, "I promise we can guide you through this, if you'll let us."

Okay, I hate to admit this, but I had that annoying prickle in the corner of my eyes that alerted me to the fact that if one more kind word was spoken, I'd be wallowing in a pool of tears. I know, it makes no sense, but people being nice to me always hits me right in the vulnerable spot. Even if that niceness was being delivered in a cultured, smooth-as-silk accent. I gave a little nod, since I knew from experience if I tried to speak, the tears would Niagara out of my face.

"Good. Now, I want you to think of me as a sort of guidance

counselor. I believe that's what you call them."

"Yeah," I muttered, thinking that the only guidance counselor I'd had was in high school and she'd told me I was a moron who belonged in remedial classes because I hadn't given a cat's behind about nailing a high score on my PSATs.

"So, I want to start things off by letting you ask me anything. Three questions. I'm sure you have more, but as this is the first time you've traveled so far, you'll soon be quite tired so we should keep this interview short. Now, don't be shy in your curiosity. Oh," she exclaimed, and gave a deprecatory smile, "how rude I'm being. This is London, after all." She snapped her fingers and there appeared before us a tray with a silver teapot, two delicate cups with *F & M* scrolled on the side, and a three-tiered silver tray laden with a variety of sweet treats.

Okay, maybe she wasn't so bad.

"You're not averse to sugar or gluten or chocolate, are you?"

"Not in the least."

"Then let's tuck in."

From the tray, she served two slices of a dessert I'd recently been introduced to, and to which I had quickly become addicted. Dense chocolate interior, a thick layer of apricot jam in the center, and a perfectly smooth ganache surface. "Sacher Torte," Olivia said, handing me a plate and fork. "Fortnum & Mason's isn't the best in the world, but it'll do in a pinch."

She poured a tea whose scent reminded me of Mr. Tenpenny, but with an additional citrus note to it — I told you I was becoming part bloodhound. When she saw me taking in the aroma, Olivia told me it was Countess Grey, a dolled-up version of Earl Grey.

As she added a heaping teaspoon of sugar to her cup, I took a bite of the cake, and nearly melted into a pool of chocolate bliss. It wasn't as good as Gwendolyn's, but if this was bad Sacher

Torte, the best must have people climaxing at their tables. I briefly wondered if Sacher Torte was a key challenge in the Magics' version of the Great British Bake Off.

"Even non-magics get a little boost from this," Olivia said, possibly seeing the cocoa-induced euphoria in my eyes. "It was invented by a member from the Vienna community when the Magics there had been hit by a plague. Nearly wiped out all of the community's power until this," she raised forkful, "rallied the few surviving members."

I put myself at the edge of a chocolate coma, then revived myself with Countess Grey tea before Olivia prodded like the genie from Aladdin's lamp, "So, questions. Three. Use them wisely."

I had a question in mind, but didn't want to blow everything at once. Save the biggie for last, warm her up a bit. Besides, there'd been something niggling at me ever since I started this whole magical journey.

"Why does Mr. Tenpenny hate Harry Potter references so much?"

Olivia, the graceful, elegant, sophisticated Olivia, sputtered out the sip of tea she'd just taken and gave a rather horsey laugh.

"You've noticed that?"

"An elephant dancing the tango couldn't be more obvious."

Olivia, her dark eyes glinting with amusement, set down her cup.

"He used to be acquaintances with the author. She was one of the few Norms who could scent magic on us, and somehow they struck up a friendship. Anyway, she took many ideas from things he told her. Granted, she put a delectable twist on some of them, added in plenty of her own very clever ideas, and the storylines are all her own imagination, but Busby has always felt a bit put out since she didn't bother to name a single character after him.

He couldn't even find one who resembled him, which really raised his hackles. He scoured every book of the series trying to figure out who he was, but to no avail. He's been bitter ever since."

Which explains why someone who hates Harry Potter so strongly understands all my references.

"Next?" she asked, placing a fluffy, fruit-studded scone on my plate along with a big dollop of lemon curd.

I really wanted to ask her where she got the snow globes decorating her hair, but didn't think it would be the best use of my questions.

"I'm guessing London HQ is the center of magic. So, where did you guys get your magic? I mean, why here?"

Granted, I was sneaking two questions into one, but that didn't explain the suddenly tense set to Olivia's jaw. The moment I asked my question, I regretted it. Not because of her reaction, but because I should have asked straight out what that look had been between her and Busby when she'd mentioned my needing to show improvement within a month. Or, maybe about this person I was being assigned to work with — and Alastair's odd reaction to the news. Which goes to show you just how distracting sweets can be.

Olivia shifted in her chair then hid the stain of embarrassment that had crept into her cheeks by sucking down half a cup of steaming Countess Grey. I kept my eyes fixed firmly on her. If she was going to squirm this much, the answer had to be good.

"Not all magic history is happy history," she eventually said.

"I've gathered as much." I'd learned not long ago that the slave trade may have begun because of a magical greed for sugar.

"This really isn't my area of expertise, but I'll give you the basics. And you mustn't judge us on how we behaved in the past." I continued watching her with increasingly judgmental eyes just to guilt her into giving the full story.

"We stole it. People think the Elgin Marbles at the British Museum are controversial, but they're nothing compared to—" She caught herself, then asked, "You're familiar with them?"

I was. The Elgin Marbles weren't a collection of small, glass balls. They were giant marble carvings that had once perched above the Parthenon in Athens. Lord Elgin, or rather his workers, showed up in the early 1800s, took down about half the friezes, and sent them back to England. You know, as you do when you can't find just the right postcard for your souvenir collection.

Elgin claimed the ruler of the Ottoman Empire, which Greece was a part of at the time, told him this bit of redecorating was okay. But when questioned, Elgin could produce no evidence of this agreement.

Now, personally, I don't think you're going to be able to pull down massive hunks of marble from a prominent ancient structure without drawing the notice of someone official. So, either Elgin and his team were some really slick operators, or somewhere along the line he must have gotten some sort of permission. But that hasn't stopped his taking of the friezes from drawing loads of criticism, especially once the Greeks shook off the shackles of their Ottoman overlords in the 1830s. The newly independent Greeks wanted to restore their ancient works, but by then the marbles had been sold to the British Museum who really pushed the claim that possession is nine-tenths of the law.

"The debate about who really owns them rages on, right?" I said.

"Exactly, but if they only knew the depth of what we Magics have taken from others, those carvings would seem no more questionable than us displaying the Roman coins mudlarkers find along the banks of the Thames." She took a bite of scone and licked lemon curd from the corner of her mouth before continuing.

"I'm talking about Ireland. It's referred to as England's first colony and there's a reason for that. We had some magic here — remind Alastair to tell you about the Druid Debate some time — but that magic was already dwindling before we could figure out how to make use of it and strengthen it. Merlin knew how, but he was a real curmudgeon who didn't like to share his knowledge, so all magic in England was at risk of dying out.

"However, on his death bed, Merlin told of a people in Ireland: the Tuatha Dé Danann. We were desperate, we knew we were losing something that could benefit us and we wanted more, so we went over. We invaded. We pretended we wanted nothing more than to learn from the Tuatha. But as soon as we'd perfected our magic and enhanced it with our own brand of power, we forced them to submit. Some fought. Most lost. The few survivors went underground. The majority of them never came out again, turning their back on the upper world. We're slowly repairing relations, but magic memories are long."

She stopped talking for a while, as if contemplating her own part in this history. I moved a tall slice of a seven-layered cake onto her plate, partially to be polite, but also to butter her up and get her sugar drunk for my next question. We ate, we made small talk (not my specialty, but I was swimming in sucrose by this point). Then, just after Olivia told a surprisingly off-color joke about a troll and a pixie, I launched my third question.

"Can you take me to my parents? Or tell me where you think they are? I know you have information on them."

Olivia immediately resumed her businesslike detachment and pushed her plate away. She took another long sip of tea before setting her cup back on its saucer so carefully the china didn't even clink. Then she looked me squarely in the eye and said, "That information was not meant to reach your eyes or ears. Who told you?"

"I found the letter," I said, instinctively protecting Alastair. "I'm kind of snoopy, so don't blame Mr. Tenpenny. I'm not asking for anything special. I just want to know what you know."

"I can't tell you anything about that until we verify it's true and that it's safe for you to know it."

"You said three questions."

"I said you could ask three questions. I did not say I would answer them."

I scowled at her, thinking, "Tricksy Magicses." Still, while she wasn't directly telling me what I wanted to know, she also wasn't confirming my parents were dead, which did answer part of my question.

"Now, I believe we've given each other a pair of good first impressions," she said as she stood and smoothed down her eggplant-colored skirt. "You'd probably like to get settled in. Your room will be down that hall." She pointed to a doorway to her left. "Head up the stairs then go to the left. Room forty-two."

Knowing a dismissal when I heard one, I got up, grabbed another scone, and trudged up what felt like ten stories' worth of spiraling staircase, all the while wondering what Magics had against elevators.

When I opened the door to my room, I literally could not move. And not because of all the damn stair climbing, but because of pure and utter shock.

Keep in mind, this was the White Tower, built by William the Conqueror himself way back when the year 1200 seemed like the far distant future. Hundreds of years of history supposedly surrounded me, but there I was, staring at what looked like your standard-issue hotel room with nondescript, easy-to-clean carpet, a side nook for coats and luggage, a small table with two stiff-backed chairs that looked painfully uncomfortable, and a door just within the entryway that opened onto a small bathroom.

My bag had been left at the foot of a crisply sheeted, single bed that was situated underneath a bland landscape print and opposite a low dresser topped with a tea service. I picked up the bag, moved it into the bathroom, and as I unpacked a few things, I wondered how hard it would be for an American with no passport and no money to get back to Portland. I felt very far from home and very out of place, and I already missed Pablo using me as his own personal sleeping cushion.

Despite having left Portland well before lunchtime, the grounds of the Tower were empty of tourists, and the London skyline outside my window reflected the warm glow of the sun being closer to setting than its zenith. It would seem that even a magic portal couldn't get around time zones. I wanted to explore the city, but Olivia had been right. Even though I'd just had enough sugar to send most Norms into diabetic shock and which should have left me bouncing off the walls, I was exhausted.

I stared at the view. Below was a small expanse of lawn. Through the gap of a couple trees were the Tower's inner and outer walls with the River Thames flowing past. A raven hopped amongst the branches of one of the trees, even though it seemed late enough for the bird to have returned to its enclosure for the evening. The bird paused in its gymnastics, looked my way, dipped his head toward me, then took off, heading up and over the White Tower.

I wanted to go out, maybe wander the grounds, but my eyelids suddenly felt like lead weights had been stitched into them. I closed the curtains and crawled into my narrow bed.

CHAPTER FIFTEEN

SOLAS CHARM

The next morning a tapping on my room's door woke me. I say *woke*, but I'd been awake since about three in the morning. Apparently even magic travel results in jet lag as my body tried to figure out why it had been suddenly thrown nine hours into the future without being consulted about such matters. And, with sugary treats not being the most substantial of meals, I'd also been kept awake by a stomach grumbling for proper nourishment.

Dressed in a t-shirt and a pair of boxer shorts, I answered the door and was immediately hit by a sharp aroma that reminded me of lightning. What stood before me was a very small woman, the skin of her cheeks so pale I could see veins inking their way underneath it. She was dressed head to toe in a gown of some sort of floaty material, big Audrey-Hepburn sunglasses nearly covered the entirety of her tiny face, and in her hand she clutched an umbrella that shaded her from I don't know what.

"It's bad luck to open an umbrella indoors," I told her.

"It's bad luck to open a door to a stranger without asking who it might be," she said, her wispy voice bouncing with a melodic Irish accent. "And rude not to invite a guest in."

"Are you a guest, then?"

"I'm Banna. I'll be overseeing your instruction." She looked past me. "Ah good, you remembered to keep the curtains drawn."

I stepped aside, and she drifted past me as she pulled in the umbrella and took off her sunglasses. I had my hand on the string to pull open the curtains, but Banna shrieked in fright and I jumped away. When I turned to ask her what in the world her problem was, I met her eyes. They glowed with a blue-green light that made me think of pictures I'd seen of glaciers brightened by an eerie sort of internal illumination.

"You cannot open the curtains," she insisted.

"Why? How are you supposed to teach me in the dark?"

As if in answer, she opened her hand. A heartbeat later, an orb about the size of a softball appeared in her palm. The orb glowed with the same cool, aqua luster as her eyes. Then, like some sort of magical MacGyver, she gave her umbrella a little jerk. From the handle popped three legs. She stood the umbrella on its end and balanced the orb on the tip. With a little wave, the orb shone more brightly to light up all but the farthest corners of the room.

"I'm very light sensitive."

"So I gathered." Luckily she lived in a land known for rainy days and cloudy skies.

"Now, if you'd like to get dressed, we can begin our first lesson."

The orb's light didn't extend to my windowless, ensuite bathroom. Once I shut the door, I could see nothing. I was tempted to turn on the light, but I worried some photons might escape under the door. How sensitive to light was Banna? Her reaction when I'd wanted to open the curtains gave the impression that light could cause her pain. I certainly didn't want to kill or maim my mentor.

At least not on my first day.

So, I literally got dressed in the dark. I knocked over the drinking glass housekeeping had placed by the sink as I fumbled for my toothbrush, it took two tries to get my tights on the correct way, and my underwear felt off kilter the rest of the morning. But, once suitably attired, I sat down across from Banna who had conjured up a pot of tea. Well, she either conjured it or the White Tower had room service.

"Do you have any questions for me before we begin?"

"Only about a million."

"You may want to limit that as we have only an hour this morning."

"Okay, not to be rude, but what are you?"

"I'm one of the originals." She stared at me and I thought of what Olivia had told me. My eyes went wide.

"The Tuatha Dé Danann?"

"Yes, I was brought here as a prisoner, but that's since changed and I am free to come and go now."

"Now that your people are extinct," I said, recalling Olivia's quick history lesson.

"Are they?" Banna said in a coy way that told me she might have more up her gauzy sleeve than she was letting on. "But that's a topic for another day. Next question?"

"What are you going to be teaching me?"

"I'm going to teach you about you."

"I already know about me."

"Do you? You didn't even know you had magic until a few weeks ago. Sure, you know your ownself, you know what has happened in your life, but you really don't know why, do you?"

This was getting too metaphysical for such an early hour of the morning. Needing something to tamp down my hunger, I spooned two spoonfuls of sugar into my tea as Banna began her lecture.

"The Mauvais has been a part of your life far longer than you've known. Do you understand how magic works? No, let me rephrase that. I know Fiona is a very good teacher, and I'm sure you have a decent grasp of the physics of magic, but what I'm asking is, do you know the mental components of magic?"

This all seemed a bit mental to me, but I merely said I didn't and took a sip of tea. My mouth puckered. The brew was horribly bitter and I almost spat it out. Instead, I forced myself to swallow, then heaped a couple more scoops of sugar into the cup.

"To know your magic, to access it, you must have a sense of self-worth and confidence. The Mauvais did all he could to keep you from gaining either."

"How?" I asked, curiosity instantly shoving aside the foul taste of the tea lingering on my tongue. Then I remembered how evasive Magics could be regarding important questions. "Or is that something you're not allowed to share with me?"

"It's never been a secret. See what I mean about you not knowing yourself." After a short pause and an adjustment to the light orb to keep it out of her eyes, Banna continued. "You went missing as a small child. You were four, I believe." I nodded in agreement. "Lola LeMieux was meant to watch over you, but one day she got distracted. Even she can't recall what it was that stole her attention that day, but she swears it was only for a moment. When she turned back, you were gone." I knew this much and feared Banna was just going to tell me the same slim information I'd already gleaned. That fear turned out to be entirely misplaced as she added, "This was terrible news because only a year before a curse had been put upon you."

I'd always joked that I must have been cursed to end up with my lot in life, but to have truly been cursed? Doesn't that just figure.

"How? I mean, how could my parents let anyone curse their kid?" Maybe I didn't want to save these people.

"I'll make a note that you need to study curses," Banna said contemptuously. "But let's just say, curses do not have to be made in person if made by a strong enough Magic. In that case, the very writing down of the curse is enough. Your parents, on your third birthday received a card stating if you remained with the Magics, you would be loved but you would die young.

"On the other hand, if you ever fell into the hands of the magically challenged, you would survive, but you would never know love, you would never feel wanted. That curse made certain that if you left the community, you would end up with families who would be harsh on you, who would treat you like dirt, who would unwittingly repress your magic."

"There was one good family," I said, thinking of the Roberts who took me to museums and gave their twins a perfect Christmas.

"Norms?" She spoke the word referring to non-magical humans as if it tasted of moldy kippers. I nodded. "And what happened to them?"

Images of a mangled car hooked onto a tow truck, of a social worker coming to the door, of finding myself in a new home and on a dirty bed that very night. My chin trembled.

"But Mr. Wood?" I said shakily. He had shown me kindness, and now he was in a wheelchair. "I felt wanted with him."

"Again, you need to study. Curses have expiration dates. Thirteen years is the maximum. You were sixteen when it ended, an age when, if your average Magic hasn't been trained yet, he or she is unlikely to be able to master any spells."

"Why wouldn't the Mauvais just kill me?"

"In Rosaria, in the magic world, when the Mauvais was at his height of power, you were guarded. As with most magic children, you were well-protected. As soon as possible, mothers take a lock of their baby's hair and place it in a charm. This charm, a symbol of maternal love, is kept closely guarded by the mother, or other caretaker, until the child reaches age twelve. That's when training begins and the child can learn to defend his or herself. Most mothers choose to put the cutting in—"

"A locket," I said, my voice full of awe and my gut full of apprehension. Yet again, I had to wonder if Alastair had told me the truth of how he'd obtained the locket that was now dangling from a slim chain under my shirt.

"Correct again. And as to why the Mauvais didn't come after you once you'd left Rosaria, by then, thanks to your parents," she said, with a slightly critical tone under her lilting accent, "he had lost the strongest aspects of his power."

I didn't want to ask the next question, but at the same time I had to know.

"Who took me? Did they ever find out?"

Banna spoke as if choosing her words carefully.

"It was never determined with any certainty."

"How can you know all this?"

"It's what I do. I know all Magic history. I know the stories of the Magics. Even the stories they don't know themselves. I've had quite a few centuries to study up." She paused a moment, then said, "By the time you took the job with your Mr. Wood, the Mauvais's curse had already worked to plan. You had a landlord who hated you, you had a shoddy apartment, and you had no friends. You did have yourself a defensive sort of confidence, but not the self-worth that could bring forth your magic which seemed to be fully suppressed before you ever reached adulthood.

"But not everything can fall into line. Who would have known that you'd enjoy the work at the funeral home, or that Mr. Wood would be kind to you, or that that job would stir something in you."

"I thought it was the watch that did the stirring."

"The watch helped, but it wasn't everything."

"But why would the Mauvais care? Just to be a jerk?"

"We have as many prophecies running around the magic world as mice scuttling through a cat-free grain silo. He may have heard one regarding his own end. These things can be vague, but he must have tied the words to you."

"That's ridiculous. He ruined my life for that, for a suspicion? And what exactly am I supposed to do with this knowledge? I mean, it's pissed me off, but anger's not going to help me contain my magic, is it?"

"It's just a reminder of how far you've come and that you can go much farther if you think you can."

Great, so I was the Magical Little Engine That Could. "Can you teach me that?" I asked, pointing at the orb. Banna hesitated, perhaps at the abrupt change in conversation. She then grinned as if I'd asked exactly the question she'd been hoping for.

"I can. It won't look quite like mine. What color are your eyes?" She leaned forward and the orb shifted with her. "Hazel. Yes, that will do. People with very dark eyes can't perform the spell, it runs the risk of creating black holes. They have to find other means of illumination, but you should be able to produce a nice, warm light with the Solas Charm."

"Is there any danger, you know, with my extra-strength version of magic? I'm not going to burn the place down, am I?"

"It is possible, but your first orbs won't be much to worry about. Once done with practiced skill and control, it's similar to LED lighting. There's no heat, otherwise I wouldn't be able to stand it, but if you have a pair of sunglasses, you may want to slip them on."

I went into the bathroom and scrambled through my bag because, even though I may come across as completely pessimistic, I had enough optimism somewhere in my bones to dare to bring sunglasses to London.

"Practice saying the word," Banna said once I'd rejoined her. "Then imagine the orb. Don't try to go as big as mine, just picture something the size of a marble."

I slipped on the sunglasses and did as she said. Nothing happened. On the bright side, I hadn't blown up the room. I tried once more. Again, nothing, not even a spark, which was really frustrating because I'd been able to do most other spells — or at least ones that didn't involve a potion — quite easily, even if I hadn't done them with much finesse.

"This is stupid. Couldn't I just use a Shoving Charm to flip a switch if I need to turn on the lights?"

"Confidence, Cassie. I may have thrown you by telling you about your past. Try not to think about that. Think only of something that's made you happy, made you feel worthwhile."

Irritatingly, I had a sudden image in my head of Tobey coming to help me clean my apartment after it had been ransacked and I'd nearly been killed. An odd choice of memory, but it was the only one sticking. Holding onto the moment, I said, "Solas." My heart thudded in my chest, waiting, anticipating, expecting nothing. But then, twelve pounding beats later, a small pinpoint of light appeared just above my palm. I tried not to shout with delight. I tried not to let doubts about Alastair creep in. In another few seconds, a luminescent, gold-green ball the size of a pea hovered above my hand.

"Well, done, Cassie." Banna circled around my tiny orb, scrutinizing it. "It will get larger and come more quickly with practice, but it's tight and compact, not misty and loose like some first efforts. Very promising. That must have been a good memory."

Not really. Very soon after that evening, Tobey had proven himself a complete jerk by pressing himself up against Vivian in an alleyway of MagicLand. But I had the orb now. I wondered what might happen if I hurled it at him. At that thought, the orb faded away.

CHAPTER SIXTEEN
ACROSS THE UNIVERSE

Banna had me practice turning my light orb on and off several times before declaring our lesson was done for the day.

"So what's next?" I asked, removing my sunglasses as she slipped hers back on. My eyes had grown sensitive by this point and I noticed the room darkened slightly once the tinted lenses covered her eyes.

"Well, you've had enough of me. I believe Olivia wants to meet with you in her office. I'll leave you to finish getting dressed." Even with the sunglasses on, she managed a skeptical glance at my hair.

Half a second after Banna left, I darted into the bathroom, flipped on the light, and groaned at the horror show looking back at me in the mirror. Even though my straight, in-need-of-a-trim hair doesn't take a lot of work, trust me when I say I can achieve some impressive bedhead tangles.

Since I hadn't been able to see what my brush had been doing when I got dressed, my whole lesson with Banna had been spent with the left half of my bangs sticking up at strange angles like some sort of modern art sculpture. Using a comb and cold water, I dismantled the disaster and reshaped it into my usual forehead-hiding fringe.

The work with the orb hadn't been too strenuous, but I also

hadn't had a proper meal since leaving Portland the morning before. The whole way down the winding stairs, the sound of my growling stomach echoed off the cool, stone walls.

The idea of facing Olivia didn't exactly comfort me. She had been easy to talk to, but she carried the cool demeanor of someone who could be harsh if you did something wrong. Really harsh. With hunger and nerves gnawing outward from the center of my gut, I entered Olivia's office.

Did I say she could be harsh? Not at all, she was a wonderful person who clearly understood my needs, because on her desk was a full English breakfast. Not just beans and toast, but eggs, fried tomato, the British form of bacon, and rounds of sausages that Olivia called puddings.

"Why call them puddings?" I asked, taking a seat and barely refraining from picking up the plate and dumping the entire contents into my mouth. "They look like sausage."

"Because they're pudding," she said as if this should be obvious.

"Then what's the sweet, goopy stuff old people eat for dessert?"

"Pudding."

I let the argument die in the firm belief this was a language conundrum that would never be solved, but I reminded myself to always clarify what exactly I might be getting if someone offered me a pudding cake.

Olivia poured us tea and my hand once again thought it was fully functional. As I reached for my saucer, I bashed the stupid appendage into the front edge of Olivia's very solid desk. Grunting in pain and biting back a scream, I clutched the hand to my chest.

Olivia watched me with a mixture of sympathy and consternation.

"This will not do." She pressed a button I hadn't noticed on her desk. A crusty sizzle of electricity came from what sounded like the teapot. Then, on the teapot's shiny metallic surface appeared the face of a man with rich, warm-toned skin and prominent cheek bones. "Rafi, is Chester handy?"

"Sure, he's in here with me."

In the teapot? Was this Rafi a genie?

"Good, send him in." Olivia pressed the button again and Rafi's face vanished from the pot.

I stared at the teapot, half expecting Chester to come crawling out. When the lid failed to rattle, I looked up at Olivia.

"Have you never seen a tea-lephone?" she asked.

Before I could answer, Chester thudded his way into the vast office.

"You needed me, sir?"

Olivia bristled a little, but only said to him, "Ms. Black could use a little help. Cassie, let Chester see your hand."

Chester was big, looked more than a little clumsy, and well, didn't seem like the sharpest knife in the drawer. Plus, he seemed to really enjoy breaking the bones of the Tower's rat population. So I might be forgiven for being a little hesitant to let him handle an already delicate part of my body. I clutched my hand tighter to my torso.

"What's he going to do?"

"Among other talents, trolls have healing powers. Some have been instrumental in our Medi Unit."

I thought of Morelli. I thought of Mr. Wood's abnormally brief trip to the emergency room and of his being able to stand after only one night at Morelli's apartment. I slowly released my protective grip and held out my hand.

Which Chester shook as if in greeting. And he had a very firm handshake. I shrieked in agony.

"Chester, no!" Olivia cried out, then fought to bring her voice down to a normal level. "You've already met her. Heal it, don't shake it."

"You could have told him that first," I grunted.

Chester, flummoxed now, eased his hold on my hand as he bubbled out several apologies. His cheeks and ears burned red, and I thought he might spontaneously combust with embarrassment. Once Olivia convinced him it was alright (it wasn't, I wanted to throw up with the pain throbbing from my fingers to my shoulder), he took my hand in both of his, gently this time, and scrunched his face up with concentration.

Within seconds, the pain subsided. I was about to call that a job well done, no more need for any further Troll Triage, but Chester held on. It was like our hands had become two strong magnets that couldn't be easily pulled apart. A strange sensation hummed from my finger bones to my wrist bones. Almost as if they were moving. It felt good, but it also felt incredibly creepy.

When the sensation stopped, so did the magnetic hold, and Chester held up my hand. He gave a confident nod and peeled open my cast to remove it. I flexed my fingers, as amazed at the movement as I would have been if I'd suddenly sprouted daisies out of my fingertips.

"Thanks, Chester," I said.

"No problem, sir." I gave Olivia a questioning look.

"It's a habit he can't unlearn. You've done very well, Chester. You can have an extra TV break today."

Chester's eyes went wide, and he even clapped his three-fingered hands with glee as he thanked Olivia and told her there was a *Black Adder* rerun he'd been hoping to catch.

Once he'd gone, Olivia said, "They're so easy to please. I can't think of why Morelli didn't volunteer to take care of your injuries." Before I could respond that Morelli had probably enjoyed watching my misery, Olivia indicated the pile of food. "Go on. I'm sure you're starving by now."

I gave my newly healed hand a test run by spooning beans onto my toast. Olivia spoke of the weather while I maneuvered the crisp triangle of bread to my mouth. I then bit into my toast, spilling most of the beans I'd piled on top of it back onto my plate. Olivia had the poise and manners to ignore my idiocy and continued on discussing the tides of the Thames.

Once the food was gone, Olivia flicked her hand as if shaking water from her fingers. The plates disappeared and she pulled out a file from a desk drawer. She then flipped open the file and ran her index finger down a list.

I say *list*, but the sheet was blank until her fingertip slid over it. Then, line by line, words would appear. They'd stay on the page long enough for her to scan them (and not long enough for me to read the jagged handwriting upside down) before disappearing again. She closed the file and rested her hands on it with her fingers entwined.

"Now, you've proven yourself a strong absorber, but I also hear you have the ability to give, which is rare. Most absorbers can only absorb. Your goal while you're here is to fully tame both sides of your magic. This will include using the Shield Charm, Membrane Charm, and other advanced spells."

I thought about mentioning that Alastair and I had already started working on some of these spells, but I didn't know what Alastair was and wasn't supposed to be sharing with me, so I held my tongue.

"You will be required to do some background work, but most of your time will be spent on practical work, since," and here she tapped the file, "it seems you enjoy that type of training."

"This isn't going to involve cleaning windows, is it?" I asked, thinking of all the practical work experience I'd gained during my lessons with Lola.

"Not unless you'd like to volunteer with the Historic Royal Palaces. No? Didn't think so. Now, the first thing to know before we start is that you have two opposing forces in your magic. If you find a balance, neither can take over. However, thanks to the watch, your absorbing is so strong right now you're a risk to other Magics. But there is a caveat: If you control your absorbing side too much without gaining balance and control, your poles will, let's say, flip." She turned her hand from palm down to palm up. "Your giving side will be your stronger aspect. Magic will quite literally flow out of you and into whoever is nearby. Good for them, not so good for you. And with both the Mauvais's and the watch's power in you, not so good for Magics as a whole."

A knot that had nothing to do with the six thousand grams of fat I'd just ingested formed in my gut. Had Alastair been teaching me how to control my absorbing side in order to strengthen my giving side? Was he trying to make me magically incontinent? Before I could stroll too far down the adult diaper aisle, Olivia continued.

"The first order of business will be teaching you to easily switch back and forth between giving and absorbing. It's a challenging exercise, but once mastered, it makes balancing your two sides come as naturally as walking."

I was about to comment that I was a certified klutz and walking didn't always come naturally for my long limbs, but before I could speak, Olivia had placed a beaker full of what, I kid you not, looked like the night sky, complete with galaxies whirling around inside.

"What is that?"

"The universe, but only a small portion of it."

Of course it was. Silly me.

She continued on without hesitation or explanation as if everyone had a five-hundred-milliliter jar of the universe stashed in their desk drawer. "Now," she said, pointing at the beaker, "absorb."

This was easy, I barely gave a second thought to the command before several grain-of-sand sized stars zipped out of the jar. They flew toward me and stuck to the skin of my arm. I froze, holding as still as possible.

"I didn't just kill an entire alien species, did I?"

"No, this section of the universe has been certified to be a dead zone. Now, give."

This took more concentration, but it was something I had been practicing with Alastair even if he didn't know it. Whenever I noticed him starting to look weary, I'd try to put some magic back into him. Unfortunately, as Olivia pointed out, I wasn't a natural at giving and doing so required me to squint my eyes and strain with the effort. Alastair may have felt better after I gave him these secret boosts of magic, but he probably wondered if I had unresolved gastro-intestinal issues.

With Olivia watching me, I squinted at the stars on my arm. I pinched my lips, tensed my arms, and balled my fists, picturing myself pushing the magic out of my pores. Finally, the stars lifted a couple centimeters off my arm, but they fell back the moment I dared to congratulate myself.

"A good effort," Olivia said in a non-committal way. "We'll keep at it until you're tired, then tomorrow we'll practice finding a way to shield yourself to prevent others from tapping into your magic."

"Tapping into my magic?"

"Yes, it's not an easy feat, but a clever enough Magic could figure out how to absorb from you or pull power from you. We call it *tapping in*. Much like a maple tree being tapped for syrup.

And once a Magic is tapped for the first time, it becomes easier to continue doing so. The tapped power can then be kept or passed on. But with a Shield Spell around yourself, it should help stopper the spigot."

"Is this what other Magics have to learn? Other absorbers, I mean."

"No, but then again, absorbers are rare, and most get training from a very early age so they barely have to think about what they're doing. It's like a child growing up in a bilingual household. They can automatically switch between the two languages without giving it a second thought."

So basically, Cassie is not smarter than a magical fifth grader.

We continued on for another thirty minutes after which I could barely think from sheer exhaustion. But I had managed to move the stars a foot closer to the beaker before Olivia finally plucked them off my skin and dropped them back into the container. I guess she assumed they'd just find their way back to their proper place in their respective galaxies.

"You've done well," she said after the beaker's dark sky swallowed the final star. "We still have a few matters to sort out with your schedule. Banna has some ideas of her own, but now that I know Busby and Alastair's schedules, I'll need to coordinate everything with Rafi. Why don't you take a walk around the grounds? The Tower's still not open to Norms at this hour. Once they start showing up, return here. We should have at least your first few days planned by then."

I didn't ask why they couldn't have done their planning last night, or perhaps when they made their politely demanding request that I come to London, but that didn't mean I wasn't thinking it. Still, free access to the Tower of London without tourists? I wasn't about to complain.

CHAPTER SEVENTEEN
MEETING NIGEL

Olivia explained the route to get out of the White Tower, and after spiraling my way down another staircase, backtracking along a few hallways, and turning several wrong corners only to end up on what looked very much like the hallway I'd started from, I found the exit — a door on the west side of the building at ground level that Olivia told me only Magics could access. Or see, for that matter.

With relief to be free of the interior maze, I stepped out of the White Tower and into the calm of what might actually become a sunny day. Maybe it wasn't so stupid to pack those sunglasses.

My phone pinged the moment the door shut behind me, making me wonder if the interior of the White Tower was a no-call-no-text zone like MagicLand. Sent the night before at nine p.m. Portland time, the message had one line of text:

Pablo is settling in well.

This was followed by a down arrow emoji.

I scrolled and nearly cried out in horror when I saw what the arrow was pointing to. It was a picture of Pablo. Dressed in a cowboy hat. A pink cowboy hat.

I would have demanded Mr. Tenpenny take me home immediately so I could save my cat from this feline embarrassment, but Pablo had a look of proud contentment on his face that I'd only ever seen once after he extracted the treat bag from its hiding place, tore it open, and ate the entire contents.

I texted back a smiley face emoji and hoped that was the end of Pablo's fashion show.

After slipping the phone back into my pocket, I strolled over to Tower Green. Once I'd taken in the execution site memorial where Anne Boleyn had a little taken off the top, I wandered to the nearby Chapel Royal of St. Peter in Chains where Anne's bones and those of a few other historic royals rested.

I paused, taking in the arched windows and letting my imagination roam. What if I could wake up Anne? What would be her final desire she would want taken care of? Would it be to clear her name? Would it be an uncontrollable urge to run about slashing all the portraits of her wife-murdering husband, Henry VIII? You can bet she wouldn't waste her borrowed time grabbing a bouquet of bacon. Still, she might at least get the vengeful satisfaction of knowing her daughter, Elizabeth I, showed everyone a thing or two by becoming one of the most famous royals in English history.

A chill crept along my arms. Likely a breeze coming in off the Thames, I thought, then wondered if it was worth the stair-climbing effort to head back inside and grab a jacket.

"This chapel, St. Peter in Chains, was built in—"

A squeal of fright escaped from me and, I'm not exaggerating, I jumped back three feet, clutched my hand to my heart, and wished I hadn't left my baseball bat behind at Mr. Wood's. Okay, not the expected reaction from someone who has befriended the dead and fought an evil wizard, but it had been eerily quiet and I had been thinking about zombie queens.

What stood before me, looking just as taken aback as I

probably did, was a white man who looked to be in his mid-fifties. Other than a slight middle-age paunch, he appeared fit. Although with his heavy, knee-length overcoat that was black with red trim, evaluating his frame with any precision proved a challenge. On his head perched what looked like a squat top hat, also black, also trimmed in red. Emblazoned across the chest area of his coat was a crown and the Roman numeral II flanked by the letters E and R. Which, no, does not stand for Emergency Room.

"You scared the life out of me," I said, my heart pounding against my palm.

"Apologies, I do forget how quiet I am these days." This was a Yeoman Warder, also known as a Beefeater. I knew they guarded the Tower and served as tour guides. I also knew they had to have quite a few years of exemplary military service under their belts to apply, but I hadn't heard anything about them being trained in stealth. "Would you like a tour?"

"I don't think I have time. I've only got until the gates open."

"Then, let's get started. We've got enough time to do the tour from here to the raven enclosure."

I assumed his time was limited because the selfie-stick-wielding hordes would soon be flowing in, but it seemed he might have better chores to tend to, or at least not want to start in on a spiel he'd have to give several times over the course of the day. But as he encouraged me to join him, his bright eyes spoke of someone who really liked his job. He carried on a couple paces ahead of me. As I caught up, I glanced down at his feet.

And then froze in place.

Before I could speak, the raven from the conveyor belt, the one with the white eyebrow, swooped down and landed on the warden's shoulder.

"Well hello, Winston." The bird rubbed its beak against the brim of the man's hat. "Did you enjoy your trip to the Edinburgh community?"

"What are you?" I asked.

"Oh, how rude of me. We're supposed to give our names at the very start of the tour. I'm Nigel Knighton. And this is Winston."

Winston hopped onto Nigel's hat, then with a quick flap of his wings, soared over to my shoulder. The bird weighed more than I expected, and his claws dug through my shirt and into my skin as he balanced himself. If I wasn't distracted by Nigel, I might have given a hearty, "Arrghh, matey."

But I was distracted. Nigel's feet were most definitely not touching the ground.

"No, not who. *What* are you?"

Nigel stood at attention, floating feet held tightly together, chest puffed out, chin tilted up. "Yeomen Warder of Her Majesty's Royal Palace and Fortress the Tower of London, and Member of the Sovereign's Body Guard of the Yeoman Guard Extraordinary." Then some of the air deflated from his chest, his chin tucked down, and he pulled off his hat. "Or, at least I wanted to be. I kept failing the test. Then, well, it became too late for me to qualify."

"Too late?" I asked warily.

"Yes, well, death does tend to make you a less desirable job candidate."

Oh crap. Where did they keep the dead Beefeaters? I racked my brain. I knew they had a doctor on the premises, but surely they didn't store corpses on the grounds of the Tower. Or did they? Had I gone and taken my Waking Dead Tour international? Winston hopped back over to Nigel and rubbed his beak against Nigel's chin almost as if comforting him.

"You died?" I asked, proving there were stupid questions.

"Yes, about twenty-five years ago. But I quite like it here and the living Yeoman Warders do need to sleep, so they allow me to guard the Tower at night. During the day I'm free to do what I like as long as I don't scare anyone. Although some of the other Yeoman Warders do ask me to play tricks on particularly rude visitors. But for the most part, I'm to stay out of the way of Norms." He paused, suddenly unsure of himself. "You know about Norms, yes? I hope I haven't bunged things up before the gates even open."

"No, you're fine. I'm a Magic."

"Ah good, thought I detected something on you."

Twenty-five years. I know I had just been contemplating the bones of Anne and her queenly friends, but even with my new super powers, I was pretty sure I couldn't wake people who weren't freshly dead. I'd even tested this theory one evening by heading over to the nearest cemetery to my apartment. Okay, maybe it wasn't the smartest test. After all, if I had woken up all the in-ground residents, mayhem would have ensued, or at least a remake of Michael Jackson's "Thriller" video.

Luckily, no matter how many graves I walked past, no one woke up from their long nap. I wasn't sure what the exact timing was, but my not-so scientific inquiry proved there was a cut-off period between time of death and my being able to return the dead to a more lively status.

"So, would you like the tour?" Nigel asked. He sounded so hopeful, so eager, how could I refuse?

"Sure, but just a short one. Olivia told me to be back before the gates open."

"We certainly can't do much of a tour in that amount of time. Are you sure you have to go back so soon?"

I shrugged. "I better do as she says."

"Well, we'll have to make do, won't we? Come along."

And so I came along. And I soon discovered why Nigel had failed his test so many times. While he did have an engaging style of delivery, he kept messing up his history. He had Richard II becoming imprisoned some time after Richard III supposedly killed the Princes in the Tower. He had Elizabeth I facing down Oliver Cromwell. And he wasn't quite sure if Lady Jane Grey had been married to Henry VIII or not (she hadn't been).

With every mistake, Winston shook his head and turned back to look at me as if to make sure I wasn't really believing all this.

It was a relief when, once we reached the ravens' enclosure, an announcement was made that the Tower was opening for the day. I thanked Nigel for the tour.

"We can do another one later today," he offered. "The Wall Walk is my speciality."

"I'll have to see what my schedule is like. I might have another lesson with Banna," I said, vaguely grabbing at the first name that popped into my head. "Do you know Banna?"

"Yes, well, I shouldn't tell you this, but we don't get along," Nigel said, almost apologetically, but Winston snapped his beak with a vicious clack.

"Why?"

"Do you know, I can't recall. Avoiding her just seems to have become a habit."

"She does take some getting used to."

"Quite. But I do love giving tours, so if you can, I'll meet you at Tower Green this afternoon. Cheers."

"Right, cheers," I said. Before hurrying off, I glanced at Winston and I would swear he was grinning at my expense.

CHAPTER EIGHTEEN
YOU DID WHAT?!

When I returned to Olivia's office, I thought about bringing up my encounter with Nigel, but didn't want to risk getting him fired — or would it be exorcised? — for spreading bad history. After a polite greeting, Olivia handed me a sheet listing where and when my classes would be for the day.

I rolled my eyes when I saw my next lesson would be in room forty-nine, seven doors down from my own room. Yep, it was another trip up the stairs for Cassie. If nothing else, I'd be leaving HQ with improved cardiovascular fitness.

I'm not sure why, perhaps because we were on his home turf, but I assumed this lesson might be with Busby. Once I'd trudged up the stairs and caught my breath, I knocked on the door and crossed my fingers that it wouldn't be Tobey who answered.

It wasn't. It was Alastair. My cheeks, already warm from the climb, burned a little hotter. He smiled and stepped aside to let me in. He'd somehow managed to book himself a double bed, whereas I'd only gotten a narrow, single bed, but in every other aspect his room was an exact twin of mine. Whoever had turned the hidden rooms of the White Tower into lodging must have formerly worked as an interior designer for Best Western.

"If you're going to be one of my teachers here, couldn't we have just done this in Portland?" I asked, stepping over to the window to see what view he had. It looked to be nearly the same as mine, even though I would have sworn his room was on the opposite side of the hallway.

"I'm able to build strength here since we're near the source of all magic."

I turned away from the window to face him. "What exactly does that mean?"

"It means you won't be so exhausting to be around," he said with a grin as he wound a tiger-shaped timer and set it stalking across the table.

"Don't be too sure of that. So what exactly are you teaching me?"

"In addition to working on how to control your absorbing and your giving, we're continuing on with the defensive lessons we've already started. You'll also be working with Busby and doing some classes with Rafi."

"Isn't he just Olivia's assistant?" I asked, remembering Olivia calling him earlier.

"He is, but he also serves as troll liaison and research coordinator. You'll meet him soon. He's a great guy. Anyway, they've decided to have you start with me today since I have special knowledge in this area." I gave him a questioning look. "I'm one of the few people who understands the Mauvais's fighting tactics. Or, at least, I used to."

"What do you mean 'his fighting tactics'?" I asked, glancing over to the small counter beside the mini-fridge. Even though I'd eaten less than an hour ago, a lesson with Alastair without snacks didn't seem right.

Seeing no cake, I opened the twin packet of cookies that had been left beside the electric kettle and offered one of the wafers to Alastair. He refused it. A Magic denying sugar? He really was feeling good. I slipped the second cookie back into its plastic sleeve, taking it with me as I sat down at the table near the window.

"Because I used to work for him. With him," he added meaningfully.

"What?" I blurted through a mouthful of chocolate-hazelnut biscuit.

I'd known Alastair had interacted the Mauvais on some level, but to have worked with him? And I was pretty sure *work* didn't refer to secretarial duties. Which meant I was sitting in the same room as someone who had been in league with the person who may have killed my parents. My jaw clenched so tightly my teeth ached. At the sight of my glower, Alastair quickly fumbled to explain his despicable actions.

"I'm not proud of it, but I don't know, I was so young and felt so out of place when my teachers advanced me in school. My own parents had no time for me and I craved an adult to look up to, to tell me I was doing well. I think it made me a bit clingy when someone did pay me attention."

"Clingy? That's your excuse for, for whatever it is you've done?"

"It's no excuse, but I wasn't even twelve years old at the time. I idolized your mom, Simon too. I had a crush on Chloe. I knew she was too old for me, but that didn't stop me from latching onto them for some form of adult connection. Maybe I saw them as surrogate parents, or perhaps older siblings." He watched the tiger timer a moment, nudging it with his index finger as the beast neared the edge of the table. "Still, they didn't always want some kid hanging around, and I felt left behind by their pairing up.

"When your parents had less time for me, I transferred my need for an adult in my life to the Mauvais. He had such bravado, such profound ideas — or so they seemed at the time. I was impressionable and didn't have the reasoning skills to question if he was what a real leader should be." Alastair paced over to stare out the window. His chocolate-raspberry scent radiated from him. When he continued, he spoke like someone trying to explain why they once liked canned sardines with strawberry jam. "The Mauvais, he had this swaggering charm, he made you feel like you were important to him, and I gravitated right to that."

"But how did you not recognize him as Kilbride?"

"When he was on the streets of Rosaria, he was Devin Kilbride. Big and bold, but not the type of guy you'd think would amount to much. When he was operating as the Mauvais, he had either been using a Morphing Spell to hide his face, or he kept his followers under a Confounding Charm to keep us from recognizing him. I'm guessing it was the latter, or perhaps some sort of potion he wore that worked like a Confounding Charm because I swear none of us could describe his features when we were interrogated later."

"But you just went along with him?" I scooted forward in the chair. It was the same style as the ones in my room and I'd been right in guessing they'd be uncomfortable. Spots in my back were already going numb from the rigid, poorly positioned backrest.

"No," Alastair said without conviction. He shifted away from the window, then plunked down on the edge of the bed. "I mean, yes. I kind of thought what he was saying was wrong, but I wanted to fit in, so I didn't argue. And the more I was around him, the more I liked being part of his crowd, and the more the idea of Magics being the highest form of humanity started to seem spot-on.

"I wanted to impress him, I didn't want to be sent drifting alone again, and so I joined him even though a voice in the back of my head kept telling me he was wrong. A voice echoed by warnings from your mother who begged me to stop hanging out with the Mauvais. By then, I was angry with her for always being busy, either with Simon or with her police training. So I ignored her pleas, told her she was one of the backwards thinking sheep."

"Did you..." My words trailed off, my throat too tight to speak. I swallowed hard. "Did you kill people just to hang out with the cool kids?"

"No," Alastair said so quickly it seemed like a lie, or at least like a half-truth. He glanced down at his fingers, drumming them nervously on his thigh. With a sigh, he admitted, "He used some of my knowledge to kill non-magics and even some Magics who didn't agree with him. It was right after I turned thirteen that something clicked in me, something told me I was on the wrong path. I began distancing myself from the Mauvais and worked to reforge my friendship with your parents."

"So noble of you," I said bitterly. I was now glad I'd stolen his cookies. He didn't deserve them.

"Like I said, I don't consider that time a high point in my life. And it wasn't without danger. You don't just walk away from the Mauvais without him noticing. I had to stay in for a time, and during that time your parents were invaluable in keeping me on the right path. They had already worked their way up in the police force and advised me to play the fool. I hated it. I was a cocky teenager who wanted to be thought of as this young genius, but I slowly swallowed their advice. So whenever the Mauvais called on me to do something bad, to kill or hurt people, I made excuses that I didn't know the proper spell or would purposely fumble the charm, that sort of thing.

"It worked. He already had what he'd wanted from me, so he began shunning me. Eventually, when I stopped showing up to his gatherings, he didn't question my absence. I witnessed some terrible things, things I could have probably prevented with one twist of my hand, but what I've seen, what I've experienced does make me useful. No one can really know the Mauvais, but I know how he fights and how he can use others and his own power to manipulate people, to get into their heads. Now, if you'll stop slapping me with that judgmental look, we should get started."

I handed him the second cookie in a show of truce. And even though Team Brain was insisting on more evidence of Alastair's innocence, Team Heart was clearly willing to forgive him because it gave a little jump when our fingers touched as he took the treat.

CHAPTER NINETEEN
GREAT BALLS OF FIRE

Alastair finally began the lesson by explaining that HQ had decided one of the skills I should master was to form a wall around myself that would act as a barrier to prevent me from accidentally giving away my magic (or from having it stolen), and to reduce my chances of accidentally absorbing someone else's magic.

A nice idea, but it didn't work.

The wall I conjured blocked all my magic and kept me from performing even the most basic spells. Alastair admitted it was a complex concept, but seemed to have no problem doing the trick himself. Seeing my dismay and frustration at his easily formed wall, he decided to change tack and appeal to my science-loving side.

"Think of it as more of a membrane to contain larger particles of your power and prevent them from escaping."

"Isn't that just the same thing as a wall?" I asked sarcastically.

"No," he said, raising his eyebrows and smiling as if he was about to clue me in on a wonderful secret. "Because this is a semi-permeable membrane. It will hold back the larger particles while still allowing smaller bits of your magic through."

I'll admit, I was skeptical, but having this visual in my head did help. A little. It was a challenging task since it required doing two things at once: holding the membrane, while also executing a Shoving Charm or whatever magical stunt Alastair tested me with. It was far harder than anything I'd tried before, and my frustration with myself was being made worse by jet lag — or rather, portal lag. By noon it already felt like it had been a long day, and I called it quits well before the timer went off.

"You've done well," Alastair said.

"You're a really good liar."

"No, I mean it, which means you get a reward."

"Does it involve cake?"

"Sorry, no, just information. Last night I had a little chat with Chester."

"He chats?"

"Eventually. It does take a bit of patience to wait for him to get around to what you're asking, but apparently Rafi has been working with him to be a sort of messenger, which means Chester gets news that doesn't always make it to the rest of the magical communities. He said that before we arrived, Olivia had indeed gotten information about your parents not being dead. She seemed to think it wasn't just a hoax."

"That's good news, right? We can go looking for them. I'm sure there's got to be more information—"

"Cassie," Alastair said sharply enough to interrupt the verbal lava flow spewing from my mouth. "I'm not telling you this for you to go after them. It's too dangerous for you to do that. You promised we would do this my way, and Olivia has given me the perfect opportunity to do just that."

"What opportunity?"

"The historical research she mentioned? It gives me every excuse to sift through the old files. If I go through HQ's papers on your parents' disappearance, you and I can compile what I find. We can then take it to Busby who'll help us argue the case to rescue your parents."

"Wait. Compiling? Consulting? My parents are in danger and you don't think we should hurry up the process of finding them?"

"That's not what I mean. I just—" He caught himself, his cheeks flaring red. He fiddled with the crinkling plastic wrapper left over from the cookies, then glanced up at me through his lashes. "I don't want to put you in harm's way. I've only ever wanted to protect you," he said quietly. "No matter how clumsily I've gone about it."

I stared at him, touched by the sentiment. The really intense sentiment, if I'm being honest. But I was also annoyed by his lackadaisical attitude toward the main reason I'd come to London.

"I don't need you to babysit me, okay," I said, trying to sound patient when all I wanted to do was run down to this file room and have a poke around. "I need you to be an ally, but it seems you're still trying to fit in with the big kids. We don't have time to wait for HQ to debate this. If you get information, we need to act on it. And if you won't, I will."

"You can't go hunting down the Mauvais on your own. Besides, you probably wouldn't make it past the outer wall."

Alastair abruptly stopped speaking and jerked his head up to meet my eyes. He opened his mouth, the look on his face was that of someone who desperately wanted to hit rewind on their words.

"Wait, am I a prisoner here?"

"No. I mean, not exactly. I only found out this morning, but they don't want you to leave. It's not imprisonment. They just don't want the Mauvais to get to you, so you're not really allowed to leave the Tower on your own."

"This is ridiculous," I snapped, my irritation churning harder than an industrial washing machine. "They invited me here and now they're treating me like a juvenile delinquent?"

I used an array of curse words that included what anatomically impossible things the Magics could all do to themselves. Then, as I made an emphatically rude hand gesture, something that looked like my orb from earlier in the day burst from my palm. Only this orb wasn't green-gold. It was red. It was also flying across the room, directly toward the door.

Alastair flicked at the air with his fingers, sending a jet of ice after the fiery ball. But my orb had a head start. It hit the center of the door and burned a hole straight through before Alastair's spell caught up, put out the flames, and coated the damage in ice.

"What was that?" he asked.

"Banna taught me the Solas Charm this morning," I said cautiously.

"She should not have taught you that spell. It's not part your curriculum."

I glared at him. Not seeing the handsome face, not seeing the endearing demeanor, but instead seeing someone who was going along with people who seemed to want to do nothing but control me.

"I'm so glad everyone has decided everything already. Am I allowed to pick out what I wear tomorrow, or has that already been decided for me as well?"

"Cassie, please. It's just—"

"I'm out of here," I said, throwing up my hands in defeat. "First, I don't do magic and you get mad. Then I do do magic and you still get mad. I don't know what you people expect from me."

I whipped open the door and slammed it behind me.

Or, well, I tried to slam it. As with any modern hotel room

door, this one was equipped with hinges that eased the door shut to keep the hallways silent.

But I was a witch who knew her way around a Shoving Charm. I thrust out my hand and the door banged shut. When it did, the ice from Alastair's spell cracked apart and *thunk*ed onto the carpeted floor.

CHAPTER TWENTY

A STRANGE FRIENDSHIP

Refusing to play the role of prisoner, and feeling more than a little paranoid that Olivia would unleash her fury on me for flinging a fireball through a door, I marched down many, many, *many* stairs and made my way out of the White Tower.

Not knowing exactly where to go, and with crowds of tourists already filling the grounds, I decided to continue my tour from the morning and headed toward the ravens' enclosure. Winston was nowhere to be seen, but a couple of birds were busying themselves by playing with a set of house keys. I imagined someone would be going home that evening and finding themselves in need of a locksmith.

"They're ravens," a voice said behind me. I grit my teeth. Why did it have to be him?

"Yes, very good, Tobey," I said as if he were four years old and had just recited the alphabet. "Maybe you ought to be a wildlife biologist."

"Don't throw your attitude at me, Cassie. Come on, let's walk, it'll clear both our heads."

Walkies with Tobey? Hadn't I already met my daily quota of odd behavior and strange news without adding Tobey Tenpenny to the mix? Still, walking with him would keep anyone from questioning what I might be up to, so I shrugged an assent and fell into step alongside him. We climbed the walls and joined the throngs of visitors strolling from tower to tower. I wondered if Nigel knew the names of any of the structures, or if he just made them up as he went along.

With the Thames to our left, Tobey and I said nothing to one another as we wandered toward Wakefield Tower. I found I enjoyed the silence, plus it allowed me to eavesdrop on the family ahead of us. Their pre-teen son kept asking where they tortured people, where they mounted the severed heads of traitors, where the weapons had been kept. I was just sizing up this serial killer in the making when Tobey finally spoke.

"You'll probably be pissed at what I have to say, so promise me you won't hurl me off this wall." He added a magical finger flourish to the word *hurl*.

"I can't make guarantees like that."

Tobey rolled his eyes and instead of risking anything, he clammed up again. Eventually, we stepped back down to ground level. The pre-teen axe murderer was now asking when they could get something to eat, and his father's weary sigh showed he'd had just about enough of his progeny.

Tobey and I passed St. Peter in Chains, the squat little chapel where I'd encountered Nigel and where a couple of garden gnomes had been situated at the base of one of the windows. We then strolled around to pass by the crenellated building where the crown jewels were kept. Once we pushed through the crowds waiting to get in to see the sparkly things, Tobey had again worked up the gumption to say what was on his mind.

"You do know Alastair worked for the Mauvais at one time, right?"

"Of course I do." I'd known for all of sixty-three minutes. "What's your point?"

"Nothing. Go ahead and hang out with him if you want, but I

just wonder how he couldn't have known Vivian was the Mauvais if they used to work together. It's all a bit convenient, don't you think? I mean, he had to recognize the Mauvais's scent."

"Vivian smoked and wore gallons of perfume. You probably noticed that when you had your face smashed up to hers."

"Look, that wasn't— Never mind, I don't need to explain myself to you. But it wasn't what you think. My point is that Alastair was close to the Mauvais at the time your parents died. And now I hear Alastair convinced you to come here by telling you your parents might still be alive. I just—"

"Just what? Want to be a meddling lunkhead?"

"Why do you have to be so impossible?"

"Because I don't know why you're telling me this. Do you not think this has already gone around inside my head?" Tobey looked about to speak, but I cut him off. "And hearing it from you isn't helping since I don't know if you're spreading your little conspiracy theories because you want to help me, or because you want to be a jerk."

"How is warning you being a jerk?"

By now people were staring, and some were pulling out their phones to record our tiff. I needed to ask Busby if there was a spell that could instantly shatter the lenses of phone cameras. I lowered my voice, gripped Tobey's forearm, and tugged him along.

"Because," I said once we'd gone several paces, "you still act like you have a chip on your shoulder about me, and that's not fair. I didn't ask to be Magic. You didn't ask to not be Magic. I thought maybe you were telling me this because you were jealous of Alastair, but it's more like you're jealous of me. We're not friends and we won't be until I've tossed aside all my power or you suddenly gain some. Neither of which are going to happen any time soon, so please stop taking it out on me."

"I'm not taking it out on you. And I kind of thought," he said hesitantly, almost as if he didn't like the taste of the words in his mouth. "I kind of thought you'd want a friend in here."

"Are we friends now?" I said with a mocking laugh.

"I keep trying to be, but, well, talk about someone with a chip on her shoulder." He punctuated this quip with an arch of his eyebrows and a know-it-all grin.

I told him he wasn't clever, and we continued along past the Fusilier's Museum to head back toward the raven enclosure where Winston had shown up while we'd been away.

Tobey was right. He'd come by to help me clean my apartment after it had been ransacked, he'd tried to help me with Pablo, and he'd been sort of nice about it. I was the one who got bent out of shape over him smooching Vivian. I was the one who kept throwing my attitude around. He had no reason to be here, and he had his new girlfriend back in MagicLand. Had he really come to London as a friend? I swear I didn't think I'd ever sort out this whole human socializing thing.

"Okay," I finally said. "I'm sorry. I'll try to play nice, but that doesn't mean I'm not going to make fun of you from time to time."

"I would expect nothing less. So, do you want to know a secret?" I crossed my arms over my chest and stared at him. I was in no mood for guessing games. "You're not much fun, you know. Anyway, there's a file room in the lowest levels of the White Tower. It supposedly contains information on every Magic who ever existed."

"I thought they had Banna for that?"

"Magics like to be thorough. Banna is impossibly old, but she's not immortal. The file room is sort of a backup system.

Anyway, I think I can get you into it. They know me here and wouldn't question me showing you around."

I stopped. My heart pounded in my ears, thudding over the metallic jangle as two ravens played tug-of-war with the stolen set of keys. Alastair would be fuming if he found out I was even thinking of going behind his back to do this. I'd promised him we would find my parents his way. But really, I wouldn't be looking *for* my parents. Just information on them. That wasn't against my promise.

I know, I'm the Queen of Loophole Finding.

"When do we begin?"

"Soon," Tobey said, his voice revealing a hint of delight. "I've got to wait to get the key from my grandad."

"I could just..." I waggled my fingers.

"No, they'd smell your magic on the lock. You'd think you'd know that by now. Anyway, I'll find you once I get it." This was followed by an awkward lull in our devious conversation. "Don't you have a class to go to or something?" he asked waspishly.

Did I mention Tobey was impossible to figure out? I pulled the sheet out of my pocket.

"What the—?" Where there had been three classes listed for this afternoon, the sheet had gone blank except for a check mark next to Alastair's time slot and a note at the bottom telling me Chester would collect me early the next morning. "I guess not. Did you—?"

Before I could ask him if he wanted to grab some lunch, the ravens began cawing loudly enough to be heard across the river. The sound echoed off the Tower's stone walls and sent a shiver down my spine. The crowd of tourists nearest the enclosure hushed.

Winston turned his attention to us. Suddenly, he began flapping his wings as if preparing for flight and snapping his beak with sharp clicks. Tobey glanced around as if looking for the source of the noise and stepped back a pace.

If it weren't for the weird sensation charging through my spine and into my toes, I would have teased him about being afraid of birds. Before I could say anything, Tobey muttered, "I've got to go."

And with that, Tobey — apparent sufferer of ornithophobia — turned on his heel and strode hurriedly away. When I looked back to Winston, he was standing proud with his wings sleek against his body. He then gave a sharp nod of his head as if to say, "Good riddance."

Since I couldn't stand around staring at birds all afternoon, since the day was too nice to hole up inside my room, and since I needed some sort of distraction, I headed back over to the Tower Green and spent the afternoon being regaled with Nigel's inaccurate tales. Who knows, maybe if I corrected him enough, he might earn his place as one of the Yeoman Warders.

CHAPTER TWENTY-ONE

STRAIGHT FROM THE HORSE'S EAR

With jet lag still making a mess of my circadian rhythm, the sun was only just rising when I pulled myself out of bed the next day. I dressed, and when I emerged from the bathroom, a tray of breakfast had been left on my table.

A chill ran up my arms at the realization I'd heard neither the door to my room open, nor the sound of the china clinking. But by Merlin, did the eggs and toast smell tempting. And the small slice of crispy ham made me wonder how Mr. Wood was getting along.

My stomach growled. I poured a cup of tea and was just lifting a fried tomato to my lips when a heavy fist thudded on my door. The sound startled me and the tomato plunked into my tea.

"Miss Black, sir, are you ready?"

As promised, Chester was at my door to guide me down to the room I'd be training in. So much for breakfast. I grabbed a piece of toast, holding it between my teeth as I pulled on my pair of thrift store Doc Martin's.

Chester fidgeted with his hands and kept muttering to himself that, "It would be okay," as he led me down the staircase, along various hallways, down some more stairs, and through a couple arched entryways. When we reached a broad, wooden door, he stopped. His hand shaking as he reached for the iron latch. Again he repeated his mantra that it would be okay.

"You doing alright there, Chester?" I asked, wishing I'd brought more of the toast with me since the first slice had barely made a dent in my hungry belly.

"I don't like going in here alone." The guy who trampled rats in the dark was scared of this room? That did not bode well. He glanced over to me, a watery smile on his big face. "But you're with me. It'll be okay."

"Let's hope so." And still he didn't open the door. "What's in there?"

"Lots of sparkly things."

Dear Merlin, had we somehow reached the room where the crown jewels were kept? HQ couldn't possibly expect me to train in there. What kind of idiots were these people? They knew I had control issues. What if I disintegrated millions of dollars worth of gold, diamonds, and rubies?

"Where exactly are we?" I asked.

"The armory," replied Chester as he flipped the latch, opened the door, and swept his arm to usher me in.

With Chester sticking close to my side, I entered. And gaped in stunned surprise. The room was full of life-size horses made entirely of wood and wearing battle gear from across the ages. Chester's hands twisted and fretted against one another as we passed by full suits of gleaming armor, jewel-hilted swords as tall as I was, and a block of wood, which seemed absolutely out of place amongst all the *sparkly things*, as Chester put it.

"I think someone forgot to tidy up," I told him and pointed to the wood block.

Chester, who need I remind you was big, brawny, and well-muscled, shimmied back from the object and pressed himself as close to the opposite wall as possible as he hurried along. All the while, he kept a wary eye on the hunk of wood as if it might fling itself at him. Which, given that I was in the room, it just might, but I don't think Chester knew of my super powers. Just to be safe, I kept my own hands firmly pinned to my sides.

"That's the block," he said, his voice a trembling whisper. "They used to chop people's heads off on it. People, and trolls. Lots of trolls who wouldn't behave. Even some who would."

Slaves, invading other countries, troll genocides? Magic it seemed had a really dark past.

"Cassie, over here," called Mr. Tenpenny from somewhere amongst the suits of armor. Chester's ears twitched, and he honed in on the sound with me following close behind. "Ah, Chester, thank you for showing her the way. With all its hidden rooms, the White Tower can be tricky for new arrivals."

"I still can't keep track of them all sometimes," Chester admitted. "Rafi has to remind me. Don't tell Mr. Olivia that though, she gets mad at me sometimes."

"I promise not to say a word. Feel free to go now. I'll take matters from here."

Chester gave a curt nod of his head to both of us. Then, muttering again to himself that it would be okay, he headed back the way we had come. At one point I heard his footsteps pick up the pace, and I'd bet it was when he had to pass by the chopping block.

"You certainly do know how to pick a place for training," I said. "So what are we going to do? Joust?"

Mr. T arched his left eyebrow. "How did you know?"

"You're not serious."

"Well, we're not going to gallop toward one another with

lances at the ready, but you will learn how to exert and control your power by moving those horses a few paces. They have special properties we'll get to in a moment. But first, something light to practice with." He gestured toward the suit of armor nearest us. It looked big enough to fit a giant. A fat giant. "Make that walk, turn around, then return to its current position."

"Whose is that?"

"King Henry VIII's."

"He was a big boy. But do they really just leave this thing out in the open? Tourists come through here, don't they?"

"The keys that unlock the gates at the start of the day also trip a protective spell that brings up glass cases and security systems around most of the items in here. And yes, Henry was a bit on the portly side. Now, make him get some exercise."

I was sorting through the spell I'd need to use and what spin to put on it, but a question kept getting in the way.

"Why not just keep the cases up all the time?"

"Then how would we play dress up in the evening?" he said, showing no indication he was joking. "Now, get to it, we haven't much time."

And so, I made Henry's silvery suit march ten paces. This took a great deal of concentration since I had to make each leg move one after the other. If you think the act of walking is easy, ask an expert in neuroscience just how tricky it is to coordinate brain, muscles, and inner ear to put one foot in front of the other without falling on your face.

Henry's first few steps were as halting as a toddler's, but the massive amount of focus had one up side: It was keeping me from using too much magic at once. Thinking about every minute action meant I was doling out precise amounts of power.

"Very good, Cassie. Keep that up as you turn him."

I really wanted to cheat. I could have just made Henry walk backwards to return him to his spot, but I did as I was told (first time for everything, right?) and turned him around to head back to where he'd spend the day being gawked at by the masses.

"That showed an excellent amount of control. You had to think, didn't you? You didn't just react. You really put some thought behind what you were doing. That's what we're aiming for, but for it to come naturally even when you're reacting without thought to a situation. Now, let's try the horses."

We headed back to where I'd entered the room. When we passed the block, even I felt a small shudder run through me.

"This will be more difficult."

"Why?" I asked. "I mean, it's the same idea, isn't it?"

"Well-trained animals," Mr. Tenpenny explained, "especially ones trained for battle, were expensive investments. No one wanted to lose the time and money they'd put into their mount, so the armor decorating these models was enchanted to protect the real horses the armor was intended for. It makes the steeds, even these wooden ones, more resistant to magic, much like the sparring vests you'll be using later. But go on, get that second horse to take three steps forward and then back."

So we're just going to gloss over this whole sparring thing? Mr. T watched me expectantly. Yep, guess so. I focused on the second horse.

Okay, Seabiscuit. Let's get you trotting.

It did take more effort. Much more. See, I can feel my magic coming from inside me when I use it. It's kind of like waving your hand through a gentle breeze. There's an infinitesimal amount of resistance, but nothing to prevent you from moving your arm.

This however, felt like when you put your hand out the window of a car as it zips down the freeway. Much as your arm will do in the fast-moving car, I immediately felt my magic whipping back. But, just as in the car, if you angle your hand the right way, your limb glides through the air like an airplane wing soaring through the sky. Using this image, I shifted my magic to get under that resisting flow coming off Seabiscuit and he stepped forward three paces, his hooves clopping against the wooden platform he stood on.

"Have him go back," Mr. T said quietly, his voice carrying a sense of awe.

After Henry and after pushing through Seabiscuit's magic barrier, this lesson started to seem easy. And so, dancing my fingers like playing a piano, I signaled the horse's legs to step back to his original spot, even though I was ready for him to have a go at the racetrack.

And that's where I screwed up. I wasn't concentrating. I mean, I was, but not with the all-out effort I'd used earlier. In my cockiness, I allowed too much magic to flow out.

And that thought about the racetrack seeped out as well.

Seabiscuit reared up and charged forward. I tried to force him back with my go-to Shoving Charm.

Big mistake.

The wooden, full-size horse went hurtling back, his legs flailing and trying to find purchase like when you see horses being airlifted to safety.

Mr. Tenpenny cursed, but the exact words were drowned out when my poor racehorse crashed into his friends. Luckily, these things had been built solidly. Some wood chips went flying, some rivets from the armor popped out, but none of the steeds broke their legs. Okay, one lost an ear, but it was a clean break and could probably be fixed with a couple drops of Super Glue.

Still, the whole horsey exhibit was now a jumbled mess of wood, cloth, and metal. An emerald from one of the bridles came loose, bounced across the floor, and rolled to my feet just as a buzzer sounded and glass enclosures went up around some of the exhibits.

Olivia burst in. "What the hell happened? I heard the crash from down in my office."

Down? Wasn't her office above this room? I really needed a map of this place.

"Cassie had… That is to say, to her credit, she had been doing quite well prior to…" Mr. Tenpenny trailed off.

"Prior to destroying one of the most popular exhibits in the whole Tower?" asked Olivia, her dark cheeks made even darker with fury.

"Well, yes. That."

Olivia stared at me. Thinking of the pre-teen axe murderer from the day before, I wanted to point out that the torture exhibit was also quite popular. But I held my tongue.

Olivia looked like she wanted to shout at me. Her nostrils were flaring, truly flaring. Her jaw muscles quavered from clenching her teeth so tightly. She closed her eyes and pulled several deep breaths through her nose. When she opened her eyes, she looked only at Mr. Tenpenny, as if looking at me might set her off again.

"I will go inform the guards that the exhibit will have to be closed today. I will then send the pixies in to work on tidying this up."

"I could help," I offered, trying to be useful. I probably wouldn't be allowed to magic anything back into place, but I knew how to use a broom.

"We will manage without your help, Ms. Black."

And with that, Mr. Tenpenny showed me out of the White Tower. Tourists were already heading in our direction. They all let out a collective groan when one of the Yeoman Warders told them the White Tower's armory was undergoing some renovations for the day.

That's right, it was barely half-past nine in the morning, and I'd already ruined a historic display and put a giant hitch in hundreds of people's sightseeing plans. This was not how I imagined spending my first trip to London.

CHAPTER TWENTY-TWO

THE FILE ROOM

As soon as I'd been shown out of the White Tower, my phone pinged. I found a bench, checked my messages, and my gut plummeted when I saw several were from Mr. Wood. All I could think was something terrible had happened. Either to him or to the funeral home. Had Morelli's interference set Mr. Wood's recovery back? Was he now in worse pain than before? Had the health authorities come snooping again? Were the medical bills too much and he'd filed for bankruptcy?

My fingers flew over the keypad to tap in my passcode. But other than a single, "Hi, Cassie," there were no other texts from my boss, just a series of pictures.

I scrolled through the photos. Several were of ever-increasingly tall variations on the classic BLT. I don't even know what was inside some of them, but I swear one was sandwiched between two maple bars instead of bread. Most of the other photos were of clumps of yarn that were starting to look more like squares and circles rather than one of Pablo's hairballs, but just barely.

I texted back that it looked like he was having fun and keeping fed. I also told him I was sorry for missing the photos earlier but my phone hadn't alerted me to his messages. I asked how he was feeling, hoped he was doing well, and told him I'd be home soon. Judging by my horsey fiasco I might not be, but I wouldn't have him fretting.

Below all of Mr. Wood's photos was a single image from Lola with the caption, "Having a roaring good time with Auntie Lola." The image? Pablo dressed in a fluffy lion's mane and posed before a Serengeti-style background. And again, the cat looked quite pleased with himself. I texted back that I would report her to the Humane Society if this kept up, but added a winking emoji to show I was only joking.

Then, feeling like a complete imbecile as more people grumbled their way away from the White Tower, I wandered toward the Waterloo Barracks to see the Crown Jewels. Unfortunately, about ten tour buses worth of tourists were queuing up to get in. The sea of people was so deep I couldn't even see the entrance.

Deciding it wasn't worth the effort, I turned on my heel and strolled around the grounds, counting garden gnomes (six) and catching snippets of speeches from various tour guides who held bright umbrellas or silly flags above their heads as a signpost for their group to follow.

As I came around the back side of the White Tower, I saw Alastair. My gut did one of its annoying little jumps of excitement at seeing him, but I managed a show of nonchalance as I strolled casually over to catch up with him.

"Cassie," he said with delight. Clearly he'd decided to forget my little outburst from the day before. Which was good because the warmth in his eyes at the sight of me, the look in them that said his day was already better for my having found him, the tilt of his head that looked almost like he wanted to bend down to kiss me, all wiped away any thoughts of my Seabiscuit screw up. "I heard you had a little trouble."

Well, that was a nice few milliseconds away from my angst.

"I'd rather not talk about it. Look, can we, you know, meet later?" My words prodded the warmth in his eyes into glowing hot embers. "I mean, sort of like a briefing. I want to keep on track with what you've found out about my parents."

"I— Yeah, sure." Those intense eyes shifted to glance over my shoulder. Alastair smiled brightly and waved his arm to signal someone. "Rafi, over here."

Damn you, Rafi.

"Hey Al. And you must be Cyclone Cassie. I'm Rafi," he said in a voice that carried a pleasing mix of Indian and Welsh accents. He held out his hand to shake and, as the scent of sandalwood enveloped me, he wore a grin that showed he thought he was being terribly clever. "I'm just heading over to grab a coffee. You want to come?" This invitation was made to Alastair, as Rafi angled his slim shoulders just enough to exclude me.

"Sounds great. Cassie, you want to come?"

"I'll pass," I said, annoyed that Alastair was ignoring my question about my parents to go have coffee.

The two walked off, laughing about something and leaving me wondering if Alastair had been doing anything to search for information on my mom and dad — the people he said had been his friends.

"Cassie."

Completely lost in my grumpy thoughts, the sound of the voice behind me scared me so hard, I whipped around and nearly let loose a Shoving Charm. Nearly. But I didn't. See? Control. I am a master of my own magic at least once a day.

"What's up, Tobey?" I said, then scuttled aside as someone with a selfie stick kept backing up right into the spot where I'd been standing. I was tempted to magically tie the stick in a knot, but performing magic in front of non-magics isn't allowed. Still, I think selfie sticks should be the exception to that rule.

"Look," he whispered, "everyone's busy either cleaning up or discussing the mess you made of the armory horses."

"Does gossip defy the laws of physics to travel faster than the speed of light in the magic world?"

"We do really like our gossip," he said with a dismissive shrug. "Anyway, they're occupied, which means I can get you into the file room and we can get a start on a few of the drawers."

So while Alastair, the guy who was supposed to be here to search with me for my parents, was off having a latte with his little buddy, Tobey the Terrible was actively doing something to help me out. I will never understand people.

"Are you serious?" I asked, somewhat surprised.

"Yes, I'm serious." He then told me how to find the file room. As he spoke, from the corner of my eye, I caught a raven swooping low, then soaring back up with a croaking cry. Tobey glanced up at the sound, then started backing away from me. "I'll meet you there in fifteen minutes," he said quickly. "It'll be less obvious if we don't go together. Got it?"

I told him I did, and Tobey headed off toward the White Tower, using the side door you wouldn't know existed if you weren't part of the magic world.

I strode across a small, grassy area, biding my time by pretending to be looking at the remains of an old gate.

"These are the foundations for a scaffold that was built to execute Oliver Cromwell," said Nigel. Perched on his shoulder was Winston who was shaking his head as if he couldn't believe how inaccurate Nigel could be with his history. Nigel glanced up doubtfully at the bird, then to me. "Is that not correct?"

"Close, but not quite."

"Do you know," said Nigel after I'd explained to him what the stones once were, "you remind me of an old friend of mine.

Didn't know her long, but she always took the time to help me with my facts. I guess they just didn't sink in. But enough nostalgia, would you like a tour?"

"As entertaining and educational as that might be, I have to be somewhere."

"I don't think you should go." This time Winston was bobbing his body and nodding his head.

"Why shouldn't I go?"

"Because the tour is really spectacular. And I just think you should wait for Alastair to help you."

"Were you eavesdropping on me?"

"No. Winston may have been, though," he added cheekily.

Before I could question how Winston might have relayed his information to the ghostly warden, from the other side of the lawn, I caught sight of Alastair and Rafi, coffee cups in hand, chatting and chortling away.

"Well, Alastair's a bit busy right now. Hold on." I pulled the sheet that was supposed to list my classes from my pocket to see if anything had been added. The page was still empty. "Look, I won't be long and I'm free afterward. As soon as I'm done, you can give me the tour and we can work on your version of events."

This pleased him immensely and his apple cheeks warmed with pride. Winston, however, was again shaking his head.

I told Nigel I'd meet him in the same spot sometime after lunch. As I jogged toward the White Tower's door, Winston let out a blood-curdling series of caws that got the other ravens squawking from all corners of the Tower. Several children started crying and one wailed that he wanted to leave "before the pterodactyls" got him.

* * *

I made a few wrong turns and I swear I was going down a staircase only to end up looking out over Tower Green from two stories up. Then I had the sensation of going up stairs only to end up in one of the lower levels of the White Tower. I was just cursing Tobey for playing a trick on me when, down a corridor that seemed to go on forever, I found a door labeled File Room.

I looked up and down the hallway. No one was around, so I darted into the room. A bank of half-hearted incandescent lights ran the length of the narrow space. One wall was covered in a yellowing map of London, a table where people could look over files stood a few feet in from the door, and lining each side of the room were your standard-issue, five-drawer, metal file cabinets.

"What took you so long?" Tobey asked impatiently.

"Nigel wanted to give me a tour."

Tobey pulled a strange face at this. "You probably want to avoid that guy." Apparently Tobey was aware of Nigel's trouble with historic facts and figures. He then gestured toward the file cabinets. "Ready to get started? I say we go alphabetically to make sure we don't miss anything."

"That'll take too long. Can't we just look under S for Starling?"

"We could try, but it would probably only pull up their personnel file. Most anything they did would have gone under a code name. Why don't you take one side and I'll do the other. We probably have an hour, but be ready to go when I say."

Tobey pulled open the top drawer of the cabinet nearest him. He wanted me to start on the cabinet behind him, but the area was so narrow the drawers extending from the cabinets would have left no room to work. He grumbled a bit when I told him I'd start at the other end to keep out of each others' way, but grumbling wasn't an unusual response from Tobey Tenpenny.

Moving away from Tobey not only gave me more elbow room, it also meant I could satisfy my own curiosity. I didn't know anything about my parents, so even if it didn't provide any clues as to their current whereabouts, I wanted to see their personnel file. I headed down the row and stopped at S, then found the St drawer.

The moment I opened the drawer I caught the scent of chocolate with a hint of raspberries. Alastair had been here. And recently. If he had found something and hadn't told me, if he had found something and decided to go off and have coffee with stupid Rafi—

Fuming, I jerked open the drawer and sifted through the files in search of my parents' dossier.

Stark, Starkly, Stenton, Sturgious.

What the—?

I thumbed twice through all the tabs with names that started with St, but there was no *Starling*. Had Alastair taken it? Furious with his do-it-my-way attitude, I threw the drawer shut, stomped down to the end of the row, and started in on the Z files.

Big surprise, there was no file for *Zeller* either, Alastair's surname. But neither did I scent him on this drawer. Maybe HQ didn't keep files on people who weren't agents. Or maybe he got rid of it long ago.

Oddly, in the magic world, there are a lot of people with names that end in Z. My eyelids felt heavy, probably from the time shift, but I willed them to stay open. I'd just gotten to *Zollo* when Tobey called down that we needed to get going. I don't know if he had a timer or if he'd heard something, but I eased my drawer shut and hurried to join him.

"Anything?" I asked.

"No, we can start in again tonight if you want."

"Can't I just come any time?" I was exhausted and imagined

there was an early bedtime ahead of me. "I mean, you probably have better things to do here."

"Not really. Besides, it's my grandfather's key that lets me in. He'd know if it went missing for more than a couple hours. So, later tonight?"

"Yeah, we'll see," I said noncommittally, forcing myself to accept that Tobey was now part of my covert operation.

At least he was proving useful for once.

CHAPTER TWENTY-THREE

MAKING PLANS

After a long, roundabout trek along corridors and stairways, I found my way back to the White Tower's secret exit. That morning's slice of toast was long gone, and my hunger joined in with the weird tiredness that had hit me in the file room to deliver a throbbing headache.

Recalling the direction Alastair and Rafi had gone to get their coffees, I slipped around the White Tower and followed my nose to a cafe. My appetite took over as I moved through the food line and I ended up loading my tray with a double portion of fish and chips, a green salad, apple juice, black tea, and a pile of cookies. It was only as I reached the cashier that I hoped my debit card would work. After all, in the rush of Mr. Green's funeral, packing, and getting Mr. Wood settled, I hadn't exactly thought to put a travel alert on my account.

The cashier, dressed in a colorful sari, was an older woman of Indian descent. I held my little rectangle of plastic out to her, but she took one sniff and waved the card away.

"No need to pay."

"But…" I wasn't normally one to question free food, but this was a tourist site, places not generally known for handing out meal bargains.

"I have a line of customers, so please move along." She then lowered her dancing voice. "And next time you choose to eat here instead of in your room, don't make it during the lunch rush. I hate having to explain to Norms why the person ahead of them got a free meal."

She snapped her head to the side in a sharp get-out-of-here gesture. Duly chastised, I got out of her sight, but as I scanned the dining area for a table, I heard her telling a disgruntled diner that I had won a free lunch voucher from BBC Radio 4.

Once finished with my gut-busting meal, I left the cafe and headed back to where I'd left Nigel that morning. Even if his facts were completely inaccurate, I needed something to take my mind off things, especially after seeing tourists still approaching the White Tower and being turned away. Some simply shrugged their shoulders and went off to snap pictures of other parts of the Tower, but some (embarrassingly, mostly ones with American accents) were declaring they'd sue for false advertising. And the poor Yeoman Warders were having to take it all in stride.

With it being the middle of a summer day full of sunshine, the Tower was crowded with tourists. Despite the warm weather, a familiar chill brushed over my skin just before Nigel appeared beside me. To avoid being jostled by other humans as well as to avoid looking like a nutter who spoke to herself, he guided me around to an area behind the main buildings that was off limits to visitors.

He recited a speech on the founding of the Tower and I corrected him that it wasn't William of Orange who started construction, but William the Conqueror; that William had won the Battle of Hastings, not the Battle of the Bulge; and that the White Tower was named for the bright white stone used, not because white people were the original occupants — although, technically, that fact wasn't entirely off the mark.

In between the history lessons, he pointed out where his

friend had resided while she was here, showed me the gate she passed through the last time he saw her, and made little jokes that if she hadn't already been married, he might have had a chance with her. I wondered if this woman had been the wife of one of the other Yeoman Warders who had long since retired.

It was late afternoon by the time we worked our way back around to Traitor's Gate where Nigel thanked me for helping him with his history and made his goodbyes. Once he'd vanished, I passed under a gateway that led to the heart of the Tower.

"Cassie, hey, there you are," Alastair said, greeting me with a warm look in his eyes as if he hadn't seen me in weeks.

"Done with your coffee?"

"Sorry about that. Rafi oversees some of the historic collection and he was eager to tell me about a hoard of Viking treasures they recently found just beyond the walls."

I made a noise in my throat to show I was listening. Listening, but not caring. He caught the hint and some of the air fell from his sails of nerdy excitement.

"I said I was sorry," he said, glancing through his lashes in that way that could almost make me forget all the doubts that kept a lock on my heart. A lock that was slowly loosening with every interaction. He darted a glance over both shoulders. "Look, I think I might have something. It's not anything about the night your parents went missing, but I think it gets us a little closer."

If you knew how much control it took for me not to say I knew he'd been in the file room, that I had detected his scent on the drawer where my parents' file should have been, you would march yourself to Olivia's office and say, "See, Cassie Black does know self-control. Stop being so hard on her and making her do stupid tasks. Moving wooden horses, indeed. What use is that for anyone?"

Instead, I played it cool by asking, "Did you find a file on my parents somewhere?"

"No, not a file, but there were some photos. We should have time tonight if you want to look over them."

Before I could agree — and I felt a very enthusiastic agreement at the top of my throat — Chester thudded up to us.

"Sirs, I'm supposed to tell you Alastair has to go to his room. Or you have to go to your room," he said, turning to me.

"What do you mean?" I asked. "Which of us has to go?"

"One of you. You're not supposed to be together. I was told to tell you that. You have to stay apart from each other until it's allowed."

"Chester," said Alastair, "you're making no sense."

"I know. I'm sorry." Chester scratched his head and scrunched up one side of his face as if that might help him remember. Then Rafi strolled up, moving with a gracefully smooth gait. He did have striking features. Maybe he'd once been a model. Did the Magics have fashion shows?

"Did you tell them, Chester?"

"I tried. I got confused. But I did get three rats this morning."

We all muttered vague sounds of admiration at this feat. Then Alastair asked, "What's this about, Rafi?"

"There's some talk going on about Cassie's trouble this morning, and something about a hole in your door, Alastair." Did you hear that? That was my stomach plummeting straight through the bedrock and into the River Thames. "I'm not sure what they're planning, but you might be involved, so they want to keep you two separated until everything can be sorted out."

"But we had plans," I said. Alastair grinned at the disappointment in my voice.

"They'll have to wait. Look," Rafi said to me, "they don't really want you wandering. You're supposed to go to Olivia's office, then I guess just stay in your room until tomorrow."

"Why can't this be settled today?" Alastair asked. "She's done nothing wrong. A few things got knocked over. Nothing was damaged."

"There was an ear," I offered, pleased that he was sticking up for me when it seemed like everyone else wanted to make a mountain out of a horse turd.

Alastair laughed. "See, an ear. Wait, from one of the horses, not from a living human, right?" I glared at him, letting him know he was not funny.

"I'm just the messenger," Rafi said apologetically. "Olivia seems angry, but if I'm being honest, it doesn't seem like she's angry at you, Cassie. Just go along with it. It's one night. I'm sure by tomorrow you two will be able to do whatever it was you were planning."

His rakish smirk sent heat into my face and, as if he'd been nailed with a paint gun, a splash of red colored Alastair's cheeks. I was about to say it was just some paperwork we had to go over, but that would only make it sound like I was covering up something. Something that involved getting naked.

"It's not what you're implying, Rafi," Alastair insisted. "And you're right, it can wait until tomorrow. As long as someone keeps her promises."

He leveled his gaze on me almost as if he knew I'd been in the file room. And almost as if he knew I'd planned to go back. Crap, if I was under house arrest, I couldn't go wandering the hallways.

"Sirs, we should go. The message is delivered, isn't it?" Chester asked Rafi, who sighed with exasperation and said it had been.

Alastair gave me an apologetic smile and went off, yet again with Rafi who was explaining to Chester how much trust he was putting in him to get these messages right.

I turned back to the White Tower, trudged my way inside, then headed to Olivia's office.

CHAPTER TWENTY-FOUR
STRANGE ENCOUNTERS

The door to Olivia's office stood open. Even so, I knocked and hesitated. Maybe she'd be too busy to scold me. Maybe she had short-term memory issues and had already forgotten why she'd sent for me.

No such luck.

Olivia looked up, her face revealing nothing of her mood as she waved me in. After I sat down, she tidied some papers, laced her fingers together with her hands resting on her desk, then spoke to me with surprising calm.

"From what Busby told me about this morning, you did well. Showed some real control, so I don't want you to think what I have to say next is any reflection on your work today." Like I said, this was spoken with calm poise, but it still did not sound good. "You will be tested the day after tomorrow."

"A test? So soon? I thought I had a couple weeks."

Olivia responded with a flash of annoyance, but for once, it wasn't caused by me. "Someone," she said, acidly biting back a name, "insists the test be done as soon as possible. *Someone* wanted it to happen tomorrow." She paused, and it seemed like she was debating whether to tell me more. Apparently she decided against it. Her face softened, and she said, "I have, however, argued that you will be allowed a full day of our most rigorous defensive training, especially as you have never formally sparred before. Have you?"

I didn't even know what she meant by sparring, so I shook my head.

"You'll be working hard tomorrow, so I want you to get some good rest and build up your energy tonight."

With another of her hand flourishes she produced a wicker basket with a latching lid and a large, black *F & M* printed on the side. It didn't take any magic to smell the sweet and savory treats inside. Something chicken-y was in there along with something filled with lemon, strawberries, and honey. My mouth started watering.

"We have our own chefs here, but that," she pointed at the basket, "is top grade magic fuel. If you need it, there's always more where that came from. Now, promise me you'll pay attention tomorrow, that you won't get flustered, and that after your test we'll celebrate because I'm confident you'll do just fine."

As with Alastair, as with all these HQ people, I could tell from the overly bright way she said this that she definitely was not confident I would do fine.

This time when I headed up the many stairs to my prison cell/hotel room I had to lug a picnic basket loaded with what felt like twenty pounds of gourmet treats. I considered using a Lifting Charm, but it wouldn't improve my chances of passing muster with these people if I ended up sending a few hundred dollars' worth of Fortnum & Mason food and beverage through the roof of the White Tower.

When I reached my hallway, my legs were begging me to stop moving. Marveling briefly over having two functioning hands once again, I stopped for a moment to switch the basket from my left hand to my right. It was then I caught sight of Banna heading my direction. With a pair of too-large sunglasses perched on her tiny face, she reminded me of an overgrown insect.

"I heard what happened and that they're being right dunderheads by telling you to go to your room like you're a child. Olivia has no sense of humor. Never has. And you with plans tonight."

Which plans was she talking about? Operation Alastair or Operation Tobey? I thought it best not to speak, no sense condemning myself.

"Anyway, I don't see any harm in leaving your room. As long as you stay in the White Tower, it's not like you're going to vanish, is it?"

"Well, it is possible. Magic, you know."

"Quite right, but you'll try to avoid that, won't you?" I nodded, wondering what in Merlin's name she was going on about. "I'll let Tobey know you'll meet him, then."

"You know about me and Tobey?"

"Yes, and a more charming pair could not be found. Far better than you and that Alastair," she said with a sneer. "There's the little matter of— Well, but that's not forbidden, is it?"

By forbidden I assumed she meant a Magic and a non-magic hooking up. But still. Me and Tobey?

"Tobey and I aren't—" I stopped talking. If Banna was going to give me permission to explore because she thought Tobey and I were a couple, that provided the perfect excuse. A disturbing one, but still perfect. "You're sure it's okay for me to be out?"

"I won't tell if you don't. Meet him in an hour. The others will be planning your work for tomorrow then."

And with that, she turned and shuffled back down the hallway.

After delighting in the world's best chicken pie with chips, an imperial pint of British ale, and a thesaurus-sized piece of lemon cake loaded on the top and in the middle with fresh strawberries and whipped cream, I flopped onto my stiff mattress. I was tempted to take a nap, but there were secrets to discover, so after too little time, I pulled myself off the bed.

Despite my legs declaring they were going to start a coup against the rest of my body if I even looked at another staircase, I darted as stealthily as possible through the White Tower's maze of corridors to meet up with Tobey in the file room.

As I headed to the cabinet where I'd left off, I made a quick search through the Ma drawer, hoping for something on the Mauvais. Again, the chocolate raspberry scent. And again, an empty spot where the Mauvais's file should have been. Alastair had obviously taken it despite what he'd told me. I wanted to know what was in those stolen files, but couldn't risk going to Alastair's room. Damn Olivia for her stupid demands.

Annoyed and disappointed at my lack of success, I continued on and worked through the Ys and Xs. I didn't know exactly what I was looking for, but I knew I hadn't found it by the end of the hour. I bid Tobey good night and, although utterly exhausted, I managed to return to my room without making a single wrong turn. Quite a feat given how much brain power was being devoted to pondering what magical challenges I faced the next day, and how long it would be before I could talk to Alastair in private.

CHAPTER TWENTY-FIVE
MORNING WORKOUT

At some point while I was in the bathroom getting dressed the next morning, another full English breakfast had appeared on my room's table. I know I should have probably been more wary, but the previous day's toast hadn't killed me, so I doubted the food was poisoned. Besides, the only person who might want me dead would be the Mauvais — well, him and a few home-care nurses back in Portland. And he needed to capture, not kill me to get his magic back. After which he would likely kill me.

I know, such happy morning thoughts, right? I made my way through the eggs, the beans, the sausage, and half the toast, but before I could finish, there came a knock on my door. My first thought was it might be Banna, so I shut the curtains and turned out the bathroom light before answering.

Instead of a tiny, light-sensitive woman, I stood face to face with Busby who wore a look of annoyance.

"Are you not awake yet?" he asked, peering over my shoulder at the darkened room.

"No, I just thought you were Banna."

"Hardly," he said derisively. "If you're ready, then let's get you to the training room. You'll need to spend today practicing for tomorrow."

I rushed back in, opened the curtains, and grabbed the final two triangles of toast. The empty plate instantly disappeared. It's not one of my prouder moments, but the vanishing flatware made me yelp and sent me jumping back two paces. In my defense, I was already on edge. A little snort came from the doorway and I glanced over to see Mr. T biting back laughter.

"Oh yes, Cassie nearly had a heart attack. Very funny." As we wound our way, not down, but up the staircase (seriously, how many levels did this place have?), I said, "There's something more to this test than you're letting on, isn't there?"

"What makes you say that?"

"I may have the social skills of an earthworm, but I can recognize when people aren't giving me the full story. So, are you going to tell me or not?"

"It's a placement test of sorts."

"Of what sort?"

He stopped on the stairway and turned to me, his face sterner than I'd ever seen it.

"Of the very important sort, so please take it seriously."

Well, that certainly put me at ease.

When we reached the top of the stairs, we passed by a door with the words "Magical Medic" to the left of a caduceus decal, but instead of a snake twisting up a staff, it was a winged dragon doing the twining.

Mr. Tenpenny ignored this door and opened another at the far end of the small, poorly lit space. When the door opened, I was blasted with bright sunshine, and Mr. T became nothing more than a silhouette to my newly blinded eyes. Squinting and blinking, I followed him. The moment my eyes adjusted to the light, my jaw dropped at the view.

We were on the roof. From ground level, the top of the White Tower appeared to be nothing special. But the area I was looking at sported a tinted glass awning and had been screened in with some type of mesh fabric — both of which I later learned had been enchanted to prevent any spells from going beyond them and to block the view of any passing planes or drones. The smooth floor was painted with the markings of a tennis court around which ran an oval track.

"Is this a magic gym?" I asked.

"No, just a recreational area, the gym is on one of the lower levels along with the pool. It's been decided that the armory, while back in order now, may not have been the best place for your, well, your level of power. And really, it's too nice to be cooped up in the indoor training room."

I wondered briefly what William the Conqueror would have made of the Magics' improvements to his White Tower. Mr. Tenpenny didn't give my imagination much time to wander.

"Now, the rules of the test are that you cannot employ any of your absorbing side. You'll have to defend yourself using the techniques we'll be working on today."

"Why can't I absorb? It's my skill, isn't it? That's like saying a tall person has to crouch down during a game of basketball."

"Because it is also your liability. And we don't know how far the Mauvais might have infiltrated the magic community. After all, he was walking around right under our noses in Rosaria."

"Are you saying I could be fighting the Mauvais and not know it?"

"No, but there will be people watching, any one of whom might be influenced by the Mauvais, even without their knowing it. We believe that's how he got so many Magics to go to his side before." I looked at him questioningly. "How can I explain it? Anyone in the audience could be given something that, if you absorbed it, could either hurt you or make it easier for the Mauvais to get your magic, the watch's magic, for himself."

"Like a computer virus."

Mr. T clapped his hands together. "Exactly. And like a computer virus, it could get in and allow the Mauvais to access your power, his power. Which is another reason you must find a balance between your absorbing side and your giving side. That balance will keep you from doing either unintentionally."

The Mauvais mucking around inside my head? Yeah, I was a little more motivated to get to this training.

"So where do we start?"

"Where you left off with Alastair." Sexual tension mixed with unrelenting suspicion? No, probably not. "I'll be working you rather hard on some basic defensive spells this morning." He stepped over to a supply closet and began rummaging for something. My first thought was magical medicine balls.

"I thought Defense Ag—" I bit off the Harry Potter reference before Mr. T caught it. "I thought defensive training was Alastair's job."

"It is, but you need a full day of training and he can't be around you that long. Others can." He made a sound of triumph and pulled out two thick, black shirts that reminded me of darker versions of the things fencers wear. "I will show you the most useful spells as well as tactics for when to use them. You will then have a break for lunch, after which you will spar with Olivia and then finally Rafi."

"Is that safe? For them, I mean."

"Olivia is quite strong. You don't get to her position without having supreme control over your magic." I didn't miss the admiration in his voice.

"And Rafi?"

"He's an elf. Their magic is a little different than ours, which means they have a unique ability to be around Magics like you. They're usually the ones we employ to teach and train young absorbers. Plus, with these," he handed me one of the vests, "it will be even safer. For everyone."

The vests, similar to the Kevlar vests worn by police, were able to absorb the majority of an impact from a spell. Unfortunately, just like its Kevlar comrade, it did nothing if a spell was aimed at your head, your arms, your throat, or your legs.

"That's why they're really only good in sparring where you will be directing your spells at the chest only," Busby told me. "Any spells aimed otherwise would be cause for immediate dismissal."

"But what if I aim for the chest and my opponent ducks and I end up hitting their head?"

Mr. T tapped the center of my vest. His fingers made a hollow *thunk*.

"This vest has sensors that detect where a spell has been aimed. It then pulls the spell to that point. If you aim at the chest, it will always hit the chest."

"So why not just make it so the vests pull every spell to the chest?"

"The technology is being developed. You know," he said, again with admiration brightening his words, "you come up with some ridiculous ideas, but also some brilliant ones. You might look into magical engineering if, well, if the test is a success."

Before I could ask him to elaborate on that hesitant little "if", Mr. Tenpenny was describing a Shield Spell, a Binding Spell, a Throwing Spell, a Stunning Spell, and what seemed like an entire year's worth of self-defense classes all rolled into a single exhausting morning.

Each hour on the hour, a cake with two spongey layers and a center filled with strawberry jam appeared. This hunk of deliciousness, called a Victoria sandwich, was the only thing that kept me on my feet as I moved over and over through the spells until they became almost a dance. They reminded me of the graceful forms I once learned when I took Tae Kwon Do for my P.E. credit during my stint at community college. Graceful, yes, but the moves in those forms were meant to give you the muscle memory to fight in a sequence of punches, kicks, and turns with wicked efficiency.

A series of bells finally tolled the noon hour.

"We'll stop there," said Mr. T. The sky, while still bright, had slowly filled with high, thin clouds, making the air warm and humid. I felt like a disheveled mess from my exertions, but Busby still looked as fresh as he had at the start. His steel grey hair hadn't even moved a millimeter out of place. The only concession to our physical efforts had been when he rolled up the sleeves of his dress shirt. Maybe being dead wasn't all that bad. "You did quite well, Cassie."

I'd been hunched over, hands on knees as sweat dribbled down my forehead, but at his compliment I glanced up. "Well enough for you to tell me what this test is really about?"

"Not that well, no," he replied with a rueful grin. "Olivia will be here after lunch, and don't be shy about filling up. Wait, why am I telling you this? Food is one aspect where you are never shy."

"A girl's gotta eat." And when you've missed as many meals as I have, you don't turn down free food. To prove the point, I popped the remaining piece of Victoria sandwich into my mouth.

A whole new cake appeared on the platter.

"Whoa!"

"Yes, quite a convenient amenity of the Tower."

"It only works here?" I asked, full of disappointment.

"And only if you're Magic. Otherwise the tourists would never leave. Now, while I'm glad we've discovered an aspect of magic you actually approve of, you do need something nutritious." He picked up the cake platter and a new plate appeared on the table with a mound of fries and a thick sandwich that was practically overflowing with chicken, tomatoes, and lettuce.

Test prep training was hard, but it did have its benefits.

CHAPTER TWENTY-SIX

BUTTING HEADS

After Mr. Tenpenny left — taking the cake with him, much to my disappointment — I finished my sandwich then began testing out the food replenishing thing to see how quickly more fries would appear once I'd eaten the last one. My experiment was disturbed when the door to the rec area opened.

"Cassie, there you are."

"Hey, Tobey," I said through a mouthful of fries. Tobey's interruption was probably for the best since I'd already eaten so many, I was at risk of turning into a potato.

Tobey sat beside me on the bench and took the last fry for himself. Without even asking! Oh well, there was more where that came from, I thought as another mound popped onto the plate.

"Look, while you were keeping my grandad occupied, I made a little progress."

"You went to the file room without me?"

"Well yeah, I didn't think you'd mind. You can help more tonight. Anyway, I may have found something."

I sat up straighter, ready to run to the file room right that very second.

"No, don't get all keyed up. It's just a lead pointing me to another file. Kilbride's file."

"We should have started there."

"Maybe, but I still think it's better to go through all the files. I mean, they've got plenty of stuff on Kilbride, but since they didn't know he was the Mauvais until just recently, there may not be much of importance in there. But it's still worth a look, right?"

"Sure," I said and pushed the plate away.

"I thought you'd be pleased," he said moodily.

"I just keep feeling like this is completely pointless. If they knew anything, they'd have acted on it."

"But they do know something. There are rumors. There's got to be information they've overlooked. Come on, say you'll come tonight and we can look it over together."

"Fine, but I can't stay up too late." I put up my fists like a cartoon boxer. "I've got a fight tomorrow."

"Don't worry, it shouldn't take too long. Still, this test is good for one thing."

"Which is?" I prodded, hoping Tobey knew something more about the test than Mr. T would tell me.

"It's keeping Alastair away from you. I just don't trust that guy. And neither should you."

"You're being ridiculous." Is what I said, but hadn't I thought the exact same thing about Alastair multiple times? Wasn't I the one always whining about his true motives? Still, I didn't need Tobey Tenpenny telling me what to do.

Tobey eyed me as if he wanted to say more but knew it was best if he held his tongue. He shrugged, then polished off the rest of the fries, all but one to keep the plate from refilling.

Not long after he left, Olivia showed up as a one o'clock bell chimed in the distance. Where Mr. Tenpenny had been encouraging and offered explanations on how to adjust my actions to better execute a spell and avoid a curse, Olivia put me through my paces.

I missed deflecting so many of her spells that my sternum under the sparring vest was aching after only an hour. The tolling of the two o'clock bell started a full-on Pavlovian response and my belly rumbled at the thought of cake. My attention went to the side table where desserts had appeared before. Just at that moment of distraction, Olivia hit my legs so fiercely with a Binding Spell I tripped over my own feet and crash landed on the ground.

"You're not supposed to go for the legs," I complained as I checked the scrapes on my elbows.

"And you're supposed to be able to defend yourself from that." She held out a hand to help me up. Despite my sweating brow, her hand was cool to the touch. "Come on, let's see what they've conjured for your afternoon snack."

The afternoon snack turned out to be raspberry scones. The scent of them reminded me of Alastair. As I ate, Olivia lectured.

"You already know you need to find a balance between your two sides. But what you also need to imagine is a membrane around you that allows only magic for spells out, and doesn't allow someone else's magic to be taken in. Alastair told me he worked with you on this." I nodded and admitted I'd had some trouble with it. "That's to be expected. We'll work on that next, but I am worried about your progress. By now, with the training you did previously with Alastair, you should at least be able to hold a Shield Spell throughout any fight. Unless you've been seriously cursed, a Shield Spell should be your immediate line of defense."

"I know that in theory, but it's just not the first spell that comes to mind."

"What is?"

"Shoving," I said, somewhat embarrassed. It was the first spell I'd learned — well, besides bringing back the dead, but that was more accidental mishap than trained skill.

"Shoving is effective, but perhaps try to picture shoving out a shield instead. You need to take what you're good at, then put a new spin on it to make other spells work with it. Eventually, you'll be able to do most any spell without falling back on your stand by, but falling back is a good place to start."

"Better than falling forward," I said, holding up my elbow to show the scrape.

"Yes, sorry about that, but you really must learn these things."

After another couple hours, and another five thousand calories' worth of treats, Rafi took over from Olivia, and the afternoon of torture continued.

Unlike Mr. Tenpenny and Olivia, Rafi seemed not to care one lick about the rules of sparring, and I took blows to my legs and arms. One of his spells — a Flaming Arrow Curse — whizzed past my ear so closely, I could smell my hair singe.

Sometime after the five o'clock break, I'd had enough of playing by the rules and of getting battered by a cheater. I don't know what Rafi had been trying to hit me with, but I responded with a sharp nod of my head, using a combination of my giving side and a Shoving Charm to send out a pulse of power as I pictured head butting my elvish opponent.

Rafi staggered back three paces, then rubbed his forehead. I fought back the urge to cheer my success.

"What was that?" he asked.

"Olivia said to use what I know. I've head butted a few people in my time." In fact, it was a head butt that taught Foster Dad Number Six not to grab me by the arms and shake me so violently I thought my teeth might fly out. "I sort of pictured the Shoving Charm while doing the action."

"That's exactly what you need to do," he said with delight. "And now that I know what to expect, maybe I can defend myself from it. Which is an important lesson not to forget. Magics are quick learners, so don't get too reliant on any one spell. Your opponent will observe what you use and will quickly adapt to it. You want to always keep them on their toes. It's sometimes the only way to win against an enemy."

The temptation to ask about the Mauvais, about what people had used against him, about his signature spell all churned inside me, but Rafi had already assumed his fighting stance, signaling it was time for more work.

"For the next hour, neither of us will use the same spell more than once. Are you ready?"

"No, but I don't think that's going to get me out of this, is it?"

"Not in the least," he said with an infectious grin.

Even with another pile of scones, I thought I might just lay down on the bench and sleep for a month after that hour. But on the other hand, there was a small sense of pride in me that I hadn't repeated any spells. Sure, I copied some of the ones Rafi had used on me, but that wasn't against his rules.

"You did great. Not perfect, but if you do tomorrow what you did today, you should pass the test. No guarantees, though."

These Magics really could use a class in the proper ways of giving encouragement. But before I could complain, a plate of pasta tossed with black beans, roasted vegetables, and cheese appeared.

Rafi then placed his slim hand on my arm. The gesture came as a shock as most Magics avoid touching me because they don't want to get sucked dry by my super-absorbent brand of magic. "I do hope you'll do well tomorrow," he said with warm sincerity. "I can see why Alastair won't stop talking about you. Now, eat up and get some rest."

CHAPTER TWENTY-SEVEN
CHECKING IN

Of course, Rafi was already out the door before my gobsmacked mouth could ask what exactly Alastair had been saying about me.

And as for resting? I had files to sift through. I had parents to find. I figured I could get a quick, carb-induced nap, breeze through the Kilbride file with Tobey, then try to get some sleep before my ordeal the next day.

Once I'd finished three plates of pasta — leaving a single black bean to keep the plate from refilling — I started down the stairs. And promptly realized I didn't know how to get back to my room. How many flights had Mr. Tenpenny and I climbed that morning? Which corridors in this maze of a place had we crossed?

Needing to get my bearings, I emerged from the stairwell. I'd hoped to find a window so I could see how high up and on what side of the building I was on, but the hallway was fully dark. Eerily dark, because I knew it was still light outside and would be for a few more hours. Somewhere beyond the walls a raven cawed.

"Lost?"

My entire body tensed as a faint hint of ozone tickled my nostrils. From several yards down the hall, a small point of sea-colored light grew and expanded.

191

"Banna? Is that you?" I asked, but I held my arms up, my fingers buzzing with magic and ready to throw out one of the billion defensive spells that were bumping into each other inside my head.

"Yes, very good."

The light grew brighter, glowing above the small woman who approached me.

"Don't tell me I have another lesson."

"No, not at all. I just wanted to wish you well. How are you and Tobey getting along? Finding anything interesting?"

"You know what Tobey and I are doing?" And, I wanted to say, no, I wasn't finding anything interesting because all the interesting files had gone missing.

"I do." She said this with a mischievous smile on her face. "I gave him the idea to help you with your research." She began walking back toward the stairwell. I followed her, assuming she would guide me back to my room. Then I remembered what she had told me when we first met.

"You could speed the process up, you know. You said you knew the history of all Magics. You have to know about my parents."

"Of course I know about your parents, dear. But that doesn't mean I know everything. After all, I can't know events that weren't witnessed by another Magic, and I can't know feelings or intentions. Besides, not every piece of paperwork crosses my path." This seemed contrary to what she had implied before when she had said straight out that she knew the histories of all Magics, even the stories they didn't know themselves.

As if reading my thoughts, she said, "I know the general histories. I know when things happened such as your parents going missing, supposedly killed, but I don't know the details of what they did that final day, of where they went, that sort of thing. Is that information somewhere in our files? Perhaps. Perhaps not. But I figure you deserve time to look, which is why I haven't told Olivia about your little exploits."

Banna left the stairwell through a side door that would have been easy to miss. The hallway we entered had a hotel's carpeted blandness and the first room we passed was numbered thirty-nine. And oddly enough, someone had left a garden gnome outside that door. I wondered if the gnomes were sold in the souvenir shop and this was some sort of product-placement advertising.

"Now, I know you had plans," said Banna when we stopped at my door, "but I don't think going tonight is the wisest idea."

"Not tonight? Are you kidding? Do you understand how important this is?" I was tired, I was sore, and if I dared to admit it, I was scared about what was going to happen tomorrow. All this, plus the underlying emotional strain of wanting to find my parents, of wanting to trust Alastair, of wanting to be home, added a quaver to my voice.

"I do understand, but they've got a watch on you tonight. If you leave your room, they'll know. Besides, you really do need your rest, dear. You're practically in tears as it is."

In truth, the effort of the training had hit me with full force as I'd been speaking with Banna. I was exhausted. Too exhausted to bother questioning why I was under surveillance. And even the hard bed in my room seemed like an island paradise compared to trekking down hallways and stairwells to locate the file room. I nodded my agreement and Banna wished me a good evening as I staggered into my room.

I collapsed into bed and passed out. When I woke, it was fully dark out and someone was knocking on my door. I groaned a curse. It was probably Tobey mad at me for being late. I'd assumed Banna would have told him I couldn't come. I bumbled over to the door, pulled it open, and was greeted by a cupcake.

"Open wide," Alastair whispered. This isn't a command I take readily, so I just stared at him. He held the treat out and placed it in my palm. "Eat it."

"I just had dinner." I think I did. What time was it?

"You didn't have this."

I have to say it smelled wonderful, not too sweet, but still rich with vanilla and maybe a hint of citrus. I ate the cupcake, and I don't know who had made that little treasure, but it tasted like an entire cake shop's worth of goodness had been crammed into it. I closed my eyes, trying to concentrate all my senses into my taste buds.

When I opened my eyes, Alastair had stepped closer. This time, I was the one who backed away. Alastair glanced to his toes in embarrassment. I cursed Tobey for getting into my head.

"I've been told I can't be around you until after the test," I said to his confused expression.

"Right," he said disappointedly.

"Is there a reason why?"

"Because I'm the one giving you your test." I didn't see why this should be an issue. Possibly sensing my disregard for Olivia's rule, Alastair darted his gaze up and down the hall, then whispered, "Quick, let me in before someone catches us."

I gestured him in and, as the door eased its way shut, turned on the lights. The curtains were still open and the night view over the river caught my eye before I asked, "Giving the test? As in, you're one of the people overseeing it?"

"No, I'm sparring against you. Which is why I came. I want to know how your training went today. You have to pass this thing."

"And if I fail?" I asked.

Alastair's jaw tensed and his shoulders gave the smallest

flinch. He played it off with a forced smile that I think was meant to be encouraging.

"I really can't say, but I don't think it's simply a placement test. There's something more behind it. But," he said, changing to a brighter tone, "you'll be glad to know I'm getting closer to finding out some concrete information. Information I think we can act on within a few days, so let's make sure you get through this with flying colors. Are you up for a little work?"

I wasn't, but the cupcake had given me a boost and, what can I say, when my mind stopped spewing out doubts and conspiracies, I liked being around Alastair.

I agreed to a brief bit of work. Alastair explained how to put a Silencing Spell on the room, telling me it would last until the next time the door was opened. It proved to be a fairly easy spell that required nothing more than spreading out the air molecules surrounding the room and thereby making them poor sound conductors. From the closet nook, the nook I was certain contained only my bags, Alastair pulled out two sparring vests.

"Where did—?" I asked. "Never mind. I know. Magic."

We donned our vests, and I started out by showing him the fighting moves Busby, Olivia, and Rafi had gone over with me. Alastair approved of what I'd learned and of the easy way I moved through the spells. He also got a good laugh when I told him about head butting Rafi.

Then it was time to go up against each other. We ran through the moves in the prescribed forms, but Alastair also threw some unexpected spells my way. And I have to admit to a bit of pride when I managed a few improvisational shots of my own. I parried three attacks — a series of Punching Hexes — but got too cocky, and his next strike, a Stunning Spell, hit me with full force.

I stumbled backwards. The vest absorbed the blow, but my head still swam and my ribs under where the spell had landed ached from the hits I'd taken earlier in the day.

Alastair rushed over to me, concern darkening his face. He reached out, sweeping his arm around my waist to steady me. Even through the vest, I sensed his fingers on me as well as the electric charge I felt whenever he touched me. My first thought was that I was absorbing from him, that the tingle was me sucking power from him. I angled my head to see if he was showing any weakness.

"Are you okay?" we asked each other at the same time. And at the same time, we both laughed. We were so close, I could make out silver flecks in his dark blue eyes. Any closer and we'd be—

Oh god, were we about to kiss? We were about to kiss! Time for Cassie to go all awkward.

"Thank Merlin for this," I said, thumping the vest where his spell had landed. The motion of my arm put me out of Alastair's embrace. We both reached up and rubbed the backs of our necks as if massaging away the tension filling the room.

Yet again, I struggled against a dual tug within me. Part of me wanted to see if that kiss might not be the perfect way to end the day, while another part told me to keep my distance.

"You should have caught that one, the Stunning Spell," Alastair said. "Are you tired?"

"No, let's just try one of the other spells," I said, irritated with myself. Now that his arm wasn't around me, Team Heart was left standing confused by the sidelines. Which meant Team Brain took over and questioned why Alastair was really here. What might he have taken from that kiss?

And what was with that hit? It had thrown me off more than it should have. I didn't expect to block every attack, but Tobey's comments about Alastair barged into my head, adding to Team Brain's sniping voice insisting that Alastair's spell shouldn't have hurt so much.

Alastair and I sparred for another few rounds. I was thrown off by the hit. I was thrown off by the almost kiss. I was annoyed over my persistent doubts. All this meant I couldn't focus and ended up taking more blows than I blocked.

"I think that's enough," Alastair said, even though he didn't look a bit tired. We removed our vests, and after he placed them back in the closet, he waited by the room's door.

"What happens if I fail this test?" I asked, approaching him as he reached for the doorknob.

"You won't fail."

"You can't guarantee that. You have no idea how good I am at failing."

"You have to pass. No, you *will* pass." Alastair looked up from his hand that hadn't yet turned the knob. "Trust me," he added, the words full of meaning.

Something jumped in my gut. Was that what this had been about? Rafi said Magics can learn other Magics' fighting moves. Had Alastair come here to see what spells I was best at so he could turn the test to my advantage?

Don't get me wrong, I didn't want to fail. It was actually starting to sound pretty ominous if I failed, but I also didn't want to pass just because someone had made it easy for me.

"Is that why you came here?" I asked sharply. Before he could answer, I said, "Don't do anything to help me tomorrow. I'm not a charity case."

"Cassie," he said, dropping his hand from the knob, "that's not what I was implying. You're—"

I leaned forward. Reaching past him, his breath whispered across my ear as I turned the knob and jerked the door open. I hated myself for accusing him. I wanted answers about my parents. I wanted not to worry about the Mauvais or this stupid test. I wanted to rescue Pablo from a life as a feline fashionista. I wanted to be alone, but I also wanted Alastair to stay so I could tell him everything. My mind was an absolute mess of wants.

Right at that moment, though, temptation had me desiring nothing more but to turn my head. With Alastair still so close in the narrow entryway to my room, only the slightest movement would have had my lips on his. But he was easing past me and stepping into the hallway before that movement could begin. He watched me for a moment and I hated that I couldn't read the expression in his eyes.

I moved toward him into the threshold. Surprise flashed across Alastair's face and melted his chilly stare. He eased forward like someone cautiously approaching a stray cat. Closer now, his chocolatey scent drifted over me. Team Heart definitely had Team Brain bound and gagged somewhere as we inched nearer.

A door slammed at the end of the hallway and we both leapt back. Of course, his leap only hopped him back about a foot, but my move knocked me into the door, jamming the handle into my left butt cheek.

"I better go," he whispered, darting a glance either way down the hall. "The guard will be back any minute." I grunted my agreement and watched him hurry away in the opposite direction of the damn, kiss-interrupting noise. I shut the door, jumped in the shower to run cold water over my throbbing butt, then settled in for the long night ahead of me.

CHAPTER TWENTY-EIGHT

THE TEST

The next morning I was up early. After all, what's the point of staying in bed if your nerves are nipping at you so doggedly that you can't sleep? I had just gotten dressed when a light knocking sounded at my door. My empty belly lurched. I wasn't ready for this. I was most definitely not ready for this.

With my hand on the doorknob, I glanced over my shoulder. The room wasn't all that high up. I could probably jump. Then I thought of Mr. Wood's cast-bound leg. Magical Medi Unit experience or not, the very idea of having to move into Morelli's apartment and being under his care was enough to make me abandon my escape plans. I opened the door. I managed a weak smile when I saw who it was and even came close to warmly greeting the person with him.

"Are you ready for this?" asked Mr. Tenpenny. My gaze flicked back to Tobey who sported a sneer on his face. I didn't understand him at all. One minute he acted like he wanted to be my co-conspirator, the next he was going around looking like he wanted to throw me off the top of the ramparts. Lacking the mental space for sorting out Tobey Tenpenny, I ignored him.

"Oh sure," I said, allowing the door to close behind me as I stepped out to join Busby. Side by side, we headed down the hallway with Tobey skulking along behind us. "I've had a whole day of defensive training. How could I not be ready?"

"You've had more than that before you came here. Just remember, you're going up against someone who doesn't want to hurt you." Tobey made a scoffing noise, then pretended to cough when I shot him a warning look over my shoulder. "But he will be testing you. If you think it's difficult, just remember how hard it might be if it were the Mauvais or some other enemy you were facing."

I always enjoy words of encouragement that start out reassuring then turn sinister.

"Good speech, Mr. T." My voice echoed up the spiral staircase. "Where are they conducting this little show, anyway?"

I expected the test to be given in one of the larger rooms of the White Tower or out on Tower Green, but Mr. Tenpenny merely replied, "You'll see."

Oh goodie, because I had just been thinking I needed more suspense and tension to start my day.

We passed by Olivia's office, then trudged down a set of stairs, and came to a door that, if I hadn't been drowning in nerves, would have made me cry out for joy. An elevator! It dinged, the doors slid open, we stepped in, and my leg muscles celebrated the effortless transition between levels.

When the elevator reached its destination, I expected to see the same stone walls as the rest of the White Tower, but what we stepped into was a narrow hall with recessed lighting and whose walls were painted a drab shade of grey. I followed Busby down the zig-zagging corridor. After a couple jogs I could see a darkened room at the end of the hallway.

Banna was waiting at the entryway. She held a clipboard and was checking something off with a purple pen. Swathed in her layers of gauzy fabric and donning her dark lenses, she looked like a very tiny version of the Invisible Man. Olivia, emerging from the dark room, joined us soon after we reached Banna.

"There you are," Olivia said, her voice tinged with annoyance that brought out her Scottish brogue.

"We got a later start than I intended," explained Mr. Tenpenny.

"Are you nervous?" Banna asked me kindly. She probably had super senses that picked up the sound of my knees knocking together as my legs trembled like blocks in an about-to-tumble Jenga tower.

"A little."

"You'll do great. I know you will." Then, under her breath she added, "As long as your opponent plays fair."

"Banna, hush," Olivia hissed. Sheesh. Who let a cockroach loose in her panties this morning? "I'm sure you'll do your best. That's all we expect."

Did you hear that? That was both of their words triggering my what-the-hell-is-really-going-on alarm.

I muttered a thanks. It was all I could do since I felt too freaked out to speak. Why would Alastair not play fair? Why wouldn't I be able to do my best? Olivia and Banna then turned and headed into the darkened space. Mr. Tenpenny gave me a gentle nudge, signaling me to follow.

I trailed after them. And promptly stopped in my tracks when I crossed the threshold.

Tobey crashed into me, but I ignored his muffled curses. I was in an arena. A real arena. But not an arena as in some modern monstrosity sponsored by an insurance company who could be charging lower rates rather than laying out money on sporting venues. This was a true Roman arena with a stone walkway leading from the hallway up to the circular arena floor, and stone seats situated in tiers. Seats that, in the glow of dozens of tiny fairy lights, I could see were nearly full with onlookers. And not a single one of those onlookers was wearing a toga. I wasn't sure whether to be disappointed or grateful.

After getting over the initial shock, it dawned on me that we were still in a room. There were no windows. Just high ceilings and dark walls. The corridor had had no windows either and I wondered if we were in a basement.

"Where are we?" I asked Mr. Tenpenny.

"Guildhall. It's in the City, not far from the Tower. The elevator is a portal."

"But it's a Roman arena."

"Yes, but only a small one."

"In London?"

"The Romans did settle here for a time."

"Okay, yes I know that, but an arena? This thing is in better shape than the Coliseum in Rome. Why isn't it on any postcards?"

"Because to Norm eyes this is just a jumble of ruins in a building few tourists ever visit," Olivia said tersely, as if I should be well-versed in magical architecture from Roman Britain. "We keep it that way to avoid attention."

"It's time." Mr. T gave my hand a quick squeeze, then gestured me forward. The seats weren't packed to capacity, but there was enough of the London community in attendance to make me feel queasy. Although I stole a few glances of this unexpected marvel of architecture, the introvert in me kept my chin tucked down as if this might shield me from the audience's stares while I crossed the length of the walkway and stepped into the center of the arena floor.

Where Alastair was waiting.

Shifting on his feet, he looked almost as nervous as I felt. I greeted him, expecting to see the usual delight in his eyes. I needed something normal, something reassuring before this started. But he didn't smile. Not even a grin.

My queasiness turned to outright nausea.

Banna announced the rules of the test, but my blood was hammering too hard through my ears for me to catch any of it. I didn't dwell on this, though. During one of the cake breaks with Busby yesterday, we'd gone over sparring protocols. I didn't think they'd have changed much in the hours since.

In too little time, Olivia told me to formally greet my opponent. Alastair and I both bent at the waist to bow to one another. Our eyes locked. His revealed nothing but determination. My stomach twisted and an acid taste filled my mouth.

I swallowed back the bile. I thought of the balance. I thought of the membrane around me allowing only enough magic in and out. Olivia called for the test to begin. I lifted from my bow.

Before I could prepare for it, before I could even take my fighting stance, my whole body felt like it had been forced into in the world's tightest pair of bike shorts. I could move my fingers but not my arms. My legs were free, but some unseen rope was pulling me toward Alastair. My feet tripped over themselves as I struggled, fighting against the bonds. I tried to resist, I tried to push my arms out as if I could burst the restraints like the Incredible Hulk, but it was near impossible.

I panicked. I was out of control. I could feel magic pouring from me. It reminded me of my draining at Runa's, but that had been a gentle tug, not this ripping, tearing sensation. I clenched my hands and pinched my eyes shut, straining with the effort to hold in as much as possible, but it was like using a tissue to dab at a gaping arterial wound.

I opened my eyes, staring with rage at Alastair. The temptation to rip my power back from him was stronger than the need to pee after drinking half a pot of coffee.

I wanted my magic back with a greedy ferocity. I was certain I could take it back, but the nonsensical rules of the test stated I couldn't use any of my ability to absorb to combat my opponent. Besides the fact that I already had enough magic in me to kill a herd of unicorns, with my lack of magical control, if I absorbed I could mistakenly pull in magic from the audience — any of whom could have been tainted with the Mauvaisian computer virus Mr. T had mentioned.

Also, this test was about proving I could rein in my magic. No lashing out, no slapping my opponent with whatever happened to burst from me. I had to win by using the spells I'd practiced the previous day and by using them with finesse and control. A nice concept on paper, but so is nuclear fusion.

Theoretically, I knew I didn't need my hands or arms free to do magic. I only needed to focus on the spell. But you try being tightly bound with magical ropes then forced along like some sort of prisoner puppet and see how well you can concentrate on the task at hand.

What made all this a million times worse was the look on Alastair's face. It held a wicked amount of concentration. None of the gentle charm. None of the shy pride. None of the warmth that had slowly been thawing my icy little heart. He also appeared stronger, more robust. And I don't mean it looked like he'd suddenly packed muscle onto his lithe frame, but the way he held himself, the vibrations thrumming off him were as though he'd gotten a vitamin boost that made him radiate strength.

Then it hit me. What if this wasn't Alastair? What if the Mauvais had regained his strength and was morphing again? The realization made me stagger. I fell to my knees. Thankfully, the arena was authentic and the fighting surface was cushioning sand, not concrete.

Angry fear roiled in me and I later realized — because right then deeper thinking wasn't going to keep me alive — that the fear hadn't been for myself but for Alastair. If the Mauvais had morphed into him, where was the real Alastair? Was he even alive?

The only way I could be certain would be to detect Alastair's scent. Even the best Magic couldn't fake that because everyone's smell was slightly different to the smeller. I inhaled deeply through my nostrils, begging my brain to find the familiar chocolate-raspberry scent.

The ropes pulled me, dragging me along through the sand. I inhaled more deeply, but it did no good. We were still too far apart and with dozens of other Magics in the confined space, their excitement was pumping out scent like a sales girl forcing you to sample Calvin Klein's latest perfume. It was impossible to pick out any one odor. I couldn't risk it. I had to fight. If it was Alastair, I hoped I wouldn't hurt him. But just in case this was the Mauvais, I had to give it all I could.

Despite everything, despite the tugging, despite my knees burning from the sand, despite getting lightheaded from all my sniffing, I dug my toes in and used every fiber in my thigh muscles to pull back and get to my feet. The audience cheered and the bonds cinched tighter.

I inched back, my steps felt like walking the wrong way on an escalator made of mud, but once I'd managed three steps, the tugging gravity of Planet Alastair weakened.

This tiny respite gave me the head space to find the balance, to form the membrane. Again, I wanted to yank my magic back out of Alastair, and had to remind myself this wasn't allowed. I wouldn't fail this test on a technicality.

Speaking of technicalities, no one said I couldn't give.

The moment the idea flashed into my brain, the binding on

my arms lessened ever so slightly. Just at the second Alastair's face registered surprise at the change, I walloped him with that magic head butt that had worked so well on Rafi. Alastair staggered back, my arms came free, and the arena floor shook with the crowd's stomping cheers.

CHAPTER TWENTY-NINE
SHOOP SHOOP

It took me a moment to catch my breath. I felt dizzy. I felt betrayed. My arms felt like they might float right off my body. I hunched over like a runner, hands on knees, sucking in air. I craved candy, cakes, cookies, cannoli — dear Merlin, why did so many sugary snacks start with the letter C?

Hands still on knees, I glanced up at Alastair. Had he enjoyed doing that? Did he like pulling power from me? No, that wasn't fair. Surely, it had been what he was required to do as part of my test. Still, that look of triumph that had been on his face.

You're being ridiculous, I told myself as I stood up straight. You're letting that idiot Tobey spend too much time in your head.

Just as this thought came to me, Alastair rushed over, threw his arms around me, and was congratulating me with pure enthusiasm in his voice. He eased back a bit. His eyes shone with delight, relief, and something more, something that made my heart swell like a dried up sponge that had been tossed into a bucket of warm water. And then his lips went to mine.

I instinctively jerked back. I was angry over how vicious he'd been during the test. I was confused. And I was more surprised than if I'd woken up to find I'd grown a tail. But he slipped his hand around to the back of my head. His fingers combing up through my hair sent a wave of calm through me that had nothing to do with a spell, a trick, or any magic. My neck muscles relaxed, and we fell into a full-on, damn-why-we-do-have-clothes-on kiss. As his tongue said, "How do you do" to mine, happy waves washed over me.

From somewhere very distant I caught the sounds of shocked murmurs and someone shouting my name. Then I remembered we weren't alone. I tightened my lips, breaking off the kiss.

Alastair pulled away, looking mischievously pleased. Something in my face wiped all the pleasure from his.

"I thought you were trying to drain me."

Even though my heart was racing and I desperately wanted to latch onto him again, there was no coyness or playfulness in my statement. The words were blunt. They demanded a response. As the song promised, that kiss told me a lot about Alastair's feelings, but I had to know what game he'd been playing during my test. I guess the "Shoop Shoop Song" didn't apply to such a cynical heart as mine.

"I was. A little," he said. We were still close, our toes nearly touching. "I wanted to hit you with the strongest spell I could muster without too much risk. I wanted them and I wanted you to see exactly what you could do."

In his eyes all I could see was sincerity. So why couldn't I just accept it? Because too many people who were supposed to care for me, who were supposed to be looking out for my best interests had been brutal to me. Plus, I was really stubborn.

"And to see what you could do?" I snapped.

He flinched like I'd just slapped him.

"No, why would you say that?"

I instantly felt like a heel, but that only made me angry with myself. And so, I lashed out again.

"You lied to me about what type of Magic you are. You absorbed from me. Was that to help the Mauvais? Or were you getting back at me for what I've been putting you through these past few weeks?"

Several Magics from the audience had stepped down from the arena seating. People who might have wanted to congratulate me or give me my magic diploma or whatever was supposed to happen next. They milled about just at the edge of being in earshot. Ours was obviously a private argument, which meant they gave every pretense of keeping a polite distance while still tilting their ears to catch everything we were saying.

"You haven't put me through anything," Alastair whispered. "I don't even know what that means. I've been happier since you came to Rosaria than I've been in a long time. And I haven't been deceiving you about my abilities." He opened his hand to show a small capsule that pulsated with a faint violet light. "It's an absorbing capsule. It takes in power just like an absorber. Empty it's red, but when it's full of magic it remains purple.

"It was part of the test to prove what you were capable of. With this pulling away your power you'd be forced to control your magic. Which you did, otherwise it would be deep purple, not pale. It was my idea to show them what you can do, not some hidden power I've been keeping from you. And while it does allow me to hold on to your magic for a time," he dropped his voice to an even lower whisper, "I was hoping to return it to you later." He grinned and touched his lips as if I didn't understand his meaning.

"Oh," I said awkwardly, knowing I should say sorry, but my tongue seemed unable to form the word. I'd have made a terrible Canadian, eh?

"You two," Olivia barked.

Alastair and I both startled. We stepped away from each other and faced her, shuffling our feet like two misbehaving school kids. Banna, who'd removed her sunglasses, stood a few paces behind Olivia, glaring at her with icy eyes. "My office. Now."

Mr. Tenpenny tried to keep up with Olivia as she marched off on her shapely legs. I caught phrases from him like, "He really wouldn't," and, "It's not how it appears." I had no idea what he was trying to apologize for. Was using my giving side not allowed? No one had told me that rule, so if it wasn't and I was being disqualified, they were going to hear a round of complaints from me.

Regardless of his efforts, Olivia's heels clicked away faster than Mr. T could keep up. Once she reached the entry to the arena, he gave up and headed back to us as Olivia disappeared into the hallway.

"I can't believe you'd try to do this," Tobey said, the sneer residing again on his face. Banna moved up to his side. "Of all the dishonest tricks."

"Tobey!" Mr. Tenpenny said. "Enough of that. I'm sure there's been a misunderstanding."

Exactly. As in I was misunderstanding what in the world was going on.

"Give Olivia about fifteen minutes," Banna said consolingly. "She'll have had time to cool down a bit by then."

"Cool down from what?" I asked. "Did I pass or not?"

"Let's just see what Olivia has to say, shall we? Afterward, we need to chat." Banna glanced meaningfully to Tobey, then smiled at me. I think she intended it to be reassuring, but with her oddly tiny teeth and eyes as frosty as an Arctic winter, it made me shy away from her. I bumped into Alastair, who placed a steadying hand on the small of my back. The warmth of it soothed me and some of the tension fell from my shoulders

Tobey threw another scowl at me and Alastair, then marched

off. It did him no good. He ended up having to wait at the elevator where Banna slipped on her eye protection, took Tobey's hand, and helped him through the portal. I didn't understand why at first, then realized he was traveling from one magical spot to another and couldn't do it on his own. His embarrassment at holding the tiny, ancient hand cheered me up immensely. Mr. T watched them, a strange look on his face. Perhaps he was envious of Banna taking his role away from him. Once Tobey and Banna had made their trip, Alastair and I stepped into the elevator with Busby joining us.

"What's happening," I asked, breaking the awkward silence.

"Let's wait to see what Olivia says," Busby replied, repeating Banna's words as if no one dared cross the line until Olivia gave permission to do so. "You really— Never mind. I should have known. I shouldn't have brought—"

Busby had his back to us as he spoke these sentence fragments, giving Alastair the chance to slip his hand into mine. His touch was like a defibrillator jolt to my heart and filled me with the sense that I could get through whatever I was about to face.

CHAPTER THIRTY

TEST RESULTS

Of course, Alastair and I dropped hands the instant the elevator bounced to a stop, but that's not to say our fingers didn't brush together now and then as we followed Mr. T to Olivia's office. Tobey had gone off to do, well, whatever it was he did all day. Which was good because I'd have hated for him to hear the tongue-lashing Alastair and I got from Olivia as she paced her office, her anger filling the room with her woodsy scent. The gist of her words: Apparently test givers are not supposed to lock lips with their test takers.

"This is not a behavior we approve of," Olivia said, standing rigidly behind her desk where a plateful of cupcakes kept drawing my eye.

"It was only a congratulatory kiss," I said, hoping to protect Alastair.

"Ms. Black if that's a kiss of congratulations, I can only imagine how you must kiss in private."

I was tempted to say how weird it was that she would be imagining me kissing anyone anywhere, but figured now was not the time for smart ass comments.

"Cassie and I formed a bond before we came," Alastair said, making whatever we were sound painfully formal. "I should've informed you of that."

"No, I should have made the rules more clear," said Busby.

"Yes, both of you should have done exactly that," Olivia said. "As it is, Alastair, you are at risk of losing your teaching license altogether."

"What's the big deal?" I asked. "We're both adults."

"The big deal is that a teacher who is in a relationship with a student is more likely to falsify things. Alastair may have gone easy on you or used a weaker version of the Binding Spell to make sure you succeeded today."

"Believe me, he was not going easy," I said. My arms still ached where the magical ropes had tightened against them.

"Were you, Alastair?" Olivia asked crisply.

"No, quite the opposite. I want Cassie to be able to fully protect herself. I always have, as you'll remember from my trial." Trial? Wait what trial? Oh, okay, so yet again we're not going to explain things to Cassie and just let Alastair continue blabbing? Guess so. "I used a harsher spell than I would have conjured for a final exam, let alone a placement test." Alastair paused, casting a quick glance at me before returning his focus to Olivia. "I care very much for Cassie. I would never make her feel stronger in her magic than she is. I want her safe, not overly cocky."

"I'd like to believe that," Olivia said. Her voice was calm and sincere, but her face remained resolute as she sat down in her plush, leather chair. "But as it is, we can't accept the results of Ms. Black's test."

"That's bullshit," I blurted. I kind of expected Alastair and Mr. Tenpenny to back me up, but they remained disturbingly silent. "Believe me, Alastair was not pulling any punches on that test." I pushed up my sleeves and showed her the rings of bruises on my upper arms.

"Then you will do fine when you test again," Olivia said evenly.

"Against who?"

"We can't tell you that."

"Is the—" Alastair began, his throat sounded dry. "Are the goals the same for the next test?"

"Not exactly."

"Would anyone care to explain what this test is for? It's obviously not a placement test."

"In a manner of speaking, it is," Olivia said apologetically. "It's why I'm so angry with you two. Cassie, I wanted you to pass this test without any question of the results. Now another test is required. Likely within the week." I started to protest, but Olivia cut me off. "I'm sorry for the short time frame. I advised giving you more time. I think it only fair we provide you the training you deserve. But other… Well, there are higher ups who believe it's safest to get you sorted before we allow you into more formal training."

"Sorted?"

Olivia took a deep breath and Mr. Tenpenny patted my shoulder. I didn't like this one bit.

"If you are unable to contain your magic, to prove you can control it—" I nearly burst out that I had just proven I could control it, but then decided that shouting an interruption wouldn't be the best proof of being in control. "You will be drained and you will be asked to leave the magic community."

"Draining? Expulsion? Just like that without even giving me half a chance to learn a damn thing?"

"Cassie, that's—" Olivia started to say, but I'd had enough.

I got up, and I really wanted to try out the magic head butt thing again, but instead I took my anger out on her cupcakes by turning them into a pile of Brussels sprouts. I then stormed out. Too rankled to think of what to do or where to go, I traipsed to the end of the hallway and stared out the window over the

Green. From the office, I could hear Alastair offering an apology before saying a hurried goodbye. He came up behind me and I whipped around.

"Of all the—" I started, but Alastair pulled me to him. The kiss was quick, but only because Alastair started laughing.

"That, the sprouts, her face."

"I have my moments," I said, and Alastair's giggling fit ended up being contagious. It felt good. It certainly felt better than crying, which was running a close second in the race of my emotional reactions. After the intensity of the test, the stupid results, and my doubts about Alastair crumbling by the minute, the laughter seemed to bond us back together. He took my hand, but he stepped back.

"I do care about you, Cassie."

"But..." I prodded.

"We should be careful while we're here."

"Are they really going to kick me out?"

"Not if someone sticks to her lessons and learns to fully control her magic." He kissed me on the nose and I caught his chocolate-raspberry scent. I was hoping we could talk, that I could try to explain all the fears and suspicions that had made me keep him at a distance. And to remind him that since I was at risk of being booted out of this world, we had limited time and I wanted to get cracking on finding my parents.

But before I could suggest anything, his phone pinged to remind him he was already late for a mandatory lecture on the ethics of the use of magic in political campaigns.

CHAPTER THIRTY-ONE

SEARCHING AGAIN

Once Alastair took off for his lecture, I debated what to do. I could continue working on Nigel's education or I could sulk in my room. But before I had a chance to decide, the heavy curtains framing the window swished closed, the hallway darkened, and with her orb providing just enough light, Banna was at my side.

"The others are all in that lecture, you know." All trace of her earlier icy attitude was gone, replaced with a conspirator's friendliness.

"And?"

"And I've told Tobey to go fetch Busby's key. Now would be a perfect chance to search for the files you need. That is," she paused and lifted her glasses to give me a knowing look, "assuming they're still there."

"What do you mean?" But did I really need to ask? I'd already found the empty spots where two important files should have been.

"Let's just say that you and Tobey aren't the only ones using that room lately. A certain someone has been in there. Who knows what he might not want found."

"Alastair, you mean?" My stomach plunged down into the depths of the dungeon. Okay, I didn't really know if there was a dungeon in the White Tower, but there had to be, right?

"I wouldn't like to name names, but it's best you get in there and find what you need before anything else wanders off." As proof of how thrown off I was by the test, by Alastair's kiss, by the possibility of being drained, I didn't even think to ask why, if she worried about their being stolen, Banna couldn't just bring the relevant files to me. "I'll tell Tobey to meet you there, shall I?"

"Yeah, you do that." Confusion charged through my veins. I had just allowed myself to truly think of Alastair as an ally, as someone I could trust. And now this. Should I cry? Should I scream? I wasn't sure, but I did know that Team Brain was jeering, "I told you so!" and gloating over Team Heart's stupidity.

Team Brain's triumph filled me with a rigid determination. So, despite the test and the previous day's preparation leaving me aching, and despite my belly demanding breakfast, I trudged my way to the records room.

As before, Tobey insisted we work through the files alphabetically.

"That's dumb," I told him. "You yourself said we should try the Kilbride file. If we don't find anything there, we can move on with names and places we know, like Rosaria, Tenpenny."

"Tenpenny?" Tobey narrowed his eyes with disapproval.

"Your grandfather oversaw my parents' last mission." An idea struck me. "Was there a name for the mission? You know like Operation Save the World, or something?"

Tobey shook his head. "Yeah, maybe, but it's not exactly something we discuss around the dinner table."

"Right. I wonder if Olivia has a list of missions somewhere."

"Look, it'll just be more organized if we go alphabetically. That way we won't miss anything. Now, can we get started? That lecture only goes for forty-five minutes."

I rolled my eyes at him and headed to where I'd left off. As I passed the file cabinet with the Te drawer, I caught the scent of chocolate. I glanced up the row. Tobey was busily sifting through his own cabinet's contents. I inhaled once more. Raspberry.

Damn it.

I tried to tell myself that Alastair had only taken the files to study what was in them in the comfort of his own room, or perhaps to organize them to compile his case. He'd said he'd found something we could act on in a few days, but why wouldn't he just tell me what he'd found? Why be so vague, so covert? Was he taking the files to help or to hinder the search for my parents?

I was tempted to pull open the Te drawer and see what they had on Mr. Tenpenny, but Tobey had seemed annoyed with me ever since he and Busby showed up at my door that morning. And that foul demeanor had only increased. One little annoyance might set him off, might make him unwilling to let me in here again.

I didn't have the energy to deal with a grumpy Tobey. I was also dizzy with hunger and not in the mood to waste time where it wasn't needed. So, I started where I'd left off, making a show of flipping through the documents, and giving only cursory glances at the contents as I rushed my way to the Tenpenny files.

Even in my haste, I did catch a few tidbits, including the original business application for the Wandering Wizard. The first branch — I had no idea it was a franchise — dated back to 1266, and had been set up by a real wandering wizard by the name of Merkle Morningstar to commemorate his hundredth birthday. Each century, he broke ground on a new branch of his cheery pubs in a new community. The one in MagicLand had opened in 1866 as part of Merkle's six hundredth birthday celebrations. Sadly, he died before he could expand his empire further.

I did little more than brush my fingers over the files starting with U. Although, out of curiosity, I did check for Umbridge.

Turns out there was one and she did have a thing for cats, but there was no mention of her being a sadistic monster. Quite the opposite: She was the driving force behind the first flying cat veterinary clinic.

I had just opened the Te drawer, when Tobey's phone went off with what sounded like the world's loudest alarm.

"Time to go," he called. It looked like he was still standing in front of the same cabinet he'd been at when we started. Slacker.

"Let me just finish this drawer."

"Make it snappy. My grandpa's due back any minute."

To which I thought, *So what?* I mean, it wasn't as if Tobey was a five-year-old who couldn't go wandering around the Tower grounds on his own, maybe pop into the pub for a pint. Did Busby immediately check for the file room key the moment he returned from anywhere? But I held my tongue and searched for Mr. T's file. Tennison, Tenopin, Tenrider.

Oh, you have got to be kidding me.

I flipped through the names once more, scanning the drawer front to back. No Tenpenny.

"Cassie, come on, wrap it up."

I slammed the drawer shut.

What was Alastair playing at? Did he find something? Was he searching for something? Was he hiding something from me?

"Find anything?" Tobey asked when I stormed up beside him.

"No. You?"

"Nothing of interest." He opened the door and scanned the hallway before we hurried to the stairwell. "Want to grab something to eat?" he asked once we'd stepped out onto the level I recognized as being the one Olivia's office was on.

"Not really." I chided myself for the snappy response. It wasn't Tobey's fault he wasn't a fast reader and hadn't gotten through many files. It wasn't his fault Alastair was stealing the very files I wanted. It wasn't his fault I was cranky from my test results and from not sleeping well the night before. "Sorry, I'm just insanely tired. I'll catch you later."

Tobey shrugged off my response and headed toward the stairwell that would take him back to his room. I, however, had a score to settle.

"Where was the lecture being held, do you know?" I called after him.

"St. John's Chapel. Second floor." He pointed to the stairwell we'd just come from. I hesitated. I didn't want to admit to Tobey that I had no idea which floor I was currently on. "Down two flights," he finally said, and I didn't miss the *well-duh* tone in his voice.

I hurried down the stairs, but when I reached the stunning chapel with its cream-colored stone and graceful Norman arches, it was empty except for a few tourists.

I wanted to find Alastair, but the need for food hit me more keenly than it had since I started drawing a regular paycheck. I figured breakfast had reliably appeared in my room before, so I grunted and groaned my way back up what felt like half a million stairs. Given my day was going horribly, I was pleasantly surprised when, only moments after I entered the room, another full English breakfast appeared on my table.

I had just bitten into the last slice of toast when I caught sight of Alastair out my window. He was striding away from the White Tower and toward the walls. As tempting as another plateful of fried protein sounded, I dropped the last bite of toast and raced down to confront him.

I don't know who I was kidding. I might have long limbs, I might be physically fit from cycling all over Portland, but only magic could have gotten me through the interior maze of the White Tower and out to Alastair quickly enough. And as yet, no one had taught me a thing about teleportation.

Still, it was the first time I'd been out of the White Tower for over twenty-four hours, and my phone pinged so many times with messages it sounded like I had a pinball machine in my pocket. I ignored it, racing over to where Alastair had been headed. I passed through a gateway in the inner walls and reached an entryway in the outer walls. I raced over, ready to run to catch up with Mr. File Thief. But before I set one toe into the exit, two Yeoman Warders and the sari-wearing woman from the cafeteria blocked my path.

Stupid me. I forgot I was the latest prisoner in the Tower of London.

I didn't say a word. I didn't argue. I didn't see the point. Alastair had to come back sometime.

I headed back to the raven enclosure to check my messages. Two were photos of Pablo: one of him dressed as a dragon, the other of him donning a space suit. Mr. Wood had sent some more BLT food porn and an image of a crocheted length of red yarn that looked like (if you tried really hard and if you were told in a caption what it was) a strip of bacon.

He also said they had three clients lined up.

Because of the time difference, if I did text back, I couldn't expect a response for at least another few hours. But right then, I didn't know what to say. I honestly hadn't expected any work to come in while I was away. I suppose I had hoped Mr. Wood wouldn't take on clients without me, that we were partners in a way. It was a stupid and selfish assumption. He needed the money and he needed to keep his business viable.

But the real question eating at me was: Would Morelli be able to do the makeup without turning someone's dearly departed into Bozo the Clown?

CHAPTER THIRTY-TWO

THE MUSEUM OF LONDON

I spent most of that afternoon with Nigel. Since I had dead bodies and prisoners on my mind, we went over the use of the Tower as a prison. And surprisingly, with my help, by the time the gates were closing for the day, Nigel managed to recite a pretty decent speech in which the only inaccuracies were your typical tour guide's embellishments.

I never did locate Alastair. He wasn't in his room when I pounded on the door, he wasn't in The Keys (the pub for the Yeoman Warders and Tower residents), and by the time the sun began to set, I was too exhausted to keep searching.

I woke the next day with my arms aching, my shoulders throbbing, and my mind wondering what would be expected of me now that I hadn't managed to graduate Magical College after only a few days of study. I eventually pulled myself out of bed and winced at the bruises and scrapes on my knees.

When I emerged from the bathroom, a tray of breakfast showed up on my table. Propped next to the teapot was a folded note. I slathered a piece of toast with strawberry jam and munched on it as I read:

> *As we are uncertain what to do with your practical studies at the moment, we have decided it would be best*

you spend the morning on some background work. This coursework will take place at the Museum of London.

The prisoner freed! Huzzah!

I stabbed a piece of sausage...sorry, pudding, with my fork and continued reading that I was to meet my instructor at ten a.m. at the Guildhall portal door, the same door I'd used the morning before to go to my test. He would then show me the way to the museum.

In other words, I'd be chaperoned. So much for freedom. I was, however, grateful for a chance to get out of the Tower. After all, I'd been in London for well over eighty hours and had only visited two attractions. That's no way to whirlwind your way through a trip abroad.

It was already half-past nine — apparently my body had finally gotten over its jet/portal lag. I hurried through my breakfast, helped by Winston who showed up at my window to sample the bacon and steal my fried tomato. He then clacked his beak as if saying thanks before flying off.

My knees protested down the first flight of spiral stairs, but once they realized I wasn't giving in to their demands to stop moving, they slowly quieted down. I seemed to be getting the hang of the White Tower's confusion of stairwells and hallways, and found my way to the Guildhall portal without making a single wrong turn.

Unfortunately, this was the extent of my good luck for the morning because I soon discovered my newest teacher had been in the audience during my test. So, as we strode along the City's sidewalks, passing modern office buildings and historic churches, he teased me about my display with Alastair.

"Now, you control yourself around me. I might be tempted to hand out easy tests just to celebrate," he said after introducing himself, his voice filled with a Monty Python-esque wink-wink-nudge-nudge tone.

To be fair, Alvin Dodding was cute… for a guy who looked to be in his late nineties. He had a small frame that might have been taller about fifty years ago, but not by much. His white hair leapt out of his head like it was trying to launch its own space program. And he had a strange habit of adjusting glasses that weren't there. In between his teasing, he explained to me that Olivia had convinced him to allow Chester to magic his eyes into proper form about ten years ago and he still hadn't broken the habit of fiddling with his spectacles.

Despite his age, Alvin had a quick, lively step as we zigzagged around the City's businessmen and women. I wondered if Chester might have also worked his wonders on the old man's arthritic joints. It took only ten minutes to reach the museum where Professor Dodding had no problem jogging up the steps leading to his office, one wall of which was almost entirely window and looked out over the remnants of a stone wall.

"Is that part of the arena?" I asked.

"What?"

"The big hunk of ancient ruins in your backyard."

"Oh, no, just a wall, another part of the old Roman infrastructure. You hardly notice it after a time, I suppose. Now," he said, climbing up on a very wobbly step stool and reaching for a book that looked like it might weigh about as much as he did. If he donned a diver's weight belt and a backpack full of bricks, that is.

I rushed over to help, but he hopped off the stool, balancing the book in the palm of one hand.

"You're very spry," I commented.

"Ah, that's the Floating Charm. Ever try it?" I said I hadn't. "It adjusts the gravity around you. Does wonders for people my age."

I almost asked him what that age might be, but even in the magical world I was pretty sure it was rude to pry into how many years someone had been roaming around on Planet Earth.

In Portland — and boy, did it seem like ages since I'd been there — I'd already learned that magic did something to slow people's aging. But as was evidenced from the wrinkled old man across from me and from Mr. Tenpenny's grey hair, Magics did age. I almost wished I could stop by Dr. Dunwiddle's and pester her about the magic aging process, but I'd have to leave that conversation for another day.

Alvin flipped back and forth through the book while he explained the theory behind his low-gravity talents. Which he demonstrated by leaping up and drifting down into his creaking leather chair like a feather. Finally, he seemed to find what he'd been searching for and settled into his seat.

"It seems my job is to teach you a bit about why you're in London."

"I thought I was here to control my magic," I said before he could continue. His fluffy eyebrows showed his displeasure. "Aren't I?"

"That's what you will do here, not the why of it. Do you always interrupt like that?" I was about to apologize when he got a teasing glint in his eyes. "No wonder Alastair kissed you. It was probably to shut you up."

He gave a good laugh at his own quip. A dry, old man's laugh that stirred up his underlying scent of sage. Once he'd composed himself, I pointed at the book, "Does that say why I'm here?"

"Oh no, I just like the feel of leafing through the pages. Now, I'll ask you some questions to get an understanding of what you already know. Have you learned what the watch does?"

"Brings people back to life."

"Correct, but what is the problem with that?"

"There's already too many people on the planet?" I said doubtfully.

"That is very accurate. Can you imagine the parking situation if all the dead came back? But the real reason is that the watch lends the person who owns it an amazing amount of control over time, over life, over magic itself. With enough strength, the possessor can make themselves immortal; they can kill a person with only a tiny twist of the wrist; a grander twist, and they can wipe out an entire city. With the watch, a Magic is in control. Too much control."

"So why was the watch made if it's that dangerous?"

"I thought I was asking the questions." Amusement filled his voice and eyes, making it obvious that Alvin Dodding adored teaching. "But since you wouldn't have known the answer to that one anyway, I'll tell you. The watch was only meant to be a way to, oh how does one put it, *channel* magic into an object. I'm sure you've heard of magic wands?"

I nodded, biting back any reference to Ollivander's Wand Shop. See, I was learning.

"Well, one does look terribly silly carrying around a little stick and waving it about, so the magic community had long been trying to come up with some other form of portable, transferable magic. And before you ask, yes, transferable. That was the main point of a wand. As you've seen, you don't need a witch's wand or wizard's staff to do magic, but say you're feeling under the weather or have gone sugar-free for some ridiculous reason. If you've put your magic into another object, you can call it up even when you're feeling low. It's like keeping a spare loaf of bread in the freezer in case you can't get to the shops. So, why would the watch be dangerous, given what I've just told you?"

I thought for a moment, fighting back the image of a magic loaf of bread. "If the Mauvais had the watch," I said slowly, working out the idea in my head as Professor Dodding's pale grey eyes gave me an eager look of encouragement. "And the watch already had some power put in it..." The magic loaf exploded in my head. "The Mauvais put more of his magic into the watch than he intended to."

Alvin Dodding clapped his hands. "Very good. And that is why when we got our hands on the watch we thought the Mauvais had been defeated. After running some tests, we were certain the Mauvais had put nearly all his power into that object. He would have done so to allow the watch to enhance his power, but he didn't take into account our getting our hands on it. We had his magic," he said emphatically. "He should have been weak, too weak to pull that little morphing stunt. What did he call himself?"

"Vivian," I said, picturing the busty, bombshell floozy changing back into the broad-shouldered, hairy-legged Devin Kilbride.

"That's it. With the majority of his magic in the watch, to do that trick he had to be gaining power from somewhere. Or someone. Which is more than a little troublesome. But I've gotten ahead of myself." I wanted to tell him he hadn't, that I needed to know who he suspected might be passing power to my arch nemesis. But Dodding was in lecture mode and couldn't be stopped.

"When the watch was built, its special qualities quite surprised its maker, but the Mauvais immediately saw the potential of that pesky object. I don't believe it had been constructed to be evil, but in the wrong hands, even a pencil might be dangerous. So, not long after the Mauvais allowed his magic to blend with that of the watch, his power increased exponentially and we were subject to his whims, to his quite horrible whims.

"There's too much history to go into today regarding the details of all the investigations and attempts to get the watch from his hands into ours, but you will be proud to know your parents were a part of that wonderful event."

I already knew some of the story of my parents being on the team who came to London to secure the watch. They'd come, they'd succeeded in getting what they were after, then they were betrayed by their partner Devin Kilbride.

"But you had the watch," I said. "I still don't understand why you couldn't just destroy it then and there. Why take the risk of holding onto it for so long, and then of sending it to Portland?" I'd been told something of this. There was some difficulty with destroying the watch by, say, whacking it with a hammer, but I wanted to see what Dodding might add to what I already knew.

"First, let me ask you what you think would happen if we destroyed the watch. Consider that the Mauvais has imbued his power into it."

"It would destroy him, right? Or at least a good portion of his magic."

"Exactly. But his magic isn't the only magic in there. The maker of the watch filled it with his own power to get it started. Destroying the watch would not only kill the Mauvais, but very likely the maker of the watch as well."

"Okay, so why not destroy it? Wouldn't it be worth the loss of one life to save so many?"

Professor Dodding flipped the book shut with a *thump* and shrugged his shoulders. "I suppose it would, but we can't. There are only a few who know this, but HQ had weighed the options and were going to destroy it without telling the maker. It was thought it would be better that way." I was slowly coming around to the full-strength conviction that HQ was a very creepy place. "Trouble was, the watch wouldn't give up no matter how much magic we threw at it. We had been able to channel away some of the power, but even our strongest people couldn't manage a full extraction. The essence of magic remained within the gears.

"So we kept it safe, knowing one day we would figure out how to untangle the power. We had research teams working non-stop on some very clever ideas. And before you judge us, by this time it had been agreed to alert the watch's maker that we were attempting to destroy his creation and therefore risked killing him as well. And you'll be glad to know, it was your Rosaria community where the solution was found. So, the watch was sent there through regulated channels, but as you know, the watch never made it to its proper destination."

Yes, I certainly did know. Why did I ever take that stupid courier job? Life was far better when I wasn't being hunted by an evil wizard, wasn't doubting every feeling I had for someone, and wasn't knocking holes in walls with uncontrollable magical power.

"Then the watch reappeared and seemed to be quite reanimated under your influence." He gave me a wink to show this wasn't meant as a criticism.

"Finally, you had your little scuffle with the Mauvais, during which you — although none of us had been able to do so before — took in all the watch's combined magic, even its core essence, and now here you are," Professor Dodding concluded. As if that summed up everything.

"If I don't get my magic under control, if I don't prove myself. What happens?"

"Besides the Mauvais possibly using you to ravage the world?"

"Yeah, besides that little detail."

"We will have to destroy you. But don't take that personally.

You seem very likable." Trust me, that's a phrase I've never heard in my lifetime, but the surprise was completely overshadowed by that whole *we'll have to destroy you* thing that had come before it. "So, I do hope HQ's training gets you to the point you need to be."

"Wait, back up. You're going to *kill,* not drain me if I don't sort this out?"

"No, no, of course not. Not kill. We'd only extract you to the point of imbecility. But don't let that wear on you. I'm sure you'll do fine."

He said this as if we were merely discussing how I'd do at my piano recital.

"How long do I have?"

Professor Dodding counted on his short fingers. I was encouraged by how many times he was tapping his thumbs against his other digits. It had to be quite a long time indeed.

"About three or four days, I believe."

"You're not serious."

"Maybe a little less. Whenever your next test is."

"What's to stop me from running away? I could leave here right now and just keep on walking."

"Well, we are on an island. You'd only get as far as Cornwall. And, now please don't take this the wrong way, but we can track you. The scent, you know. Plus, we can tap directly into all the CCTV cameras around town quite easily."

With that cheery bit of news and my stomach growling for some sandwiches, I asked if we were done for the day. He said we were and gave me some homework regarding how the watch might have been made, and told me if I'd like to grab some lunch in the cafe or to browse the gift shop, he'd meet me in the lobby in time to escort me to my next class.

I agreed and stood to leave. Just as I got to the door, I paused and turned back. Professor Dodding was tossing the book back into its spot on the shelf and leaping up to claim another. He caught me watching.

"Waiting for that kiss, dear?"

"Not this time. I was wondering, who made the watch?"

"Oh, I assumed you knew. It was your Alastair. He was very precocious. Still is apparently."

CHAPTER THIRTY-THREE

A LUNCH DATE

I don't exactly remember leaving Dodding's office, nor making it down to the ground floor of the museum. I could have tumbled over the railing and landed on my feet after a perfect gymnastic triple flip and I wouldn't have known for all the thoughts pounding through my head.

Alastair. He built the watch. The watch that led to my parents' deaths. The watch that might end up getting me killed as well. All those timers and trinkets of his. I should have seen it, shouldn't I? But I didn't. And despite all the opportunities to do so, he'd never told me he'd made it.

Circular thoughts of suspicion, of the desire to trust him, of that kiss, of the missing files, of his true motives flew round and round my head as I plodded through the lobby of the museum. The race came to a halt when someone called my name. My instinct was to instantly put up my magic defenses. I don't know if that shows my training was paying off, or if I was just exceptionally paranoid.

I whipped around toward the sound, then breathed a sigh of relief. A strange reaction since it was Tobey Tenpenny waving at and striding toward me. Strange, because I'd normally have wanted to keep marching straight out the door to avoid him. But I was so relieved it wasn't Alastair, that seeing Tobey seemed like winning the lottery. As for Alastair, I had too many questions to sort out before I saw him again.

"What?" I asked, perhaps more testily than was warranted. But I did just find out the guy whose lips I could still feel on mine was responsible for ruining my life. I'd also learned my brain had only a few days left of forming coherent thoughts. That kind of news really plays on your mood. Plus, I was famished, and that always boosted my innate grumpiness by a factor of ten.

"Bite to eat?" He gestured toward the museum cafe, the entrance of which was flanked by two garden gnomes. "My treat."

"Sure, why not." I considered joking about what garden gnomes had to do with the history of London, but Tobey never appreciated my humor, so I remained silent as we got in line for what was a surprisingly good selection of food.

I still hadn't satisfied my post-training, post-test hunger, and ended up loading my tray with the largest pastry on offer, two sandwiches, and an orange juice. Tobey opted for an overpriced grains-and-greens salad. With the lunch rush already taking up the tables next to the windows, we settled for a seat in a corner nearest the cafe entrance. I inhaled the first sandwich before asking Tobey why he'd followed me to the museum.

"The others all had some meeting to go to, so I went to your room to see if you wanted to hit the file room again. But obviously you weren't there. I decided I'd go for a swim instead." He paused to take a bite of his salad.

"And?" I goaded, not really wanting to drag out this retelling of A Day in the Life of Tobey.

"And to get to the pool you have to go past Olivia's office. She wasn't in there and the door wasn't shut, so I went in. Your schedule for today was on her calendar, which is how I knew you were here. And maybe," he said with a sly grin, "while I was looking, one of her desk drawers sort of opened when I bumped into it."

"I don't think they'll buy that in a court of law. I assume something good was in the drawer to drag you here."

"A file," he said. Then, just to be even more annoying than usual, he didn't continue.

"Which file?" I demanded. Instant thoughts of Alastair's possible innocence in the whole file affair bloomed in my head. Maybe Olivia had taken the Tenpenny, the Starling, and even the Zeller files. Maybe Alastair's scent on the cabinets was nothing more than his being in the file room to do research.

"Not one of the main files like the ones in the file room, but sort of a general dossier compiled from various sources," Tobey said, bursting my hopeful balloon of maybes. "A dossier on the watch, on you, and on your parents."

"Shut up!" I was so shocked I dropped my pastry. "Are you serious?"

Tobey nodded as he shoveled a bite of food into his mouth. He stole a sip of my juice to wash it down. "They're alive, I'm pretty sure of it."

"Pretty sure?"

"There's not a single record of their deaths. The very absence of a death record is a sign HQ thinks your parents didn't die that night. You've seen how Magics love their record keeping."

"Which makes no sense in a world where you can change documents with the flick of a finger." I pulled off a chunk of my pastry and popped it in my mouth. I could almost hear the magic in my cells humming Beethoven's "Ode to Joy."

"Want some?" I offered. I mean, he paid for it, I should at least see if he wanted any since his salad couldn't possibly be satisfying.

Tobey pulled a face. "No, I don't eat sugar."

"That is so wrong," I scoffed. "So very, very wrong. No wonder you can't do magic." I added an elbow nudge and quick smile to show him I was only teasing.

"Very funny, Black. Anyway, they can detect changes like that, can't they?"

"Yeah, my landlord caught me out. He's supposedly skilled at such things."

"Maybe we can have him verify the paperwork at some point, but these reports seem official and I've overheard Grandad referring to them more than once to Olivia since we got here. I get the impression they don't want you to know what they've found."

"No, they don't." I recalled Alastair bringing me the letter from HQ and telling me he wasn't supposed to share the information. But he had wanted me to know. So why wasn't he being more helpful? The whole situation cast storm clouds of doubt about everyone's motives. "So why do you want me to know? Why are you helping me? No, never mind. I'm sure it's so I'll owe you some favor later on."

The look of angry dismay bit into Tobey's face for only a few moments during which he slowly and methodically finished off his quinoa and kale salad. Every itty bitty grain of it.

"Okay," I finally said, "I'm sorry. Go on and tell me what you found out."

He finally put down his fork and said, "Your parents were last seen in London. They're thought to still be here somewhere, and if they are, there's a chance they're not far from where they were last seen."

"Which is?" I asked through a mouthful of coronation chicken on wheat bread.

"There's mention of a building with close ties to the Tower and within view of the walls. Then there was some reference to ravens, but I didn't quite get it. Anyway, I'm not sure which building it is exactly." I glared at him. Why tell me this if he didn't know anything? "It can't be far, though, because the file says your parents went out on foot that night. Look, you're smarter than me." That was certainly something I never thought I'd ever hear come out of Tobey Tenpenny's mouth. Tobey pulled a folded scrap of paper from his shirt pocket and slid it to me. "I copied that from the sheet in the file. I figured you'd be able to sort it out. But if you do, you can't tell Alastair."

I hadn't intended to. First off, I didn't know if I could talk to Alastair without shouting at him. I mean, he made the damn watch! And hadn't mentioned it in all the conversations we'd had. Second, even if Alastair agreed with what Tobey had found out, he would probably tell me not to go.

Still, I am in the habit of being stubborn, and the very fact I was being told *not* to tell Alastair totally made me want to tell him.

"Why not? He's like an ally in all this."

"Ally," Tobey said critically. "Is that what you think he is?"

"He wants to help me." And I really wanted that help to be motivated by his caring for me, not by his trying to trick me. "That's more than a lot of people have done in my life."

"Don't be so sure of that. Look, Cassie, I don't know what that was in the arena, but keep in mind Alastair and Vivian were close. Very close."

"As were you. Or does making out in alleyways behind your grandpa's house not count as close?"

I chewed the last bite of my sandwich with a satisfied grin on my face as Tobey's cheeks flared with embarrassment.

"I'm going to tell you this once and then you have to drop it," he said. "I'm not sure what that was. I mean, now I know it was probably the Mauvais messing with my mind. I was never attracted to her, him, whatever, but that night I just felt pulled in." I made a disgusted face. "What happened between us only happened once, not that it's any of your business. But she and Alastair were seen speaking together. A lot. Those conversations shut up very quickly when anyone passed by them. And of course, you know of his history with the Mauvais."

I sipped my juice, thinking, afraid of commenting. Alastair made the watch. Vivian was the Mauvais. If Vivian and Alastair were in league together once…

A bright, yet raspy voice called my name from the lobby. Alvin Dodding stood next to the reception desk, waving his arm to signal he was ready.

"Crap, I need to get back. Thanks for the lunch. And the info."

When I stood, Tobey got up as well, then reached out and grabbed my arm. A shock went through me. It startled me to say the least. It felt too much like when Alastair or one of the other Magics dared to touch me, but then I realized his thumb had caught a pressure point in my biceps. He pulled me closer to him. If he dared to kiss me—

I groaned at the thought. Plus, I couldn't imagine how much ribbing I'd get from Professor Dodding.

Luckily, Tobey only wanted to deliver one more piece of overbearing advice.

"We'll figure out the building thing together and we'll go there together. Just don't do anything stupid, Cassie."

"Wouldn't dream of it."

Mentally cursing Tobey for being so damn weird, I twisted my arm out of his grasp and hurried over to join the jovial professor.

CHAPTER THIRTY-FOUR

THAT AFTERNOON

Alvin delivered me back to the arena/Tower portal and said to return to my room for my next lesson. I figured if this was a class with Olivia, it would be held in her office; if it was with Mr. T, we'd go to the rooftop or to his room, which I just bet was a massive suite; and if this was a lesson with Alastair…well, I didn't think they'd be assigning me classes with him anytime soon. Thank Merlin for small favors.

Using those brilliant feats of deduction, I decided it had to be a lesson with Banna. As such, once I got back to my room, I set about closing the curtains, unplugging the overly bright digital clock, and even placing my phone face down so it wouldn't light up if a signal happened to get through to it.

When I answered the knock at the door, I almost cheered my super duper Sherlockian skills. It was indeed Banna, wearing darker than normal sunglasses and sporting an umbrella whose canopy was made of thick canvas. She was in too much shadow for me to see any expression on her face, but she gave a quick nod of approval, stepped in, and pulled down her umbrella once I'd shut the door on the dimly lit hallway.

"You knew I was coming?" Her tone was uncertain as she removed her sunglasses and placed them on the low dresser next to the tea service.

"Lucky guess."

"Very clever," she said appreciatively while conjuring a light orb and propping it up on her umbrella. "Now, personally, I don't see where background work is going to get you. Practical work is what you need, and practical work is what you'll get from me. I thought we'd go back to day one. Back to the Solas Charm. Have you been practicing?"

I admitted I hadn't, then added, "I was told you shouldn't have taught me that."

"Who said that? Alastair? He just doesn't like the Solas Charm because he's not good at it. He'd rather build some contraption to make a light."

Okay, I know I was angry at and confused about Alastair, but I still wanted to think of him as my friend. It should be my job to question and insult him, not hers, and my hackles went up at her harsh tone. But I had a feeling I didn't want to get on Banna's bad side, so I played along.

"Or a contraption to kill us all," I said.

"Yes, good point. That was a clever use of his skills," she said admiringly.

Have I mentioned Magics are impossible to figure out? And I thought normal humans were bewildering.

"Right," I said, dragging out the word. "Anyway, Solas Charm?"

"Yes. I think it would be good for you to practice it. You see, the Solas Charm requires concentration, especially when you first start doing it. I can produce a light orb without giving it much thought." She generated a second orb as if to demonstrate her magical prowess. "But I have been doing it for several hundred years. As for you, let's think of it as a form of meditation, a way to let your magic concentrate on something while also keeping your mind free. We've all been debating how to teach you that, but I'd like to give my idea a whirl. If you don't mind."

"Whatever it takes." I considered bringing up what Professor Dodding had said about what would happen if I didn't pass my next test, but I didn't think I could take hearing any false denials. Better to practice and keep these people happy.

"Alright then. You remember how to do it?"

I nodded and pictured a glowing orb the size of a marble. As with the first time I tried this spell, I'd just been smacked upside the head with uncomfortable news, making it difficult to concentrate.

"Focus, Cassie Black. Think of a good memory."

Surprising even myself, the memories that popped into mind were of Alastair kissing me, Alastair handing me that first slice of Sacher Torte, Alastair telling me he cared about me, that he had always done what it took to protect me.

Banna gasped. I opened my eyes. I hadn't even realized I'd closed them. What I saw made it impossible for me not to smile. A glowing orb. But it wasn't the greenish hazel of my eyes. Instead, it gave off a warm pink light that throbbed in time like a heartbeat. And it wasn't the size of a marble. Unless it was a marble for a giant. The light was the size of a bowling ball and I swear I caught the scent of raspberry coming from it.

"Unusual, but we'll work with it. Now, pull it in," said Banna. "Control it. Don't just let it wink out."

This took a little ingenuity. As I've pointed out before, Magics are great at telling you what to do, but not so great at explaining how to do it. It was up to you to find your way around a spell. I pictured a dimmer switch and slowly turned it until the orb was only a pinprick of light.

"You haven't been around Alastair, have you?"

"No, when would I have? I've been with Professor Dodding all morning."

"Last night? Did you invite him to your room, or go to his?"

Sheesh, was I a promiscuous sixteen-year-old, or something? "No. What's the big deal?"

Banna shrugged her shoulders and gave a dismissive toss of her head. She then spoke in a gossipy tone that was a sharp contrast to the accusatory one she'd just been using. "Of course, I don't mind, but Olivia has her rules, and she hates to have them broken. That orb you just made shows signs of you being in love. Or maybe it's not Alastair. Could it be Tobey Tenpenny?"

"Definitely not. I'm not in love with anyone," I said, a sudden wave of fatigue adding a cranky tone to my words.

"Maybe you just don't realize it yet. Sometimes the magic knows more than the mind." She watched me for a moment, the eerie blue of her eyes felt like it was drilling straight to the back of my skull. "Regardless. How did you feel when you were doing the Solas Charm?"

"Focused." And like I really wanted to be in Alastair's arms, but I didn't think that was the best answer at the moment.

"Good. And I felt very little of your magic affecting me. The Solas Spell does seem to rein in your absorbing side."

"But I can't walk around making light orbs all day."

"No, but if you can find that level of focus you use to make one, you'll be on the right track. And they are handy things when you need to find your way in the dark."

After a few more demonstrations, Banna concluded the lesson.

"What class do I have next?" I asked as she slid her sunglasses back on.

Banna snapped her fingers, and with a crackling pop, three books appeared on my table.

"It would probably please Olivia to know you've studied those for a while. Give it an hour or two, then feel free to explore the Tower. You probably haven't had much time to just wander."

What? Did she think I'd spent every bit of free time holed up in my room practicing spells? Wait, maybe I should have been. "I hear some find it an interesting place," she said, her tone making it clear she couldn't fathom the idea. Clearly she hadn't done one of Nigel's tours.

Once Banna left, I opened the curtains and discovered two of the books, both written by Professor Dodding, were on magical history: *How the Irish Saved Magic Civilization* and *The Making of the English Magics*. The other was titled *The Zen of Membrane Magic and Power That Flows Like Water.*

I followed Banna's advice and, after reading over the sheet Tobey had given me, I perused the history books for a couple hours before heading out. It was a summer day. The sky was clear, the temperature hovered right around perfect degrees Celsius, and by this time of day, while still crowded, the heaviest crush of tourists had left to cram in a few more London sights. I did want to explore, but I also wanted to think.

But first, I needed to check my messages and, now that the West Coast would be awake, I could text Mr. Wood to find out exactly how he planned to get his clients ready for their funerals without disgracing the entire funerary business.

I'd had my phone on silent while I'd been at the Museum of London, but turned it back on as I wound my way down the stairs. The moment I'd stepped outside, three messages chimed their way through. Seriously, the Magics had the power to do so many cool things, so why couldn't they get decent cell service within their little realms? Maybe, I grumbled to myself, that's what Alastair should have been focusing on instead of building evil watches.

Not surprisingly, one message was from Lola. This time Pablo was dressed in a tuxedo sitting next to a glass of champagne. The message read: *Cheers to you!*

I wondered if she'd sent it before or after my test and what news had reached the Portland community regarding my results. Apparently none had, otherwise I would imagine she'd have sent something more sympathetic and less congratulatory. Rather than worry her, I merely replied that I hoped Pablo didn't have a hangover.

The other two messages were from Mr. Wood. No sandwich photos. No crochet creations. Just one with a single line in all caps: *WE HAVE ANOTHER FOUR CLIENTS!!!* The second message: *We'll show those medical bills who's boss.*

I replied back: *Yes, but is Morelli up to the task? Can he really do the makeup? How can you handle so much work?? Hope you are well.*

A response came before I could return the phone to my pocket.

Mr. Wood: *Eugene has found someone to help. He does the heavy lifting. She does the dressing. And I do my usual meet and greet. It's quite doable. And they don't even expect to be paid, so all the money is going to my bills.*

Oh great, I'd just been pushed out of my job by free labor.

The phone pinged.

Mr. Wood: *Don't worry, I still prefer you. As long as...you know...*

Yep, I knew. As long as I could keep his clients from wandering off. I replied with a thumbs up emoji. Then, with my head full of mopey thoughts, I strolled around the Tower grounds.

I knew I should confront Alastair. Ask him about the watch, ask him if he was getting anywhere with the search for information on my parents, tell him what Tobey had found. Banna gave the impression that Alastair was still supposed to be off limits, but I didn't see what would be wrong with speaking to him since it was highly unlikely he'd be the one testing me again. We were two grown adults and if we wanted to overstep the student-teacher line, that was up to us. Or maybe there was another reason for keeping us apart.

I let out an audible grunt of frustration and annoyance that drew the eye of a cluster of old ladies, all wearing pink visors to shield their eyes. This was ridiculous — both the visors and my roundabout thoughts. I had to talk to Alastair. The air needed cleared.

Of course, you have to know the gods of decision making like to have their laughs. The very moment I resolved to confront Alastair, who did I see heading toward the Tower's main exit with Rafi? Yep, the watchmaker himself.

Just as I took off toward them, a massive tour group oozed out of the White Tower and stopped right in my path. I worked my way around their sprawling bulk, darting toward the gate, but Alastair and Rafi had already exited. One of the guards watched me, ready to act if I tried to make a break for it, but I knew it was pointless. With the twisting tangle of streets in this area of London, I'd never be able to find them if they turned a block or two. And if they got on the Underground, all bets were off.

So, instead of giving chase, I fell in with the tour group who were doing the Wall Walk next. All the while, I took mental notes of facts I could share with Nigel. But my note taking wasn't terribly in depth because the tour members kept asking silly questions, demanding their guide repeat herself, and complaining about the cost of the cafe food.

Nevertheless, I found myself enjoying the ease of being with people who had no clue of the magic all around them. Once the guide regained control, it turned out to be a pretty good tour. In between her explanations I had time to scan the paper Tobey had given me. And to sort out what it meant.

The ravens were the clue. From the area of the wall above where their enclosure stood, I had clear views of several buildings across the river, but only one could be seen on the Tower side of the Thames from this vantage point. A four-story, red brick building that, from its boarded up windows, looked unoccupied.

The only problem was that the building was beyond the walls of the Tower. Walls that proved to be well-guarded.

Obviously, I had to escape my imprisonment in the Tower to get to the building. The Wall Walk had given me good views of where I could possibly get out, but I needed more details. So when I came down the steps from the tour, I headed back to the raven enclosure.

While I waited, another message from Lola came through. It must have been too early in the day for her to come up with a costume since the photo she'd sent showed Pablo dressed only in his usual fur suit. Well, and a toothy cartoon grin where his mouth should be. The caption read: *Having a great time. Wish you were here.*

I choked up a little at that. I wished I was too. I blinked away the tears as I sent a message back, telling Pablo he did not have to do any chores no matter what Auntie Lola said. There was an immediate reply of a laughing emoji, a winking emoji, and a hands-out shrugging emoji, which convinced me that Pablo was at this very moment pushing a cat-sized mop around Lola's kitchen.

A light shiver danced up my arms.

"Are you here for another tour?"

I clicked the phone off. Exactly the ghost I'd been waiting for.

CHAPTER THIRTY-FIVE

SNEAKING OUT

That night, I slipped out of the White Tower, crossed through the archway near Wakefield Tower, then skirted along the space between the inner and outer walls.

During my time with Nigel that afternoon, I had asked questions about where someone could access the top of the outer walls (through a hidden stairway near Cradle Tower) and about who guarded the Tower at night. Proud to an absurd degree over knowing the answers to my questions, Nigel explained in great detail the location of CCTV cameras, how many guards were on duty each night, and the route and timing of the Ceremony of the Keys — the official locking of the Tower's gates.

Assuming Nigel had his facts straight — and Winston's head nods seemed to imply he did — I had a nearly encyclopedic knowledge of where and when I could jump from the walls undetected.

Yes, you read that right. I planned to jump. What? Like I was going to tie my bedsheets together and scale the walls?

Professor Dodding's Floating Charm had given me the idea, and I tested out the spell in my room after dinner. It took a few tries, and Banna would have been proud of the amount of focus I'd employed, but it really did work. Once I made it to the top of the outer wall, marveling for a moment at the view of Tower

Bridge at night, I visualized all my cells spreading apart, distancing themselves from one another and making them so wispy that gravity barely affected them.

And then I leapt.

And quickly realized my mistake. Better late than never, right?

Okay, maybe I should have taken more time to perfect the spell and maybe I should have practiced by jumping from a height greater than my bed. But for a brief moment, I was in the air, floating as if gravity had no hold on me. But it's just that moment when you begin to enjoy magic that magic comes back and bites you in the butt. Hard.

See, right when I thought of myself as a dainty butterfly floating on the breeze, I noticed I was indeed floating on the breeze. I'd overdone my gravity defying and was at risk of being blown across the Thames. In a panic, I pulled all my cells back into their proper places. As it tends to do, gravity took hold. I plummeted down to the concrete riverside walkway, landing with full force on my knees.

The pain of what felt like both legs shattering shocked up into my brain then plunged back down into the pit of my stomach, doubling me over. The urge to vomit and the urge to scream fought a miniature nuclear war inside me until, shuddering and clamping my hand over my mouth, I forced both into peace talks where a truce was called without any shots being fired.

Slowly, agonizingly slowly, like a sloth would have made fun of how slowly I was moving, I got to my feet. My tights were torn, but oddly enough, I had nothing more than a few scrapes on my knees. No bone fragments poked out, and there was only a tiny bit of dribbling blood. Still, I did really like those tights.

I hobbled-walked around to the east side of the Tower,

grimaced my way down a few blocks, and it didn't take long before the building was in sight. A square, brick thing you'd more expect to see in the eastside industrial area of Portland than in London.

The place had a low retaining wall around it and the south side was full dark with no streetlights illuminating the shadows. A perfect place to hide. I crouched down beside the wall to plan my next move.

I was confident I could get in without a problem. Lock Picking Charms weren't exactly a challenge. But once I got in. What then? I had to free my parents right away. Wait, or did I need to take out the Mauvais first? Yes, definitely take out the Mauvais. But what if he went for my parents just to be a jerk? Okay then, free my parents. But they might be too weak or too brain damaged to escape with any haste. That settled it: Take out the Mauvais.

Something scuttled along the wall. I jumped back, picturing some sort of land shark attracted to the scent of blood coming from my wounds. Or just your ordinary city-dwelling rat. After wishing Chester and his vermin-stomping feet were with me, I conjured a Solas Charm with surprising ease. The light orb revealed what form of wildlife I was up against.

"Winston," I scolded, "you nearly gave me a heart attack."

The bird hopped along the edge of the wall, grabbed my shirt sleeve in his beak, and began tugging.

"Hey, stop it. I can't have all my clothes in tatters." It took some effort since I didn't want to hurt him, but I pushed the bird back until he finally relented. Impatiently, he snapped his beak at me.

"I can't go back yet. I've got stuff to do."

Winston then proved that birds can pout by tucking his head down and giving me a dirty look, but he stayed quiet except for a few murmurs that sounded very disapproving.

Despite what some of the Magics might think, I'm not a fool. Instead of rushing in like some testosterone-loaded action hero, I practiced the hand motions for the defensive spells I'd worked on with Busby, Olivia, and Rafi — going through each one in order, then reverse order, then skipping every other one to make sure I could call up each spell without a second's hesitation. Winston seemed to think I was directing an avian dance and bobbed along with the gestures.

It was just when I was about ready to stand and make my move that I saw someone going into the building. Tall, dark-haired, and looking very much like Tobey.

What the hell?

Enough with practice. Tobey had said he couldn't figure out where this building was. Had he known and not told me? It didn't matter, Tobey could not go in there alone. And why was he walking straight in like he owned the place? Did he think I was already inside?

Winston cawed and ruffled his feathers, shaking his head as if agitated.

"I'll never understand him, either. Now, scoot aside. Long legs coming through."

I stood up and put my hands on the wall to vault myself and my torn tights over.

Just as my legs left the ground and I was tucking them to my side to clear the top of the brick wall, Winston made a croaking sound. Then, strong hands grabbed me, jerked me backward, and pulled me down into the grass I'd just been crouching in.

I punched at my attacker. So much for magic. I guess my first instinct was a non-magical form of fighting, which after all that practice, kind of disappointed me. Still, I did land a hard left to my assailant's gut. A rush of air went out of him, but he caught it back just as quickly. From the wall above me, I could hear Winston flapping his wings. When I raised my fists to deliver another punch, my attacker grabbed my hands and held them tight.

"Cassie, stop. It's me. Breathe. You know it's me."

I inhaled. That chocolatey scent.

"Alastair, what are you—?"

Before I could finish my question, Winston cried out with an alarming *squawk* as Alastair threw himself on top of me.

Then came the rush of heat, the swishing whisper of black wings flapping.

Followed by the boom of the explosion.

CHAPTER THIRTY-SIX
JAMMIE JAMS

"Get off me." I writhed under Alastair, which wasn't nearly as much fun as it should have been. "Tobey's in there."

Alastair eased back and let me up, but the moment I started for the wall again, he threw a Binding Spell to lock down my arms. Both the shock of being trapped and of him restraining me sent me staggering. He caught me before I did a face plant into the brick wall.

"You can't go in there," he shouted.

Just as I was about to tell him not to tell me what to do, another explosion knocked us off our feet.

"Tobey!" I tried to get up, but Alastair held me close, pressing my face into his chest to shield me from the rush of heat. With his arms tight around me, my heart pounded in my chest. My breathing came in shallow, choking gasps.

"He's not in there, Cassie," Alastair said quietly, reassuringly, as he stroked my hair. "No one is."

"I saw him go in." I pushed away, putting some space between us and fighting back a sob. I mean, I didn't like Tobey all that much, but I never wanted to see him burnt to death in a fiery inferno.

"You didn't. I left the Tower not more than ten minutes ago and he was in his room, wearing pajamas, and sitting with Busby having hot chocolate."

Later I would have a good laugh at the image of Tobey in his jammie-jams sipping his cocoa, but at that moment I was torn between wanting to stay in Alastair's arms and wanting to scream at him that he was a deceitful liar.

Alastair then placed his hands on my shoulders and turned me around to face the smoldering building. A figure. A man. Tall, dark-haired, and looking very much like Tobey was strolling into what used to be the building's main entryway.

"What the—?" I turned to Alastair, then looked back at the building. The guy was walking into the non-existent door once again. "Is it a hologram?"

"No, it's your basic Projection Spell. That is Tobey, but it was Tobey from earlier today. Maybe when he was walking around the Tower grounds." Sirens wailed in the distance. Alastair took my hand and scanned the darkened street that led toward the back of the building. "We should get going, emergency services will be prowling this area at any minute."

He started walking in the direction he'd been looking, tugging on my hand to get me to go with him. I planted my feet, tugging back, and pulling my hand out of his grasp.

"We can't leave. My parents are in there. And if you had passed on what information you've taken about them, maybe I would have gotten here in time. You were supposed to share what you knew with me. Instead, you just hide everything from me."

I pushed Alastair away and started toward the scorched edifice. This time, Alastair not only locked me in a Binding Spell, but also did the pulling-back thing. I was like a dumb dog getting jerked back after forgetting, yet again, how long his leash extended.

"Stop doing that!" I said. "You still have my magic, don't you?"

"Your parents are not in there." The sirens squealed louder. "Cassie, please, just stop being so stubborn and listen to me. I swear to you, I'm using my own magic and all this touching we've just been doing, while nice, is really kicking my ass."

He eased back on the spell. In the glow of the building's fire I could see sweat beading on his forehead and dark circles showing under his eyes.

"You've been tricked into coming here. I don't know if that explosion was meant as a warning, or if it was meant to kill you, but I don't like the idea of either possibility." Pulsing lights began cutting through the darkness. "We're going to have to answer a lot of awkward questions if we're around when those patrols get here, so can we go get some cake and talk like sane people?"

"Sane people do not magically strap other peoples' arms to the sides of their bodies, nor do they use a magic tractor beam to keep that person from running away."

"Sane people don't run into unoccupied, burning buildings. Please, will you come with me? Let me explain? Do you trust me?"

"Two out of three of those things, yes."

Alastair didn't ask which one missed the mark, but he did unleash me, leaving my arms with a weird, floaty feeling. I briefly wondered where Winston was, but then recalled the sound of him flying off. I could only hope he'd stayed safely out of the blast.

We headed down the side street. When we reached the rear of the building, three patrol cars screeched to a stop at the front of the building and a fire crew began shouting orders to get the hoses ready. We slipped around the corner and were halfway down a curving street before I heard a gush of water spraying onto the flames.

I didn't know where we were going. Even the Marks & Spencer bakery would be closed at this hour, but I merely followed along, somewhat dazed and angry with myself for being so easily tricked. But that didn't explain what Alastair had been doing there.

"Were you following me tonight?" I asked.

"No, of course not. The gnomes told me you'd gone."

"Gnomes? Like garden gnomes?"

"Yes, you commented on them soon after we arrived."

"So, what? They have cameras in them?"

"Good god, no. They're living beings. The ones at the Tower serve as elite spies for HQ, but it takes them years to work up to that rank." A fact it might have been nice for Nigel to include when I'd questioned him. Then again, it had been foolish of me to expect all his information to be on the nose. "Most earn their chops by doing mundane surveillance. I mean, you have seen how many of them hang around people's gardens. There's one right outside your apartment building."

"But they just stand there."

Right as I said this, I recalled that Morelli's gnome had gone missing on occasion. I had always assumed he'd taken the thing in for a sad sort of companionship while he watched his game show reruns.

"They *appear* to just stand there," Alastair explained. "They've got a very organized system of dispersal. Once they receive their orders, they show up to where they're needed and they wait. They're incredibly good at holding still, but when they have news to tell, they can hustle. It helps that gnomes are terrible gossips."

"And one just happened to gossip to you that I'd gone?"

"No, and you're lucky for that. The one who saw you leave was heading toward Olivia's office to tell her, but he came across me first. That's the one downside with gnomes. It's usually trained out of them by the time they climb the ranks to work in the Tower, but some want to spill their news so badly, they just blurt it out to the first person they find. I happened to be that person. Snellton—"

"Snellton?"

"The gnome who saw you leave. He's also heard you and Tobey talking several times. Have you really been going through the files with him?"

"Trying to."

I was about to add that certain files had been missing, but Alastair cut in.

"Anyway, earlier today a couple gnomes told Snellton you'd gotten some information about that building." Alastair gestured in the direction we'd just come from, and I recalled the out-of-context pair of gnomes from outside the Museum of London's cafe. "Information from Olivia's files. Please tell me you weren't going through her desk. She is not someone whose hackles you want to raise."

"Of course I wasn't. It was Tobey. He told me what he'd found when we had lunch at the museum."

"You had lunch with Tobey?" Alastair sputtered, clearly knocked for a loop.

"Jealous?"

"No," he said abruptly, then paid an unnecessary amount of attention to a street sign we were approaching. "Okay, yes, I am, but I'm more concerned with the fact that Olivia suspects the information in that file is fake. We're bringing in an expert to verify it, but Tobey's involvement does concern me. At lunch, what did he smell like?"

"I can't say. I—"

"Did you smell magic on him?" Alastair insisted.

"No, I mean, it's Tobey, it didn't cross my mind to sniff him out." I'd also just gotten two hits of strange news, both of which I still needed to confront Alastair about. "I was hungry, and I wasn't paying attention, and it's not like we were swapping spit with our sandwiches."

"Thank you for that disgusting image. Although I am glad to hear it." He darted a shy glance at me, but the warm quirk of his lips dropped before it could turn into a full smile. "I trusted you not to act without me. I'd heard you'd been seen on that level of the Tower, but I didn't think you'd be stupid enough to do anything so risky as to go after your parents on your own. When Snellton told me you'd left and what he'd heard from the museum gnomes, I knew where you were headed. As it is, I barely made in time. That was just dumb, Cassie. Really dumb."

Chastised and feeling like an utter heel, I remained silent the rest of our walk, which ended in front of a cake shop. It was closed, but Alastair undid the lock and we stepped in.

"Breaking and entering? You do know they have CCTV cameras everywhere."

"It's not breaking and entering. My cousin owns it. She won't mind."

CHAPTER THIRTY-SEVEN
TRUTH AND CONSEQUENCES

Once he'd served up two huge slices of an almond-and-raspberry studded Bakewell tart, Alastair asked, "What did you mean when you said you've been *trying* to go through the files? It's not the best room to work in, but things are never out of order."

"At least I am trying," I said. Alastair looked at me questioningly. "It just seems like you spend most of your time going to lectures and the cafe, when I thought you came here to help."

"Believe it or not, except for a couple times out with Rafi, I have been using most of my free time compiling various sources of information about the Mauvais and the night your parents went missing."

"Then why are you stealing files? Do you think I haven't noticed the gaps? Or that your scent is on the very drawers where the missing files should be?"

I expected to see him squirm, to take a bite of tart to bide his time while he came up with a lie, but he did neither of these things. Instead, Alastair lowered his fork and stared at me as if I'd started crowing like a rooster. He spoke directly to me, eyes locked on mine, not darting away, not hiding a damn thing.

"Cassie, I know you're really good at thinking the worst of people, but first off, I got everything I needed from the file room on the first day we arrived. I haven't gone back. My other work has been in the library, in the historical records room, or in conversations with other Magics. Even with your super powers, my scent should no longer be lingering anywhere near that room."

He took a bite of the tart. My ill humor had done nothing to quell my hunger, and I'd already eaten half of mine. Alastair chewed and swallowed, then said, "Second, you might be able to remove an individual sheet, but entire files can't be taken from those cabinets. And I mean that literally. Rafi put a spell on the room so if any file gets within a foot of the exit, it swells so much you can't fit it through the door even if you could keep hold of the thing. Which files haven't you found?" he asked, his brow furrowed with concern.

"Both my parents' and Mr. Tenpenny's are gone," I said, trying to inject accusation into the words, but failing. How could the files be gone? What had I really smelled?

"I never went through Busby's folder. I read through two files and that's the Starling one and the Kilbride one." He continued to watch me, as if driving home the honesty in his answer. I lowered my gaze, fiddling with the crust of my tart in ashamed defeat. "You're smarter than this, Cass. Besides the files, there's whatever it was Tobey showed you about that building. Your cynicism knows no bounds, and with your magic being so strong, if there's some trickery going on, you should have been able to detect it."

"Like I said, I never saw the info about the building myself, only what Tobey copied down. And you can't expect Tobey Tenpenny to detect anything more than the fact that he has ten fingers. And that's on a good day," I added.

At this, a quick breath of laughter escaped Alastair, but the concern quickly returned to his face.

"Look, don't take this as being jealous or overbearing, but I have a feeling you shouldn't work with Tobey on this. Intentionally or not, he's already fed you bad information. And I can't explain why my scent would still be on drawers I haven't touched in days, nor why you can't find files that should be impossible to remove. Besides, neither of you really knows what you're searching for. Okay?"

"Okay," I agreed, half-heartedly.

"Look, Cass, you've got to be more wary and you need to take your studies seriously. You need to focus on your lessons, your balance, your control."

"Yeah, I heard why." I swallowed back the sob that threatened to escape, but my voice still quavered. "Extraction? Really?"

"There are people on your side who won't let that happen. Trust me on that. Just promise me you'll work on your magic and leave the investigating to me until your test is done. I want to help you and I want you to stay alive. You need to be alert to the danger around you. I don't have anything concrete, but I'm coming to agree with Olivia's idea that someone within HQ itself is passing power to the Mauvais."

He reached out and took my hand. I wanted to enjoy the warmth and electrical thrill of his touch, but I pulled away.

"You worked with him once. More than worked. Dodding told me you made the watch." Now that my verbal dam had been breached, the flood waters of all the secrets I'd learned came spilling out. "Oh, and he's the one who told me about being extracted if I don't get my magic under control. He, someone I've never met before, let me know what I was up against if I fail. Did you know?"

Alastair nodded. The tart solidified into a brick in my gut. But at least it was his turn to look ashamed. He pushed away his plate even though half of his pastry remained untouched.

"Since?" I prodded.

"It was in the original letter."

"You lied to me?"

The words came out as a whisper filled with both disbelief and disappointment. I wanted to shout. I wanted to scream this question at him, but it just hit too hard. So much in me wanted to trust Alastair, but every time I began to do so, something came up to rip the rug of faith right out from under my feet.

"I don't know exactly when it's scheduled, but believe me when I say this all-or-nothing test wasn't supposed to happen until you'd been training here for at least a month. Then we show up and barely two days later, Olivia insisted your magic was too strong and HQ needed to test you to keep everyone safe. I argued against it. I argued you should at least be told the stakes. I argued until my throat ached. You deserved to know and I would have told you, but Banna threw a Confidentiality Spell on Rafi, Olivia, Busby, and me."

"And that does what exactly?"

"If we told you, we would be extracted immediately and mercilessly. But since you've found out through Dodding, through someone who wasn't bound by the Confidentiality Spell, the spell on me and the others has broken. And just so you know, Rafi and I had just come up with a way to get around the Confidentiality Spell this afternoon. When Snellton found me, I'd been on my way to tell you what was really going on. I swear, Cassie. I've said this before, but I will protect you. I will fight for you."

Okay, yeah, my throat got a little clenchy at this point, but the needles of distrust were still jabbing me.

"And the working with the Mauvais part? The watch? How could you? You say you want to protect me, but you built the very thing that has ruined my life."

Alastair took a while before answering. When he spoke, the words were thoughtful, careful.

"I've explained to you before about my working for the Mauvais and about how I fell into his circle. I was younger, and he acted like he was my friend. I don't want this to sound arrogant, but my talent was recognized at an earlier age than most. That's why they advanced me to the equivalent of a high school level when other kids my age hadn't even been called up for training. I was smart and clever, but with no friends and no adults to lean on I also felt entirely out of place.

"Your parents took me in as a friend, or maybe as a mascot. When they got more serious, I wasn't jealous exactly, but I did feel abandoned. I didn't understand why they didn't have room for me in everything they did together.

"The Mauvais was rising to power right at this time. He drew me to him like a butterfly hunter with a net. It's likely he was using me from the start. He was a strong wizard, but not clever, not inventive. I was. He praised me, he needed me, and his attention was hard to resist. I'm sure a psychologist would tell me I was in need of some type of parental figure. I wanted to impress him. I wanted him to like me so much he wouldn't abandon me. If I was a rich kid, I'd probably have bought him things, but I wasn't wealthy.

"I did, however, like to tinker with things and I liked coming up with silly ideas, and one day I built this amazing watch that could mess with time and affect magic. To me it seemed no more wicked than a joy buzzer. I was too young, and I suppose too proud, to realize the danger it might pose. I made sure the Mauvais saw it. When he showed his interest, I boasted about what the watch could potentially do.

"I was completely joking around, of course. Like when you brag about something you're going to do but you really have no intention of ever doing it. The Mauvais zeroed in on that potential, though, and told me to make it work, make it do the things I was only joking about. I knew it was wrong, but I didn't want him to dislike me, so I did it anyway.

"Again, I was showing off, wanting approval, craving attention. Which meant I imbued the watch with a power it never should have had, a magic I should have been smart enough to stay away from. To demonstrate what I'd done, I brought my pet parakeet — who'd died just that morning — back to life.

"The Mauvais wanted me to do more with the watch, make it even more powerful, but by then I'd already proven myself with the thing. I was bored with it and impatient to move on to something new to impress him with. I gave him the watch, which he soon filled with his magic. It wasn't long before he was using it in ways I'd have never imagined.

"By that time, your parents had finished their training with the police and we'd been slowly rebuilding our friendship. Their support and the things they told me about the Mauvais brought me around to realize I needed to distance myself from him.

"So yes, the watch I designed had some evil tricks hidden inside its gears. I'm not trying to pass blame, but he built on those bad aspects. His power and his intention made the watch what it came to be, not me."

I thought of what Dodding had told me about the watch. Alastair had made it. He was the first one to make it work. His magic had jumpstarted the watch. I toyed with the remaining sliver of tart, but couldn't find the desire to eat it.

"So your magic was in the watch. The Mauvais's power was in the watch. I took on the watch's power, so both your and the Mauvais's power is in me," I said slowly, trying to wrap my head around the implications. I recalled what Fiona had told me about how strands of magic intertwined, making them near impossible to separate. "Does that mean our three magics are bound together?"

"That's what I had been working on. It has to do with the membrane concept I've been trying to teach you. Well, not a membrane, more of a filter. It would have finally been a way to separate entangled strands of magic.

"I thought I had it figured out when I asked for the watch to be sent to Portland. Then you came along." He smiled in a way I think was meant to be teasingly flippant, but fell a little flat. "Now, the magic has been blended in a way no one ever expected. You, me, the Mauvais, our magic is now tangled together. My magic within the watch should have dissipated over time. It's hard to say how much, but now that your power has boosted all the magic in the watch..."

He didn't complete the sentence, but there was no need for him to. My interference had ratcheted up all the magic in the watch, even magic that might have been nearly absent. I thought of the times I'd caught the scent of cinnamon on Alastair. Faint, but there. The same scent I'd detected on the Mauvais when I fought him. Was the scent of the Mauvais hovering around me as well?

"Can I just," I waggled my fingers in front of my chest, "filter out your magic from his and give it back to you?"

"That would be great, but no. Once magic combines within a person like that, it's difficult to section it back out. It would have been challenging enough to do it with two strands of magic, but add in a third and..."

As his words trailed off, a couple strode by outside, laughing, holding onto one another, living and enjoying their non-magical lives. Their arms twining around one another made me think of the magic twining within me. A thought struck me.

"So you could die if I'm killed while the watch's magic is in me?"

Alastair nodded slowly. "Which is another reason I'm really keen to keep you alive. Not my main reason, though." He squeezed my hand then let go. Distractedly, I took the final bite of my dessert, finding no enjoyment in the nutty sweetness on my tongue.

CHAPTER THIRTY-EIGHT
AN UNWELCOME LESSON

After Alastair walked me back to the Tower, I went straight to my room and cracked open the books Banna had left. There's just something about the idea that your brain will be wiped clean if you don't do your homework that adds a keen motivation to your studies.

I also produced no snarky comments and no grumblings when, early the next morning, I had back-to-back lessons with Rafi and Mr. Tenpenny, nor when I was told to expect more of the same that afternoon. I was then left to go back to my room for lunch where Mr. T told me to use the time on background work, not just seeing how many times my lunch plate could refill.

With a maelstrom of new information roller derby-ing around my head, the time I should have spent sleeping the night before had been spent thinking, and apparently it wasn't quite ready to stop. Too full of nervous energy to sit, I paced my room as I munched on a thick Cornish pasty. I kept wondering about Tobey, about whether he had lied to me about the building, or if he'd just made a stupid mistake.

Also, what if Tobey wasn't really Tobey? What if the Mauvais was up to his Morphing tricks again? It wasn't a comforting idea that I might have been in the cramped file room with the

Mauvais, but in some ways it was better than thinking Tobey had deliberately deceived me. And if the Mauvais was using the Morphing Spell again, well, that just struck me as vastly unoriginal.

But could he have even done a Morphing Spell? It was, after all, a trick that required a fair amount of magical strength; and by pulling the watch's magic, I had taken a good chunk of the Mauvais's power. Still, he had been weakened before. If, as Alastair had said, the Mauvais was gaining power from another source, from someone in HQ, then he could be strong enough to morph again.

I shook my head at this line of thought. I couldn't accept Tobey might be the Mauvais. After all, where was the scent? If the Mauvais was using the Morphing Spell, he'd have to cover his scent up with cologne, with cigarette smoke, or with plain old body odor. But Tobey just smelled like Tobey. Sort of that clean, forgettable scent you get when walking down the soap aisle in the store. Tobey smelled like nothing more than well-scrubbed human because he had no magic to hide. His own or the Mauvais's.

All this rattled around my head while I stared out my window, mindlessly caught up in watching a couple on the wall trying to get someone to take their picture, then making wide, emphatic gestures as they explained to a volunteer how to use their camera. I told myself to snap back to attention, planted my butt in the back-breaking chair at my table, and pushed my lunch plate away.

I needed to study and couldn't be distracted with the antics of tourists, with endless servings of food, or with sifting through files in the dead of night. The sooner I could control my magic, the sooner I wouldn't be extracted out of existence, and the sooner I could search for my parents.

I focused on the book in front of me. *The Zen of Membrane Magic and Power That Flows Like Water* was a bit more philosophical than I'd prefer, but it was helping me understand the concepts of balance. Plus, it had lovely drawings of pools, ponds, and waterfalls in Asian-style gardens.

The calming scenes reminded me of being around Alastair. He had protected me. Again. It was hard to remain suspicious of someone who kept intervening to save your life. And holy Zen waves, when he had held me to him....

Studies be damned, I couldn't stop replaying it. If I hadn't been so freaked out about Tobey or my parents being trapped in a burning building, I'd have wanted to stay crushed up against Alastair for at least a few hours. I couldn't deny just how good I felt when I was near him, and there was also no denying that the attraction between us was getting more difficult to resist. Again, came the thought that the sooner I controlled my magic, the sooner we could—

Could what? A relationship with Alastair would mean facing up to my own fears of trusting someone, of opening up to someone, of being vulnerable to someone. Thanks to the cruelty of my endless parade of evil foster parents, none of those concepts were ones I'd had much luck with in my life. Mr. Wood had been the rare exception, but even from him I kept myself guarded, never opening up too much.

Book, Cassie. Read your damn book.

I had a choice, I thought after managing to read half a paragraph: Alastair could be my teacher, or we could test out how our lips fit together. And since that second option would be exhausting for him until I was better able to contain my magic, and because Alastair had shown he was a dedicated and skilled teacher, I opted to forego the smooching for training. Of course, that was easy to promise myself when the man himself wasn't right next to me.

Since my attempts to read were going nowhere, I decided to do some practical work on my own. I flourished my way through the motions Mr. Tenpenny and Rafi had gone over with me that morning, and was just about ready to try a Binding Spell on my pillow when someone knocked on my door.

I checked the bedside clock. I had more work to do with Busby and Rafi later, but it was only two o'clock. I approached the door cautiously, my fingers tingling in preparation to defend myself.

"Open the door, Black. I can smell you in there."

I blew out an annoyed huff of air through my lips, then opened the door and found myself face to face with the unlovely sight of my landlord.

"Where's Mr. Wood?" I asked immediately. If Morelli was here, who was taking care of my battered boss?

"He's fine. He's got a physical therapist in early this morning."

Which could only mean Morelli was here to get his rent, or to tell me how many days I had before rent was due.

"I told you when I left that I set up my rent payment to come to you automatically."

He grinned. "That's not why I'm here, Black." I did not like the sound of that. "You gonna invite me in?"

"Why should I?"

"Because I get to be your teacher today."

I groaned, but stood aside to let him in. It only made sense that I should have to spar against other creatures, but if I was going to have to go up against a half-troll, couldn't it be Chester? It'd be a breeze, all I'd have to do is distract him with a particularly lively rat.

Nevertheless, best to get this ordeal over with as soon as possible. I made some space by pushing my chair against the wall.

"Alright, Eugene, let's do this," I said as I took my stance, bowed, and raised my hands to signal I was ready.

"What the hell are you doing? I'm not fighting a girl. Put your bony arms down. And don't call me Eugene."

"Then why are you here?"

He pulled a stack of papers from the envelope he'd been holding and dropped them on the table. He then took a good look out the window.

"Nice view. Anyway," he turned to me and thumped a meaty index finger on the file, "you get to learn how to detect forgeries. Hear you're not so good at that despite your supposed gifts and what you're meant to do."

"Meant to do? The balance thing?"

"Nah, forget I said anything."

I stared at him, then shook my head. I needed to spend my mental energy learning, not trying to make sense of whatever was bouncing around my landlord's thick skull.

"Is this a one-time lesson, or are you going to be showing up regularly?"

"You can learn the basics today, but I might come back just to annoy you." He opened the envelope and pulled out several pieces of paper of various sizes, quality, and color.

Morelli first had me sift through ten documents ranging from handwritten letters to bank statements to passport applications to see if I could determine right off the bat which one was fake. Needless to say, I failed.

"You're looking with your eyes, not your magic," he said, actually taking on a teaching tone, not a Cassie's-a-dunce tone. "Drift your fingers over the words, smell the paper, talk to the document."

"Talk to it? Pick it up and ask it if it's fake?"

"You really have no sense of nuance, do you?"

"Says the guy who I can hear farting from an entire floor away."

"The documents, Black."

I tried again. I wasn't about to talk to the papers, but I smelled each sheet and made a pile of possible forgeries with Morelli rumbling out exaggerated sighs of impatience. Then I hovered my fingers over each line of these possible positives. Something like, but much fainter than, the tingle of static you sometimes get when you take off a sweater danced up my middle finger as I ran it over a certificate of completion for someone's day-long training in Microsoft Word. I drifted my finger over the lines for the date, the course title, and the person's name.

"This one," I said. "The name's been changed."

"Good. Slow, but good. It's rare for someone to get that precise on a first try."

"So, I pass? We're done?" I asked hopefully.

"You're sufficient, but a snail would seem fast compared to your detection speed. If you had a file drawer full of paperwork, it would take you weeks to get through it all. I could do it in about ten minutes."

"So, no magical secretarial work for me. Let me tell you," I said, coating my words with sarcasm, "that's really heartbreaking."

"It's an important skill," Morelli said defensively. "I'll mark down that this isn't something you need intensive training in, and that you have some natural aptitude for it. But you need to work at it, so don't think I won't throw a pop quiz at you now and then."

"Speaking of important skills, what's with all these clients Mr. Wood has gotten? Or, more to the point, who's this interloper doing the cosmetics?"

"Daisy."

"Tobey's girlfriend?"

"Yeah, you've seen her. She's a whiz with magicking up some beauty. Even on dead people."

"I knew that perfect hair and skin couldn't be natural."

Morelli made a snide comment about green-eyed monsters. After explaining a few other principles of forgery detection, he declared we were done for the day, and that he was supposed to take me down to Olivia's office.

As we circled our way down the stairs and through the myriad of corridors the White Tower seemed to grow each night, Morelli made small talk centered on the latest news about Portland. When we entered Olivia's office, it was empty, but Morelli still didn't leave. Was he worried I was going to run off or something?

"So, how is Mr. Wood?" I asked to break the silence. "Cholesterol levels out the roof yet?"

"He's doing remarkably well and his cholesterol levels are well within the normal range." I wondered if it was some sort of magic, cholesterol-free bacon my landlord used for his BLTs. "Oh, and he told me to give you this." Morelli pulled a wad of purple and pink yarn from his envelope. He gave it a shake, then handed it over.

I turned it around a few times. It wasn't squared off, it wasn't round, it was just sort of a...shape.

"What's it supposed to be?"

"I think it's supposed to be a cat. Turn it just so and you can see the tail."

I did, and if I squinted my eyes, I could see the vague shape of a cat. Okay, a cat who had possibly lost all nine lives in a tragic car accident, but cat-like nonetheless. As Morelli was relating Mr. Wood's crochet enthusiasm, someone knocked on the office door.

CHAPTER THIRTY-NINE

OFFICE MEETINGS

Morelli and I both tensed. Olivia would not knock on her own office door. He gave me a stern stay-put stare and went to answer it. It turned out to be Alastair who strode toward me with Morelli close by his side.

"Finished?" Alastair asked us. "I don't want to intrude."

"She's all yours," Morelli said with a grin as he gathered up his envelope. He then headed back to the door, pausing at the threshold to add, "Or at least that's what I hear."

"You are not amusing," I said, to which he responded by displaying the single finger he probably used to tally his IQ.

Alastair came over and we were close enough to touch. I wanted to reach out for his hand — a strange desire for me since I did not make first moves. Too much of a chance of rejection. But that fear of making a fool of myself wasn't what forced me to jam my hands into my pockets. I was resolved to be a student and not to be distracted. I took a step back and asked what we were working on today.

"Olivia and I were going to try some new membrane tactics with you, but I just found out I have another lecture to attend. I can't believe how many talks these London Magics sit through on a weekly basis, and half of them seem spontaneous. A lecture's announced and we're expected to go. It's annoying." He darted a glance at me, a sparkling light in his eyes. "For more reasons than one."

Don't be distracted. Don't be distracted. Damn, his eyes were blue. Stop it, Cassie!

"Yeah, I've noticed Magics aren't big on schedules. It's a wonder Runa is so stringent about her appointment keeping."

"Well, at least this one should be interesting."

"What's the topic?"

"Prophecies: What to Believe and What to Ignore."

"It does sound good, but don't worry, I'm sure they'll find some way to make it boring."

"Look, Cass," he said in a whisper as he glanced to the door, "I'm not supposed to say anything, but I'm tired of keeping secrets from you."

"This doesn't sound good. What is it?"

"Your next test?" I nodded. "It's this Sunday."

"Sunday? But—" It was already Wednesday afternoon. Olivia had said the test would be within the week, but I'd just assumed, with so much at stake, I'd be given the full seven days. "Are you giving me the test?" I asked, then chided myself for being so stupidly hopeful. Of course they wouldn't allow Alastair to test me again.

"No, and I swear I don't know who you're going up against, so don't ask me." He took my hands, but lightly enough that we could jerk apart if anyone walked in.

"I thought you and Busby were working on something to get me out of this. I'm not a criminal." He arched an eyebrow as if to say, *You kind of are.* "Okay, I stole the watch from Runa's, but it was for the greater good."

"I know. We still have a few days, but this isn't Portland where things are a bit more lax. This is HQ."

HQ, the place that had once planned to destroy the watch at the risk of Alastair's life without even telling him.

"That's why they were so angry about you kissing me. They knew you knew what the test was really for."

"Yes, and I swear to you I did not throw that test in your favor. I'm sure they'll be putting you up against someone stronger than me to make sure. But you proved yourself once; you'll prove yourself again."

I released Alastair's hands and slumped down on the edge of Olivia's desk.

"Can't I just toss the extra magic into a freezer bag?"

"Magic isn't like storing leftover Thanksgiving turkey. If it worked like that, I would have insisted you do so a long time ago. Unfortunately, the strength of the magic in you is why you can't just be drained."

"Why not? Runa drained me."

Well, she tried, but a breakfast of donuts had thrown a wrench in her efforts.

"Before, you could be. Now, with the watch's magic in you, if even a scrap of power is left in you, it— How do I put this?" He pondered for a moment, searching for the right words. "It will refill itself within you. It's why, for the most part, you no longer get tired during your training. The magic you use just pops back up."

I thought back to my first days of trying to do magic, back when it was only my magic inside me. Those efforts left me exhausted. But ever since taking on the watch's power, sure I'd felt hungry after doing hard spells, I'd felt like I needed a break on occasion, but I hadn't felt wiped out by using magic. Except, of course, for those first couple trips to the file room, but that had probably just been jet/portal lag since it hadn't exactly required any magic to thumb through drawers full of paperwork.

"And that's why I'd need to be extracted." I stood up from the desk. "Because they can't risk any of the Mauvais's magic growing in me."

Alastair nodded solemnly. "And if the Mauvais gets even a small amount of your power transferred to him, it will grow there too. He wouldn't need much to gain strength once again."

"Here's an idea," I said, trying to lighten the mood. "You build a magic centrifuge, then we give my blood a spin and separate out the Mauvais's magic from mine."

"I'll look into that," he said, and his eyes brightened with his smile. "But for now, let's get you through the test. After that, we'll work on more subtle aspects of separating out your magic. We will get the watch's power out of you, and if we can't, we'll make sure you know exactly how to use it."

My hands again in his, Alastair leaned forward. Heat surged from my fingertips to my toes. I reminded myself I was supposed to be his student, nothing more. But it was getting a little difficult to stick to my resolve as his breath brushed against my lips. Then, from the hallway, came the *click clack* of heels on stone flooring. We both jumped back at the sound, and I conjured a Shield Spell just as the door creaked open.

"That's exactly right, Cassie. Good job," Alastair said, far too stiffly. Like a bad actor reciting his lines.

"Cassie, I've got other matters to attend to, but Busby is ready for you," Olivia said, her eyes narrowing as she cast a skeptical glance over me and Alastair. "He's in the practice room down the hall, if you're done here," she added in a tone that indicated, *You most definitely are done here.*

"Yep," I said, taking down the Shield Spell. "Only so many shields you can whip up in one day. Enjoy your lecture," I said as I hurried toward the door.

"Yes, our lecture," Olivia said coyly, but it wasn't directed toward me. She'd already turned toward Alastair. A familiar pang of worry bit into my gut.

CHAPTER FORTY

BETRAYAL

Telling myself I was being a paranoid and jealous lunkhead, I headed down the hallway. Several rooms lined the dim corridor, and Olivia hadn't told me which one I was supposed to go to. I decided it must be the one at the end farthest from her office. Not because I'd suddenly become psychic or anything, but because it was the only room whose door Tobey was loitering in front of. When he turned to face me, his look was so stony, I jerked to a stop and tripped back a pace or two.

"What?" he asked.

"Nothing," I said casually. "I'm supposed to have a lesson with your grandfather. Is he in there?"

"No, he's got a thing to go to. You've got a lesson with Rafi in an hour. Rooftop. I told him I'd let you know."

"Okay, thanks."

Annoyed with everyone's inability to stick to a schedule, I figured I'd go out to get some fresh air. Clouds had crept in during Morelli's lesson and I wanted to stretch my legs before a rain storm kicked up. I moved to step past Tobey, but he blocked my path.

"Did you hear everyone talking about that building blowing up?" he asked.

"Kind of hard to miss." Especially when you've been tricked

into standing right next to it. "That information you gave me from Olivia's files was fake, did you know that? The whole file might have been."

"Sorry, I didn't know," he said, not sounding apologetic in the least. "Wait, you didn't go there, did you?"

I was glad to see Tobey wasn't burnt to a crisp, but something made me hesitant to tell him about the previous night. Both the sneaking out, and the conversation I'd had with Alastair.

"No. I was wiped out from all the training and went to bed early."

"Right. Look, I wanted to ask you something." He gestured down the hall in the direction I'd just tried to go. With the looming clouds closing in outside and only one window to light the long space, the hallway was as dark as twilight. "Come on, let's talk down there."

"That's not a question," I said. He sighed in a way that said he wasn't in the mood for my smart comments. "Fine," I relented. "Off we go."

"Look," he said, stopping and turning toward me even though we'd only gotten about halfway down the hall, "I was wondering if maybe we could go out sometime. I hear the galleries around here are open late on certain nights."

Tobey. Asking me out? What in Merlin's beard was going on? And then, to make the situation even weirder, he reached up and brushed the back of his fingers along my right cheek.

"Like a date?" I scoffed, flicking his hand away as if swatting aside an annoying fruit fly. "I thought you had a girlfriend." And what would Daisy do if she found out Tobey was two-timing on her with me? Would she exact her revenge with cosmetics, making Mr. Wood's clients look like something akin to drunken mimes?

"No, not like a date," he said, cramming his hands into his

pockets and sounding flustered. "Why do you have to be so impossible?"

"Everyone's got a talent."

"I shouldn't have asked." He stopped walking and stared at me. "I should have known you'd be a jerk about it. You do know it's a lost cause with Alastair, right?"

"You know nothing about it."

"Don't I?" He pointed to the door we'd stopped in front of. It was Olivia's office, and the door was partially open, providing a clear view of her desk. The desk Olivia was leaning against as Alastair pressed against her. Her fingers tugged on the back of his shirt. His face was buried in her neck. Her head tilted back and a soft moan escaped her lips.

I wanted to barge in. I wanted to shout at Alastair, rip him off of her, and ask them what the hell they were doing. I wanted to tear Olivia's braids out by the roots. But I couldn't.

I'd been right all along. Alastair had been using me, he was playing me, he was not to be trusted. It would have been better if he'd just snatched out my heart and fed it to the ravens. I stormed off to the window at the end of the hall, crossing my arms over my chest and staring blindly out at the cloud-darkened grounds. Tobey followed close on my heels.

"You're a jerk, Tobey Tenpenny," I said and slugged him in the biceps. He grabbed my hands and pulled me to him. Then his lips were on mine, and his arms were around my waist. My first thought was to knee him in the groin, but my next jumbled thoughts were, "Wow, he is an amazing kisser. He won't get weakened by me. Alastair can go straight to hell." With my mouth clamped on his, the only way to breathe was to inhale. There was no scent. Only that clean, soapy smell.

A shadow crossed before my closed eyes. Then something scratched and scraped against the window. I ignored it. Team

Brain and Team Heart had been completely stunned into silence, both by what I'd just seen and what was happening.

Wanting Tobey to press himself against me, wanting pleasure and anticipation to drive away the anger and the hurt, I pulled him closer. He slipped one hand under my shirt. His lips moved to my neck. In one ear he whispered my name, in the other came the scrambling of claws trying to find purchase and the batting of wings against glass. The noise made me think we needed to find somewhere private.

I opened my eyes to see Winston practically attacking the window. He cried and cawed and crashed his beak against the pane. I pulled back, dizzy from the kiss, confused over what I'd just been doing, over what I had just seen, over what the hell I'd just wanted to do with Tobey Bloody Tenpenny. The bird relented his attack and gripped onto the window ledge, but he didn't stop watching us. I suddenly felt very tired.

"I need to go," I blurted. I then darted into the stairwell and sprinted on burning legs back to my room.

Once inside, I bolted the door. I didn't want to see anyone. I didn't want to go to my lesson with Rafi. I wanted to go home. I wanted to cuddle up with Pablo, to have an IPA, and to lose myself in a library book.

Instead, I was in London. Alone. Both betrayed and a betrayer. And, glancing at the clock, it would appear I'd even missed my magically appearing tea time.

Exhaustion like I hadn't felt since my first days of training overwhelmed me. I wanted nothing more than to throw myself onto the bed, to fall asleep and forget about the rest of this day. But before I could flop properly, Winston showed up at my window. I let him in and he hopped onto the stiff back of one of the chairs. I broke open a large packet of cookies, handed him one, then nibbled half-heartedly on my own.

After we'd eaten our way through the entire package of treats, I was still bone-tired, but my head felt much less loopy. I still had time to kill before Rafi's lesson and I needed something to do. I needed to not think about Alastair. I needed to not think about Tobey. Of course, this was impossible as these were the only two subjects rampaging through my brain.

Like a gift from the gods of stationery, distraction then appeared. On the dark carpet just in front of my door was a square, cream-colored envelope. In my rush to lock myself away from everyone, I must have missed it when I'd come back.

When I'd come back from…

I groaned as the image of me smashing my lips against Tobey's flashed into my mind.

"That didn't happen. That just did not happen," I muttered as I crossed the room. I bent over to pick up the envelope, feeling ready to keep lowering myself until I reached the floor where I would sleep for at least a dozen hours. But curiosity kept my eyelids propped open.

Taking the envelope back to the table, I felt none of the tingling I'd felt on the forged certificate. I glanced around, you know, like someone might be in the room with me, then asked, "Are you a test from Morelli?"

The envelope said nothing in reply.

I think the stress was getting to me.

Winston hopped from the chair over to the envelope and cocked his head as if questioning it himself.

"What do you think? Safe to touch?"

He chattered his heavy black beak and bobbed his head. This was the point I'd gotten to: I was talking to envelopes and taking advice from a bird.

I peeled open the flap. Inside was a sheet of paper, the top third of which had been torn off. What was left had a series of lines like an order form, then a large box at the bottom to write in details. I sniffed the sheet and ran my fingers over it, but detected nothing other than your standard-issue cheap paper and low-quality ink.

But this wasn't an ordinary form for supplies. It was an intake report. For people.

Two people.

FORTY-ONE
REPORTS AND UNICORNS

The name "Simon Starling" had been typed on one of the lines. Poorly centered on the line below was "Chloe Starling".

But it was the detail box that turned my stomach:

> Subjects collected and questioned without remorse regarding the news they'd obtained at the—

(here the ink was smudged)

> Subjects have given up no information. A full draining was undertaken to see if we could extract any lingering knowledge from their magic, but none could be found.

A sharp, feminine hand, writing in purple ink, had added:

> However, after the annoying and inconvenient deaths of so many test subjects, we finally discovered our technique is on the right track. Subjects were kept alive. They're to be stored here until further notice.

Along the bottom of the sheet, next to a black "HQ" stamp, someone else had written:

> This sheet was found by one of our agents. We have visited the above address. The building was empty. The Starlings are officially presumed dead.

"What address?" I shouted at the paper.

I would have gone straight there that very night if I had the stupid address. Maybe HQ had missed a room in their search. My parents were still in that building. I was sure of it. Or at least, I wanted to be sure. And I wanted to do this on my own. I didn't need any help from the lying, deceitful, evil watch-making Alastair, nor from the confusion-inducing Tobey. I could get my parents. I *would* get them. But where the hell was this damn building?

My phone's timer trilled out an alarm. I fumbled the device out of my back pocket and stabbed the screen to silence it. I'd have to plot later. For now, it was time to trudge up to the roof and pretend nothing was on my mind.

In the desperate hope that I wouldn't run into Tobey or Alastair, and especially not Olivia, I skulked my way up staircases and peered around every corner before racing down hallways. As such, I felt more than a little rattled when I met Rafi on the rooftop of the White Tower.

The two of us were the same height and I'd guess the same weight, but somehow his slim frame came across as greyhound sleek, whereas mine was more Gawky Teenager, like my limbs still didn't quite fit. He was a racing hound, whereas I was a gangling moose.

"What are we working on this time?" I asked, as he handed me a vest. From the flags whipping, the trees rustling, and the white caps cresting on the Thames, I could tell the dark clouds were indeed going to bring an umbrella-breaking storm. But thanks to the charmed netting around the rooftop, as I donned the vest, I detected only a light breeze across my arms.

"The membrane, defense, offense, whatever I feel like putting you through." He put on a menacing tone, but smiled at me, his dark eyes warm and friendly. Even though I knew Rafi would make me work hard, I needed a little friendliness right about then and some of the tension eased from my shoulders.

We went through the polite bowing motions then set to sparring. It wasn't a full-on battle, more like Rafi tossing slow-moving Stunning and Binding Spells my way then advising me on how to deflect them, which charms would be most effective, and how to switch between spells efficiently.

Actually, he was a really good teacher, and I wondered why he was in administration. When we took a break — lemon tarts were being magically served up that afternoon — I asked him.

"We all teach. No matter what our main job is, any Magic can be called in to instruct. There's some who do make careers of teaching." I thought of Fiona. "But for the most part, we're all substitute teachers. I suppose it helps keep us on our toes. I mean, I can't recall the last time I whipped up a good Binding Spell or really thought through the whole membrane thing. Teaching refreshes our own knowledge, it doesn't just add to yours."

"Glad I could be such a good public servant and help you all out like this."

Rafi laughed and finished off his piece of tart, then served us each another slice.

"But what about other defensive tactics?" I asked.

"How do you mean?"

"Besides the physical stuff. In Portland, there was this guy who had been under the BrainSweeping Charm—"

"You don't have to worry about that," Rafi said, cutting me off. "That spell can only be done on non-magics."

"Oh, right." I took a bite of my tart, feeling a little dumb.

"But you're not far off the mark. There's the Confounding Charm. It can affect Magics and Norms, makes them see things that aren't there, not see things that are there, or make them do what you want them to. It's a vile spell, and I think the Council is considering banishing it. Of course, the Mauvais loved it."

"So I've been told. But how would you fight it?"

"You have to have a strong mind." Rafi arched an eyebrow. "You have to trust your own instincts. You have to trust those closest to you and know in your own heart what they would and wouldn't do." He pushed his plate away. "Want to give it a go?"

"Sure," I said hesitantly, trust and confidence not being my strong suit. "Just don't break my brain."

"You won't even know I'm there. That's the scary part. You can't feel it."

"So how the hell do I fight it."

"Think happy thoughts?"

"Not my specialty."

"Come on," Rafi said, his eyes glinting playfully. "Stand up and let's try. I'm not quite sure how to do this, but the tart should help." I stood in front of him while he tapped his index finger on his pointed chin, thinking, plotting. "Okay, I'm going to make it so you see a unicorn standing next to me. You're going to make that unicorn vanish by telling yourself the unicorn is not there, that Rafi Singha is highly allergic to unicorns."

"Are you?"

"All elves are allergic to those horny bastards. So, if there really was a unicorn there, I'd be sneezing and wheezing. Ready?"

"Not really."

"Too bad. Now, don't try to resist it. I want you to see how unnoticeable this really is. Keep your mind open and let me in. Once you see it, once you get a good feel for it, then I want you to try to fight it."

Rafi closed his eyes. His face tightened with concentration. It took some time and at first it faded in and out, but after a few minutes there appeared a solid unicorn standing next to him.

It was gorgeous. Really, I felt like some medieval maiden wanting to touch its horn, stroke its hide, let it rest its head in my lap. It was that real.

No, it isn't.

I stared at the unicorn, resolutely telling myself it wasn't there. Insisting to myself it was only Rafi tricking me. A shock of pain pierced through a point somewhere in the center of my head. If I ended up with brain damage from this…

The pain eased back. Perhaps I was being too intentional. I relaxed my mind, concentrated on the unicorn, and asked it to go away.

The unicorn started to fade. I fought the urge to cheer my success and kept my focus. I hated to see it go. It was so delicate and I swear it was smiling at me. No, it had to go. I couldn't let another Magic play mind games with me.

The unicorn popped out of existence.

And then, just as Rafi opened his eyes with happy surprise, the unicorn popped back into existence.

"Close your eyes again," I said. "Let me—"

Suddenly, Rafi's wide-open eyes flamed red. He backed away from the animal, sneezing over and over. The unicorn itself — the alluring beast that was supposed to be nothing more than a planted figment of my imagination — began running around the rooftop in a panic. If not for the sturdy mesh surrounding the rec area, the creature would have gone over the edge.

Meanwhile, Rafi gasped for air. He grabbed at his throat in the universal signal of choking. His airways had shut.

I threw a Stunning Spell at the unicorn. It collapsed in the center of the tennis court. I screamed for help, then, thanks to the CPR lessons Mr. Wood required me to take, I started mouth-to-mouth on Rafi.

Thankfully, the magical medic office was adjacent to the rooftop court. Someone arrived within seconds of my cries, pushed me back, and conjured a Clearing Charm to instantly flush the allergens from Rafi's system, followed by a Reduction Spell to open his airways. Rafi shuddered. Then, like a vacuum on overdrive, he sucked in great gasps of air.

I wanted to stay and make sure he was okay, but before I knew what was happening, someone grabbed hold of my upper arm. I was hit with the spicy scent of spruce as Olivia led me away. She didn't say a word as she practically dragged me to her office.

I knew I was in deep trouble when no desserts appeared on her desk. Well, and the fact that she was looming over me, her arms crossed over her chest.

"I'm sorry," I said, a questioning tone in my voice. What else could I say? Well, besides demand she tell me what she'd been doing with Alastair.

"*Sorry* does not cut it, Ms. Black. You nearly killed him." She took several deep breaths, taming her voice that had risen to a shout, nearly a scream. As for me, I felt like I couldn't breathe. "Explain what happened."

I did, making sure to add that it was Rafi's idea. Not to throw him under the double-decker bus or anything, but he could have warned me what might happen.

"This is another example of your magic being too far out of control. You are really not showing any signs of improvement and it is worrying."

"I am improving."

"I have an assistant who almost died and a unicorn that will need to be relocated because of your magical power. Power that you can't seem to rein in."

"Are you kidding me?" I snapped. All the anger, all the hurt over seeing her with Alastair combined with my overall frustration at their refusal to see that I was trying, that I was doing my best. "I followed your stupid rules and didn't absorb one molecule of magic during my test. I performed a Floating Charm without any instruction." I didn't bother to add I almost blew away. "And I was able to do a Solas Charm last night with barely a second thought. Yes, I screw up now and then, but I am learning."

"Solas Charm?" Olivia asked, abruptly changing to a tone and expression of worried concern.

"Yes."

"Last night?"

Was her fury with me blocking her ears?

"Yes."

"That's how he knew you were there."

"Who knew I was where?"

"The Mauvais. At the building. Yes, I know about your little escape." I wondered if Alastair the Betrayer had told her, but she didn't give me a chance to butt in. "The light generated by a Solas Charm has a trace on it. It's often used as a way to alert other Magics if you get into trouble, but it can also be used to track a Magic. This should have been explained to you."

"Yes, it should have." I bit back my sniping tone. A little. "You want me to learn so much in so little time, but you seem to offer only half instructions. You tell me to do things, but not how. You teach me things, but leave off the important, this-could-be-dangerous bits. It's a little frustrating."

"I can imagine so, but you have to see you are a risk. To yourself. To us. I'm sorry to tell you this," she said in a cold way that implied she wasn't sorry at all, that she was just relaying news she had no vested interest in, "but your next test must take place Friday."

"Friday? I thought I had until Sunday," I protested, as if forty-eight extra hours would really make any difference.

"When he was here, Morelli detected that more than one forgery had made its way to my desk. It's a huge breech of security." Olivia's voice changed as she said this, less detached and far more critical. "And some feel it only compounds the problem you present. As such, a tribunal decided that if you made one more error, no more training time would be allowed. The test would have to take place at the earliest chance." She paused, her strong shoulders slumping almost as if she truly regretted what had been decided. "And I do worry about your ability to pass that test."

"You and me both. Are we done?" I didn't wait for her answer. I got up and headed toward the door.

"Ms. Black," Olivia called, "please understand. This isn't my—"

I shut the door behind me before she could finish making her excuses.

CHAPTER FORTY-TWO

SILENCING SPELLS

By the time I got back to my room, my head swooned. So much for the theory that my high-octane magic could keep me from getting worn out. But apparently the stress of knowing I'd soon be literally fighting for my sanity, the gut-wrenching hurt over Alastair's betrayal, the disgust with myself for kissing Tobey, and the self-hatred over nearly killing Rafi had gotten hold of me and was squeezing every bit of energy from my cells.

I looked at the intake report I'd left on the table.

The file Olivia had stashed in her desk may have been fake, but this paper…I had no doubt it was real.

In my earlier bravado that afternoon I had told myself I would act that very night, but at the moment I could barely raise my arms. There was no way I had the brain power to determine where this building was, nor the energy to fend off an evil wizard in his evil lair.

I would sleep. Tomorrow I would go through the motions of my pointless lessons while taking every chance I could to uncover the address for the intake form. Then tomorrow night, possibly my last night as a thinking human, I would rescue my parents.

Tomorrow, not tonight. My mom and dad might be suffering somewhere, but they would just have to wait.

I felt like a real lowlife for the cold thought, but it was true. Even in top form, I'd be risking my neck to get to them. Going in the state I was would have been suicide and would do them no good. They'd waited this long for their freedom. They could wait one more night. Plus, they were magical morons. Did they even have a concept of time anymore?

A plate of food soon appeared on the table. I ate it without tasting a thing. I think it was spaghetti, I can't recall. The plate filled again and I cleared half of it, leaving my window open in case Winston wanted to stop by for a meatball. I then cast a Silencing Spell around my room before falling into the deepest sleep I'd had since arriving in London.

I slept straight through the night, I slept past dawn, and I probably would have slept until noon if someone hadn't been blaring a trumpet outside my window. After a few creative, albeit sleep-mumbled curses, I got up and marched over to the window, noticing the plate was empty except for one tiny piece of tomato. Clever Winston.

Busby was down in the lawn below doing a horrible rendition of the *Reveille*. But given that he was dead and could barely speak a few weeks ago, his producing sound from any wind instrument was a pretty impressive feat. Still, it was far too early for so much noise.

"Shut up!" I shouted. Mr. Tenpenny lowered the offending horn and squinted up at me.

"You didn't respond to my knocking at your door."

"I did a Silencing Spell," I called, kind of hoping this would impress him. No control, indeed.

"Well, because of that, you missed the news that you're—" He stopped to suck in a couple deep breaths. Not so alive, after all, I thought smugly. "I can't keep shouting like this. I'm coming up."

I removed the Silencing Spell and propped my door open. In the time it took Mr. Tenpenny to get to my room, I'd managed to tame my hair into something that didn't look like it had been ravaged by a drunken pixie in the middle of the night. Mr. T gave a light tap on the door and then entered.

"Oh good, you're ready."

"Ready for what?"

"Oh no, you really didn't hear, did you? You're not supposed to make the Silencing Spell so strong. What if there'd been an emergency?"

"Would you get to the point?"

"You're being tested in," he glanced at the bedside clock, "about twenty minutes."

"They can't do that. I'm supposed to have the test tomorrow. I'm not ready."

"Olivia announced last night that you were."

Of course, Olivia the Neck Kisser. I guess when she wanted someone out of her way, she really wanted them out of her way.

"Who am I up against?"

"I still don't know." He paused. "Look, I know I've been hard on you at times, and I had meant to work more closely with you while we were here, but I think you do have a lot of talent. It is entirely unethical and unfair for them to test you like this, and I promise if you fail I will appeal any decision to extract you. It's ridiculous this tribunal won't give you more time."

"Those aren't exactly encouraging words, but thank you. For what it's worth, I'm glad I brought you back from the dead. Twice."

"Which is why I owe you a chance at life."

He hesitated, clearly fighting with his instinct to remain composed and aloof. I didn't let him. I blame the stress and the emotional confusion for the upcoming un-Cassie-like act of spontaneous affection. I pulled Mr. T into a hug. I even thanked him, but I don't really know why. His words completely freaked me out. He knew I'd fail today.

We broke out of the embrace, both of us looking sheepish and uncomfortable. I hurriedly asked after Rafi, and Mr. T seemed relieved for the change of subject.

"To tell the truth, I think he's perfectly fine, but the Medi Unit at the Tower provides some of the most attentive care and comfortable beds you can find in the magic world."

"So you're saying I've been worried he might die, and he's been milking it?"

"It's practically a vacation for him." Mr. T patted my arm stiffly. "You should get dressed now. I'll meet you at the arena portal. You'll—?"

"I won't run off, if that's what you're about to ask. You guys would just track me down anyway."

With a shrug, Mr. T agreed then left me to finish getting dressed. I hurried, but still took time to make myself presentable. No sense going to your doom without applying a couple layers of mascara first.

I glanced toward the window, looking for Winston. When I didn't see any hint of black feathers, I took a deep breath and left my room, wondering if it would be for the last time.

I was halfway down the spiral stairs, when I came face to face with Tobey. My cheeks flared with embarrassment and it took a mountain of effort to force myself to meet his eyes. Oddly enough, he showed none of the discomfort that was threatening to turn me into a clumsy heap of bones.

"Look, about yesterday," I said.

"What about it?"

Okay, so that's how we're going to play it.

"Nothing, it was just unexpected and we should forget it happened."

He gave me a look that reminded me very much of when Pablo sees me eating ice cream and can't figure out why I'm not giving him any. Tobey then shook his head and rolled his eyes as if this was just another one of Cassie's typical nonsensical moments.

"Anyway," he said as he changed direction and we wound our way down the stairs, "it's weird they're testing you again so soon. Grandpa says it's not fair. And, I guess I agree. I just wanted to wish you luck and hope there aren't any hard feelings between us."

I'd been keenly aware of something very hard between us the day before, but I bit back saying so. Instead, I shrugged and said, "It's fine."

"So, anyway," he said awkwardly when we got to the hallway that would take us to the arena portal, "the V & A has late hours tonight and I was wondering if you wanted to go."

Every single one of these words came out so fast I might have wondered if Tobey was practicing to become an auctioneer. Might have, that is, if I hadn't been dumbstruck by the idea that he was asking me out. Again.

"I might be brainless by tonight."

"They won't do it today. I mean, I'm sure you'll do great, but if you don't, Grandpa says an appeal will be made. That means you'll have a reprieve of at least a few days. So, what do you say?"

"Let me think about it. I've got a lot on my mind right now."

Why this? Why now? I did not need so much weirdness in so little time. I did not need to be in some stupid love triangle/emotional roller coaster with Temperamental Tobey and Adulterous Alastair. First and foremost, I didn't even like Tobey in that way. Second, I needed to magic the poop out of whoever they put me up against. Then I needed to find my parents without getting captured by the Mauvais. I also needed to get back to my job before Daisy dazzled Mr. Wood any further. And once all that was done, maybe I could find time to sort out my love life.

When we reached the arena portal, Mr. T greeted us, seeming pleased to see us together.

"All ready?" he asked.

"Not really," I replied, glancing around to see if anyone else was going through with us.

"Don't worry. Alastair is waiting on the other side."

Which was exactly the news I did not want to hear.

CHAPTER FORTY-THREE

CUPCAKES AND DAHLIAS

When I stepped through the portal from the Tower to the Guildhall arena's hallway, Alastair was indeed waiting. I was more than ready to give him some arctic-level cold shoulder, but in stark contrast to the dismally grey walls, he held out a bouquet of brightly colored dahlias.

"What are these?" I asked, making no effort to take the orange and yellow bouquet.

"Most people know them as flowers. I've heard they're often liked by female humans and seen as a welcome gift."

"Then give them to Olivia."

"What?" Alastair paused and dropped the dahlias to his side. "Why?"

"Because I saw you with her yesterday," I said, walking off in the direction of the arena.

"Of course you did," he said, keeping pace with me. His voice revealed no hint of guilt. What was it with men? "You were there when she showed up to her office. After you left, Olivia spoke with me about the forged files and about your test. I told her you deserved more time and she agreed, but she said there's some tribunal that's pressured her to test you without delay. She told me she had no choice."

"Yeah, I'll bet she was persuasive. Did you put up much of an argument, or was your mouth too busy nibbling on her neck?"

"What? Cassie, no. Olivia would probably drop kick me if I did that. What are you on about?"

I'm not great with people, but I do have a good instinct for when they're being lying sacks of crap. Alastair wasn't lying. He was genuinely confused by my accusations.

"How did she smell?"

"Cassie, this is ridiculous. I really like you. More than like," he added *sotto voce*. "But I can't take the jealousy and suspicion you've been throwing at me lately. I've done nothing to—"

"Alastair," I said firmly. "How did she smell? Like Olivia? Like perfume? Like cigarettes? What?"

"To me, Olivia's magic smells like ripe apples. That's what she's smelled like since we've been here. Cassie, you are at risk, but not everyone is out to get you. Olivia is not the Mauvais." His brow furrowed and the firm, yet caring tone grew serious. "What exactly did you see?"

By then, we had reached the hall at the end of which was the darkened arena. Olivia, who had been speaking with Mr. Tenpenny, caught sight of us, abruptly ended her chat with Busby, and strode toward me. She barely glanced at Alastair before handing me a cupcake. I took it, looking at it warily, as if it might be laced with arsenic or filled with spider eggs or something.

"Eat it quick," she said in a commanding whisper. "And don't tell anyone I gave it to you. I can't believe they're going through with—" Before she could finish this cryptic statement, a bell chimed a cheery, five-note tune. "It's time."

Olivia turned on her three-inch heels and clicked her way toward the arena. I looked at Alastair, he was staring at the arena entrance, a fretful expression intense on his face. He returned his attention to me. The deep worry softened, but only slightly.

"You better eat that," he said.

I sniffed the treat and could detect nothing but deliciousness coming off it. I crammed the cupcake into my mouth. The spongy, chocolate cake and sweet, creamy interior delighted my tongue, and my magic sparkled inside me as I chewed and swallowed.

Alastair took advantage of my moment of bliss and swiped his finger to remove some frosting from the corner of my mouth. He leaned forward as if to kiss me, hesitated, then decided against it. But he didn't lean back. With his eyes locked on mine, he whispered, "Much more than like, okay?"

My throat went tight and my eyes did that stupid prickling thing. I swallowed hard as if I could gulp down any tears trying to make themselves seen. Unable to speak, I nodded and walked with him down the final length of the hall.

Once we entered the arena, it took my eyes a few moments to adjust to the dark. A cold blue light orb hovered over the arena floor like a spotlight. The only other points of illumination were floating dots of fairy lights that reminded me of the slivery flecks in the beads at the ends of Olivia's braids.

With a shaky voice, Alastair wished me luck, told me to keep my head, reminded me to stay in control. He paused, and for a few seconds I thought he might stay with me, but in too little time, he strode away, the forlorn bouquet rustling with his steps.

I wanted to go after him, to grab his hand and run with him back to the portal to Portland, but I was too confused. I honestly didn't know what I had seen the day before, what had truly happened, who to trust. So, before I could go to him, before I could reach for his hand to at least get one of the reassuring squeezes I'd grown accustomed to, he had disappeared into the dark.

There was nothing for it. Like a criminal from Ancient Rome, my fate would be decided in the arena. On shaky legs, I stepped into the center of the sandy oval.

My eyes had adjusted to the darkness, but the silence of the space sent shivers through me. I had expected the chatters and murmurs and cheers I'd heard last time, but for this round of the Cassie Games all was quiet.

I scanned the seats. They were full to capacity. Full of people with pitying looks on their faces. They did not look like people who expected to see me walk out of here a happy woman. The cupcake hung like a stone just below my sternum and I imagined myself hurling the thing up whole like a mother raven feeding her chicks.

From the walkway behind me came footsteps. Quiet, soft steps like a cat walking over gravel. My legs felt rooted to the arena floor. Behind me was the person HQ had decided would test me to my limits. The person who would do everything possible to see me fail.

"Cassie Black, turn and face your opponent," came Olivia's voice.

I turned. My heart sank. It was dark enough in the arena that she didn't need her sunglasses, nor her umbrella, but she still wore her usual long-sleeved, gauzy dress.

CHAPTER FORTY-FOUR

THE OPPONENT

Banna.

One of the original Magics. A witch who'd had centuries to gain skill and build her already substantial power. This was grossly unfair. I darted my gaze around the perimeter of the arena. My eyes caught a flash of yellow dahlia and then found Alastair's face. He gave an encouraging smile, but his eyes showed his true anxiety.

Blood thudded through my ears. My gut churned, the cupcake knocking around in there like a cement block in a tumble dryer. I clenched my hands in a failed attempt to stop them from shaking.

The door to the arena slammed shut, sending up a few startled cries from the audience.

There was no getting out of this.

I returned my focus to Banna.

We bowed, we took our stances, and it began.

I was instantly knocked to the floor with what felt like a claw digging into my chest. With a speed that came almost instinctively, I drew the membrane around me. But Banna expected this. She knew what the others had been teaching me. She would know every defensive spell I might conjure.

She also knew how to make her magic assaults small enough

to permeate the membrane. What she threw at me was like being bombarded with microscopic bits of hail. Like hail hitting a rooftop, the magic pellets struck me with stinging force. And as each one bounced off my skin, it ripped out some of my magic.

Screw subtlety. I threw a magical head butt at Banna. It staggered her back a few paces, but she recovered in a heartbeat.

I thought of the hail she was sending through my membrane. Using what was essentially a Shoving Charm, I pushed the air around me, and around and around to kick up a whirlwind that spun her wicked pellets away. Banna took all of two seconds to route them back down through the top of my wind funnel. Her pelting magic rained straight down on my head. Each strike stripped away more of my power.

I was quickly tiring. Hell, they wouldn't need to extract me if this kept up; Banna was doing the job for them. I flung my wind storm at her fast enough that it sucked the hail pellets off me and right at her. She squealed with pain, but I didn't relent. I threw another whirlwind at her.

While she was distracted, while she was regaining her footing, I called up a light orb, my anger causing heat to radiate from it. But I wasn't looking to earn points for executing the perfect Solas Charm. I reshaped the flame-red ball into a lightning bolt. And, feeling very much like Zeus himself, hurled it toward her. The bright flash from the bolt was enough to cause Banna's skin to sizzle.

I could have kept at it. I could have burnt her to a crisp. I was so furious over so many things that I could have kept conjuring and reshaping orbs, using every last scrap of my power to do her in. But that wasn't the point of the test. The point was to prove I could control myself, to prove I could keep her from taking my magic. Frying my opponent would prove neither of these things.

And so I eased back on my attack.

After several more rounds of back-and-forth blows, Banna revealed that she'd only been warming up. She gave up playing, she gave up going easy on me, and she directed what seemed like the nozzle of an industrial-strength vacuum at me. I could literally feel my skin stretching and pulling when she started it up.

You know when you're in a car and the driver unexpectedly whips around a curve and it seems like all of your weight slams over to one side of your body? That's how the Banna Vacuum felt. All my magic slammed against the small area where she had concentrated the suction. It hurt. It wore me down. I couldn't control my magic. I couldn't keep it in. I couldn't fight any longer.

And so, I failed.

Since it was only a test, Banna returned my magic to me the moment my loss was acknowledged. And let me tell you, that return process hurt more than having the magic sucked out. It was like being jabbed with a hundred syringes tipped with the fattest and dullest needles the doctor could find.

Still, once my power was back, it was an amazing high.

The wooziness hadn't cleared away, but I felt keenly focused. My very bones hummed like I'd been filled with electricity. I was shaking with the certainty that I could take on the world. Shaking so hard in fact, it was a struggle to move without staggering.

Olivia came up to me, taking my arm and helping me steady myself. Pretending she was checking my eyes, she leaned in and whispered, "This was more than unfair. I thought the cupcake might help, but she's too strong."

The wooziness, instead of diminishing, had increased, and my head started spinning. Not only from what I'd just gone through, but because this did not mesh with the Olivia who had thrown herself at Alastair, the Olivia who I thought had demanded the test happen today, the Olivia who I'd assumed wanted rid of me. Before I had much time to think, Olivia was stepping back from me, her back rigid. She spoke loudly enough for the crowd to hear.

"Cassie, by the declaration of Headquarters, you must be extracted to the point of no return." Tears stung the corners of my eyes, not at my fate, but at the tremble in her voice. "You have not proven you can control your magic."

"I demand a stay," called Mr. Tenpenny from the stands. A flash of relief crossed Olivia's face, but she quickly put on her businesslike mask once more.

"Someone must second it," she said, darting her gaze around the arena.

"I demand a stay," said Alastair. The words were clear, but his voice shook with wavering emotion as if fighting back tears.

"You cannot second for her," Olivia told him, her own voice weakening. "As you are in a relationship with Miss Black, your opinion is biased."

Alastair nodded, wiped his eyes, then stared at the dahlias in his lap.

"If we have no other—" Olivia began.

"I demand a stay."

I jerked around. The voice was familiar, but not in a million years could I fathom him coming to my rescue. But there he was, dressed as ever in cargo shorts and a dingy tank top. Morelli. My heart leapt with surprise and delight. Then I remembered I was his only tenant. No wonder he wanted to keep me alive.

Olivia turned her attention back to me, her eyes showing some amount of hope. "You will have a stay of twenty-four hours while we decide your case." Olivia took my hand and shook it, sending her apologies into my head. Which was a trick I would really have liked to learn. Too bad learning was going to be a bit impossible since my brain would soon be nothing more than mush.

I nodded to show I'd heard.

And then I left the arena.

Just left.

I didn't want to hear people congratulating me for "giving it my all" and "making a good effort." I didn't want to hear condolences that it would all be alright. I didn't want to hear lies that Mr. Tenpenny and Morelli would be able to change the minds of HQ. I was through. Even though I knew my own capabilities, even though I'd realized my own potential in this very arena, I was through.

Of course Banna had won. She was the epitome of magic. She was the mother of magic, for Merlin's sake. Why did I even bother to fight after seeing she was my opponent?

It had been planned from the start. Maybe since the day I'd come through the London-Portland portal. Maybe that's why Olivia's file had been faked. To lure me here so they could do away with me.

I should have felt sad, annoyed, dismayed, but the lingering buzz of my magic being returned to me had me rippling with focus and determination. Besides, I hadn't come here to prove myself to these people. I'd come to find my parents. I'd already lost valuable time coming to this pointless test.

I had twenty-four hours left.

I didn't plan to waste them.

CHAPTER FORTY-FIVE
WINSTON THE RAVEN

Until I could act, I craved privacy. I raced along corridors and up stairs to my room, only giving in to the burn in my thighs once I'd locked myself in. I stayed silent as people kept coming by and knocking on my door. Alastair was the only one I wanted to let in, but what was the point? He couldn't console me without me exhausting him, nor could he change the Magics' minds. I was going to be extracted, and it was time to cut my losses.

I sound like I was wallowing in self pity. I wasn't. I was a dog paddling in a huge vat of pissed-off stew complete with chunks of bitterness and morsels of unfairness. The Magics may have beat me, but I wasn't down for the count yet. I refused to be magically lobotomized knowing my parents might be trapped in some sort of eternal limbo.

While I waited, while Alastair pleaded outside my door, I checked my phone. Mr. Wood and Lola had sent me more messages. They'd come through at some point, possibly when I'd snuck out the other night, but in the madness of the previous day I hadn't thought to look at them.

Without warning and before I'd even glanced at a single message, tears dripped onto my phone's screen. Pablo would have a good home with Lola. I could picture him getting grossly obese on her coconut cookies; and with his expanding wardrobe, I imagined he'd soon need his own closet. Mr. Wood was on the road to recovery. Once things were up and running, he'd have no trouble finding another assistant. Maybe Daisy was looking for permanent work. At the very least he'd be able to hire someone who had the proper licensing and didn't raise the dead. Someone who wouldn't run the risk of putting him out of a three-generation long business.

I wiped my eyes and nose, then dried the phone's screen on my shirt sleeve before checking my messages. Most of the photos from Mr. Wood were of increasingly elaborate BLTs, but there was one surprise: a single crochet creation that was actually recognizable as a granny square.

I'm going to make a blanket! He'd added below the photo.

He'd then sent another message: *Eugene tells me you might be in trouble there. I hope not. Despite your little problem, I would miss you. I never had kids, but you're just what I'd have hoped for if I did. He says he will do his best. Please call if you get a chance.*

And my phone screen was a salty, wet mess again. I couldn't reply. My hand was trembling too much, and I doubted autocorrect would be able to make any sense of what I might type if I tried.

I dried the screen and my eyes again, then went to Lola's messages.

Chip, chip, cheery-oh, guv'nuh!!

It was so stupidly silly, I couldn't help but laugh as I scrolled down to see the photo.

There was Pablo. Lola had outdone herself this time. He was dressed in the full regalia of a Yeoman Warder. Jacket, hat, neck ruff, and even a tiny toy raven perched on one shoulder.

Do you think they'll hire me?

I was about to type back that, no, they definitely would not, when a thought struck me harder than Banna's magic hail.

I needed to speak to Nigel.

I had to wait over an hour, but eventually Alastair gave up — and I have to say, even my tough-as-nails heart had been melting at his pleas to let him in, to at least talk to him. Once I heard the muffled sound of his footsteps retreating down the carpeted corridor, I skulked my way out to the Tower grounds, moving cautiously to avoid bumping into anyone I didn't want to see. Which, I'll admit, was everyone.

Despite the thick layer of clouds, it still hadn't rained, and visitors were taking advantage of the weather. I made my way straight toward the raven enclosure. Winston was nowhere to be seen, but a chill soon danced up my arms just before Nigel appeared. As ever, he was eager to impart information.

"Looking for me? I might have to start charging you for these tours."

"You. And Winston," I added.

"Ah, I believe I saw him eyeing the entry to the crown jewels. He's always had a fetish for shiny things. Come along, I'll tell you about the royal zoo that was once here. Did you know they used to keep dolphins in the moat?" I gave him a skeptical look. "No?"

"Not quite."

I strode alongside him. The idea that Pablo's photo had given me couldn't wait.

"How long did you say you've been here?" I asked as we headed around the White Tower and toward the Waterloo Barracks. I did wonder what people thought when I asked questions or spoke to Nigel. From what I could determine, only Magics could see him, so the Norms either thought I was talking to myself, or they didn't notice a thing and assumed I was just another person gabbing into a bluetooth headset.

"Oh, going on twenty-five years now."

"Were you here when my parents came? Chloe and Simon Starling. Did you ever meet them?"

"Why, yes," he said with delight. "I told you I had."

"No, I'm pretty sure I would have remembered that."

"I did. My friend who was just like you, teaching me some history. And then she left and I didn't see her again. I was fascinated by both of your parents because we don't get many Americans here," he said as a group of ten Americans passed us, each munching on a bag of Cheetos and speaking twice as loudly as anyone else.

"American Magics, that is. They were part of a very important mission. They were so brave, and, well you probably guessed, I had the most terrible crush on your mother." Nigel gave a wistful sigh. "She was, I mean, they were really your parents?" He stopped and scrutinized me for a moment. "Yes, I see some resemblance. The face shape. Don't know why I didn't see it before. Sometimes I can be so forgetful."

Which was the understatement of the decade.

We turned a corner, and as the Waterloo Barracks — the building where the crown jewels were housed — came into sight, I asked, "And do you know anything about that mission they were working on?"

Just then Winston soared down from the sky and landed on Nigel's shoulder.

"There you are, you rascal. Did you know we were talking about you? No, wait, I hadn't gotten to that part of the story yet."

"What part?" It was only then that I wondered if there was any way I could trust Nigel's information. He'd been wrong on so many other things.

"The mission. It was named for Winston here. Operation Winston."

"Winston was here then?" I asked, unable to hide my skepticism.

This was pointless. Nigel had confused his facts again. I'd seen Winston come in on the delivery system when I'd arrived. I wasn't up on my bird biology, but I didn't think ravens lived that long. Poor Nigel. Did ghosts suffer dementia?

"Well," Nigel said, reaching up to scratch Winston's head, "he had been alive. He was such a good bird, weren't you?" Winston bobbed his head in agreement. "You see, he couldn't be held back. The ravens are supposed to be the symbolic guards of the Tower, and the realm, really. He didn't want to be a symbol. He wanted to protect England. And so when the Mauvais appeared here, Winston went on the attack.

"Now," Nigel continued, sounding very much like the knowledgeable tour guide he aspired to be, "a raven is not a bird you want to tangle with, and the Mauvais certainly came out of the fight bloodier than he'd entered it. But Winston didn't win the battle. The Mauvais killed him. This wasn't long after I'd lost my own life. Ever since, we've been partnered up.

"Anyway, to honor our feathered friend, Busby Tenpenny — he was in charge of recording everything for that operation — named the mission to hunt down the Mauvais, the mission your parents were on, Operation Winston. Now, would you like me to tell you about the story behind the crown jewels? Did you know the original crown was square?"

"Sorry, Nigel," I said, charged with impatient urgency, "but I've got to cut the tour short."

"That's alright, then. We can take it up where we've left off later."

"Sure thing." I looked at Winston. Could Nigel be right, just this once? I had to get to the file room. Hadn't I told Tobey we should look up the mission names?

I made a quick goodbye, then ran back to the White Tower. Because of the tangle of stairways and hallways and floors that didn't seem to know what level they belonged on, I somehow ended up having to make my way past Olivia's office to reach the other stairwell that would take me to the file room.

I eased up to the room. Thankfully, the door was mostly closed and would be easy to get past, but from inside I could hear Alastair, Morelli, and Busby, pleading my case.

Their words, words like "talented" and "extraordinary" and "can't lose her" — words I couldn't believe were being used to refer to me, especially not from Morelli's mouth — made it suddenly hard to swallow. Morelli even said something about how "he didn't protect Black all this time just to have her brain drained." Alastair put in a comment about his efforts to safeguard me and how he wasn't about to stop now.

I appreciated those words, but they didn't matter. I knew they wouldn't change HQ's minds. The words were, however, keeping them occupied and I slipped undetected past the door, down the hall, and to the lower level.

CHAPTER FORTY-SIX

REVELATIONS

As I expected, the door to the file room was locked. Tobey had always brought the key. Still, despite being unable to defeat the mother of magic, I knew my way around a lock. The others would detect my magic on the door, but what did that matter now? A scolding over breaking and entering would simply bounce off my extracted head.

The trick with magic I'd learned is that you had to know how something worked. I couldn't just make the lock pop off, I had to know what the internal mechanism looked like so I could picture the lock's parts that needed to shift to open the door. Granted, I could have just given the lock a jolt to make it explode, but I was going for subtly and stealth, not blow-em-up, action-movie antics.

I imagined the lock's components. It took a few moments to settle on the right kind of mechanism, and if I weren't going to mentally die the next day, I would have made a note to myself to study up on these things so I could do this trick more quickly. Eventually though, the lock's tumblers fell into place and I slid back the bolt to enter.

The room was fully dark. I fumbled for the light switch, but when I flipped it, the room remained black. Sometimes the universe just hates you.

I didn't want to do the Solas Charm, not if I could be traced with it. I thought of my lessons in MagicLand, specifically those from Fiona's copy of *The Principles of Physics and Magic* she had loaned me. It had briefly covered quantum physics, explaining how it could only make sense in a world filled with magic, but that it was fun watching Norm physicists trying to sort it all out.

I'd been practicing the Light Capture Charm before I left, now it was time to put that practice into action. I don't know, maybe because it was based on physics, but I found this spell far easier than the Solas one. I imagined a light bulb with a magnet instead of filament. The magnet pulled in photons, and *voila!* I had some light. Sure, the rules of entanglement meant that somewhere someone's headlight probably just went out, but it wasn't like I pulled in enough photons to wipe out all the bulbs in a hospital or anything.

With my captured light glowing above me it was time to get a move on and find the file for Operation Winston. I went straight to the O cabinet, then opened the drawer that held the Om to Oz files.

And cursed.

The only *Operation* folders were surgery notes from the Magical Medi Unit. I slammed the drawer shut. I thought of looking up *Winston*, but I'd already gone through the Ws. I was about to try the R files for *Ravens*, when my heart jumped with excitement.

I had gone through the Ws, but in my rush to get to the *Tenpenny* file I'd barely flicked through the W drawer. If I'd seen a *Winston* file, I probably ignored it, assuming it held information on Winston Churchill. I raced to the W cabinet and whipped open the Wa to Wi drawer.

"Oh, you have got to be kidding!"

There was no Winston folder. Not for the bird, not for the prime minister, and not for the damn operation. Maybe there never was an Operation Winston. I mean, it's not like Nigel was a reliable source of facts and figures.

I kicked the drawer shut. My jaw shaking with irritation, I stared down the row.

Files, files, files.

I didn't have time either tonight or in what remained of my coherent life to get through all of them. There had to be another way, a faster way to find what I was after.

I closed my eyes and recalled what I knew of the Mauvais. When I'd fought him — or rather *her* since he was in the form of Vivian at the time — he had been coated in perfume. But when someone tries to rip the magic out of you, steals a watch from you that could help him take over the world, and grapples you to the point your hand breaks, you get acquainted with that person in a squeezed-onto-a-crowded-bus-during-rush-hour kind of way.

Under the perfume there had been a scent of something like burnt cinnamon. A smoky, spicy scent of baking gone wrong. So, like a dog scanning the parquet for a lost biscuit, I smelled my way back and forth across the cabinets. And let me tell you, that's not easy work. A couple times I thought I was going to pass out and had to remind myself to take a few deep breaths to refresh my head.

I sniffed high and low with my captured photons following along. I got down on my hands and knees, sucking in who knows how many particles of dust and mouse feces, but from the A cabinet to the Z cabinet there was no sign of the Mauvais's scent.

I suppose it made sense. The Mauvais wouldn't have handled the paperwork here. He wouldn't have been processing reports of his own whereabouts. But who would? Who was working here at the time of the Mauvais and would have been recording things?

Busby Tenpenny.

He was in charge of recording everything for that operation, Nigel had said.

I stood up. Hadn't I detected the scent of bergamot somewhere about a quarter of the way down the row? I couldn't tell which file it had been coming from at the time, but I had at least narrowed down my options.

I sniffed, honing in on the D cabinet. Then the Da to De drawer. I soon realized it was mostly filled with De files: De for "Death Report." Just briefly looking them over, I began to truly get a sense of how awful the Mauvais had been. The things he'd done would have made even the likes of Stephen King and Wes Craven seem unimaginative in their horrors.

Tucked in the very back of the drawer was a folder that didn't belong. Or maybe someone thought it did but hadn't gotten around to relabeling it: Operation Winston.

I pulled it out. There was a sheet stuck with old, crackled tape on the very top. Centered about a third of the way down were the words *Starling Report* written in slanting block letters. My stomach gave a little jolt that made my light flare brighter, which I thought interesting, but not worth contemplating at the moment.

Inside the file were full details of my parents' work, of their tracking efforts, of notes in their own handwriting about how they'd suspected Devin Kilbride, warnings from them that he might be the Mauvais — warnings that were apparently ignored because further notes indicated their frustration with the system. There was also a request made by them to investigate a building where the Mauvais was reported to hold a lease. The request was denied. They went anyway. They didn't return.

The final pages of the file had been hole punched at the top and were held in the place with a metal fastener attached to the folder. On these pages were evaluations from various sources asserting that the Starlings must be dead. But two reports stated that the Mauvais did not hide the bodies of his victims. He put them on display to show what he could do. If the Starlings' bodies hadn't been recovered, the reports stated, the Starlings were probably alive.

This was the end of the first report, but the second went on to point out that the Mauvais may have drained the Starlings. From a source who had defected from the Mauvais's side, there was a statement about a new technique the Mauvais had been working on. A cruel technique that stole power to make the thieving Magic stronger. The defector noted the technique could work on a repeating cycle if the victim's magic could regenerate itself.

The human battery, I thought. So it wasn't just speculation.

The report ended with emphatic declarations that all efforts should be made to find my parents. An investigation into the building was done, but turned up nothing. In a hand that showed clear aggravation, was written: *I quit.*

The first handwriting, the statement about the new technique, I recognized as Alastair's. The second, although sharper than usual, was Mr. T's copperplate script.

Amongst the last pages in the file was a sheet that had the creases and marks of a piece of paper that's been crumpled up and spread flat again. It was a police report — magic police, not the regular kind. I'd have probably skipped over it if not for the source of the report: the Portland community. Embossed in the top right corner was the Rosaria emblem. Centered at the top were the words, "Missing Child Report."

While some details of the report had been written in by hand, the bulk of it had been typed. It was a transcript of a witness statement.

Witness: I saw Lola LeMieux with the Starling child at the park. The girl was feeding the ducks but must have run out of food. There's that concession stand just near the pond, you know, so people can have their picnics by the water. Well, Lola tells the girl to stay put.

Officer: You heard this?

W: Well, no, but that's what it looked like. The girl nodded and Lola went up to buy something. Chips maybe, or perhaps a hot dog so the ducks could have the bun.

O: That's irrelevant. What happened next?

W: I see that Alastair kid come up and he starts talking to the girl who's looking up at him like he's the bee's knees. Can't imagine any girl liking a gawky thing like him, can you?

O: It doesn't matter for this questioning. Please continue.

W: Nothing to continue with. Like I told the lady officer, someone, a great big fat someone, mind you, walks right in front of me and stops to stare at the lake. And when I say fat, *I mean* fat. *Like at least four feet wide. Don't even know how he fit through his front door. There really ought to be laws to keep people like that from getting so big. Just a waste of space, isn't it?*

O: I would ask you to stick to what you saw.

W: Didn't see nothing. By the time Jumbo moved along, Lola was back, the girl was gone, Alastair was gone, and Lola was crying her heart out calling for the girl. Broke my heart to hear her so upset.

At the bottom of the report someone had noted: *Zeller has been put on trial for the abduction, but swears he only spoke to Cassie Starling, nothing more. He was cleared of all charges, but considering his former relationship with the Mauvais and his unusual magical talent, he will be kept on surveillance.*

The file slipped from my fingers. I fumbled, gripping at the pages to catch it. I knew I'd gone missing. I knew I'd been in Lola's care at the time. I knew Alastair had been in the area. But I didn't realize he had been right there with me, had been speaking to me at the very moment I'd gone missing. And I most definitely did not know there'd been enough cause to suspect him and put him on trial for my abduction.

Alastair had not only been in the area, he had very likely been the last person to interact with me before I disappeared. Alastair who had worked with the Mauvais. Alastair who had built the watch. What had really happened that day? And why?

I couldn't process this. I really couldn't. All the efforts to not suspect him, to try to believe he actually cared for me had been a complete waste. I had ignored my natural instincts to distrust. I wouldn't do it again. I'd be angry over his betrayal later — if I had a later, that is. Right then, I needed to undo some of the damage he and his buddy the Mauvais had caused.

In my scramble to catch the file, I'd snatched at the final few sheets, exposing the inside back cover. There, barely held in place with a strip of brittle, yellowed tape, was a remnant of torn paper. I pulled the ripped intake report from my pocket. It matched up. And this matching piece had the address I needed.

I marched over to the wall map of London. It took a while, but I eventually found what I was looking for. The address wasn't within easy walking distance of the Tower, but neither was it far from the Victoria & Albert Museum. I memorized the address and distractedly crammed the file back into the drawer.

I sent my captured photons back to wherever they needed to go next, then locked the file room door and set out to find Tobey Tenpenny.

After all, we had a date to go on.

CHAPTER FORTY-SEVEN

DATE NIGHT

"About that date," I said when, under the watchful gaze of a gnome, I found Tobey walking along the walls.

"Look, I'm sorry I asked. I didn't mean it as a date, just an excuse to get out of here."

"Either way. I'll go."

"What about Alastair?"

"I'm going to be brain dead soon. I think I should be allowed to do what I want while my neurons are still firing."

"Don't say that. Grandpa and the others are working on keeping it from going that far."

I shrugged. If I believed they could win, if I dared to think that I might be allowed to keep living my life with all my mental faculties still intact, I would lose my nerve about risking that life to save my parents. I wasn't exactly thrilled about spending any of my final hours with Tobey Tenpenny, but the only way I was allowed to leave the Tower was with someone else. If I left with Tobey, the gnome — who was certainly eavesdropping on our plans — wouldn't be suspicious.

Oh, don't get me wrong. I had no doubt the gnomes would gossip amongst themselves about my leaving on a date with Tobey; I was counting on it, because that gossip would quell any speculation that I might be, oh say, trying to escape to rescue two people the Magics seemed to have no intention of ever searching for. I only had to hope that the news didn't reach Olivia until I'd had enough time to ditch Tobey and save my parents.

And with any luck, not get killed in the process.

* * *

Not long before the hour Tobey and I were supposed to meet, I pulled on my black tights and a black sweater. I couldn't help but feel awkward walking out the main gate and over to the Tube station with Tobey. And not just because I'm normally awkward with other humans. I worried about what to do if he tried to put his arm around me or pull me aside and smash his face into mine again. But on our journey, he maintained a polite distance and gave no hint that this was anything more than two people who could barely stand one another going out for the evening.

How could he just play off that kiss as if nothing had happened? I couldn't bother to sort out the mind of Tenpenny the Younger. I had enough problems of my own to solve.

I knew I might encounter the Mauvais soon, and after failing my test that morning, I should have been nervous about such an encounter. I should have been doubting my ability. But there's something about knowing you're as good as dead anyway that lends you a weird amount of courage. If I died trying to set my parents free, I would certainly feel a lot better about my mental death (well, as good as one can feel about that sort of thing) than if I just sat in my room waiting for HQ to pass judgment on me.

As we rode the District Line, Tobey and I made little more than vague comments about how many stops were between the Tower and our destination. At South Kensington station we got off, and even then our only conversation as we trekked through a long, underground tunnel was to note the signs directing us to the Victoria & Albert Museum.

Once inside the museum, it was as perfect as I'd hoped it would be. Plenty of big sculptures, miles of corridors, and a confusing layout for someone unfamiliar with the building. But Cassie, your intrepid armchair traveller, had seen maps of the place, had "borrowed" Morelli's wi-fi to wander along virtual tours of the main galleries. I didn't have a local's knowledge of the museum, but it wouldn't be difficult to ditch Tobey once the opportunity came.

Sure, I felt like a jerk about my plan, but he was the one being weird. Actually, with the aloof way he was acting, he probably wouldn't even notice I was gone.

From the Tube station tunnel we strolled through a wide, bright exhibition hall filled with marble sculptures. We then made our way along several low-lit galleries that, although inhabited by larger-than-life pieces of art, were nearly empty of other humans, making the rooms seem abnormally eerie. After going up a level, we came across a cafe.

"You want to get some wine or something?" Tobey asked, sounding beyond uncomfortable.

"Sounds great," I replied, seeing my chance. "Get me a red while I go pee. I'll find you at one of the tables over there." I pointed vaguely to the side of the dining area, then took off.

The loo, which I did need, ended up being ridiculously far from the cafe. And of course, it was at the end of a gallery that turned out to be a dead end. Which meant I had to backtrack in front the cafe to make my escape.

As I passed the cafe, Tobey was still lined up with a group of annoyed-looking customers while a harried bartender tried to keep up with the orders. I slipped in amongst a group of art students who had their pads and pencils poised to sketch any object that caught their eye. Their drawings could use some work, but the cluster of pupils did block the line of sight from the cafe. Once past the beverage queue, I rushed my way out of the building and into the night.

Take that, you stupid gnomes.

Using the directions I'd jotted down after returning from the file room, it took me less than ten minutes to walk to the address I'd found on the map. The building was a big, square thing, sort of nondescript, easy-to-forget, and looked like it might have once been nothing more exciting than office space. As I approached the door, I caught the distinct scent of cinnamon.

And, barely perceptible under the Eau de Mauvais, lingered a hint of chocolate.

I can't find the words to tell you how disappointed I was. Even after all the suspicions I'd harbored, even after what I'd learned of his involvement in my disappearance, I had wanted Alastair to be telling the truth. I had wanted Alastair to be the good guy.

Like they say, wish in one hand, poo in the other, and see which fills up first.

I did not want to go up against two wizards, but like Rafi had told me, once you know how a Magic fights, you can anticipate his moves. I knew Alastair instinctively went for the Binding Spell. He had said he didn't throw my test, that he wanted me to know what I was capable of. Well, now I knew. I'd beat him in that test. I could do it again.

I skirted around the building. One faint light was on, but the windows were all covered by what appeared to be butcher paper, like when a shop covers their windows while preparing the interior for opening day. I couldn't find an open window to slip through, so I looped back around to the front entryway.

As I approached the main door, I ran through a list of lock possibilities, but it was my lucky night — well, if you ignored the whole Alastair-really-is-evil thing. The latch hadn't caught when the door had swung back after the last person entered. I pushed the door slowly, begging it not to creak or squeal. I prepared to use a Silencing Spell, just in case, but the hinges remained quiet. Again, lucky me! Walking into my own death was proving to be super easy.

I glanced around, then I stepped inside.

The interior was dark, so I called up the Light Capture Charm again. I pulled in only enough photons to make a light about as bright as the beam of a flashlight with nearly dead batteries, just enough to keep me from tripping over anything. It didn't take long to realize the ground floor was empty, a shell of a room occupied by nothing more than several support columns.

But there was a stairwell.

You know, because I hadn't climbed enough stairs during this trip.

I tiptoed up the steps, keeping my back to the wall as I went. The top of the first set of stairs let me out onto a broad interior landing. This floor remained intact with what were probably former office spaces and hallways leading off either side of the stairway.

In the distance, at the far end of the left-hand corridor, I heard men's voices. I wasn't near enough to catch what they were saying, but I recognized one of them and my thudding heart sank.

See, despite being the world's foremost cynic, I'd still been holding out hope that maybe the scent of chocolate on the main door had merely come from a cake the Mauvais had brought with him. I mean, who doesn't like a little snack when practicing malicious magic? But I should know better than to hope, and I swore never to do it again as I honed in on Alastair's voice.

I took another step forward, focusing intently on trying to hear what was being said. My magic was humming over my eardrums when a hand touched my shoulder. I whirled around and instinctively used the Shoving Charm. My attacker stumbled and thudded against the wall as I whipped the light around.

"What the—?" he started to say.

I jumped forward and slapped my hand over the idiot's mouth.

"Shut up," I hissed. "What are you doing here? Never mind. Just go." I pointed in the direction of the stairs with my free hand, but Tobey shook his head. "Then stay quiet and stay behind me. Did you follow me?" I asked, as if that weren't obvious.

He nodded his head, then pulled my hand away from his mouth and whispered, "The wine line wasn't moving and I was just going to go grab a table to wait for the queue to die down. When I turned around, I saw you walking by. And so, yeah, I followed you. What is this place?"

"Mauvais," I said and pointed down the hall. "You need to leave."

"No way."

"You are such a pest. Just stay out of my way, okay? And don't let him see you."

Tobey agreed. I stood up and crept toward the door at the far end. The voices became clearer, but not the words. It wasn't exactly an argument, but it wasn't a pleasant chat either. The tone was terse and clipped.

"Is that Alastair?" Tobey whispered. His mouth right against my ear. I flicked him away like a pesky mosquito. "I never did trust him."

I didn't need to hear it from the likes of Tobey Tenpenny. I had wanted to trust Alastair. I had wanted to fall for him. Who am I kidding? I *had* fallen for him. Luckily, I was used to walling up any wounds in my heart.

"Do not move away from this door," I told Tobey.

Then, with my magic tingling in my fingertips and ready to fight, I entered the room.

CHAPTER FORTY-EIGHT
WE MEET AGAIN

Both men turned toward me. One had a look of pure delight, like a squirrel who's just fallen into a sackful of peanuts. The other's face drooped with dismay.

"Cassie, you shouldn't have come," Alastair said.

"Yes, she should have," said the Mauvais with a delighted chuckle. "It's exactly what she should have done."

"You're in on this with him," I accused Alastair, ignoring the Mauvais. "You lied to me. All this time, ever since I was a little kid, you've been working for him."

Alastair's gaze flicked over my shoulder. From the corner of my eye, I caught Tobey. The King of the Idiots must have decided being behind the door wasn't for him and had entered the room. Alastair returned his attention to me, his face showing some surprise, but mostly heartfelt pain.

"Cassie, it's not what you think. Do you really not believe me?"

"I believe what I see, and that is you betraying me at every step of the way. First with Vivian— No, what am I saying? You started all this long before Vivian. Of course, then there was Olivia, and now you're here having a chat with the Mauvais. Everything you've done has been to hurt me, to bring me closer to him. Well, good job. I'm here."

I darted a glimpse at the Mauvais. He was making no move to

approach us despite this being a perfect time to attack.

"No, that's not how it was. I came here because I caught your scent on the lock of the file room. I found the slip of paper on the floor with this address. I came here hoping to—"

"Claim your reward?" I cut in.

The Mauvais, who'd been smirking over our little spat, barked out a laugh at that.

Alastair shifted to face me more directly. The move turned him away from the Mauvais. Only then did I realize why the Mauvais hadn't bothered to attack me, hadn't even bothered to take a single step forward. Alastair had been holding the Mauvais in place with a variant on the Shield Charm. But when he turned to face me, his focus on the spell broke.

The bark of laughter was still echoing in the vast room when the Mauvais walloped Alastair with a Shoving Charm hard enough to send Alastair flying into the support column behind him. It was only by dumb luck that the blow hit him in the gut, doubling him over and making it so only his back, not his head, hit the concrete support. Still, slamming against the column did knock the wind out of him.

"Do something," Tobey shouted. "He's getting away."

The Mauvais was jogging through a doorway into what must have once been a connecting office space. A powerful urge to chase after him filled me, but that was probably exactly what he wanted. Instead, I ran over to Alastair, checking to see if he was alright. I was mad as hell at him, but he was going to explain himself. After which, I might just kill him myself.

Gasping for breath, Alastair looked up at me. "I didn't betray you. I've never wanted to betray. I wanted to stop you."

"So he could get away?"

"No, because you can't fight him." He shifted to sit up and rolled his shoulders, the motion making him do little more than wince. Clearly nothing important was broken. "Don't go up against him. Let HQ handle this. Please."

"I've fought him before."

"Shut up for two minutes, Cassie." I jerked back from the sharp tone I'd never heard from him. "He has the watch. If you fight him, he's going to pull your magic straight into the gears. All of it. And he will use it. Someone else, not you, needs to take him down or we're all doomed."

"Are you able to get up?"

"Almost." The instant he answered, his face registered his mistake. I stepped away from him. He tried to grab me, but I jumped out of his reach, and before he could conjure a Binding Spell, I raced off in the direction the Mauvais had gone.

I didn't have to race far. Devin Kilbride stood in the adjoining room, waiting then grinning as he went through the formal bow and stance as if we were preparing to spar.

"Thought I'd give you a last moment with lover boy. If it makes it any easier, I'll let him live after I kill you."

"Screw you," I said and gave him the hardest magic wallop I could muster. Go big or go home, right?

The Mauvais staggered back, but then floated off the ground to keep himself from falling. I hit him with three more spells. The blows had some effect, but I had underestimated my opponent. I had expected him to still be weak. After all, I'd taken the major part of his magic when I'd pulled the watch's power into me. He should have barely been able to levitate a feather. But somehow he was full of magic. He was far stronger than he should have been and my attacks weren't doing anywhere near the damage they'd done when I'd used them before.

There had been worries about someone in HQ passing the Mauvais power, delivering him magic like a Dominoes pizza. But who? Alastair?

Wait, hold that train of suspicious thought, a Flaming Arrow Curse is coming at me.

I launched a Shoving Charm to knock the fiery projectile off course, then threw another one right at the Mauvais. It was only then I realized, in addition to not being knocked back by my spells, he wasn't blocking them. Once you knew how, it didn't take much to throw up a Shield Spell, but the Mauvais had done nothing other than shift to take my magic hits in the least vulnerable spot possible. If I aimed one at his head, he leapt and twisted and took it in the shoulder. If I aimed for his heart, he turned to take the hit in his side.

Don't get me wrong. My attacks were hurting him, but it was like a muscle cramp rather than a broken limb. After a quick grimace or grunt, he pushed through the discomfort and grinned at me like a demented Cheshire Cat.

I always hated the Cheshire Cat. Not that there's many likable characters in *Alice in Wonderland*, but that cat just irked the hell out me. His broad, toothy smile, and smug manner reminded me too much of Foster Father Number Two when he was preparing for another round of Let's Beat Cassie.

So, when I saw that same smirk on the Mauvais's face, I magically lashed out over and over, wanting with pure ferocity to knock the grin straight off his face, wanting to push him out the window he stood in front of.

The Shoving Charm and other attack spells were getting me nowhere. I was just about ready to try a new tack when someone, or rather something, grabbed hold of arms and yanked me back.

"Cassie, stop!"

I squirmed, I writhed, I kicked, but Alastair had me caught in the magic netting of his Binding Spell.

"I will kill him and then I'll kill you," I screamed.

"Stop fighting him," Alastair growled, moving in front of me to put himself between me and the Mauvais, but angling his body to keep us both in his line of sight. "It's exactly what he wants."

"Don't tell her now, Allie," the Mauvais chided. "The tank is almost full." Reaching inside his shirt, the Mauvais tugged on a chain. Hanging from it was the watch.

"Don't you see?" Alastair said. "Every bit of magic you've thrown has been the watch's magic. His magic. You're pouring magic back into the damn watch."

The Mauvais flicked his arm, but Alastair threw up a Shield Spell and the curse exploded in a cascade of sparks against it.

Despite my scowl and my fuming desire to bite Alastair's head off, he leaned in and whispered, "Whatever you've discovered, I swear I have only ever wanted to protect you. Someone's given him magic recently, but it's not been given in a way to make it stick." Another curse smacked against Alastair's shield. "He's not going to be able to fight for long unless he can keep pulling power from you. So if we're going to fight him, you need to find your balance."

I nodded and he let me go. I took a deep breath, and with surprising ease given how tired I had grown, I threw the membrane around myself to keep any more of my magic from flowing into the watch.

Alastair dropped his shield. The second it was gone, I launched myself at the Mauvais.

CHAPTER FORTY-NINE

SHOW DOWN

Despite everyone's claims that he'd been magically weakened, the Mauvais was proving himself pretty damn strong both in the physical and in the magical sense. Even as he deftly deflected the attack spells Alastair sent hurtling toward him, the Mauvais broke through my membrane. Then, snatching hold of my left arm so viciously his nails dug through the sleeve of my sweater, he yanked me closer to him.

I was too near the watch, and it was far worse than Banna's magic vacuum. The timepiece was sucking my power from me like a liposuction machine wreaking havoc on the fat lady at the circus.

The stripping of my magic wore on me. I wanted to give up, to crawl into a corner and sleep. Every exhausted instinct told me not to touch the watch. Without the membrane and without the focus, energy, or time to make a new one, there existed the possibility of the watch draining me on contact.

But as quantum physics had taught me, there was also an opposite and equally likely possibility.

I closed my hand around the watch. The Mauvais, too surprised by my actions, didn't react quickly enough. The Zen textbook had been right: Magic does flow like water. And magic now flowed from the watch into me, amplifying my power, giving me the strength I needed.

Charged with this new boost, I gave the Mauvais the most vicious magic head butt I could muster. The force of it drove him back, yanking the watch chain tight until it snapped.

The Mauvais staggered, but unfortunately didn't tumble back and out the window. Using the same gravity-defying trick Professor Dodding had shown me, my opponent quickly regained his footing then propelled himself over me.

I spun around, ready to attack. But the bastard had landed behind Alastair and Tobey and instantly threw a Binding Spell around them. Magic slammed against my fingertips and I shrieked with the unexpected pain as I barely held back the force of the Stunning Spell I'd been about to use.

Tobey struggled, but couldn't move his arms. Alastair, even though he could only move his hands, fidgeted desperately.

"Give me the watch," demanded the Mauvais as he circled around me. He was no longer amused. He no longer smirked. He wanted me dead.

"Don't do it, Cass," Alastair warned. With his unbound fingers he dug at his pocket, looking for all the world like he had a bad case of crabs but couldn't quite reach the itch.

"Leave them out of this," I said, because that seemed like the appropriate superhero response to the villain's wicked demands.

"I will, if you give me the watch."

The Mauvais had now made his way back to his original spot in front of the window. Tobey and Alastair, unwillingly moving with him, were tugged along by their magical restraints like dogs who'd been poorly leash-trained.

"Give it to him," Tobey gasped, his voice pitched high with panic.

Alastair stopped fumbling with his pocket. "Hit me, Cassie. Hit me with a spell as hard as you can and then run. Do it," he goaded. "All that anger you're feeling toward me. Send it my way. Go on. You know you want to."

The Mauvais screeched at Alastair to shut up. Tobey shrieked in pain and stiffened as the Mauvais's anger tightened the magic bindings. From somewhere in another room I heard a woman's yowling cry.

I can't say how I knew. Call it instinct. Call it a bond that can never be cut. Call it wishfully delusional thinking. But I knew that sound had come from my mother. Despite having never met her, despite having no memory of her, I knew that cry of agony had been made by the woman who had given birth to me.

"Cassie, ignore that," Alastair insisted. "Hit me and go."

"Give me the watch and you can have Mommy. You can have Daddy. You can even have both your little harem boys here."

The Mauvais was a jerk and pretty damn evil from what I'd learned, but he wasn't stupid. He wouldn't fall for the drain-the-watch trick again. My hand tingled as magic flowed between me and the timepiece like one of those machines that cleans a person's blood. In and out. In and out.

My magic was filling the watch, charging it back to full capacity. But the watch was also replenishing the magic within my cells with unnatural speed. My exhaustion vanished as the power grew and expanded within me. Free refills, anyone?

"What'll it be, girl?" the Mauvais asked, showing no strain as he maintained the Binding Spell on Tobey and Alastair.

I could hand the watch over to the Mauvais. He'd be distracted by it just long enough for me to use my supercharged power to take him out with a rapid-fire attack.

I would have my parents. I would have Alastair. And I'd even have Tobey. I didn't particularly care for Tobey, but Mr. T seemed fond of him.

"He'll kill us the minute you give him the watch," said Tobey.

My gaze darted to Alastair. I couldn't read his face beyond the intensity in his eyes.

"Can you really trust someone who used to be on my side?" the Mauvais taunted. "But wait, maybe it's you he can't trust. After all, that was quite the kiss you gave me the other night."

"Cassie?" Alastair said, agony ringing through that single word.

A strange blurriness took over the Mauvais's face. When it cleared, there were two Tobeys.

"The BrainSweeping Charm on him did wonders when you two were in the file room together, especially since I convinced him to take a few absorbing capsules with him to those little meetings. It would have been nice if you'd stuck a little closer to him like he asked, but they pulled in enough.

"The capsules made their way into my hands, and well, I felt good enough to play with my favorite Morphing Charm. So yes, that night, that was all me. Confounding you kept you from picking up my scent. And let me tell you, there's nothing like lip-on-lip, tongue-on-tongue action to get a true magic boost. Now," he growled, "the watch."

"Cassie," Tobey pleaded.

"Don't do it, Cass," said Alastair. "We'll be okay. Knock us out and run."

From beyond the room, my mother whimpered. The sound tugged at something deep in my chest.

I raised my hand, holding up the watch, dangling it from its broken chain. I extended my arm forward.

"Good, girl," said the Mauvais as he stepped toward me.

CHAPTER FIFTY

INTO THE DARK

As the Mauvais reached out his hand to take the watch, he was momentarily off guard. He'd fallen for my ruse. Really, it's hard to believe this guy had ever been a threat to humanity.

I projected my most feral Shoving Charm at him. It was so strong it knocked me back like the recoil from a Smith & Wesson. As I caught my balance, I watched the Mauvais shoot backward toward the window. Wild elation charged through me. He would crash through the pane of glass and end up splattered on the pavement below.

But my joy was short-lived. Because not only was the Mauvais falling back. Tobey and Alastair were too.

I always thought that thing where people talk about the world slowing down during intense moments was just something thrown into books so the author could draw out the scene and add in a bunch of impossible stuff. I don't know, maybe it was because I was a Magic, maybe it was because I was being trained in altering physics, but time truly did slow as I watched the three men.

The Mauvais still had his Binding Spell around Tobey and Alastair. I cursed myself for not realizing the bond hadn't been broken before I lobbed my attack. Tobey's eyes were wide open in full panic mode and looked like, with one hard smack, they might pop right out of his head. But Alastair. Alastair knew what was coming. Meeting my eye, he ordered me once again to hit him. He then twitched his fingers, drawing my eye to them for the briefest moment.

Pinched between thumb and forefinger was a small, capsule, pulsating red. An empty absorbing capsule.

If I threw my magic at him, he could catch it. He would have a dose of the most powerful magic the Magics had known: the watch's magic, my magic, and the Mauvais's magic all in one handy package. He could take my magic. He could use it to bolster his own power. He'd have a fighting chance against the Mauvais.

Or he could take it and deliver it to the Mauvais, strengthening him for more devastation.

Which was it?

To trust or not to trust? That is the question.

Alastair was falling backwards by now, but in the strange slow motion my eyes remained locked on his. The dahlias, the shy glances, that kiss, all flashed through my mind. Especially the kiss. *Shoop shoop*. This was the man who swore he'd only ever wanted to protect me. This was the man who had stayed close to me regardless of my suspicions of him, regardless of the accusations I'd thrown at him.

I nodded. Warm relief filled his deep blue eyes. This time I held nothing back, I hurled my magic at him so hard I flew back and knocked into the wall behind me.

I remember the sound of breaking glass and the impact of my body against the wall driving what felt like every molecule of air out of my lungs. The room spun and went dark.

* * *

A repetitive clacking sound chattered in my ear. Something cool and hard rubbed against my cheek. I raised my hand to brush it away and my fingers met the smooth, pliant feel of feathers. Then the bird hopped onto my chest and cocked his head at me as if wondering what this foolish human was doing on the ground.

"Hello, Winston," I groaned.

He replied with a friendly gurgle. I couldn't get up for several minutes, but I didn't pass out. Even in my dazed state I could still hear the woman yowling and whimpering. The noises sounded the exact same as they had earlier. It was only then I realized that Tobey wasn't the idiot. I was. I'd been fooled by a recording of someone crying. I'd lost Alastair for nothing.

I sat up. While my head spun for a few seconds, Winston tapped his beak on something in my hand. I looked down at it, confused momentarily about how it had gotten there.

Under my fingers, the watch vibrated with life. I had the watch. That's what the Magics wanted, wasn't it? I could return my overdose of power to it and they could go back to protecting it.

They'd be pleased, but I felt no satisfaction over it. Olivia or someone else from HQ would offer some stupid platitudes about Alastair sacrificing himself for the greater good. They would grant Tobey a posthumous magical diploma for Mr. T's sake. And they'd congratulate me for ridding them of the Mauvais.

Screw that. I wanted Alastair alive. I even wanted Tobey alive. A disturbing thought if there ever was one.

I struggled to my feet and went to the window. Glass bits littered the floor, and the frame still had jagged shards that made me think for some odd reason of the mouth of the Abominable Snowman. Winston flew over to perch on the windowsill. He then looked down over the edge and let out a loud *crooo-ack*.

"That bad, huh?"

I braced myself. It would be ugly.

Oddly enough, a small spark of hope fought through the darkness of my pessimistic nature. Alastair had the absorbing capsule, he had some of my magic. He might have had time to work a Floating Charm, or to turn the pavement into cotton, or even conjure an umbrella that he might have opened and used like Mary Poppins to drift down. Why else in his last moments would he have wanted me to blast him with magic? Maybe he was waiting below with Tobey and wondering what was taking me so long to join them.

I took a deep breath, then carefully leaned forward, gripping the watch with a fearsome amount force. I wasn't about to drop the stupid thing.

There, on the pavement below I saw—

Nothing.

Huh?

Winston made another noise that sounded as if he was as confused as me.

I pulled some photons together and directed them down to the pavement. Nothing. I mean, there was a sidewalk and a discarded napkin from Pret a Manger, but there were no bodies, no shattered pieces of skull, no pools of blood. Normally, I would have thought that a good thing, but where the hell were they?

Winston then flew out the window. I ordered him to come back. I don't know how he had escaped, but I wasn't going to be responsible for losing two humans and one of the Tower ravens all in one night. But Winston didn't go far. He flew in circles in one spot several times, then returned to the sill.

I stepped back and looked around for something with enough heft to throw and make a difference. On a table piled high with discarded and dusty office junk was an old-school stapler, the kind made entirely of steel except for a rubber base to keep it from marring your mahogany desk.

I picked it up. This was no plastic piece of junk for two dollars from the Office Depot. This was your classic if-you-wanted-to-kill-your-boss-you-had-a-perfect-weapon-at-hand stapler that weighed at least a pound.

"Show me again," I told the bird. He flapped his dark wings, made a little hop, then he was airborne and circling the same area he had before.

When he returned, I aimed and, hoping I had the trajectory right, threw the stapler through the window. The stapler went straight out about six feet, then began its curve downward. Just at the moment it began to descend, there was a small crackling noise. The stapler disappeared.

"Holy hell," I muttered as Winston hopped excitedly next to me.

A portal. But to where? And who was getting hit on the head with a stapler at that very moment?

"Move out of the way, Winston." He obeyed by perching on my shoulder. Not exactly what I meant, but good enough.

I used a chunk of brick to knock out the rest of the glass. If I was going to leap out into the unknown, which was probably just as crazy at it sounds, I wasn't going to do it with gashes across my arms and legs.

I climbed up onto the window frame. My legs shook. If this portal was small, if I missed it by even a centimeter, the police would be scraping me off the ground tomorrow morning, but probably not before several of Winston's cousins pecked my eyeballs out for a little snack.

Still, I had to try. I took several deep breaths to steady myself as I scanned the air for any sign of a disturbance that might give me a clue to the exact location of the portal. I gripped tight to the watch and crouched down, readying my legs to leap.

And then, from down the hall, a sound came again. Different this time. A woman singing, or perhaps humming. A song that dragged a fingernail of familiarity over my skin. And then the sound of a man clearing his throat and joining in, his tune coming across in a deeper register than hers.

The words *mom* then *dad* sparked across my mind.

I hesitated. If I didn't go to my parents now, who would? If I died trying to get Alastair, who would know they were here? Who would come looking for them? No one. But Alastair was out there somewhere. I needed to help him. I owed him that much and I wanted him back with a keen sense of longing.

I readied my legs once more.

And I jumped from the window.

Winston's flapping wings whispered in my ear as he held on to my shoulder. With a muffled *thump*, my boots landed on the concrete floor of the room.

I glanced out the window into the night. Jumping into an unknown portal would have to wait. Alastair had my power. I had to hope it would last long enough for me to get to him.

Yes, there I was, hoping again.

I stepped away from the window and turned toward the mumbling sound of the nostalgic tune. Tears streamed down my face as I hurried down the hallway, calling for my mother.

* * *

THE PART WHERE I BEG FOR A REVIEW
IF YOU ENJOYED THIS BOOK....

You may think your opinion doesn't matter, but believe me, it does…at least as far as this book is concerned. I can't guarantee it mattering in any other aspect of your life. Sorry.

See, reviews are vital to help indie authors (like me) get the word out about our books.

Your kind words not only let other readers know this book is worth spending their hard-earned money and valuable reading time on, but are a vital component for me to join in on some pretty influential promotional opportunities.

Basically, you're a superhero who can help launch this book into stardom!

I know! You're feeling pretty powerful, aren't you?

Well, don't waste that power trip. Head over to your favorite book retailer, Goodreads, and/or Bookbub and share a sentence or two (or more if you're ambitious). Even a star rating would be appreciated.

And if you could tell just one other person about Cassie Black's story, your superhero powers will absolutely skyrocket.

Thanks!!

By the way, if you didn't like this book, please contact me and let me know what didn't work. I'm always looking to improve.

I'D BE THRILLED IF YOU WANTED
TO KEEP IN TOUCH

If you'd like to…

- Keep up-to-date with my writing news and other random tidbits,

- Chat with me about books you love (and maybe those you hate),

- Receive the random free short story or exclusive discount now and then,

- And be among the first to learn about my new releases

…then please sign up for my monthly newsletter so we can keep in touch.

As a thank you for signing up, you'll get my short story *Mrs. Morris Meets Death*…a humorously, death-defying tale of time management, mistaken identities, cruise ships…and romance novels.

Join in on the fun today by heading to
www.subscribepage.com/mrsmorris

WHAT'S NEXT?

BOOK THREE: THE UNTANGLED CASSIE BLACK

Sometimes taking an overdose of magic is the least of your worries.

Cassie Black has just lost two people through a magic portal. Her archenemy, the Mauvais, is threatening to destroy city after city if HQ doesn't hand her over to him. And HQ isn't exactly saying no to that offer.

As HQ debates Cassie's fate, Cassie refuses to sit by and watch the grass grow between the toes of the surveillance gnomes. Biting back her life rule to never get involved, she knows the only way to stop the Mauvais is to go after him herself.

Which is exactly what he wants. Because the instant Cassie falls into his hands, the Mauvais will have unlimited power.

So don't get captured, right? Easy for you to say. Trouble is, there's a traitor within HQ who's proving to be more devious, more powerful, and to have more tricks up the sleeve than Cassie could have ever dreamed.

In this page-turning conclusion of the Cassie Black Trilogy, the curses are flying, the pastries are plentiful, and the magical batteries are charged to capacity.

Turn the page for a preview….

PROLOGUE:
LET ME CATCH YOU UP

Morelli here. So the last time you were hanging out with that dimwitted tenant of mine, she'd gone and gotten herself into a huge heap of trouble. When I heard about it, I wasn't a bit surprised. Always figured she'd end up on the wrong side of a problem.

Anyway, so here's the deal in case you ain't just read that second book of hers and you might've forgotten a few things.

The Queen of Mistrust, who's already been on this loop-the-loop ride of trying to sort out whether Alastair's a two-faced jerk or not, had gotten her panties in a twist seeing Alastair kissing Olivia. She'd also failed a pretty important test and faced the risk of being booted from the magic community (should we be so lucky). And so, as Black tends to do, she went and had a knee-jerk reaction that landed her right where the Mauvais wanted her.

This girl, I tell you. Makes me glad I never had kids.

'Coz not only did she get herself in a tricky situation, she got Tobey and Alastair in a bind. Literally. And when she walloped the Mauvais, he tumbled into a hidden portal. Along with Alastair and Tobey.

Like I said, the girl's a nitwit. That cat of hers has more smarts than she does.

But, you know, you lose some, you win some. Because while she did lose two people, she also found two people…her parents. Not sure if that evens up the balance sheet, but I'm gonna guess not.

Anyway, when you last saw her, she was running down the hallway of an abandoned building calling for her mom. Which I suppose is kind of touching. Except it's Black we're talking about, so I'm sure she'll screw it up somehow.

So that's it. I'll let you loose with the story. I've got to go whip up a BLAT for that boss of hers. Great guy that Mr. Wood. Man after my own heart. Can't believe he actually likes that nitwit tenant of mine.

Speaking of, if you see her, tell her the rent's due in three weeks, five days, and sixteen hours.

The Untangled Cassie Black is available on most major book retailers in paperback, hardback, and ebook formats. You can find your copy at
Books2Read.com/CassieBlack3

ALSO BY TAMMIE PAINTER

THE CIRCUS OF UNUSUAL CREATURES

It's not every day you meet an amateur sleuth with fangs.

If you like paranormal, cozy mysteries that mix in laughs in with murderous mayhem and mythical beasts, you'll love The Circus of Unusual Creatures.

Hoard It All Before, Tipping the Scales, Fangs a Million

THE OSTERIA CHRONICLES

A Six-Book Mythological Fantasy Adventure

Myths and heroes may be reborn, but the whims of the gods never change.

Perfect for fans of the mythological adventure of *Clash of the Titans* and *300*, as well as historical fantasy fiction by Madeline Miller and David Gemmel, the Osteria Chronicles are a captivating fantasy series in which the myths, gods, and heroes of Ancient Greece come to life as you've never seen them before.

The Trials of Hercules, The Voyage of Heroes, The Maze of Minos, The Bonds of Osteria, The Battle of Ares, The Return of Odysseus

THE CASSIE BLACK TRILOGY

Work at a funeral home can be mundane. Until you start accidentally bringing the dead to life.

The Undead Mr. Tenpenny, The Uncanny Raven Winston, The Untangled Cassie Black

DOMNA

Destiny isn't given. It's made by cunning, endurance, and, at times, bloodshed.

If you like the political intrigue, adventure, and love triangles of historical fiction by Philippa Gregory and Bernard Cornwell, or the mythological world-building of fantasy fiction by Madeline Miller and Simon Scarrow, you'll love this exciting story of desire, betrayal and rivalry.

Part One: The Sun God's Daughter, Part Two: The Solon's Son, Part Three: The Centaur's Gamble, Part Four: The Regent's Edict, Part Five: The Forgotten Heir, Part Six: The Solon's Wife

AND MORE...

To see all my currently available books and short stories, just scan the QR code or visit books.bookfunnel.com/tammiepainterbooks

ABOUT THE AUTHOR
THAT'S ME...TAMMIE PAINTER

Many moons ago I was a scientist in a neuroscience lab where I got to play with brains and illegal drugs. Now, I'm an award-winning author who turns wickedly strong tea into imaginative fiction (so, basically still playing with brains and drugs).

My fascination for myths, history, and how they interweave inspired my flagship series, The Osteria Chronicles.

But that all got a bit too serious for someone with a strange sense of humor and odd way of looking at the world. So, while sitting at my grandmother's funeral, my brain came up with an idea for a contemporary fantasy trilogy that's filled with magic, mystery, snarky humor, and the dead who just won't stay dead. That idea turned into The Cassie Black Trilogy.

I keep the laughs and the paranormal antics coming in my latest series, The Circus of Unusual Creatures, which is filled with detecting dragons, murder mysteries, and...omelets.

When I'm not creating worlds or killing off characters, I can be found gardening, planning my next travel adventure, working as an unpaid servant to three cats and two guinea pigs, or wrangling my backyard hive of honeybees.

You can learn more at *TammiePainter.com* or at that QR code, where you'll find probably more info than you could ever want or need.

Printed in Great Britain
by Amazon

37903106R00198